FANNY: A FICTION

FANNY: A FICTION

Edmund White

Chatto & Windus
LONDON

Published by Chatto & Windus 2003

2 4 6 8 10 9 7 5 3 1

Parts of this book have appeared in *The Ontario Review*
and on an internet site, *The Lodestone Quarterly*.

First published in Great Britain in 2003 by
Chatto & Windus
Random House, 20 Vauxhall Bridge Road,
London SW1V 2SA

Random House Australia (Pty) Limited
20 Alfred Street, Milsons Point, Sydney,
New South Wales 2061, Australia

Random House New Zealand Limited
18 Poland Road, Glenfield,
Auckland 10, New Zealand

Random House South Africa (Pty) Limited
Endulini, 5A Jubilee Road, Parktown 2193, South Africa

The Random House Group Limited Reg. No. 954009
www.randomhouse.co.uk

A CIP catalogue record for this book is available from the British Library

ISBN 0 7011 6971 0

Papers used by The Random House Group are natural, recyclable
products made from wood grown in sustainable forests;
the manufacturing processes conform to the environmental
regulations of the country of origin

Typeset by Palimpsest Book Production Limited,
Polmont, Stirlingshire
Printed and bound in Great Britain by
Biddles Ltd, Guildford and King's Lynn

To Joyce Carol Oates

He was extremely polite towards religion rather than a believer.
He would have been devout had he been able to believe that
he would meet his daughter Henriette again. M. le Duc de
Broglie said: 'To me it's as if my daughter were in America.'

Stendhal, *The Life of Henry Brulard*

Editor's Note

The manuscript was found amongst the papers of Mrs Frances Trollope when she died on 6 October 1863, at the age of eighty-four. Her last words were, 'Poor Fanny,' which her son Tom at first assumed must be an unaccustomed but, given the grave circumstances, fully warranted exclamation of self-pity.

On reflection, however, he suspected she might have been thinking of her old friend, Fanny Wright, the celebrated (some would say infamous) social reformer. This hypothesis was soon confirmed by an important literary discovery. Apparently Mrs Trollope had been working on this Life of Frances Wright *in 1856 at the same time that she was completing her last novel,* Fashionable Life; or Paris and London. *Perhaps she had heard that Mrs Gaskell was hard at work on her* Life of Charlotte Bronte; *Mrs Trollope was always alert to trends and often launched them.*

Soon afterwards, her mind became o'erclouded, the result of her tireless labours – six travel books and thirty-five novels dashed off in twenty-four years (she had begun to publish only at the age of fifty-three).

Unfortunately this biography was never polished by its accomplished authoress. She left many blanks awaiting time and materials for research and clarification. Does it defile her to present a sketchy work to the public? Her sons, Thomas and Anthony, think so and have done everything to stop this publication. Or does it not rather honour the names and careers of both Fannys to publish this last, precious testimony to a great friendship between two such ill-suited but devoted friends? Rather than attempting to modify this manuscript, the editor has decided the most pious wreath that, as it were, could be laid on Mrs Trollope's cenotaph would be her book exactly as she left it, as animated and imperfect as its maker. Someone should remind her sons that the ms. does belong to us – that we discovered it and, moreover, paid for it!

Daniel Hurst, Editor
Hurst & Blackett
Successors to Henry Colburn
13 Great Marlborough Street

One

Now that her life is over I have decided to write it. To be sure I knew her only for a few intense years, but our friendship was central to both of us, if only to indicate the direction each of us did not choose to take. We spent time together on the high seas and in the United States (which she admired and I despised). We seldom agreed on anything and her followers, if there be any left, will doubtless question my right to be her Boswell.

But her numerous enemies, not her few friends, are the readers I address in the hope of vindicating her honour. Nor will I pretend that this is the complete account she merits; I am too burdened with other literary projects to be able to track down the minutiae or verify even the main dates of her passage on earth. And I am writing here in the French countryside, far from a library or the confirming or abetting reminiscences of other civilized English men and women. In fact the road outside this cottage is dusty, the peasant farmer with whom I stay for the moment shouts all day in an incomprehensible patois, there's a particularly boisterous rooster . . . Fortunately in a few days I will be on my way to Florence and my beloved Villino Trollope.

Fanny Wright had undeniable virtues [develop this thought by the bye].

But she had, just as undeniably, some faults which I, as her friend and confidante, was particularly privileged to observe. Picture a blazing, ten-log fire *sans* fire-screen and you'll have a notion of Fanny Wright's heat and intensity (some would say her *glare*).

She had red hair, she was tall and slender, her complexion was as pale and lucent as opals – but she was the good kind of red-head, without freckles, though she did have that distinctive scent of the true redhead when she was overexerting herself, or as the French would say, *en nage*. [Delete remark on her bodily scent? In dubious taste? Though she gave off, in truth, the smell of a wet collie when she was sweating.]

But I anticipate. I am sitting here in *déshabille* on a broken straw-bottomed chair in a room so noisy with clucking and the farmer's screeching to his fowl and the ripe scent of damp straw (this house is covered with thatch) that I might as well lay an egg myself, except I am not up to it and am waiting here until my fever subsides and my son Tom sends additional funds to complete my overland trip to Tuscany.

Frances Wright . . .

Well, I should begin at the beginning. Her problems began with her parents and then their early exit from her life. She was born on 6 September 1795 [verify? I'm certain this is correct] in Dundee, a city almost as crowded and filthy as Edinburgh before the New City was constructed. In Edinburgh, in the Old City, though the streets were only five feet wide and the buildings ten storeys tall, the 'gentle folk' waited until ten of the evening and then, when the last watch was called, all had permission to throw their slops out the window onto the street below. Whoever was passing would be foully bespattered and the rising stench was so great one could sleep only with rose petals pressed to the nostrils. Mind you, Dundee was just as dark and densely settled as Edinburgh but the Wrights lived on a floor of an ancient house, since torn down, by the Nethergate, I believe, whence the fields and gardens were visible and where the citizens would descend and bathe directly in the cold waters of the Tay.

Fanny was preceded by an older brother and followed by her beloved little sister Camilla, but when Fanny was only three her mother died and her father passed away three short months later. Despite this early disappearance her father, James Wright, a prosperous Dundee merchant, left his mark on the child, for James was the worst sort of freethinker. He had paid to have Thomas Paine's *The Rights of Man* reprinted in a ha'penny edition available to the poor, and this infamous egalitarian tract, full of mischievous sophistry, could have condemned the rash man to Botany Bay had he not been so well connected. Mr Wright belonged to several numismatics clubs and possessed very valuable coins; typical of his Jacobin views, he wondered why the public mints employed 'the silly morsels of heraldry' in designing coins rather than 'emblems of industry and commerce.' Doubtless he wanted our shillings not to present the royal profiles but to show milkmaids plying swollen teats, and our crowns to enshrine dustmen wading through ordure.

Mr Wright would also have been arrested for belonging to the infamous Friends of the People, a communistical phalanstary in Edinburgh, had he not ridden, all alone, one misty night, out into the murky Tay, where he drowned his devilish papers . . . Years later, Fanny Wright read through the few notes her father had jotted down that had not been destroyed that night – and naturally found surprising similarities in their turn of mind. He had written, 'The spirit of law and the tenor of the conduct of governments in order to be well adapted to the mutable and ever-varying state of human affairs ought continually to change according to existing circumstances and the temper of the age.' Notice his emphasis on mutable Circumstance rather than eternal Nature and its Laws. Fanny later told me she marvelled at the 'coincidence in views between father and daughter, separated by death when the first had not reached the age of twenty-nine, and when the latter was in infancy.' I, too, alas, find a terrifying symmetry there, a family habit of reckless disregard of tradition and a total capitulation to Wanton *Flux*!

Fanny's older brother was engaged in the navy and died in a sea battle with the French off Madeira when he was not yet seventeen. Long before, Fanny and her sister Camilla (Fan and Cam as they were called) had been parcelled out to various relatives. They lived for a while in London with their maternal grandfather, Major General Duncan Campbell, an indolent and convivial man who expressed intense satisfaction that he never dined alone and that he knew nobody but lords and generals. When he dined with them, it was always with ten or twelve wines and a gaggle of tired, opinionated women in brocaded gowns and lop-sided coiffures, for his circle kept very late hours indeed.

Miss Wright was repelled by these bibulous Tory relatives in London, for if her father died when she was still only an infant, none the less she clung to her *idea* of him, and an Idea is always more tenacious than a Reality. I myself have always rejected long evenings at table with the great and good in favour of gay family gatherings, amateur theatricals, meals on the wing and ardent conviviality. I far prefer a simple farmhouse, a mulled cider, the cries of happy children and the drolleries of artistic friends to the dull panelled majesty of the Mayfair dining room with its twelve wines. Of course I did become an intimate of Prince Metternich in Vienna long after I went to America with Fanny Wright, but the prince was so temperate he ate nothing but brown bread and butter while his guests feasted. Apparently even Napoleon III hates lingering at table and gets everyone up after an hour in order to play charades and dance Scottish jigs.

We have the record (from her own hand, *d'ailleurs*) of but one conversation between Fanny, still a child, and her florid-faced old beau of a kinsman, General Campbell. One day when a starving beggar woman and her dirty child were turned away from her grandfather's door, Fanny asked him, 'Why are those people so poor?'

'Because they are too lazy to work,' the good general replied.

'But you don't work, Grandfather.'

4

'Certainly not,' said the indignant old man. 'I could not associate with the rich if I worked. It is a shame for a rich man to work.'

What a pity she did not grow up, as I did, the child of a sensible if impecunious clergyman. My dear mother died when I was only five, but Nature saw fit to spare my father, who instructed me in the beauty and moral superiority of Dante and Petrarch and introduced us, his children, to a wide circle of Bristol merchants and his fellow alumni of Winchester and New College. I spent my whole girlhood dancing, and I would have gladly made dancing more general and of more frequent occurrence than it already was.

Frances Wright's sufferings as a girl were indisputable, since she was deprived of the comfort and love of her own hearth. I myself knew the sorrow of growing up without a mother to help me dress, to advise me on my corsage, to set the *bon ton*, to warn me against the advances of one rash youth or other. But perhaps because all those clergymen surrounding my father as well as all those scientists (for Papa was also an inventor, and invented plates lined with silver to soften the scraping sound of cutlery on porcelain, a noise he could not tolerate) – because all these men had wives and I a sister, I was never deprived of female counsel and company.

No wonder Fanny, who had no gift for feminine companionship, irritated her young aunt, her mother's only sister, who took her and Camilla in charge and moved them, when Fanny was eleven and Cam nine, to the Devonshire village of Dawlish along the coast of Lyme Bay, there where the English Channel debouches into the Atlantic. This young aunt, Miss Frances Campbell, lived there in some state in a twenty-room house called 'The Cottage,' for she was an heiress, especially after the sudden, some say apoplectic, death of her father, General Campbell. Miss Campbell's brother, Major William Campbell, also died soon before or shortly after, I forget which. He was killed in action somewhere in India, and left vast estates in Bengal, Behar and

Benares [I remember these three B's] to his sister and his two nieces. Ironic that Fanny Wright's future freedom to hand down lessons to her inferiors was based on a colonial fortune founded in the Orient.

Miss Campbell hoped to raise Fan and Cam in the highly feminine eighteenth-century manner to which she herself had been submitted, but Fanny bitterly resented it. She said, speaking of herself in the priggish third person, that 'experience taught her, in early childhood, how little was to be learned in drawing-rooms, and inspired her with a disgust for frivolous reading, conversation and occupation.' Oh la! The truth of it is that this tall, red-haired girl with the low voice and solid, confronting gaze, the thin body and overly frank manner – the truth is that this paragon had no sense of humour. She knew no rhymes, played no games, sang no songs, never ogled a man or giggled at an absurdity; she alternated between noble complacency and nobler rage; if she had found a young man to her liking she would have matter-of-factly taken his hand and led him off to a corner, though in saying that I do not mean to impugn her modesty. Quite the contrary. She was lamentably without coquetry and as innocent as the wheat standing in the field.

Miss Campbell in her stately Cottage deeply offended Fanny in attempting to make her conventional. She was a lady who knew how to say three words in approximate French and rattle off a rondo on the spinet, but she took no interest in the American or French Revolutions, Fanny's recently acquired hobbyhorses. She dared to instruct her, and Fanny never forgave her for that! Fanny, after all, was Brilliant, she told us so herself, though she knew no Latin and less Greek, but Brilliant in the way of her great-great-aunt, Elizabeth Robinson Montagu, Doctor Johnson's blue-stocking muse, the woman who had defended Shakespeare when his extravagances had come under attack from the overly nice Mr Voltaire. Lucky Shakespeare to have a Montagu; fortunate America to have a Fanny!

TWO

Fanny said she resented her young aunt not because she'd been flogged or starved or neglected but because Miss Campbell had dared to introduce her into ordinary, brainless, respectable provincial society and had seen fit to instruct Fanny in the ordinary occupations of a rich young woman – pouring out tea, dancing a quadrille, paying and receiving calls and poking needles into fabric in a frame.

Nor was Fanny's anger a girlish moment of petulance but rather a form of savage indignation, nursed over five years in silence, delivered with frigid deliberation long after the fact and never regretted or even doubted in the aftermath. This sort of unfeeling dismissal of her closest living relative makes the blood run cold:

'I now sit down, Madame, to address to you a letter which it was as little my desire as my intention to have written, had you not yourself called me to do so.

'First let me say that I write as leisurely as coolly . . .'

Imagine the impertinence! As if Miss Campbell had been the ward and not the legal guardian, the kind, administering angel.

'I spare you, Madame, a review of the days of my childhood,

days that wrung such a drop from my heart – and have left me in the sad experience of life and of the nature of my fellow creatures, which, under your tuition, I, at the early age acquired, tokens of bitterness that I shall carry with me to the grave.'

Imagine invoking the grave at eighteen! The grim extravagance of it all, when Miss Campbell's only vice was that she backed the Tories.

The rest of the letter darkly hints that when Fan and Cam left the Cottage, Miss Campbell explained the departure by maligning the girls' character in letters to friends and relatives – perhaps Miss Campbell feared that she'd be held accountable for Fanny's relentless campaign against her and hoped to fend off blame.

Fanny was already her own creature. I could invoke Athena, the Warrior Goddess, but I could just as readily refer to Minerva, the deity who stepped fully formed out of her father's brow – with this difference, that Minerva embodied Wisdom not untutored Will. I forget the details, but Fanny had staged her first coup by extricating her sister and herself (and their considerable fortune) out from her aunt's control in 1813, before they were of legal age. They went back to Scotland, this time to Glasgow, to their great-uncle James Mylne and his wife, Agnes. There they lived in the good doctor's crowded but lively establishment. Dr Mylne, as don of moral philosophy, taught at Glasgow . Everything in this cramped, contentious household was to Fanny's taste. They dined richly, the women drank brandy with the men after supper, and everyone discussed ideas, the women all the more volubly the less they were instructed. It was about this time that Fanny announced that she preferred to God 'His Majesty with the tail and the cloven hoofs.' She added, with serene impiety, 'I think I have done with churches. When I can hear of one that does honour to God and good to man it shall have my presence and love.' To blasphemy she joined treason; the Glaswegians were Whigs, hated poor George III and wanted Parliament to rule in his stead. In her great-uncle's house everyone talked Adam Smith, Thomas Paine, Mary Wollstonecraft – ah, it makes me weary just to contemplate *The Rights of Man* and even *The Rights of Woman*!

Fanny, to be sure, thought she was in sole possession of the truth. She decided she was an Epicurean. I'm not too clear what that means but I gather what she had in mind was an imperviousness to Opinion and an indifference to Reputation. She published a little book several years later in London (in 1822, I believe) at her own expense. She wanted to call it 'Epicurus' but was obliged to rename it (for fear of scandal and censorship) *A Few Days in Athens; Being the Translation of a Greek Manuscript Discovered in Herculaneum.* Miss Wright resorted to this innocent little fiction in order to put forth her own epicureanism, which was not the doctrine of licentiousness one might imagine at first blush but a rather insipid tranquillity; as she put it, 'Happy life is like neither to a roaring torrent nor a stagnant pond, but to a placid and crystal stream, that flows gently and silently along.'

Poor Fanny, whose life pressed forward like a broad, cold lake that inches toward a suspiciously close horizon and then, without warning, plunges in a foaming cascade hundreds of feet down onto punishing rocks.

I suppose few people alive today can think their way back into that distant period when Utopian schemes flourished, naïve principles were fervently proposed and everything seemed possible and perfectible. The American Revolution – or the Tax Dodgers' Rebellion, as I prefer to call it – was still recent, and the French Revolution all the closer in time, and Jacobins of Fanny Wright's ilk ignored the bloody excesses and took into account nothing save the gains in rhetoric, for that was the time of talk and more talk. Fanny was only a child, she hated her Tory aunt and worshipped the Glasgow Whigs. She began to dress in simple muslin that she draped around her statuesque body as if she were an Athenian – or Athena. Her hair, which she cut short, gleamed in red curls she pressed forward onto her snowy brow and along her pure nape, which since the Terror inevitably appears to be the tenderest part of any noble body.

I myself was radical enough back then before I had made my great Voyage. Like so many others I departed for America a Progressive and came back a Conservative.

Fanny and Camilla made their first trip to America in the summer of 1818 when Fanny was just twenty-two or -three. I know little about that voyage – it was on the *Amity*, a New-York packet ship out of Liverpool, I believe, and of course the girls had all the right introductions in the New World and visited Philadelphia, New-York for certain, possibly Boston. Fanny was in ecstasies and, when she returned to England two years later, she dashed off a rather silly book called *Views of Society and Manners in America*, which even the prickly Americans found too full of praise (later they regretted Fanny's honey after I had applied my nettles).

If I seem impatient with my cosseted Miss, it's because I myself was suffering considerably during the same period. For years my husband, Thomas Anthony Trollope, *lo sposo mio*, had lived in the secure expectation of inheriting a great estate from his uncle – and given those expectations, he had moved us all out of Keppel Street near Russell Square into a lovely house near Harrow that dominated a hill (by living so close our sons were accepted as non-paying day boys at Harrow School). My husband had borrowed heavily to build a new house after his own design and poured into it all the energy he had and all the funds he lacked.

In those years I had given birth to six children – Thomas Adolphus in April 1810, Henry in 1811, Arthur a year later, Anthony in 1815, Cecilia in 1816 and Emily in 1818. I'm neglecting to point out that there had been a first Emily in 1813 who lived only long enough to be baptized. Perhaps it was an ill-fated notion to resurrect her name (and possibly a draught of her spirit) in my youngest daughter, but at first we did not dwell on dark things. In those days, despite my repeated lyings-in and our pecuniary embarrassment, we lived for fun, for gay family evenings, for picnics in summer and amateur theatricals in winter-time, and our house was abuzz with rehearsals and hissed line-readings, with suppressed whoops of laughter and the sudden charge of a children's crusade. Everything, everything was amusing, even our children's education, at least when I was in charge, for I could throw out alphabet blocks on the nursery floor and reward with a sweet the first child to piece together a word or two. I kept the children's rooms full of slates, guitars, dumb-bells, dictionaries and all the sundry items necessary for an expanded education. When they weren't learning they were quizzing. And of course our Newfoundland, Neptune, was always, true to his name, splashing through the newest stream (or gutter). We put on Molière's *Malade Imaginaire* with the children playing all the parts to improve their French. Oh, we also did speaking charades of three scenes in which the first scene was meant to suggest the first syllable of the mystery word, the second scene the second syllable, and the third scene the word entire.

If my husband was in command, the children might whimper or cry, for he made the boys recite their Latin lessons to him at six in the morning while he lathered his face and shaved. If Anthony, say, forgot a tense or muddled a case his father would pull his hair without missing a stroke of the blade. Even during a long carriage ride Trollope would open up a great grammar and set the boys to work. At night we'd all gather around a single candle and Pater would read Richardson's *Sir Charles Grandison*; I suppose in the cold, gloomy sitting-room each of us might have drifted off into his own morose but private reverie had not Mr Trollope called on us with such frequency to comment on the action and its lesson.

Fortunately we had many fêtes with our charming (and far wealthier) neighbours and artistic and political friends, for we were quite startlingly radical back then and entertained many a would-be revolutionary from Italy, France and Spain. (I'll never forget General Pepe, dear old thing, who drew himself up to his full five feet and announced with all his Neapolitan solemnity the most shattering platitudes, though he was good about giving the children dried fruits from Italy.)

We dared not invite them to a seated dinner, for that was beyond our means, but we could provide cakes and ices to half a hundred actresses, poets, Peers and dangerous exiles in evening gatherings that contrasted a banker with a mountebank or a carnival king with a king – these were my 'antithetical evenings.' So many of our friends would have been either interviewed or arrested in their own lands.

But then everything turned sour. Mr Trollope's uncle, Adolphus Meetkerke, who was almost clownishly rustic, the sort of red-faced squire who shouts from his pew up to the cleric in his pulpit to invite him to dinner following the service – well, Uncle Meetkerke lost his wife in July 1817, a good woman who had been barren. We were certain we'd soon be inheriting. Mr Meetkerke himself was in his sixties – but then, to our astonishment, just a year afterwards he married the all-too-fertile Matilda Jean Wilkinson and by December 1819, a scarce year after the wedding, she'd borne him an all-too-vigorous heir, young Adolphus – the *very* day, 22nd December, that my poor husband had signed a binding lease to the Harrow property with the unswayable Lord Northwick of Harrow Park.

Oh, I know this is not *my* biography but Fanny Wright's, yet I hope merely to explain what was transpiring in my life at the time she was gallivanting around America. When my little Emily died, when her ruby lips turned to whitest marble, I learned from Sorrow to guard my distance from the babies I bore afterwards – no, 'distance' is too strong a word for a nature as adhesive as my own, as gay and elastic and (well, why not?) as gallant, but let us say I learned to thank God for every day that was granted me with each precious Babe and to expect nothing more. Perhaps I already suspected that those days would not be many. Later I had seances to turn to in London, attended by all the most prominent writers (the darling Brownings, formidable Sir Edward Bulwer-Lytton), or in Florence, where I could communicate with my angels in a perfect whir of levitating tables, twirling lamps, rocking chairs and talking spirits, but that consolation was to come much, much later. Having witnessed the pitiable deaths of four of my children I'm convinced that they, the innocents, *know* there are moments when the two conditions touch, life and a death far less harsh than we have been led to imagine. Poor Fanny Wright was to experience a tragedy as a mother even graver than the death of an infant – but I am leaping ahead once again.

Nor should I crow since, to be perfectly blunt, my husband became more and more queer after the loss of his prospects. He'd been a barrister for years, keeping his dingy offices in the Old Square of Lincoln's Inn and riding the Home Circuit in Hertfordshire, often on the road for as long as nine weeks. But after his reversal of fortune he became more and more susceptible to the migraine and found he had neither the courage nor the health to leave his couch for long. Though a sweet man by fundamental nature, he was often short-tempered and mocking (he'd even mocked his old Tory of an uncle, which may have been the old man's motive for marrying again so inconveniently; Uncle Adolphus seemed determined not to leave his lovely house, Julians, to his contentious Whig of a nephew).

After his losses, my husband never recovered. He became irritable and unpleasant – and quite incapable of working. We were obliged to rent out our large new house and to move to a dilapidated farmhouse elsewhere on the Harrow estate, but the children treated it all as a great game, and I continued my fêtes even if we now had fewer chairs and fewer ices – half the time our guests arrived with their treats in hand. 'To carry on the war' was our expression for the suicidal determination with which we spent more money than we had.

The one great addition to our lives at that time, or at least to my life, was the eminent French artist, Monsieur Auguste Hervieu. We must have met him sometime in the mid-1820s. Auguste detested the Bourbons, fools and knaves all. His father, a colonel in the great Napoleon's army, had died in the retreat from Moscow, frozen while attempting to dismount from his horse, itself, poor beast, kneeling and frozen in the snow. The colonel left his son nothing but debts – and an undying hatred of the *ancien régime*. Auguste had fled to England after he'd been detected plotting to assassinate Louis XVIII of France; he had been tried *in absentia* and fined 15,000 francs and sentenced to five years in prison. Auguste found it expedient to remain in England.

He was a small man with a corn-silk moustache and goatee

(some would have seen it as thin and wispy). He was well made, with a lead-soldier compactness about him – small hands, always red from the cold, big feet, which only drew attention to his shoddy boots, a high-pitched chest as if the marionette strings were attached just there to the puppet's body, and a long chin and squat neck, which meant his chin almost touched his chest, as if he were an old-fashioned nutcracker, except I don't want to suggest in speaking of marionettes and nutcrackers that there was anything grotesquely mechanical about him. On the contrary, his wide-spaced black eyes, as shiny as two puddles of burnt honey, his smile as white as coconut meat and his amusing way of speaking our language – with disdainful approximation, as though English were a barbarian dialect not worth learning – all these traits endeared him to us, as did his fierce loyalty to the Trollope clan.

He was my favourite regicide.

He directed our Molière productions and assisted us all with our pronunciation. He would express amazement that we could speak French at all and would assure us that his language was by far the most difficult one in the world – cursed with an irrational orthography, a vast vocabulary and a grammar of fiendish complexity. When we would protest that he had just described English, he would contradict us with impatient finality. I was bound to advance his art and though I have nothing of the professional *salonnière* about me, nevertheless I had titled friends sit for him and I campaigned (unsuccessfully) to get *The Times* to write about his masterpiece, *Love and Folly*, which had been accepted and exposed by the Royal Academy.

Ours was a stormy household. *Mio Antonio*, my husband, had vowed that his sons should be gentlemen, which to him meant that they must go to Harrow and Winchester, as he did, and as my father did, but our son Henry had left school at fifteen. Trollope, embittered by headaches and the squalor of our cottage as well as by my gallant pace of receiving guests, became choleric against our Henry. I tried to defend him, but in vain. To be sure, Henry also had his moods and outbursts. He felt he'd

14

been humiliated at school by his wardrobe, which we could never afford to renew. It's true the poor boy stalked about in trousers that had been decuffed and which he'd so outgrown they resembled knee-breeches. His cutaway was aureoled in ink spills and his linen was a perfect disreputation, if that's the substantive form of 'disreputable.'

Worse, he found Latin and Greek a kind of torture all the more relentless because he deemed it useless. I made a point of writing to him and Anthony in Italian or French (to the point that they *begged* me to include at least a few sentences in their Mother Tongue), but I was unable to help out in the Classical Languages. I couldn't look to his Latinity.

My husband [Should I delete this part? Does it reflect badly on both my dead?] would become apoplectic against Henry, and perhaps because Henry blamed his father for all his ills and was a constant witness to his angry sloth, he'd come right back with terrible *injures* – indeed *lo sposo mio* would chase the boy through the house and Henry would just barely elude him. I can still see their two faces contorted with hate as they advanced and retreated around the dining-room table, their mouths twisted with spiteful imprecations. My poor husband would collapse in a cold sweat, deathly pale.

To make matters worse, Monsieur Hervieu was also subject to fierce moods. He was an orphan, since his mother had died when he was but three, in 1797. He had been handed about from one relative to another. When he showed the earliest signs of his considerable talent he was sent to study in the atelier first of Girodet, who had an inexplicable attraction to comely young studio assistants and, in his huge canvases, to ephebes such as the small-sexed Endymion writhing under a moonbeam [change to 'the *delicate* Endymion'?] – and then he studied with the Baron Antoine Gros, another of David's pupils, except this one was drawn to virile subjects, such as *Bonaparte Crossing the Arcole Bridge*. Both of them passed on to Auguste the great David's incomparable sense of line, though we live in such a philistine epoch that few of our contemporaries have ranked poor Auguste very high.

Auguste also offended by dressing as a 'coxcomb,' as Trollope put it, which meant he wore trousers as wide as skirts and was what in my youth we called 'an Adonis type.'

Throughout his youth, apparently, Auguste had frequently erupted in noble displays of heroic impatience with the mediocrity to be found on every side. Like Byron he laughed at ordinary human limitations – a bit easier to pull off if one is a rich English aristocrat rather than a poor French orphan. [Eliminate nationalities? Illogical?]

There is no one who has mattered more to me in this life than Auguste – his genius, to be sure, but also his loyalty to our family and his deep spiritual communication with me. I've always liked a gentleman with whom I could have long conversations about myself, and Auguste was ideal except he'd sometimes doze off due to his imperfect grasp of our language. In French he was blissfully alert for hours on end to the slightest nuance. When I met him he was twenty-nine and I cannot mention my age, but people (especially those evil-minded Americans) insisted on reading something immoral [untowards?] into our rapport.

I feel faint – I've eaten nothing for two days now but raw onions and rawer red wine and ›a few crumbs of a bad cob of bread – 'miche' – which the peasant's wife cuts off a stale loaf with a knife that trembles, she is so fearful of being too generous with me and getting cuffed by her swine of a husband, most particularly now, since I can see from their tiny red eyes that they have dismissed me as a pauper and are convinced my stories of my kinsmen sending me money are just that: stories. I don't know why that wretched editor of mine [Editor's note: My predecessor, John Murray, also known as Byron's editor] doesn't expedite me the advance he promised, God knows I've laboured long and hard for him and built his handsome London house for him, forty books in twenty years. [Editor's note: The usual authorial grumbling, unjustified, but amusing, of course.]

Speaking of swine, the peasants have just slaughtered their once-a-year pig and salted it in brine. The squealing, the trying, the hard sawing and hacking – I was quite nauseated. It reminded me of Cincinnati, but more of that anon. They resent my presence here and my furious scribbling (my sleeves are soaked in ink) which no doubt they see as satanic idleness as they process their pig in a perfect porcine factory – even the bristles are trimmed and sold for shaving brushes. [Cut this entire digression?]

In point of fact, Auguste never once touched me in an ambiguous way. Certainly he was attracted to me, but all this fascination was channelled into a chaste affection for my son Henry. Many a night Auguste would find himself too weary or *gris* after a long evening *chez nous* to make his way back to London and he'd stay with us in Harrow, sleeping with my son, and when I'd find them all tangled up together in the morning, Auguste's hairless white arm flung across Henry's hairless white chest, I could see in this filial embrace an emblem of a love for me that Auguste knew he could never live out. [Delete 'hairless'?]

The two boys were so close (for though Auguste was fourteen years older than Henry I could not help but see him as a boy, one of *my* boys) that the great French artist could not resist taking Henry's side in his quarrels with his father. Henry was determined to go to Paris with Auguste and work in a counting-house, but Auguste, naturally enough, knew he himself was *persona non grata* in France and would be guillotined *tout de suite*. The boys quarrelled with each other, Auguste making up for his imperfect English by changing moods as frequently as a barometer in a storm; both of them quarrelled with Trollope, who bellowed and took to his bed, wracked by seismic headaches. It was as if the men in my house compensated for the uniform rainy greyness outdoors by producing a whole range of interior romantic storms, earthquakes and floods – and the occasional brief burst of sunshine.

We were poor, terribly poor, since Trollope had stopped working, and when the odd client came to the house or to his chambers he invariably barked until the man slunk away – all due to excessive doses of calomel, my Henry claimed, the opium-

17

like substance Mr Trollope ingested in ever greater quantities to quell his mental pains.

Onto this stage stepped Frances Wright. She had just come back from her first trip to America. I forget who brought her to our house, for we were still engaged in 'carrying on the war,' even if we had to rewarm old tea and cut stale buns into quarters. Miss Wright was far too lofty to notice such mundane things. Once, years later, when I wrote to her complaining of being bored, she replied, 'But unless we have some fixed and steady occupation of labour – of business – of study, something which keeps in habitual exercise our physical or mental energies and the better when it is both, it is impossible to make our existence glide smoothly – otherwise we must know moments, nay hours of vexation and lassitude.'

Now *this* advice she was addressing to *me*, someone who's never known ten minutes of lassitude; I run from dawn to dusk, pillar to post, or between whatever two poles of necessity one might invent. Indeed my complaint of being 'bored' had been just an affectation, a form of social climbing. I've never had the time, the luxury, to be bored.

Just before Fanny Wright erupted into our lives my twelve-year-old, Arthur, died; he had been frail and ailing for some time. How grim it had been to watch his rosy cheeks go as white and lustreless as kiln-ready clay, to see his tubercular ribs perforate his dry skin, to wipe so much sweat from his brow I had thought I would find him one morning covered with moss.

Both my husband and I had clergymen for fathers, but nothing I had memorized or chanted or prayed to had prepared me for the loss of my Arthur. I'd already lost my first little Emily, of course, but she was nothing except an infant's hand paddling the air and large eyes turning reproachfully. Arthur was a whole person, he had loves and fears and theories and hopes and hiding-places. His loss was all the worse, perhaps, because I had only the most tepid image of the divine consolation he was swimming toward. No, I sat beside his bed so long that like a clock-face he changed, but invisibly, from the noon of life to the nadir, the six-thirty, of death.

Three

It was a mere six months later, on a cold day when the sun rose only to decline and when every one of the fireplaces at our Harrow farm had decided to smoke. I could scarcely see from one side of the sitting-room to the other, so dense was the smoke in the house, matched only by the clouds of fog outside, as if everything had been declared precious and to be cushioned in cotton, dirty or clean. Mr Trollope was groaning on his couch and begging Anthony to administer him another cup of calomel. Henry had just had a fight with his father that morning. I remember hearing Henry shout, 'You have to be rich to be a gentleman and a gentleman to be a scholar! I for one will not pretend another moment – I want an employment!' I myself was sick watching my family become encrusted with disputes like a sunken hull covered with barnacles. Nothing had ever been able to defeat me for long but now, today, I was undone. I found one of Arthur's little stockings at the bottom of a drawer; I held it up and wept at its flimsiness, as if it were a balloon that fate had emptied of its roundness. I had a horror of self-pity, and normally I had a great capacity for self-renewal, but that day (perhaps it was the irritating smoke or the realization the fog was so thick we would most certainly have no callers) I felt it would just be easier to lie down in a narrow box under the ground.

Then there was a knock at the door and our maid of all work, faithful Esther, let in this red-haired stranger, who was wearing a great black otter-skin cloak she'd brought back from the Americas. She cast it aside and revealed her startling Greek robes, worn to appear democratic, and asked for a towel with which she could dry her fog-wet hair, which threw us all into confusion because not a clean towel was to be located in the whole cottage.

I found my pulses beating and my spirit lifting as I approached this strange woman and – Who *had* brought her? Surely it was Julia Garnett who provided the wonderful connection. Julia was a girl in her late twenties whom I'd known in Bristol, where her father was a wealthy merchant. Her sister Harriet and she were friends of my family. Dissatisfied with the political situation in England, in 1787 the family had arrived in New Jersey where they bought a mansion and several hundred acres rolling down toward the Raritan River. There they had received Fanny and Camilla for weeks on end. In fact Julia and Harriet Garnett became Fanny's closest friends, and Fanny often said that it was Julia who had given her back the *joie de vivre* that her aunt Miss Campbell had crushed.

Yes, Miss Wright was travelling with Julia Garnett, I remember now, a tall, horsy girl. I knew her to have been a girl as given to swaying blue plumes as a circus pony, but under Miss Wright's tutelage she, too, had affected Athenian simplicity, which merely threw her pallid skin and big bones into pitiless relief. Oh, and they were both followed by Camilla Wright, a sweet-faced girl with auburn curls, a body as diminutive as mine in stature though not nearly so roly-poly, in fact quite angular and thoracic, for she already had the bug-eyed, sunken-chested, feverish-flushed look of the consumptive. She spoke in a nearly inaudible squeak, seldom looked away from her older sister's face and seemed, whenever Fanny left the room, at once more relaxed and strangely forlorn. She lived for Fanny, obeyed her in all things, repeated her words and bobbed in her wake like a tender behind a warship.

'Come in, ladies,' I said, struggling to work my way over to the mantelpiece where I kept bits of wax and a few missing teeth that I wedged into my mouth whenever guests came to call. Esther went off to put the kettle on the hob and to slice our stale bread into ever-finer morsels. I conducted my guests into the smoky sitting-room. 'Lord, what a day!' I exclaimed. 'The fog's rolling down so low over every tumbledown cottage that the smoke is forced back down the chimney and –' But here I broke off, as I saw Frances Wright staring at me with her big eyes, orbs utterly uninflected by irony.

The silence buzzed in the air as noisily as a winter fly. The wood sagged into the flames. I have, I must admit, putting aside all modesty, a refined faculty for orienting myself to every shift in tone. 'Tell me, Miss Wright, how did you find the United States?' I asked boldly.

Miss Wright's eyes suddenly widened in appreciation. 'Where shall I begin in speaking of that paradise?' Her voice was low for a woman's, her pronunciation hinting only here and there of a Scottish burr, the roll of terminal *r*s and the odd sudden attack on a tonic accent, but otherwise it was all the thick clotted cream of upper-class London, a tone, as I later learned, she regretted for its associations with grandeur.

'Shall I tell you about Julia's and Harry's house?' She referred to Harriet Garnett as 'Harry.'

'It's called The White House and must be as large and noble as the President's palace of the same name in Washington. Or should I tell you about New-York with its wide streets? For if the French call their streets *rues aristocratiques*, where the pedestrian poor are run down by carriages or bespattered by slops tossed down from so-called noble windows, then I shall name those wide esplanades in New-York *rues démocratiques*. There are no dark alleyways, the houses are of brick and of pleasant mien, nothing graced by art except the City Hall, but nothing dank or dangerous either. We saw no peasants trembling in hovels. We stayed in a boarding-house on Broadway where we met citizens from all over the country, for the people have free and easy manners

21

and do not hold back out of deference – in fact they resent a European who insists on demeaning courtesies.

'I could speak of the unrestrained liberty of the press, the swelling patriotism that is strong and uniform throughout the country, of the open and fiery Congressional debates, or I could speak of the Quakers in Philadelphia, or of the country's great men, especially Thomas Jefferson, a *savant* who, if he had been born European, would have devoted his energies to natural science but who, as a father of a new country, was forced to limit his philosophical inquiries and promote the welfare of the people, for which all hail him. Or I could speak of the satanic stain of slavery, which makes a mockery of America's claims to be the land of freedom, but I could also point out that this crime was imposed on the colonies by England and that the country will soon liberate its sable brethren.'

As she talked on, holding the cup of weak tea Esther had handed her, never touching it except to set it aside that she might better illustrate her ideas with simple, serving gestures – as she discoursed I felt a great burden lift from my heart. I remember that she opened her hands to each side, palms upwards, as if to point out how self-evident her ideas were. Nor did she speak abstractly, as someone does who is indifferent to the reception of her words. Frances Wright looked at me and Julia with warmth and curiosity. Sometimes she touched me – and I realized how seldom in those days I'd had any intimate contact whatsoever. Even though she was so sure of herself, she often said, 'Do you not agree?'

I understood that I had allowed my life to be fettered to the ground by Lilliputian cares, that I had forgotten that people could live *for* an ideal and not just *against* the tribulations threatening survival. The daylight sank, a breeze blew the fog away, and still she spoke, of the pirate lord of New Orleans Jean Laffite, of Indians, of the Southern gift for oratory, of women's fashions, of the black pudding the unpaved streets turned into when it rained. Later my Henry came out of the Rat Hole (my name for his room) and joined us. A sleepy Auguste sat by the fire and held his knees. Henry stared at Miss Wright with fascination and, when the delicate Camilla began to cough, he gallantly found her a warmer shawl and a rug for her knees, which was none too clean but which she accepted gratefully. Faithful Esther served us the three pheasants Anthony had shot that morning and a bottle of Madeira she'd found somewhere and more stale toast and a mash, but the rattle of plates and the handing about of food passed in a haze thicker than the smoke, for I knew I had met the woman who would change my life.

She visited us once a week during the next month and each time we celebrated her arrival as if it were a national holiday. She had a way of standing very close to me and tucking stray hair behind my ears or raising my collar only to smooth it flat again. She spoke in the most exalted terms, her eyes sparkling with tears, but her fingers were always producing less theatrical, more quotidian effects. She had studied philosophy and history and geology, her mind turned naturally to ethics and political justice – all domains that were foreign to my experience. But her way of addressing such lofty ideas to me, as her hand held mine or as her fingers massaged away a pain in my shoulder or neck that I had not previously divined – this physical attentiveness and extreme proximity somehow convinced me I was capable of understanding her, or at least worthy of her words.

Life, which had turned so sombre after Arthur's death, now became festive again, but in a new way, I might say a woman's way, except most women were blinkered and petty. But when Fanny examined my hand from every angle and paid me compliments, there was a feminine ardour, a spiritual intensity, joined to an almost domestic concern for the physical well-being of her interlocutor. Fanny made me feel worthy as a mind and attractive as a presence.

Four

In the autumn of 1823 – or maybe it was sooner or a bit later – Trollope and I travelled to Paris with Henry. We set out from Harrow at three-thirty in the morning in Trollope's gig and boarded the Calais-bound steamer at Tower Bridge. Frances Wright had promised to introduce us to the Marquis de Lafayette (she was already in Paris), and that was a great temptation and, as it turned out, a foreglimpse of heaven, but the real reason we made the trip was to place Henry in a bank, as he wished.

Auguste was distraught and clung tearfully to Henry, shaking him spasmodically. But Henry wouldn't relent and embrace Auguste, he stood there with his arms hanging empty at his sides. I knew secretly in my heart that Auguste was afraid to be separated from me and could not show it especially in front of my husband, my poor Antonio. I witnessed him sorrowfully as he kissed Henry's sturdy little chest in a wet Gallic pool of self-pity. I know it's the child's disease of the world, its *measles*, to discuss national character as if it exists, but really sometimes the French do seem to lack all stomach. They say constantly it's hot, it's cold, what's the delay, even how can you do this to me, when an Englishman would smile fixedly and stoically – undoubtedly for the better, too.

I did not know what Henry's plan was, but perhaps he thought, correctly as it turned out, that the French were bound to have another revolution before long and Auguste could come home in glory to join him in Paris. Louis XVIII died in 1828 and things did get better then. Or perhaps he had grown weary of M. Hervieu's *temperament*, so necessary to an artist but fatiguing to the entourage.

In Paris we stayed in a modest but respectable hotel and the very first thing we did was to dine with Mrs Mary Garnett and her daughters, Julia and Harriet, in the flat they had taken for the month. Frances Wright was there as well. Although I was thrilled to be back in Paris, Miss Wright saw it as the capital of vanity, snobbery and social injustice. I can remember the Garnett girls all in black, for they were still in mourning for their father.

In the lamplight Miss Wright leaned forward, her hands almost transparent, her voice thrillingly low and convinced. She said, 'We are here amidst everything that is corrupt and decadent or at least decaying.'

'Yes,' I objected, 'but, Miss Wright, we are eager to visit the Louvre to see the curiosities the Emperor brought back from Egypt!'

Miss Wright had a grave way of moving her head in one's direction as if it cost her considerable effort and to dramatize the very real mechanical trouble one was giving her. Nor did she lock glances; instead, she looked only generally in one's direction, as if she were blind and responding to the voice alone. 'I suppose', she said, 'you're telling me that by way of vaunting European culture and reproaching the United States for not possessing enough of it.'

I nodded, abashed that my interjection had indicated more than I had worked out in my weary brain. It was not pleasant to disagree with Fanny, since I lived for her approval alone, for her touch and her nod, for the answering fire in her eyes.

'To be sure,' she said, 'even the Americans have the tapeworm of European culture in their heads and cannot purge themselves of it.' She smiled very mildly but I wasn't sure I wanted my interest in Egypt compared to a parasite.

I smiled back and though I'm a merry old soul I tried to add a tincture of acid to my expression. 'But you must admit, Miss Wright, that cities – great cities such as Paris and London – make us rise above the egotism of the provinces and like great crashing waves they rub us free of our rough edges.'

'Those two cities, however, have the distinct disadvantage of perpetuating social differences and turning women into painted china dolls to be dressed and bounced on the knee, as if they were almost human.' I had been on the point of recommending Paris for its shops; now the words froze on my lips.

At this point my husband began to nod solemnly. 'There's nothing more futile and pathetic than a Paris doxy of a certain age who rushes from her stay-maker to her cobbler or *perruquier* as if she were accomplishing something more important than spending her husband's *pecuniam*. I actually heard an American woman tell another in London not long ago that she was skilled and practised at *shopping*!'

There go my new stays, I thought, even as I admired my husband's use of the accusative case in Latin, if that's what it was. My boy Henry seemed fascinated by all that Miss Wright had to say. Away from Auguste, Henry had reverted to being the sweet child, sleepy and pliable and full of shy, silky smiles. He curled up on the couch beside his father and even rested his head upon the Pater's shoulder. He studied Miss Wright with huge eyes, the child's glance that engrosses whatever it sees and soon loses sight even of its own existence.

Not that I wanted Henry to become too enamoured of America now that he was about to settle down in Paris. Through some of my husband's relations he'd been given a position as a clerk in a bank that dealt with the local English colony and our visiting countrymen. Tonight he looked too absurdly young to work at all much less to live in a vast, dirty, teeming city all on his own.

I now knew that we were ruined and that every *centime* I spent tortured my husband, but Trollope told me nothing and if I asked him where we stood, he snapped, 'Don't trouble yourself. I'm in charge of our finances,' though that was a big word for such a negative sum.

We travelled the whole day out to Versailles and spent the next trudging through the gardens as neatly laid out as an enfilade of state rooms and through the state rooms as colourful with their Aubussons and their Gobelins as a very old and ingenious garden. But though I gasped at the dazzle of chandeliers lowered on threadbare silk ropes until they grazed the parquet and sighed when I looked into an orangerie tropical with golden fruit on the drabbest autumn day, nevertheless I took an earnest dislike to Louis XIV, who though he had been dead for a century I decided had been the vainest, the most lavish and the most selfish of men – the eternal repetition of his own figure was at once ludicrous and disgusting. Can one ever wholly trust a king whose court painter was named Hyacinthe?

We visited the Louvre five times altogether – the first time entirely devoted to the exposition on Art and Industry. Mr Trollope was ecstatic and lingered in front of every display to read each placard – in that he was just like a Frenchman, who far prefers reading about something to experiencing it and in a church or at a Roman ruin will spend his whole time with his nose in a guidebook rather than just looking at the simple, ravishing reality. Of course Mr Trollope was eager to learn things technical and nautical, of which there were plenty – have I forgotten to mention that he had just published a book, *A Treatise on the Mortgage of Ships*? He'd dedicated it to Lord Liverpool, the Prime Minister and also President of Ship-Owners, and Mr Trollope had lively expectations, though his Lordship never even acknowledged receipt of the book. Pity, too, for Mr Trollope had shone a very bright light into the murkiest corners of naval law. Nor am I convinced that subsequently my poor Trollope ever recovered his zest for life.

It was the paintings, the Italian paintings, that drew me back to the Louvre so many times, for there I felt on more solid ground. I am convinced that heaven's message is encoded in Nature but that only artists of genius can decipher it; when I

27

look at an Italian masterpiece I hear God speaking. For me a Guido Reni is the Burning Bush, even if the presence of so many bad French paintings somewhat muted the divine utterance.

At the Garnetts' salon I met several interesting writers, including a Monsieur Henri Beyle who publishes under the name of Stendhal. Poor M. Beyle talks constantly of women and even said, rather injudiciously, that France is a country ruled from the bidet. He tries too hard to show how clever and sardonic he is and if there's another man present, M. Beyle reveals that he's almost allergic to the male body, male voice, male smell. He refuses to deal with men directly but rather triangulates everything through the available woman, even such an unpromising specimen of the sex as myself. Poor Beyle was in love with Julia Garnett, though she had decided to marry the Keeper of the Royal Library at Hanover, a charming young man she'd met at my house. Incidentally, Beyle and I always remained friends and years later he told me he read my books with a pen in hand.

Then there was the twenty-five-year-old Prosper Mérimée, who now, all these years later, is constantly travelling about France inspecting decayed historic monuments and deciding which ones need restoration. He is the opposite of Beyle, for he has devoted his life to the most reliable methods for pleasing women and like a good actor knows instantly how each of his actions appears to his audience. M. Mérimée was carrying his arm in a most appealing sling; he'd just been wounded in a duel by his current mistress's husband. Mérimée is witty, a protégé of Goethe and a friend to Chateaubriand. He's written verse dramas and our friend Mary Shelley praised him in the *Westminster Review*. And yet I prefer M. Beyle, though certainly Mérimée will turn out to be the better writer. When Beyle spoke to me of Napoleon, of the excitement young men all over France felt during the Emperor's reign, the pleasure in being young when the whole world was youthful – ah! *that* was the way to win *this* woman's heart, at least more than by calculated flatteries. When I asked M. Beyle what he thought of Lafayette, he said, 'A hero out of Plutarch.' My thoughts exactly.

A French man of letters is no great novelty, but Mrs Garnett had odder fish to fry: American novelists, and not one but two. Washington Irving – perhaps the first American professional writer of any stature – came across as the pillar of society, which is an unremarkable if highly serviceable kind of support. And he seemed delighted to be recognized by an English reader, even one as undistinguished as I am (or *was* at the time, since now I have my forty titles to my credit, all forgettable except the one, my first, the one about America, the very volume most likely to offend Mr Irving, elderly but still alive I believe back in his native New-York City).

Irving worshipped European culture, as well he might since he was so indebted to it. He so idealized the great dead Byron that he had recently rented Newstead Abbey for a few weeks and even searched out Byron's old servants and hired them. He was as lean as Byron could be after a strenuous diet and his eyes were set deep in his handsome face. His most famous creatures, Rip van Winkle and the Headless Horseman, he had found while ransacking the Teutonic fairy tales collected in Wieland's *Travels Through Germany* – Mr Irving did nothing but supply the Hudson Valley backgrounds, very prettily, too, I'm sure.

With me he was courtly but dim as if I were too creased with my old apple wrinkles to hold his interest for long, but when the radiant Harriet Garnett joined us he told us that his *Bracebridge Hall*, the sequel to his *Sketch Book*, was enjoying a great success. Apparently that fatuous actress, Mrs Siddons, read it and drew him aside recently in London at a party and said in her portentous bass voice, 'You have – made – me – *weep*,' as if that were at once a reproach and a compliment, certainly a miracle like the liquefying blood of San Gennaro in Naples.

'Mrs Trollope,' Mr Irving said as he handed me over to another American, '*you* know Fenimore Cooper –' the acquired French formula for introducing any two people since in Paris everyone already knows everyone worth meeting and if they don't one mustn't even hint at such an embarrassing lacuna.

'No, no –' I said, blinking and smiling, and there I was in the burning, quizzical presence of the *second* most famous writer in the English-speaking world (after Sir Walter Scott).

Cooper was a full-fleshed man whose florid face and close-shaved but bristling jowls looked almost *culinary* served up on a neat twist of whitest neck stock (the ubiquitous influence of that tragic ninny, Beau Brummell). His hair was dishevelled, romantically I suppose, to suggest storm-tossed genius but attributable more likely to an effort to diminish the gleaming expanse of brow discovered by his receding locks, shot through with grey. His left eye wandered wide and his mouth drooped on the same side – a dropsical slant he corrected by tilting his head to the right! He looked disabused and bitter, almost like a child who's just discovered that adults are capable of lying. He told me that it was difficult for him to be in crowds even as small as this one (we were twelve) since they caused him to succumb to fits of indigestion and headache. Of course he was from a country where the citizens feel that more than two settlers per square mile constitute an unbearable density.

'Mr Cooper,' I said, 'I nearly expected to find *you* in leatherstockings and crowned with plumage. But how long have you been living in Europe?' No sooner had the words flown out of my mouth than I heard the insult in them and I blushed.

'Quite long enough to have stopped painting my face blue,' he said with such alacrity that I surmised he'd already written something about European ignorance of American ways. 'You'd be surprised, Madame, to know how many Europeans have asked me if white men turn permanently black in the scorching sun of the United States. And even in Grose's *Dictionary of the Vulgar Tongue*, to be found in every Englishman's library, a "gouge" is defined as putting out an enemy's eye with one's thumb, practised commonly in Boston.' He stared at me with his one penetrating eye.

'But I still have two more years in France, Madame, before I reach the full seven that Jefferson said no American must go beyond in his European residency if he still hopes to speak with authority about his own country.'

30

'Do things change so rapidly?' I asked, delighted to be given a new topic.

'I fear they do.' Mr Cooper launched into an attack on the coarsening manners of his countrymen. He said that once Americans had been reserved and respectful but that now they'd become familiar and contemptuous of everyone superior to them. When I tried to join in the fun by summoning up some trans-atlantic oafishness I'd once observed, he cut me short with: 'But, Madame, you obviously know nothing about my country.'

As he went on I saw he was ready to contradict himself, to praise and then insult his countrymen, love them for their honest lack of manner and hate them for their beastly lack of manners – he was as restless as a puppy on a leash and alternately praised and impugned his Americans for the selfsame qualities, all by way of dramatizing his own conflicts on a *national* scale.

When I said I had noticed an intemperance, even imperti-nence, in American manners, Mr Cooper drew so near I could smell his scent (burnt almonds and vanilla) and he said, 'Many nations excel us at the arts of living, but none in the truths of human existence. In religion we are without bigotry or licen-tiousness. In morals we are consistent and sound. In politics we are purely democratic without the slightest approach to disorder. But our manners – ah! There's the rub.'

He was such a curious man. He seemed to love American class-lessness, but he told me his father, a Federalist judge, had despised democracy, wanted an elected king to rule and would challenge anyone who was for equality to a duel. The judge even said once that if anyone his size could throw him the length of his body he'd give the winner a hundred acres, and he was instantly chal-lenged and thrown and while still flat on his back he ordered the local clerk to draw up the deed. He was a representative to Congress, the judge, and he voted for Burr, and became so abusive defending him he was killed by a blow to the head. For his son, the novelist, democracy was a sacred mission, but even as he was energetically defending democracy, a more private, snobbish part of him, narrow but deep, was quite illogically

31

insinuating that there was an American 'aristocracy,' refined, conservative, spiritual, to which he belonged. He was still the judge's son.

In my usual blunderbuss way I said, 'I have been led to understand there are only two classes in America, rich and poor, and I congratulate you on belonging to the former, for you *are* Mr Cooper of Cooperstown, I believe, are you not?'

Just as he was about to tell me again how uninformed I was and that my ideas were as *louche* as his left eye, Miss Wright spoke up and asked, 'Why do you accuse your countrymen of rudeness, Mr Cooper? Just a moment ago I heard you telling Mrs Trollope how badly behaved they are, whereas I've observed nothing there but an open, hearty frankness.'

'But they've written terrible things about me and my books!' the good man sputtered, his full face turning pink as roast beef. 'I have had to take them to court. I'm involved in at least five legal actions at the moment – they're all just Vandals of the trade-talking dollar-dollar set.'

'Oh,' Miss Wright said in her grave, sweet voice, picking up her book, *Views of Society and Manners in America*, and instantly turning to the right page, 'permit me to cite myself: "The Americans are certainly a calm, rational, civil, and well-behaved people, not given to quarrel or to call each other names, and yet if you were to look at their newspapers you would think them a parcel of Hessian soldiers. An unrestrained press appears to be the safety valve of their free Constitution, and they seem to understand this, for they no more regard all the noise and sputter that it occasions than the roaring of the vapour on their steamboats."'

I was fascinated by Fanny's sweetly cerebral manner, her interest in ideas and not in fine points of etiquette. I admired her way of disagreeing with a man, even such a celebrated one. She deferred in no way to masculine opinions but treated questions as if they were abstract and uninflected by the sex of the person maintaining them.

'You're wrong!' Mr Cooper thundered. 'They gloat over every malicious word and wish nothing but ill to the two writers – Mr

Irving and myself – who've brought glory to their shores! These people need lessons in manners more than anything else – or perhaps a good thrashing. At the very least I'll sue them till they're ruined and turned out of their houses.'

Mr Cooper finished in such triumph that he himself looked stunned, then perplexed. I remember that Miss Wright and I exchanged worried glances as if we were certain he would have to hear the folly in what he was saying and laugh at his own excess of spirit.

But no . . . It was then that we both realized we were dealing with a fanatic, and to be sure in the years that ensued we heard many stories about this novelist who lost, month by month, book by book, trial after trial, all the goodwill he had won with *The Last of the Mohicans*.

I must say that intemperate as Mr Cooper was, nevertheless I envied Mrs Garnett the thrillingly high level of her salon; certainly we had nothing back at Harrow to rival her Beyle or Mérimée or Irving or her belligerent Mr Cooper, ready to wrestle us all prostrate, and as I lay in bed that night I couldn't sleep at all, so busy was I remembering all the fine sallies and piquant *mots*; I was twitching to the right and left as I chimed in with brilliant retorts, those inspired afterthoughts the French call the 'wit of the staircase,' *l'esprit de l'escalier*.

Five

The next day Mr Trollope accompanied Henry to his bank. I was proud of my men, especially Henry, who was wearing new boots shined to a mirror gloss. I was about to pin a carnation on his lapel from last night's dinner bouquet when Trollope stopped me. 'That's a shade too frivolous for a bank, my little *salonnière*,' for I'd confided to him how I'd been kept awake by the mental aftermath of the fête. 'Besides,' Trollope continued, 'carnations are bound to symbolize death or something here in France,' and now I realize he had reason.

They descended from our modest hotel near the rooms that the Garnetts had taken, and headed through the rue de Rivoli, which in those days was under construction, a noisy, dusty, magnificent arcade Pharaonic in its ambitions.

That evening Henry told me everything had gone well. He would start tomorrow at the bank but he was intimidated by the elegance of the young French clerks, their cold correctness, their dandified clothes and manners, the complete absence of anything approaching the easygoing or casual, their shameless vanity, the look of born seducers, of *coureurs d'alcôves*. He had been so intent on leaving school and defying his father that he had had no energy left to imagine the reality of working in a bank in France, which now that he had seen it with his own eyes struck him as nearly medieval in its deference to hierarchy. Poor Henry looked blue around the lips and stunned around the eyes; until now he had felt vaguely dismissive of the French, whom he'd caricatured in his mind so thoroughly that suddenly he was shocked by their sleek, supercilious reality. He also noticed that they were entirely indifferent to him.

I felt I was allowing Henry to enter Holy Orders or something equally foreign, disciplined and irrevocable, especially when after another five days we left him in the care of a respectable narrow-minded English clergyman, the kind who can live twenty years in Paris and complain it's not Clacton-on-Sea.

Mr Trollope and I then set out for La Grange, the château of the Marquis de Lafayette, a hot, dusty day's ride by diligence east of Paris, a full thirteen leagues, in a village near Brie, where they make a smelly, runny cheese, a slutty mess that leads one to long for a chaste cheddar.

It seems that Lafayette had read Miss Wright's *Views of Society and Manners in America*, which she had sent him, and he had written her an ecstatic letter. No wonder, since he wanted to hear nothing but good about the United States, which he had fought to liberate and never once visited in the ensuing forty years. As the reality of the place receded into his imagination, he glorified it not only as the emblem of his heroic youth but also as the Utopian alternative to all that he detested in France. Just as Voltaire attributed everything good to a China he had never seen, so Lafayette idealized an America he had forgotten.

I came to revere Lafayette, but no amount of hero-worship could blind me to the septuagenarian's fascinating contradictions of character. As the Duc de Broglie told me years later, 'There was something noble and imposing in his manners, a dash of the *ancien régime*, which contrasted oddly with the revolutionary ideas and the turns of phrase with which his way of speaking was imbued.' It's true that I had to laugh as I heard Miss Wright and the Marquis talk revolution as they were served by powdered lackeys! Miss Wright initially appealed to Lafayette because in her book she had found America perfect, but after he saw her in the flesh – the pale, slender, classically pure flesh – he found her all the more entrancing. He and she spoke unendingly of the spirit, but it was the flesh they very much had in mind. [Amend this? I should guard against negative reflections that might disabuse the reader about this great man. Readers need and like their Great Men. And I make too many references to the flesh.]

He was there to meet us at the picturesque entrance to La Grange. We had rolled in our carriage down a wide, beautiful lane bordered with young, vigorous apple trees. The lane turned abruptly to the left and went through a dense forest of chestnut trees, mysterious and almost wild, just before it opened up to La Grange itself – the farm, an ancient chapel and then the un-imposing château, more a manor house. We crossed a stone bridge, outfitted with little parapets, which spanned a moat that had been largely filled in with gardens. The château, three storeys tall, was surmounted by a slate roof in excellent repair. There were five round towers flying pennants. The entryway was thick with ivy, which had been planted by General Fox. Ivy on honey-warm sand-stone seemed so English it made me feel instantly at home.

I had seen so many paintings and etchings of Lafayette as a gaunt young man with black eyebrows, short, lightly powdered wig, dress uniform unbuttoned over white waistcoat, gold hoop in his right ear, his whole body long and lean, that I had some difficulty recognizing him now with his short black hair brushed forward into fangs on a face thickened and reddened by age. His grey eyes looked at me with a reserved kindliness under strongly arched brows. He'd been thrown by a horse, or in any event he moved stiffly on a cane though he held himself straight with military correctness.

Despite the democratic convictions, he habitually had an aristo-cratic disdain imprinted on his features – except when he talked to Fanny. Then he glowed and glittered with boyish excitement. If she spoke his lips moved. If she smiled slightly he grinned hugely. If she sighed he looked downcast.

36

Trollope and I were led by the hobbling master of the domain and his American Indian *valet-de-chambre* (who kept calling Lafayette 'father,' in English) to our suite – charming, the bed covered with heavy crimson satin quilts that at night were carefully folded and stored on a special rack. Curtains of the same vivid colour lined the windows; when we came in sunset was streaming through them. The Marquis showed us another, adjoining room, smaller, that also contained a bed ('For Monsieur if it were preferred,' Lafayette said in English, since obviously he had to spell out such sophisticated contingencies to middle-class English people like us).

We unpacked with the help of a maid in a starched cap who was right out of an operetta with her cinched-in waist and tinkling laugh. After she helped me don my only gown, we wandered down to the great salon, a round room at the base of one of the towers that was well lit and richly furnished. The General was there with all twenty-one members of his household whom he presented to us with old-fashioned solemnity – his two married daughters and his son, named George Washington, their husbands and George's wife and their children and many other relations and guests, all of them dressed *en grande tenue*. They were gathered to greet us and if a painter had pictured the men standing behind the seated women one would have imagined it was just another soirée of chic Parisians. The women had their shoulders exposed to the world and their hair mounted in glossy chignons, the men stood erect with upturned white collars pushing into the jaw-line. Each man wore a loosely knotted white tie above dark evening clothes.

They had those easy manners that only the French have mastered – intimacy without familiarity, spontaneity that eschews anything hectic, a knack for being amusing without ever saying anything impertinent, though the French adore innuendo and scandal and scoff at us for our Puritanism. In the General's salon, however, nothing frivolous was uttered and the only thing scandalous was the General's smile when Fanny Wright entered the room.

37

She came in last and I noticed she had abandoned her Athenian garb for a wine-red silk gown – little Camilla bobbed behind her in something pink that looked like a weak dilution of her sister's *toilette*. Camilla's shoulders were concealed against the night under a shawl, not that there was any chill in the air given that the day had been excessively warm for autumn.

The General kissed Fanny's hand but defied all well-bred practice by kissing it truly, holding it to his lips instead of merely bobbing toward it. I noticed that one of his daughters flushed a bright red as crimson as Fanny's gown, but whether from vexation or embarrassment I had no way of knowing.

I was given the place of honour but Fanny was seated immediately to the left of the Marquis. Although etiquette might have dictated that he converse first with me, then after the fish with Fanny, he preferred to confuse all those following his lead and to address us both on a general subject: glory. His own. I enjoyed the phantom sisterhood he conferred on Fanny and me as his attentive, worshipful English daughters. He spoke in an English mixed freely with French as did all the members of his household, an eccentricity that I found much to my liking.

'I've always been most *exigeant* about the *genre d'honneurs* that I would accept. You say *exigeant* in English?'

Just as Fanny said, 'Absolutely,' I murmured, '*Demanding*. We say *demanding*.'

And the General ended up by shrugging in a purely French gesture.

He told us that he'd always been most particular about the honours that were conferred on him. 'Thomas Jefferson offered to make me the first *gouverneur* of *Louisiane*, but I feared I'd be compromised by my dual citizenship.'

'Dual?' I asked.

'French and American, Madame,' he said, bowing gravely.

'Of course,' I whispered.

I suddenly saw a funny little snaggle-toothed old woman with ratty hair peering out at me from the shadows and I wondered who it could be, had they let the peasants in to gawk? Until I realized with a start it was me – my own reflection from a wall mirror. I had been so absorbed in the brilliant company, the delicate aroma of the *sole nantaise*, the taste of the cool white wine with its flinty *arrière-pensée*, the look of all the elegant company that I had entirely forgotten the sad reality of me.

Fanny said, 'The Americans are clamouring for you to return to their shores, Marquis, and they are prepared to offer you the exact shade of glory you desire. They are all dedicated Fayettistes. You will even be welcomed in Fayetteville!' Suddenly I was seeing Fanny in a new light – as the worldly flatterer. Her suavity in this capacity did not strike me as disappointing hypocrisy but rather as fluent worldliness.

I could feel the glaring gaze from Lafayette's older daughter, a middle-aged woman named Anastasie de la Tour-Maubourg, whose husband was a great radical but penniless. Anastasie had her father's regal manners and when she saw me looking at her she raised her glass to toast me with a small sweet smile, but I knew it had not been sweetness or smiling that had engraved those deep worry-lines into her gaunt face.

After supper the General gave us a tour of the castle. Fanny took his right arm and Anastasie the other, although her father, who truly needed the help of his cane, was only annoyed by the arrangement, which he could not execute successfully.

I cannot recall all the things in that house, but I remember it was a museum to his own life, especially his American adventure. I even recollect a ring marked 'Pater patriae' that contained hairs from the venerable heads of Mr and Mrs George Washington. I remember as well Washington's reading glasses and the parasol he'd planted into his horse's saddle when he rode through the blazing sunlight of the Carolinas [or was it Virginia?]. There was Mrs Washington's very last bit of embroidery. In the library there were many miniatures of men who'd played a role in Lafayette's life, including Franklin and Washington, and impeccably bound on the shelves was a specially honoured collection of American books, including Irving's and Cooper's (not that there were *many* American books at that time).

It was odd how in that most Gallic of French aristocratic households there were so many reminders of the *second* world Lafayette claimed with the sobriquet, 'the hero of two worlds.' There was jasmine from Virginia, American flags grouped on the wall, even a little house in the garden to store an Indian canoe! And of course there was the Iroquois butler who was named Mr Antelope or Ant-Eater, and he glided rather than walked and when standing behind the Marquis's chair gave no sign of life, not even his chest rose and fell with breathing. [Will my new oh-so-susceptible readers or rather readeresses object to the word chest? People have become so *correct*.] I made Mr Aardvark smile by grinning fiendishly at him and pulling his braids but when he broke into a grin it was mirthless and bloodthirsty and I definitely preferred his usual facial immobility to *that*!

During our tour the Marquis showed us his bedroom and library on the second storey of one of the towers, but as we were descending Anastasie peeked into the bedroom below his and asked, 'Papa, who is staying here?'

'Miss Wright.'

'Oh, Miss Wright,' Anastasie exclaimed, 'how rude you must think us, putting you in this damp, cramped room; before we can use it we must burn fires in it for at least a week. I can't imagine how this happened. What must you think of us?' She turned to Mr Alligator and said, 'Remove Miss Wright's things to the Yellow Room next to my own.' She smiled back at Miss Wright: 'You'll see, we'll be so cosy – do you know we French even say *cosy* all the time now, we have no other word for it?'

'No!' the Marquis said, turning to the Indian, who crossed his hands on his chest, inclined his head and said, 'I understand, Father.' Then, looking around at all of us, a bleak smile – well, not playing but *working* across his lips, Lafayette said to no one in particular, 'The present arrangements are perfect since they allow Miss Wright and me to discuss our plans whenever we wish.' Then he patted Fanny's hand. 'We deserve to be *cosy* too, do we not?'

Fanny nodded, smiled, patted the venerable hand, turned to Anastasie, said, 'I hadn't noticed any damp, if indeed there is any. You are overly nice.'

'Not *overly*,' insisted Anastasie. 'One can never be too nice about the proprieties.'

The Marquis laughed a dry little indication of a laugh and said to me, 'Do you hear that, Mrs Trollope? Do you see how even those of us from old families became bourgeois under Napoleon? I think I almost prefer the reckless frivolity of the past to this new fussing over the proprieties.'

Anastasie bit her lip and surrendered her father's arm. She fell back behind the others and walked beside me. I saw how she suffered at being humiliated in this way by her father in front of so many family members and guests.

To be pleasant I said, 'And have you travelled as extensively as your father, Madame de la Tour-Maubourg?'

'Never to America,' she said in a low tone but with determination as if she were a concert pianist who had just banged out a very loud wrong note but who was now plunging into the next, preposterously difficult variation. 'I lived in the prison of Olmütz with my father, my sister and my mother, the late Marquise.'

'You did? Where? Old . . . ?'

'Olmütz. In Austria. My father had been captured and sentenced in perpetuity by the Austrian Monarch for his role in founding the French Republic. He was imprisoned in 1793. My mother was thrown into prison in France by the Jacobins for being an aristocrat. No way to win. When she was released she went to Vienna with my sister and me and petitioned the Austrian Emperor to join my father in prison. We lived there, behind bars, for two years. We were finally rescued only thanks to Napoleon. The real loss in my father's life –' and here Madame de la Tour-Maubourg lowered her voice and took my arm – 'was his wife, our mother, Adrienne, who died on Christmas Eve, 1807. She was never able to recover her health after Olmütz. On her death-bed my mother, who was very pious, said to our father, 'You are not a Christian.' When he said nothing, she added, sadly, 'Ah, I know, you're a Fayettist!' And he said, 'You think me very vain, I see, but are you not something of a Fayettist yourself?'

'"Yes, indeed," my poor dying mother whispered, "I feel that I could give my life for Fayettism," and she did at that moment. That's why I was a bit shocked at table to hear Miss Wright refer so lightly to Fayettism.'

We were now crossing the great lawn beside the château and I looked at Fanny, sauntering beside the very tall, slightly corpulent, stiff-legged Marquis. He had gout in one foot and the other had been crushed, but he held himself very erect and there wasn't a line in his face. We were hushed into silence by the grandeur of the scene – the full moon bending down over us like a mother's face over a cradle at night, the huge, solemn trees stencilling their small black twigs and their tiny black leaves against the night sky, which was at once dark and floodlit, a ripe void, a pulsing vastness. [I mean the night was filled with stars – am I raving? Have I become incoherent with hunger and poetry?] All this grandeur reduced us to our most private thoughts, bleak because we'd left behind the henhouse glare of the château with its light, heat, wine and chatter and now we were just frightened chickens exposed to the wolves of the night. [I must cut all this, I've had too much bad wine and too little bad bread and too many throaty screams of the rooster outside my window. It's all crept into my prose.]

Anastasie squeezed my arm and said, 'My father seems quite taken by Miss Wright. I'm afraid that all his life he's given free rein to his animal nature – perhaps that's his most *ancien régime* characteristic. He thinks nothing of keeping a very young, pretty servant girl in the next room while he is drafting his letters to enter every thirty minutes and embrace him.'

I knew that Madame de la Tour-Maubourg expected me, as an Englishwoman, to be shocked, but I started giggling. 'But why does he want a servant to do that?'

'I imagine it keeps Papa at his desk for hours on end if he knows he'll have his little reward every half-hour. Grains for the pigeon. But I hate the idea that a noble soul like Miss Wright might be drawn into this minor economy of sensual rewards, that she should be the nightly *bonbon. That* is why I made the fuss about her room.'

'I am certain Fanny has no idea she's at risk. Surely she sees him as a mentor and father.'

We kept sauntering back and forth across the lawn. I could smell the grass in the air – dusty, toasted, slightly sour. The moon was so bright and low that we cast long shadows as we strolled here and there. The Marquis took us down to the little house beside a stream that we could hear and smell but not see. Then the Indian came trotting up with a lantern that dropped dazzles on the swirling and pooling stream and next he glided into the little house where we saw the canoe, covered with birch bark, a solemn thing worthy of a primitive tomb.

That night I hung out of my window in one of the towers, unable to sleep, and saw two – no three! – men darting through the trees, wrapped in black cloaks and sporting wide-brimmed black hats. They were running along the property walls, whistling like birds to one another. It was the night scene in an opera, patriots in soft boots tiptoeing into the citadel to free the Prince before his execution scheduled for dawn.

I did not want to be too 'magic casements' in my romantic reveries lest these men were robbers or assassins, so I tiptoed down the winding stairs of my tower, slid silently through a shuttered, stuffy drawing-room and eased open another door, only to see a swarm of torchlight and to hear the Marquis and Miss Wright speaking French and Spanish and whispering greetings to these weird interlopers, who replied in a vocabulary I failed to understand (I remember a reference to *charbon*, 'coal'). They urged the men to mount the stairs to the Marquis's study – and after the sound of boots and muted conversation died away and the dance of the swinging lantern and the glow of the torches faded, suddenly everything was silent and dark: extinguished.

Who could these people be? I knew Lafayette had spent his life welcoming every radical element in his country. His multiple misfired plots had even cost many young co-conspirators their lives. But their deaths didn't seem to trouble the General. He was seeking a tragic death for himself but all he could manage was a very long, some would say farcical, life.

I went back to my room, slightly affrighted, but I found that by leaning out of my window I could see the rigid beam of light cast across the lawn through curtains that had been too hastily closed within the Marquis's window, curtains that left a diagonal line of brilliance to rake the grass, a bend sinister cutting across a field verdoy.

Six

The next morning – as every morning thereafter – we rose not very early. The breakfast bell rang only at ten-thirty, but then it summoned us to – to a *dinner*, we might call it, of soups, roast mutton, coffee, tea, toast and butter. At noon another bell rang, which banished everyone back to his or her room, to while away the time writing letters or reading or drafting national Constitutions. Whence we were recalled at five-thirty to a copious supper, one served in the French style in tedious courses, though the Marquis himself waved the five servants away from his side and ate abstemiously, contenting himself with a piece of fish, a chicken wing and a glass of water. In the evening we sat around the drawing-room and listened to a M. de Ségur, member of the Academy, read his own verse tragedy about Clytemnestra (I had a hard time keeping my eyes open and stuck myself in the thigh with my crocheting hooks). Later Lafayette's daughters played piano duets and sang in their reedy voices. If the weather was fine I took long walks with those daughters, during which we discussed the relative merits of French and English literature. The daughters placed Racine, Corneille, Voltaire – and Ségur! – above our Ben Jonson and Shakespeare. I was called on more than once to apologize for the Bard's barbarisms. When I boasted that Shakespeare had a vocabulary of 50,000 words, Madame de Lasteyrie said, I suppose caustically, 'And imagine poor Racine had to content himself with just 4,000 . . .'

I might have been vexed by this difference of opinions had I not been in ecstasies over the high level of discourse. I knew not where to find so intellectual, so amiable a set of beings as these I had been living amongst here. I wasn't altogether unhappy for once that Mr Trollope usually retired early with a bilious headache. His absence left me free to chatter along in French, which he spoke with so much more deliberation, and to reinvent myself as a coquette of twenty which I felt even if I was tragically far from looking it.

At table and in the salon there were often as many as twenty-five guests and relatives (one night a pianist who had just taken first prize at the Academy serenaded us with some rather predictable, thump-thump sonatinas by Kuhlau). But despite all this competition for the Marquis's attention, Fanny seemed to monopolize it. She and Lafayette spoke in rapturous terms about the United States, which they declared a Utopia where fraternity ruled, equality was as elemental as earth and liberty flowed as freely as air, water and fire. I loved to watch the pleasure and purity lighting up Fanny's face. Her hands were busy indicating intellectual distinctions, as if she were saying, 'No, but on the other hand,' or 'Do not rush to conclusions,' but her face shone forth with a simple affirmative. If America earned their full-voiced *elemental* praise, other subjects caused them to lower their voices to conspiratorial whispers.

Fanny could be cold and abrupt with people she held in no esteem (I'd seen her raise an eyebrow of faintly quizzical amusement when one of our local ladies at Harrow made a silly observation about our Savage Parliament, for in those days we'd just lived through Radical riots calling for universal suffrage and annual parliaments, claims that the government had ruthlessly suppressed). In every case I sided with Fanny's scorn, although

46

I might not have had the courage to show it.When Fanny idolized someone, however, as she did Lafayette, then her voice became rich as a muted horn and her eyes as grey and vivid as a storm. [Verify: Did I say earlier her eyes were green? I cannot for the life of me remember them, except they were big and penetrating and surprisingly *expensive*-looking in that pale face, like maharani emeralds floating up out of a dish of thin milk.] Perhaps the difference between her and me was that she always felt that she was sitting for history's portrait, whereas I knew that I wasn't being observed at all, except I wasn't aware that my youngest son, Anthony, the future novelist, was memorizing every absurdity I uttered and that like Osiris, whose body was dismembered and scattered across the land, I would be distributed over his books in portraits of 'the triumphant feminine'.

That night, after the dinner and concert, I asked Miss Wright to accompany me to my suite and to help me adjust my corsage. She looked slightiy irritated, as if I were a mother imposing a curfew on a girl just coming out into society and inebriated by masculine attention, but she couldn't refuse me. Her hesitation wounded me, since I never felt a difference of age and interest separating us. Fanny had such powers to make men and other women love her and share in her current adventure – and she rendered her friends such happy accomplices – that when she withdrew her affection or even held herself slightly apart the distance could count as a painful alienation.

Once we were alone I told her how much I revered Lafayette. Fanny said, 'He is the father I never had.'

I could hear Mr Trollope rustling about in his little antechamber; I was pleased that he was safely sequestered there. Fanny was seated on a small love-seat next to the window, which I'd opened wide. Unlike the French maid, who had a medieval fear of the night air, I loved to swallow great gulps of the country breezes until I was quite drunk on nature.

Miss Wright was dressed in a Wedgwood blue and white organdy dress with ample folds that dramatized her supple waist by swallowing it. She was holding a midnight-blue hat with long

47

strings that went under her chin – I think she'd brought her bonnet to remind me she was about to go out for a walk with the Marquis, since ordinarily she braved the elements uncovered even in unseasonable weather. She shook drops of rain out of her long red hair with an unforgettably poetic motion. On her arm she carried a reticule into which she'd stuffed a book – she never wasted a moment and always came provisioned with intellectual work, as a normal woman might have pulled out her embroidery frame.

'But is the Marquis just a father to you, Fanny dear? I am afraid people are whispering that there's an intimacy between you that is too fervent, that there are too many *attouchements* and *empressements* and *tutti quanti* to be explained away as just filial devotion. I speak to you as a mother concerned with your reputation,' though I wasn't feeling the least bit maternal.

Miss Wright stared at me angrily and suddenly I could well imagine the defiance she'd shown Miss Campbell, her aunt, when that thoroughly ordinary lady had tried to clip her niece's wings.

'Not that *I* think such things, Fanny dearest,' I hastened to add. 'As I said to one busybody, "What might look like impropriety in any lesser woman is just an overflowing of intellectual ardour in Miss Wright."' I mimed indignation as I faced down this purely imaginary critic.

She smiled at me slightly. 'Mrs Trollope,' she said in a weary whisper. That's all. Just my name, as if the notion of explaining herself or descending to the level of the world's suspicions fatigued her in advance.

'Yes, dear?' I was seated next to her now on the little love-seat and we could breathe in the whole rustling life of the outdoors, smell the sweet linden trees and even hear the brook beyond the trees trickling its liquid mercury and jet into the veins of the sleeping night.

'Where to begin?' she murmured. 'You see, the Marquis and I are in such constant reciprocity, such intimate accord – he says two words, I think the third, he whispers the fourth, I sob out the fifth and together we *think*, just *think*, the sixth, seventh and

48

eighth until a look of spiritual rapture dawns in our eyes, bright with tears.'

I was so exalted that I seized her hand, but I was repulsed when I looked down and saw the contrast between hers, pale white where it wasn't diaphanous, and mine, a dirty grey, soft thing covered with brown liver spots, creased with rings in the flesh when I bent it back and scored all over with small, greasy diamonds when held up to reflect the lamplight. I've always been like that – I surround myself with beautiful young creatures and so immerse myself in their lives that I forget how I look; I read my own feelings not off the tawdry landscape of my own body but rather from the *lisse* map of their fair physiognomies. 'How marvellous that sort of mental communication must be!' I said with feigned dreaminess, since I was still reeling from the sight of my own hand.

People were walking below our windows and murmuring in voices that took pleasure in their tranquil complicity, their portable indoorsiness, so marked in the owl-hooting immensity of the silent night. I knew I had to engage Miss Wright or she'd be off to join the Marquis.

'I suppose it is America that has bound you together?'

'Yes,' she said, 'for we both cherish a dream of equality in a land that lies far beyond the meddling of senile potentates. We know that human beings are essentially good and capable of living together in harmony if they are allowed to enjoy the fruits of their own labour. The terrible laws of England and Europe, which render the poor ever poorer; the importunate parliaments, elected by only a fragment of the population and in any event seldom allowed to congregate; the vain, useless, greedy aristocracy who think it their –'

And she continued on in that vein for quite a long moment as I nodded, held her hand and attempted to keep my eyes as alert as ever even as my spirit drifted off to baser questions: Was she sleeping with the Marquis? Who were those cloaked conspirators sneaking last night into the château – no, not sneaking, but welcomed by the infernal pair?

49

I scarcely knew how to introduce the first question, but I saw my opening for the second and leapt on it when Fanny turned to survey the moonlit park below.

'Does the General hope to bring monarchy to an end here in France?' I asked.

I noticed that Miss Wright's head snapped back toward me and her eyes widened for a second. She then lowered her gaze and said smoothly, but without much conviction, 'What enlightened Frenchman wouldn't detest Louis XVIII?'

'Would the General take, uh, *definite* steps to dethrone the Bourbon antique?'

She looked hesitant so I rushed forward: 'For I must confess I saw some men entering your tower the other night and I felt they might be . . . *well* . . .' I cleared my throat and pretended my vagueness was discretion rather than a very real ignorance.

'Very well.' Miss Wright withdrew her hand and stood up, as if she could sort out her ideas properly only if she held herself at some distance; and she was right, for surely an upright posture and physical independence are necessary if not sufficient conditions for clear thinking.

'After all that France has suffered and known during the last thirty years, the Bourbons are trying to turn history backwards and to resurrect all their old sins and crimes. The other day the General publicly denounced the whole Bourbon programme of religious persecution, cruel and excessive punishments, the censorship of the press – and above all the ruinously *expensive* monarchy.'

'Why isn't the Marquis tried for treason and sedition?' I asked. 'Why doesn't a letter of cachet confine *him* to the Conciergerie?'

Miss Wright walked back and forth. She made certain she had my full attention before she said, 'Because he knows something the King doesn't want bruited about. Lafayette possesses a document in the King's own hand that proves he conspired to kill his own brother, Louis XVI.'

'How extraordinary!' I exclaimed, genuinely shocked by this sign of how the reins of power can bind more tightly than sacred family ties, not that I'd ever had to choose between them. The spectacle of royal treachery rather thrilled me.

'Yes, that Memorandum is all that stands between Lafayette's freedom and incarceration,' Miss Wright said.

'Fanny, dearest,' I said, looking at her with what I intended would appear as a *mélange* of sweetness and gravity, 'as I mentioned I saw a band of *bravos* entering the château. Are *they* revolutionaries?'

'Yes.' She stopped pacing and said, 'Your own friend General Pepe was one of the founders of a secret society pledged to overthrowing tyranny in Italy, Spain, France – even England!'

Oh no, I thought, not England! And instantly I feared I might be implicated in General Pepe's bomb-throwing and slogan-hurling, though fortunately his cries would be gargled in his preposterous, incomprehensible English.

Fanny was plunging ahead. 'In Italy the society is called the *Carbonari*, the charcoal burners, and in France the *Charbonniers*.'

'But why?'

'Because the language ensures secrecy. The members are organized into "Sales," which are governed by "High Sales" and then "the Supreme Sale," *la Vente Suprême*. Every charcoal burner carries a dagger, owns a firearm and twenty-five cartridges, pays a subscription of one franc a month and promises to obey any order coming down from the Salesman above. They've all sworn an oath to overturn the present government. Two young Frenchmen, who were initiated into the *Carbonari* in Naples, brought the whole movement to France.'

I said dryly, 'How exciting,' in a tone that visibly irritated Fanny.

Perhaps she'd bridled because I'd put my finger on a truth. Only the preceding fortnight, she confided, shortly before our arrival, Lafayette had set out with a small force (including his son George Washington, faithful to his father in every scheme). They had planned to capture the Château of Vincennes and ultimately Paris, but the manoeuvre had gone awry. The *Charbonniers* were captured and executed. Lafayette was still safe but he

51

needed to find a new cause, a new form of insurrection. No wonder the Duc de Broglie said that Lafayette was a monument who strolled about in search of a pedestal, even if the pedestal turned out to be a scaffold. The worst of it was that the Duke made this observation to Lafayette himself, who just smiled and said, 'Perhaps you're right.'

After our discussion Miss Wright prepared to join the Marquis in the garden. On her way out she said, 'I know I can trust you, Mrs Trollope. Several of the *Charbonniers* have fled to England and I want you to convey to them the General's messages.'

Excited and frightened to be included into history at last, I nodded dumbly, unsure what my expression might be conveying. Now I was not one of the perceived but Perception herself.

Seven

Life at Harrow seemed provincial and precarious. Away from Fanny time silted over, colours dimmed and my pulses slowed. Mr Trollope worried over the farm, but since winter had set in there was nothing he could do. He pored over the farm accounts for hours on end, as if he hoped that study alone could make up for barren fields and ailing animals. He seldom went into town, though he complained of our isolation in the country. Since he was no longer in the business of practising law, I suggested he not waste time and should devote himself to the study of Italian! This he did, surprisingly, and with such a degree of hearty application that soon he'd outstripped me, at least in his knack for reading Dante and Alfieri. I wrote Tom that we must concentrate on our Italian or soon Papa would surpass us both.

General Pepe visited me and I delivered my coded messages from Lafayette. He wouldn't tell me what they contained but he did inform me that Lafayette was the commander of the entire French *Charbonnerie* and that his château had been designated the central *baraque* or 'shanty' in their language.

Auguste Hervieu visited me much less now that little Henry was no longer at home. Oddly enough, Auguste seemed to be receiving more letters from Paris than I did, since it was often he who gave me Henry's latest news.

* * *

There! I'm back in Florence. My eldest son, Thomas Adolphus, finally bailed his poor old mother out, paid off my French peasant 'hosts,' who were deeply solaced the instant they touched solid cash and saw the back of me; their insolence changed to shameless, comedic toadying in what the Germans call an *Augenblick*. I was soon packed with my few frocks and the pages I'd written about Fanny Wright placed under my best bonnet, the one with the pale flowers picked out in azure thread along the broad brim. I found a seat on the diligence to Paris and from there I made my way south down the Rhône and along the coast to Nice, thence to Ventimiglia and eventually into Tuscany. By the time I reached Florence and the Villino Trollope I was exhausted but the weather here is sublime, hot in the direct sunlight but with a cool *fond de l'air* in the shade. Everything smells of wet clay – the crude but civilized odour of the potter's wheel – and in my *camera*, if I take off my spectacles and unfocus my eyes toward the big barred window, there's nothing but a carmine blaze of geraniums, a general conflagration.

In the courtyard down below, the *portiere*'s boy, Gugliermo, is speaking on and on in such a piping, pedantic way to his funny little three-legged dog, which regards him with the self-forgetting, timorous awe usually reserved for an older brother. Gugliermo's voice resonates off the stone walls with the solemnity of God dictating the Apocalypse to St John of – where was it? In a cave on the island of Patmos, I recall, but is that right? I keep forgetting things, things I used to know. All the other windows are shuttered and release just the thinnest lines of light across the varnished red majolica tiles. These tiles are so old, hundreds of years old, that mops and passing shoes have worn them down here and there into nearly black seams, hollowed them out, until they resemble clotted and dried bandages. Nothing moves me more than the traces of so much human labour, centuries of it, not the brutal clangour of *condottieri* but the simple housewifely application of women at work.

Oh, let me lie here another day or two in bed, before I must begin my writing again. I've written so much in the last twenty years that I recall almost nothing of it and when flatterers cite my own words to me, it's all wasted on me. 'Mrs Trollope, that's a passage from your brilliant *The Blue Bells of Scotland*.'

'It *is*?' I demand in blank surprise.

In the past my body has failed me often enough but always my mind has remained sharp, scurrying about if soundless as a mouse urinating in cotton. [To be reworked, evidently, but here I'm writing for myself, not You, the eternal Second Person Reader, receptive, even passionately so, but only if one finds the proper key, which makes it sound as if you were protected by some sordid chastity belt of squeamishness.] But now the damage seems to have invaded even my mind. Its ligaments are torn. My will can no longer lead my thoughts – it's as if the rails had sunk under the soft soil and the heavy carriage of my spirit had rolled into tall grass and come to a bucolic standstill. Stalled. Invaded by butterflies.

[*Editor's note*: Mrs Trollope was observing a true enough decline in her powers, for after her Calvary in the French countryside she never fully recovered her powers of recall and analysis; the reader will remark an increasing vagueness in the narrative as well as a childish surrender to queer metaphor, for the pleasure of mere invention, not to mention an ever more chaotic practice of introducing foreign words at random into her perfectly serviceable English and for no good reason – e.g. *Augenblick*, the ordinary German word for 'instantly,' into a passage about French peasants.]

Everything we attempted in those years, the mid-1820s, came to naught, even ended in disaster. Lord Northwick continually importuned us to pay the back rent on our farm in a manner that was less than noble. Off in Paris Henry soon succumbed to

55

a homesickness comparable to a wasting disease, for it nibbled at his bones and hollowed out his cheeks. He begged to come home and at last we permitted him to do so, especially since he paid his own passage from France and was arriving with a few sovereigns he'd managed to save. Mr Trollope's highly innovative farming methods did not extort any profit out of the Harrow acres. My little Anthony complained he was the poorest, dirtiest boy at Winchester; Thomas Adolphus, who was five years older, was supposed to look after Tony but only recently did I discover that Tom had beat him roundly every morning for a year. 'Oh, Mother,' Tom said not long ago, 'you can't imagine what a disgrace he was. He refused to bathe. His face was a vat of grease boiling with spots. He stank and he greeted every insult with a green, scummy smile, proudly bared. He invited contempt and the world accepted the invitation.'

Before he arrived at Winchester (to the mortification of Tom, who was a prefect and a rugby man), Tony had attended the Sunbury School briefly, which seemed to us to be better than Harrow, just a mild, unimportant village school near us on the Thames where most of the students were day boys, though Tony boarded. Soon after his arrival (he told me this whole story only recently, thirty years after the event), ten-year-old Tony was falsely implicated in a sodomy ring. Yes, that's what they called it, the filthy-minded adults: a 'sodomy ring'; imagine, a ten-year-old! The Sunbury schoolmaster was certain that Tony, coming as he did from an aristocratic school, Harrow, was thoroughly vicious and had corrupted the other three boys, all older than he. Poor Tony had no idea of what the Headmaster was accusing him. He was caned. The other boys did nothing to exonerate him, though to be sure they were eager enough to soothe his inflamed buttocks. Tony kept scratching his head, completely bewildered. [*Editor's note*: The reader will forgive this passage of senile rambling and pornography. That Mrs Trollope apparently judges this anecdote amusing is a sure sign of her mental disarray.]

While we were beset by our economic woes, Fanny Wright and Camilla had set sail again for the New World. As Julia Garnett wrote me, the Marquis de Lafayette had been denounced in the Chamber of Deputies for his treasonous adventures. Though the Crown still feared to prosecute him, he had failed to be re-elected by his shocked and disapproving neighbours (he lost office by just a hundred votes). Perhaps he was as celebrated in the Old World as Bolivar was in the New, both of them Heroes of a nearly antique grandeur whom tourists visited as frequently as the Tuileries Gardens or as, I can't say, the Niagara Cascades? But the Marquis's misadventures (and his truly noble hospitality) had drained his coffers, just as all his miscalculated plots had nearly turned him into a figure of fun (at least to his compatriots).

He needed America.

Fanny told me during a lightning visit to England on the Marquis's business that she had had a terrible to-do with the Lafayettes. He had decided to pay his first visit to the United States in forty-five years and Fanny hoped to accompany him. His daughter Madame de la Tour-Maubourg had put her tiny aristocratic foot down.

'She said that the Marquis's reputation would be destroyed for ever in the New World if he travelled with a red-haired adventuress a whole generation younger than he,' Fanny repeated with a certain neutrality. She was not like other women who hold up their hand and whisper shocking things with a suppressed smile. No, she spoke almost mechanically of events that touched her intimately. I think she was a genuinely impartial, philosophical person, rare enough in any form but virtually unknown amongst women. I can remember her sitting beside me in my dusty, shoddy Harrow drawing-room that an unusually bright sun was giving a white-glove inspection. My room had failed dismally and risked court martial . . .

'I pointed out', she said, 'that I'd be accompanied by my sister and that no one before had ever questioned our reputation. The General's daughter said she was talking about appearances not reality. She flew into a rage and said that her father was not a private individual, an old free-lance philanderer, but that he belonged to history and as a hero. And then she screamed at me

57

that I should remember that Madame de Staël had observed how remarkable it was that the flower of the old French aristocracy should have produced a Republican such as the Marquis. I couldn't tell of which she was prouder – their rank or his efforts to destroy it.'

'What did the Marquis have to say to all this?'

Miss Wright smiled. 'Poor old dear, I think he was fiercely chagrined by the noise and racket and red faces. I knew his gout was giving him trouble, not to mention his other infirmities, and no doubt he longed for a nap. In the end his son George Washington, ever the diplomat, suggested that Cam and I sail on a different ship so as not to *spoil*, as it were, Lafayette's triumphant return to New-York. The Americans had offered to bring him over in a state ship, but the General has refused out of modesty.'

'Modesty?' I drawled sceptically, but Miss Wright chose to ignore my innuendo. She said, 'So it's now all been arranged. Lafayette will embark on thirteenth July from Le Havre and will disembark a month later in New-York, where he will officially be received as the Nation's Guest.'

'And you?'

'Cam and I will sail on the *London* at the beginning of August and arrive in New-York early in September.'

This was the short, rational version, but in subsequent conversations with Cam, who came to stay with me for three days, and in long talks with Julia and Harriet Garnett, back for a week from France to see relatives of theirs in Bristol, I cobbled together a much stormier scenario.

Apparently Anastasie and her sister Virginie put pressure on Lafayette and forbade him to receive Miss Wright ever again at La Grange or at his *hôtel particulier* in Paris on the rue St Honoré. Nor must he travel with her in America. We English middle-class people cannot begin to imagine how disagreeable a French *marquise* can be once she is determined.

On her side Fanny was insisting that the Marquis adopt her and Camilla. They both called him 'Father' (I can well imagine she called him that even in the privacy of the bedchamber, not out of sauciness but with her grey-eyed Athenian intensity). And he liked to call them his 'adopted daughters', though he was careful not to do so in front of his, shall we say, *true* children. In any case, he showered any willing young woman with *familiarities*, if that word encompasses physical endearments bestowed in the name of the *family*.

He told her he couldn't adopt her, that his family meant too much to him, after all there were dynastic considerations (here the Republican stopped short of crossing that last, crucial line by abolishing distinctions of blood). And his daughters had lived with him through the horrors of prison, surely he owed them something? I imagined the pain that Fanny must be suffering, she who had never known a father and who as an adult had courted one – how terrible this rejection must have been!

There was so much pressure exerted on the poor old man that back in Paris he fell into a stupor for two days, sinking into unconsciousness and coming out of it only briefly – and when at last he emerged from this state, vomiting followed to an alarming degree of violence.

Fanny of course rushed back to his side. His daughters, discovering how close to death the Hero of Two Worlds had approached, feared the title might come to refer to this world and the next.

The daughters relented, covered Miss Wright with compliments, joked gently with their father and insisted that Fanny share his American triumph (though at a discreet distance). Fanny wasn't consoled. She'd been the last to suspect dissension at La Grange; now wounded deeply by the noble daughters, she refused to believe their honeyed words. All she could do was mutter to Lafayette, 'There must be another life where we may be united in peace.' In a brooding letter to me she wrote, 'His countenance and complexion still retain the evidence of the force of his late seizure' – a sentence typical of Fanny's *heavy* style (picture a brass-bottomed hot-air balloon incapable of getting off the ground).

When Fanny brought up the question of adoption again – 'but *lightly*', she assured me, as if such a proposal could ever be playful – the Marquis told her that he had promised his children he would never tamper with their status, as Louis XIV had tampered with his children's by ennobling his bastards. Not a very flattering analogy for Miss Wright and one that betrayed Lafayette's own delusions of grandeur. I must say I was surprised that Fanny found this argument dissuasive.

* * *

Today I am feeling better. My mind has cleared a bit in the Florentine pottery-wheel odours and I was even exposed to the Tuscan sun on a balcony outside the *salotto* as if I were a dusty old house-plant. I call it a 'balcony', but in fact it's a grand loggia where I like to spend most of my time, surrounded by plants, visitors, children, dogs. Thomas Adolphus makes a great fuss over me and decks me out in bonnets, scarves and plaids even though I'm fairly *steaming* under them all. Embedded in the walls are bits of ancient Roman inscriptions.

The dear Brownings called on me, Robert and Ba and little Pen, who looked absurd in his lace skirts and sausage curls, especially since Ba *will* stroke his hair with her tiny hands. She appeared to be far more ill than I feel, despite the fact that Browning assured us she is getting better every day. She actually said, 'My appetite has vastly improved – I am able to eat a whole egg every morning. Then at night I have a *tumbler*, yes, an entire tumbler of Chianti, which is a sort of claret.' I thought it pure affectation to tell an old Tuscan like me what Chianti is. 'I've come a long way from my days in Wimpole Street,' she said, 'when I would give my dinner to Flush.' She has a peculiar naphthalene smell.

I asked her what she had to eat during the day and she said the trattoria downstairs served them a dinner at three in the afternoon of soup and three dishes besides vegetables and pudding all for two shillings and eight pence a day (she still thinks in shillings). 'And I nibble on everything, despite the terrible heat. By six, when the first breeze blows in, I am prostrate. Dear Robert seats me in the deepest chair we have and pours eau de cologne into my hands and fans me till my eyes shut, for six is the hour of our siesta.'

I must say all of this nibbling and these cologne-soaks, this spineless napping during the day, depress me just to hear about. Ba continued, 'At seven-thirty, after our siesta, we drink coffee and walk and walk –'

'But wherever to?' I asked, thinking of the dusty, narrow streets canyoned by high façades.

'Why, on our balcony, of course,' she said, 'which is just wide enough for two. We walk until the moon comes up.'

Robert, as usual, was twitching – his eyes never stop blinking. He's frank and hardy, never very funny, but he has a great critical faculty – I've never dared show him any of *my* humble pages, you can be certain. He looks as if he could never grow old whereas she, worn out by illness and nibbling and applications of cologne, is already old, poor angel. The marks of pain are stamped on her face and body, the undeniable stigmata of suffering. It's as if she wept into her hands and the lines on her palms came off onto her face. She has covered her six-year-old boy with cockades of satin ribbon attached to his lace cap – no wonder she dotes on him, he was born after twenty-one hours of labour when she was already forty-three. I must say seeing Mrs Browning always makes me feel fitter and more normal than I am. She is working on *Aurora Leigh*. His conversation is like his poetry, but comprehensible.

For years I have imagined I would someday be writing an account of Fanny Wright's voyage to America with Lafayette, a trip that preceded my own by just a short while and that set the terms, as it were, for my disastrous odyssey. I kept newspaper clippings and relevant letters all stored in a box in my study in England and then up in the attic here in Florence, but just today I wept when I had them brought down and I discovered they were all water-stained and shattered and severely *eaten*, not that I've ever seen or even heard a mouse here in the Villino.

Now I haven't the energy to ferret out fresh information about the General's trip, which in any event is public knowledge of a historic occasion of world-wide renown – the General wouldn't have needed my widow's mite to add to the treasure-house of his glory, though who knows, he seemed insatiable when it came to glory. Prince Metternich once told me that Lafayette considered noise to be fame, an event to be a success, a sword to be an uprising, and believed that he alone was the author of both the American and French Revolutions. As a popular ditty put it,

> *Honneur à Lafayette*
> *Sa tête toujours nette*
> *Car il ne pense à rien*
> *Aussi dort-il fort bien.*

> All hail the mighty Gilbert
> Whose head's as shiny as a filbert
> The sum of his thoughts amounts to zero
> And he sleeps as soundly as a hero.

Now, here's a clipping that says the United States have a new word for an universal ovation, *lafayetted*. Once in Tennessee I met an illiterate farm boy, his mouth full of corn mush, who told me his name was 'Fate'. I thought that rather ominous, and only later did I realize he was attempting to say 'Fayette'. Someone in Memphis even named her baby, 'Welcome Lafayette'. Oh, yes, after a crossing of thirty-three days he arrived in New-York Harbour in a simple American packet, the *Cadmus*, since, as I mentioned, he'd refused President Monroe's offer of a governmental frigate.

A ship, the *Chancellor Livingstone*, sailed out to greet the *Cadmus*, carrying the President and many notables as well as a band playing '*Où peut-on être mieux qu'au sein de sa famille?*', 'Where can one feel better than in the bosom of his family?' Eight steamships transporting 6,000 dignitaries formed the General's cortège. For the Americans, Lafayette was a beloved uncle who had had the good grace not to visit often or overstay his welcome; he exerted no influence, usurped no one's power and was content just to be worshipped. He also had the stamina to travel up and down the country and to stop in every village, eat a badly cooked meal in every town and stoop to be crowned with flowers in every city by the local matrons splitting out of sweat-soaked silk dresses. In New-York he was accompanied by the Lafayette's Guards, each man wearing the great soldier's portrait in a medallion pinned to his chest. Bands were playing 'See the Conquering Hero Comes'. Common wisdom held that a republic is always ungrateful to its benefactors; the United States were determined to prove the contrary.

The General arrived in New-York in the sweltering heat of 16 August 1824, an inferno unknown to Europeans, just as American blizzards are equalled only on the Russian steppes. Fanny and Camilla arrived there on 10 September. By then the Lafayette circus was in full swing, a welcome unparalleled in American history, more a way of consecrating the wealth and dignity of the new Republic than of staging the deification of an individual.

Fanny had promised the Lafayette family that she would tag along behind the General at a discreet distance, but her arrival was announced in the New-York papers as the author of a book praising the United States – *and* of a play, *Altorf*, a sort of Swiss tragedy, if that is imaginable; it had been staged in New-York during her first visit and to much acclaim. That she'd been unable to arrange a London presentation had only proved to her the irreversible degeneration of the English stage, nay of English civilization, indifferent to her drama of Alpine republicans oppressed by Austrian monarchists. Now, as a returning admirer of America and as Lafayette's friend, Fanny was not allowed to book a room in a hotel. The erstwhile wife of the on-again, off-again mayor of the city, a certain Mrs Cadwallader Colden, put up Fan and Cam. Later Mr Colden would help Fanny in innumerable ways.

Lafayette (or so he averred) had begged the New-Yorkers to delay their ball in his honour until the Miss Wrights should arrive to share the pleasure. If I express a shadow of doubt I do so because this master careerist had surely already detected the first hints of the new American prudishness. Even Miss Wright had noticed that in the four years between her first and second visits American women had become less self-reliant and outspoken; they were now civilized enough to afford a simpering deference to their men – and a new conformity to mincing, blushing conventions they'd once been too busy to observe.

No matter. The ball had been delayed (on account of bad weather, one of my mouse-nibbled newspapers suggests), but if Lafayette preferred his gallant explanation, so be it. I certainly don't mean to quibble except to suggest that his intoxication with his own apotheosis had given him a new *raison d'être* that outweighed the charm of his long, frenzied and idealistic conversations with his red-haired Scottish 'daughter.' Even on their first day in New-York the Marquis did not manage to visit Fan and Cam before midnight. He'd been delayed by a long dinner and play offered by the Frenchmen of New-York and he arrived seeping brandy fumes and smiling foolishly with that antic gaiety one always feels upon seeing one's old friends in an amusing new setting. In New-York no matter how still and oppressive the day-time heat, at night great salt winds sweep the whole island clean and it was in this skirt-billowing, hat-stealing freshness that the three friends sauntered down the deserted streets. Once they were back in their quarters, Fanny was ready to take her familiar perch on her papa's stiff knee but he demurred out of deference to Mrs Colden, although she was a woman, apparently, on whom all the proprieties were lost.

The New-Yorkers, as a sign of their newfound Francophilia, decided to call their ball for Lafayette 'The Fête.' The Hero of Two Worlds made his grand entrance (all alone, nowhere close to Fanny) into the decorated hall of Castle Garden near the entrance to the harbour, I believe. He marched in to the screech and blatter of the usual out-of-tune American band. He ascended a sort of throne in a blue and white makeshift pavilion designed for him. Behind him a painting that showed Lafayette defeating Cornwallis at the Battle of Yorktown some forty years earlier was slowly rolled up to reveal a transparency lit from behind of La Grange – or, as Cam wrote, 'the château as imagined by someone who'd never seen it, a vast pile of many aery spires reflected in a swan-strewn moat, whereas our real dear La Grange is just a tidy working farm.'

Fan and Cam were not allowed to approach the throne. They were half-amused, half-amazed to see Lafayette's visage imposed on every belt, glove and fan, even on the stocks of rifles – but his countenance as it was when he was a young man with bony features, a gold pirate's earring and a powdered wig. Every man and woman in the room, and there were thousands, drew near him for a few words, if they were of the gentry, or for a mere smile from the nation's saviour, if they were more humble. A few old men were content just to touch his boots. 'One would say he's become the king he beheaded,' Fan remarked sourly to Cam.

At two in the morning the Marquis seemed to awake from an evil spell and to recall his 'daughters.' He asked them if they were amusing themselves, but he spoke in French in order to conceal his exact degree of rapport with these young, attractive women. In any event Americans always assume French is a language used to convey risqué meanings and when they hear it they invariably smile with a little tilted grimace of indulgence toward naughtiness.

The Marquis hurried his girls off into a steamboat, the *James Kent*, which conveyed them up the Hudson to Albany and back, a five-day trip. Fanny had just been waiting for this moment to fall back into her nourishing old ways with her venerable friend, though it must have occurred to her that they'd only ever had but one subject, America, and how it had United their own separate States into a spiritual domain. Now they were, alas, in the real vulgar America, the General as its Hero, Fanny as an almost unwelcome accessory, and their glorious tricolour dream of Red Indians, white settlers and blue stockings (or blue-bloods) had been replaced by a noisy, eternal Fête, soggy bunting and very long orations.

Oh let me glance through these clippings before their yellow lacework shatters under my thumb. The widow and son of Lafayette's old comrade Alexander Hamilton were aboard the *James Kent* and their reunion was tearful, enacted before the avid eyes of reporters and the broad-chested contentment of republican dignitaries. Fanny once again had to walk the deck alone and watch the dawn creep up over the stifling forests engulfing the banks of the Hudson and listen to the paddle-wheel slapping the muddy waters.

A week later and they were in – where? I think it says Newark, where the General received large peaches from the extensive fruitery of Mr Taphagen. In Bergen, New Jersey, he received – yes, it looks like a *cane* made from an apple tree under which Washington and Lafayette had dined forty-three years earlier. The mayor of Bergen had the morbid effrontery to say, 'And may you, Sir, after ending a life of usefulness, be admitted into the regions of everlasting joy and felicity.' So much for American delicacy.

In Elizabethtown, the Nation's Guest benefited from 'a most charming and tasteful display of fruits of various climes, and countries, ice creams, jellies, etc.'. The Masons of that town hymned him with yet another allusion to his imminent death:

May he live
Longer than we have time to tell his years
And when old Time shall lead him to his end
Goodness and heat fill up one monument.

N'importe quoi, as the French say, rolling their eyes: any old thing at all must do. In another poem recited the same day Lafayette was rhymed with 'ere yet' and 'forget.'

In New Brunswick he was besieged by citizens wearing a special Lafayette badge. He dined at Follett Hotel with about one hundred others, including poor Fan and Cam who were banished below the salt. At Princeton the sheep-eyed ladies were assembled on the right, the goatish men on the left, leaving a central aisle by which Lafayette could approach a brand-new temple at the centre of the Campus where, this time, it being a learned institution, he was addressed in Latin (*'Salve, Dux clarissime, nobis amicissime, nobis carissime, La Fayette'*). A local lady, granddaughter to Ben Franklin, presented Lafayette with a ring that Franklin had once worn. There was also a brooch with some of Franklin's hair stuck in it. Poor Fanny saw almost nothing – she was pushed to the back of the horde. In the next city the Marquis was especially delighted by twenty-four virgins, clad all in purest white, representing the twenty-four states. In Trenton he was reminded once more of his imminent death. What was this New World obsession? A willingness to honour someone only if one could be certain he'd soon be dead? A private club of old soldiers, the New Jersey Cincinnati, were quick to announce, 'May death, which soon or late must come to us all, come late to you.' Thankfully the Marquis's English wasn't up to these subtleties.

While in New Jersey Lafayette and his 'suit', as the Americans call it, visited the estate of Napoleon's brother Joseph, the ex-King of Spain and of his son-in-law, Charles Lucien Bonaparte, nephew of the Emperor and married to his own cousin, Joseph's daughter. To give Charles his full operetta title, we must call him Prince of Musignano and Canino. Unlike so many members of his family, the Emperor's brother had emerged out of the Napoleonic Wars with a fortune and Charles with an interest: descriptive ornithology. He was well placed in New Jersey, where he could have confined his study to the ladies' hats.

Joseph's estate, Point Breeze, encompassed seventeen hundred acres turned out in ornamental Spanish gardens and ponds as well as swan-shaped boats, the real birds competing with their simulacrae. The grounds were covered with twelve miles of winding carriage paths. The rooms were outfitted with paintings by François Gérard of Napoleon as Emperor of France and of Joseph as King of Spain.

Fanny was disgusted by the dinner of nine courses served on heavy silver salvers by *bearded* servants in livery and prepared by the ex-King's French chef – Joseph, she wrote, called himself, 'out of *modesty*,' the Count of Survilliers and on the occasion of Lafayette's visit opened up his grounds and rooms to the locals, whom he referred to as 'our American peasants.' She added, scornfully, that when his original house had burned down two years earlier the 'peasants' had rescued his many treasures from the collapsing palace – 'and later returned them all, without stealing a thing, which so astonished his ex-Majesty that he thanked them in a paid advertisement in their *Bordentown Journal* for their amazing *honesty*, which only vexed them that he'd ever questioned it.'

I can't help wondering what caused what – was Fanny irritated by Lafayette's neglect or did she find these European ceremonies and displays repellent?

New Jersey was a bounteous land, rich in forests and wildlife – Charles Bonaparte had killed and studied falcons, woodpeckers, ducks, grebes, rails, cardinals, wood thrushes, flickers and passenger pigeons. He'd also catalogued 174 native plants unknown to Europe. He'd been made a member of the Philosophical Society in Philadelphia, a small group of natural scientists, one of whose members, Thomas Say, was the distinguished Quaker entomologist (though not a pacifist; in fact Say's family were 'fighting Quakers' and had backed the American Revolution).

Charles introduced Fanny to Say, who spoke to her for the first time of New Harmony, the atheistic Utopian colony that her fellow Scot, the industrialist Robert Owen, wanted to establish in Indiana on the banks of the Wabash. This proposed experiment in socialism delighted her – especially as she was fuming with anger over her nine-course dinner.

When Lafayette entered Philadelphia on 25 September 1824, Frances and Camilla were left behind in the dust as the Great Man reviewed the gathered throngs – the Red Men of Pennsylvania, Cordwainers, Weavers, Rope Makers, Ship Carpenters of Kensington, the German American Beneficial Society, Butchers on Horses

– but there: the paper has just splintered! At this event the *Gazette* called Lafayette 'the great expected,' as if he were the Messiah. Lafayette travelled in an elegant barouche drawn by 'six handsome cream-coloured horses' while Fan and Cam walked, jostled by 'fifty thousand free men,' as they watched the curious cortège, including the Printers in one carriage, at work at their trade, pulling impressions of an interminable Ode in which Washington was called 'Sainted.' Lafayette, the 'observed of all observers,' was called 'god-like.' Next: Coopers making casks in a carriage bearing banners of adzes. Along the parade route hundreds of stagecoaches were drawn up and rented out as viewing stands to the horde of spectators.

Poor Fanny had a mouthful of dust by the time she'd battled her way back to her lodgings, which she quickly discovered had been pre-empted by a certain Carrol of Carrolton. Eventually in the mêlée cots in the attic, amongst the servants' quarters, were freed up for her and Cam. Of course they were not invited to the Masonic Dinner, judged the most sumptuous ever served in America. An azure tapestry of subtlest fretwork was suspended from the ceiling to separate the orchestra from the four hundred diners. Gas lamps, turned down to their dimmest, had been placed on every table; they all sprang into brilliancy the instant the Nation's Guest entered the hall. The floor was covered with sand shaped to resemble baskets of fruit and wreaths of flowers.

Fanny, of course, cared nothing about display and pomp, but she was highly alert to every sign of Lafayette's love or indifference. She must have suffered from his ignoring her – and from so much evidence of his rather childish vanity.

Fanny was with him the next day, however, when he headed overland to Baltimore and eventually to Washington. Little Cam was feeling the stress of the journey and longed for the nation's capital, where they were planning to spend several weeks. They would have slipped unnoticed into Washington early one evening but the Marquis took pity on his escort, whom he judged to be exhausted. They reined in before a country inn but discovered it was called the Waterloo, which so angered his American hosts on behalf of the Nation's Guest that they were forced to go on to the next establishment. Some members of the Marquis's 'suit' wanted to burn down the Waterloo, but Lafayette, with a soft smile, reminded them of the freedom of speech. As it turned out the inn, the property of an unregenerate Tory, almost never attracted any custom, but the Tory was rich and could well afford such pleasantries in poor taste, *les lubies d'un loyaliste*.

Although the Marquis talked of his escort's weariness, I'm certain he wanted to enter Washington the next morning in full daylight before a cheering crowd, properly forewarned, and he needed time to sort out his costume and restyle his coiffure.

Lafayette took all this very seriously. Every noble word and deed and tribute was being meticulously recorded by his faithful secretary Levasseur, who would eventually publish a handsome tome with a leather binding and marbled endpapers, *Lafayette en Amérique*, which would seem an addition to the genre inaugurated by the holy psalms: all praise. Though Levasseur lacked the divine inspiration, of course, and oh, the sublime poetry.

Lafayette had been led to think that Congress might reward him – with money – for his youthful help to the emerging Republic (or treasonous, cheese-paring colonies, depending on one's vantage). He badly needed fresh coins in his private coffers, depleted by revolutions at home and his own absurd extravagance. Yet he had reason to doubt the munificence of a country founded on tax evasion.

In Washington he played everything very cautiously. He was taken up by Martha Washington's granddaughter, 'Nellie' Custis Lewis. Nellie had been the first President's darling and had enjoyed the deference of the nation while the capital was still at New-York and Philadelphia; when the government wasn't in session the Washingtons all removed to Mount Vernon where Nellie delighted her grandfather with her whims and antics as much as the Duchesse de Bourgogne had ever amused her great-uncle,

Louis XIV (these grumpy old men *need* pretty girls to hop about and chirp like pet birds).

Nellie was no longer a pretty, fetching child. She had become an overconfident if startlingly plain political hostess. She had married unhappily, lived on a vast estate near Mount Vernon, wrote awkwardly metred poetry, maintained a gossipy international correspondence and had given birth to eight children, only one of whom outlived her (poor woman!). She'd been raised at Mount Vernon with Lafayette's son George. They were old friends and enjoyed the cosy intimacy of brother and sister. As soon as Lafayette and his party arrived in the capital, George warned Nellie about the scheming Miss Wright, who was determined to force the old man to make her a *marquise*, either by marriage or adoption.

'Fine,' one can just hear Nellie exclaim. 'Leave her to me. I'll stop her. I'll go the whole hog!' for that's the sort of democratic expression even the grandest ladies in the New World employ.

Nellie swung into action. She kept the old General beguiled with little luncheons and teas and suppers where pretty ladies who spoke some French served the old man choice morsels and swooned over his historic exploits. After all those Baptist sermons and Masonic handshakes and long dusty parades, the General was at last served tasty food and impudent but admiring conversation. In those days Washington was just a few elegant houses on muddy streets in Georgetown and even fewer massive government buildings and monuments, as if its population was made of swarming fellaheen living at the base of the pyramids whilst constructing them, but despite its marble halls and shabby boarding-houses, its *gratin* was richer and crustier and more cosmopolitan than elsewhere in the United States. And the Capitol building, though barely completed, had bolder proportions than I ever saw before. The elegant eastern front, to which many persons give the preference, is on a level with a newly planted enclosure which, in a few years, will offer the shade of all the most splendid trees which flourish in the Union, to cool the brows and refresh the spirit of the law-makers.

When Lafayette asked if the sisters Wright could be invited to

71

an intimate supper one night, Nellie said, 'Well, Papa –' for she, too, had taken to calling him her father – 'they wouldn't feel comfortable there for there will be nothing but respectable women.'

'My dear Nellie,' the General sputtered, 'I assure you –'

'Oh, you men are all alike, always fascinated by these red-haired *schemers*, and I, too, find Frances and Camilla delicious and, well, *original* –' here she leaned on the pejorative French meaning of *originality*. 'But at our little gatherings, which aren't at all intellectually *demanding*, there's really no room for Miss Wright's Philosophical Questions. And then, dear Papa, is it wise for you to be seen running with these Maenads, these mad, unchaperoned women, for Washington is a bit stiff and you will be addressing Congress any day now and we want your honour to remain unblemished, don't we? Remember, America is not as sophisticated as France.'

When he objected again, but a bit less confidently, Nellie said, 'When you talk that way, so pure yourself in refusing to see anything compromised in another human being, especially someone you so indulgently refer to as a *lady*, I can only remember my own dear grandfather with his perfect posture and somewhat *wooden* smile and his uprightness which made us all dissolve into a *fou rire*, so touched were we by his kindness and beatific outlook on fallen humanity. No wonder he was able to found a nation, even if he was no better a judge of character than you are, darling Papa!' And here Nellie would have crawled up on Lafayette's lap had she weighed somewhat less.

Lafayette then fell to reminiscing about General Washington's astonishing rectitude. Yet a third time he came back to Miss Wright's plight as a woman on her own in a new city and now Miss Nellie rapped him playfully on the knuckles with her closed fan and said, 'Hush! I can't have you plague me any more with your Hebridean Harridans. I know exactly what she's up to, any other woman would, she's husband-hunting without wanting to acknowledge that you already had a wife, the noblest of them all, to whom –' and here Nellie lowered her head, wiped her smile away and solemnly engaged his glance – 'to whom you promised your *eternal* fidelity.' Then Nellie laughed recklessly and let her Tidewater accent drawl all the more coquettishly: 'And I'm not sure I'm all that captivated by your Fanny, who's so uncharming – no matter what other virtues one might accuse her of, charm would never be one of them – and so *tall* and *masculine* and no longer in her first youth. In fact she's gone off already as redheads so often do, sooner rather than later. Can't you see, Papa, she just wants in on history!' Nellie pronounced the last word as 'Hiss-truh.'

Nellie rang a silver bell and provided the gouty old darling with a drop of sherry before she sent him off to bathe and dress for the evening.

As he let his manservant pour water from a silver bucket over his thickening, undraped torso, Lafayette had a whole new set of opinions to absorb: Fanny as a humourless man-eater, an ageing, raddled beauty intent on desecrating a sacred widowerhood – these were unfamiliar but penetrating images. The reader may wonder how I'm privy to such thoughts and tête-à-têtes, but I am a woman of wide experience, after all, and I much later had a long talk with the Marquis's secretary, Levasseur, who gave me the drift of what was said in Washington. Levasseur, by the bye, never once mentions Miss Wright in *Lafayette en Amérique*. The family made sure she was expunged from the record.

At first and from a long distance, Nellie had been kind to the Wrights, and had helped them find suitable accommodations in New-York and Baltimore, for instance. But after she'd been given her 'assignment' by George Washington Lafayette, she took relish in making life difficult for Fan and Cam. She had another reason for disliking Fanny. In Philadelphia, Fanny had met an agent of the brand-new Haitian government, Jonathan Granville, an attractive mulatto who was staying in a private home since he knew he'd never be given a room in a boarding-house. There he was able to receive Fanny, whom he treated with hand-kissing suavity, possibly because she was part of Lafayette's intimate circle.

Granville had spent several years in Paris in the French army and had the manners and speech of a European gentleman. When a white man of Philadelphia apologized for having mistreated him, Granville replied, 'Benefits I engrave on marble, insults always on sand.'

He made a strongly favourable impression on Fanny, who exulted in this eloquent proof that Negroes could be the equals of whites, a conviction she had held as an a priori before its truth was demonstrated. At this point she still believed that racial prejudice would gradually diminish in the United States if whites could meet a man as brilliant and courteous as Mr Granville. He explained to Fanny how Haiti was eager to welcome freed slaves from the United States since revolution and civil war had greatly depleted the new country's population. 'But now,' he said, 'we have peace and prosperity and we await our dusky brothers with open arms. I am here to find American freedmen to help us repopulate our country. We find that American blacks are superior to all others . . . ,' a bit of pointless snobbism that temporarily flummoxed Fanny. She assured him that she was Lafayette's personal representative and would speak for Haiti's cause to the General. 'I hasten to add', she said, 'that the General is as appalled as I am by American slavery. I've never yet seen men and women in chains, much less a slave auction or a public thrashing . . .' She suddenly wondered whether she was afflicting the sensitive mulatto with her harsh words. 'But that such things exist at all makes a mockery of American claims to be the land of the free. Lafayette and I are determined to find a solution to the slavery question.' Mr Granville bowed his head in acknowledgement of such generosity of soul, but was it also to conceal a half-smile at Fanny's naïveté?

As they spoke in a little solarium at the back of a big brick house off Rittenhouse Square, the sun was setting and no one had brought in a lamp. Fanny studied Mr Granville's long hands which looked blacker and more velvety in the half-light and raised her eyes to his full lips and extremely white teeth. She no doubt found him to be as handsome as the Cincinnati freedman I later

74

so admired, Mr Jupiter Higgins, a strong broad-chested buck who would aid my family in its darkest hour and offer me personally his sincerest friendship. He's somewhere in Canada now – how I would love to be able to write to him.

Well, Nellie was most displeased when she heard about Fanny's private tryst with a Haitian. She was convinced the rendezvous had been of a romantic, even a sensual, nature; in any event, as a Virginia slave-holder herself, living, as it were, atop a powder keg, she could not accept any encouragement of Negroes' aspirations toward freedom. Like all Southerners she was horrified by the very idea of a Negro nation, one that had been founded after the slaughter of hundreds of French colonists.

Nellie decidedly did not invite the Miss Wrights to the Georgetown house of her older sister, Martha Custis Peter, nor, three days later, to her own mansion, Woodlawn, in Arlington. When Lafayette went to Yorktown with Nellie to watch a re-enactment of his victory there, Fan and Cam were not notified. Nellie wrote a friend in a letter I had a copy of, 'The fair Ws did not go to Mt V—n with the Gen'l or to York with him, or Alexandria. Entre nous do I not deserve well of my country for this good deed, cost what it may to *myself*? They were resolved to go, and he could not say *no*, until I taught him how to set his mouth and pen to a *negative* position.'

Although Lafayette spent little time with the Miss Wrights, they amused themselves by frequently attending the House of Representatives, where a special gallery has been set aside for women – which shows, in this one regard, the superior gallantry of the Americans, since in England women are entirely forbidden in the House of Commons as distracting temptresses. American men are bluff, gruff creatures who turn to women only for actual breeding and otherwise prefer one another's company, but by way of contradicting my theory, in Washington the most distinguished Representatives were endlessly crowding upstairs to the Ladies' Gallery to wait on Fanny and Camilla. And to be sure Fanny had opinions on every subject they were debating, which only drew more and more men around them, partly to laugh, no doubt, and partly out of astonishment that the woman could think.

When I attended the debates a few years later I was shocked to see that the Representatives all wore their hats indoor, leaned dangerously far back in their chairs and threw their legs up on the desks in front of them, dozed and talked – above all, *spat*. Every man in America spits and when one visits the White House, for instance, one sees that the hems of the women's gowns are all soaked in the brown expectorations as are the little Aubusson carpets, for nothing anywhere is immune to the terrible habit of spitting.

Foreigners laugh at the grand schemes the Americans have hatched for their capital city and point out that so far only one boulevard, Pennsylvania Avenue, has been realized, with the Capitol at one end and the White House at the other, surrounded by a few other government buildings and a handful of foreign embassies. But Fanny and Cam found plenty to do in the tiny city. They visited the national Post Office and attended the President's *levées*, held every other Wednesday.

The Miss Wrights also visited, as I did subsequently, the Bureau for Indian Affairs where the walls are entirely covered with portraits of all those chiefs who came to Washington to negotiate peace. They can be seen in all their strange finery and noble stoicism of expression – inexpressibly engaging, all the more so because their trusting hearts were betrayed by their Great Father, as they called the President. I need hardly add that between the betrayal of the Indians and the flogging of black slaves one had little opportunity for admiring the much-vaunted *freedom* and *equality* declaimed in Congress, from the stage and even in taverns.

Fanny's greatest interest, even this early on, further prompted by her encounter with Granville, was slavery and she used this free time in Washington to read up on all the laws of the various states governing the slave trade and the legal and civil status of the slaves themselves.

She devoted herself to taking careful notes about American politics, history and geography with an objectivity, a profundity, that I could never hope to rival, given my sketchy education and all-too-rapid and quintessentially *feminine* approach. But she had one ambition I can well imagine emulating – she wanted to meet all the notable men of the day, especially Jefferson.

She had by now accepted that the Lafayette and Washington families had mounted a cabal against her and her sister. But one morning she forced her way into Lafayette's rooms, past his shocked manservant and into the Marquis's very *chambre*, where he was reading, glasses on and teeth out, some of the six hundred-odd letters that had been waiting for him in Washington. As a *vieux beau* he was alarmed more at being discovered *en déshabille* than he was vexed by the forced entry. '*Mais Fanny –*' he mumbled before he eclipsed himself behind a screen and re-emerged an instant later in a robe and with a *full*, brilliant smile. 'What brings you here so early?'

'I want to go to Monticello with you. You must write to Jefferson to ask if we can come. Here is some paper and a quill . . .'

She sat him down at a desk and fished his half-moon spectacles back out of a pocket embroidered with his crest. Lafayette's hand fluttered hesitantly above the paper and he raised troubled eyes toward his tormentress.

'Write to him', Fanny said, 'that you and he are the two men in the world I most esteem.' She waited for him to trace out the words and she read over his shoulder. 'In English *esteem* has a double *ee*, it's not *estime*. Now say, "I wish greatly, my Dear Friend, to present these two adopted daughters of mine to Mrs Randolph and to you. That's right, to you. They being orphans from their youth and preferring American principles to British aristocracy, they have passed the last three years in most intimate connection with my children and myself and have readily yielded to our joint entreaties to make a second visit to these states. Miss Wright has a small fortune and a large ambition to solve the problem of slavery, which she is eager – "

'Really, Fanny,' the Marquis objected. 'Wouldn't it be more polite to leave your programme rather vague? *Tu insistes trop, ma chère.*'

'Very well. Write what comes to you naturally, so long as it isn't pure hypocrisy.'

The Marquis stood up indignantly. 'I *forbid* you to speak to me in that tone.'

Fanny looked at him sadly before replying in a low voice, 'I will change my tone to please you so long as you will get us introduced to Monticello.'

The Marquis, who had not anticipated this strange slackening, as it were, in Fanny's gait, from gallop to a broken little trot, sat back down, bemused. He wrote out a fair copy, signed it with a flourish and gave it to Fanny to read. She strode about the room, perusing it, then closed it, heated the wax that fell on the envelope and grabbed his hand and pushed the Marquis's ring down into its molten impressionability. She even rang for the servant and told him to see it was sent off by a mounted courier to Virginia.

Once the servant had left the room Lafayette had opened his arms to Fanny. He even sat again and patted his knee, but she took a chair on the other side of the room and folded her arms tightly over her bosom.

'Oh, Fanny,' he said, 'come reward your good Papa with a little *calin*.'

But Fanny didn't budge. She just smiled at him sadly, as it were through a veil, indistinctly. 'Good Papa, perhaps,' she said, 'but bad friend. When we would discuss America by the hour back at La Grange, holding hands, our eyes brimming with idealistic tears, we saw it as a Utopia free of artifice, devoid of angling for advantage or of petty social airs. We would kiss and sigh and long to be in, say, Washington, where we would no longer fear to declare our love. But now –'

'Oh, Fanny,' the Marquis groaned. 'I know how disappointed you are. How little time for enjoying our *intimité* we've had. But don't you see – I am not only your Papa but the father to an entire nation?'

Fanny shook her head sadly. 'Your friend Washington, I thought, was considered the founding father of the republic. And *he* had the good sense to retire from office after two terms and to refuse to become King. I wonder if you would be able to refuse a crown?'

'Fanny, Fanny,' the Marquis said, leaping up and pacing up and down, as if his body had become as impatient as his spirit. 'You have known me for several years, yet with the first inconvenience, the first competing claim on my affection –'

'Oh,' she said, standing and moving to the door. 'If you think my objections are trivial and *personal*, you've misjudged the gravity of the situation.'

The old Marquis rushed over to her to prevent her leaving. There was a brief tussle and then Fanny, by walking back into the room, her head lowered but black with blood and anger, ended the struggle by conceding. That filled Lafayette with foreboding. 'You, my dear General, have not befriended the poor, homeless workers of New-York, the brutalized slaves in Virginia, the landless masses excluded from the vote, the women deprived of all rights, even the right to bestow the favours of their bodies as they see fit – no, you have received the plaudits of men, men, men. Of white men, the fat and enfranchised, and out of your infinite vanity, you have even been lavishly received by slave owners. Do you feel no shame to be waited on by these poor creatures whose bodies – even those of their women – can at any moment be flayed or fornicated, whose children can be sold and shipped off like livestock, who can be whipped quite literally to death?'

The Marquis shook his head and slumped in the chair by the window as if she'd become nothing but an irritating buzz in his ears.

'My poor Gilbert,' she said, once again regaining her isolated chair, though this time she did not hug her breasts. 'You have become an operetta Frenchman, a wind-up aristocrat doll to kiss chapped democratic hands, a platitudinous puppy propped up to review the troops, any troops, and at the same time a sort of rouged harlot looking out for a particularly large *petit cadeau* that Congress may or may not offer you.'

The Marquis had now taken to cleaning out the traces of wax

that had adhered to his seal ring, his *chevalière*. He was working quite conscientiously with a spare quill. When Fanny at last subsided he looked up through his massive brows and said, 'Fanny, Fanny, it's frightening when you get into these moods.'

She rose, went over to him. He cringed, as if she might do him harm, but she merely touched his shoulder lightly, as if ascertaining he was still a physical being. She reached the door and went through it, saying, 'I hope you get everything out of Congress you want.'

And indeed a day later, when Lafayette went before Congress he even managed to inspire those oafs to doff their hats, stand upright and stop spitting for an instant. There they stood, wadded mouths open, as he told them exactly what they wanted to hear, flatteries cut to their measure, and for his pains he was given 200,000 dollars, a baronial treasure, and a barony, or a township, of 20,000 acres in northern Florida which the Americans had just stolen from the Spanish.

And Fanny got her wish. She and Cam were invited to join Lafayette and his secretary at Monticello. Fanny was delighted because to the degree she'd become disillusioned with Lafayette, to that same degree she'd begun to pin all her hopes on Jefferson. After all, Jefferson had been born in America and though tainted with aristocratic manners during the period when he'd lived in Paris as Ambassador, nevertheless he was a true Cincinnatus, a virtuous farmer who had served the state and then returned to his fields not richer but considerably poorer than when he took office. Jefferson, for her, was the author of the Declaration of Independence, not the owner of slaves, an inherited taint he, no doubt, reviled more than she regretted. In fact, for Fanny, Jefferson held the clue to abolition; she was certain he'd thought about it longer and harder than anyone else. She would learn from him what she could do to free the slaves.

Eight

Fanny was such a mental creature that the inconveniences of American travel – the rough roads, the springless carriages, the nearly unfordable rivers, the inns and their *tables d'hôte* where men and men alone supped and spat – these inconveniences she scarcely registered, so intent was she to reach Monticello, so captivated was she by her anticipation of conversations with Jefferson. She knew he was old and ill, but her response to his decrepitude was not sympathy but avidity – she was eager to have his last thoughts, to possess his last moments. Fanny liked old men because they responded to her and they had wisdom to impart. If men like to take girls' virginity, women lust after men's senectitude. [Omit? Vulgar, and probably not even true.] Younger men knew less than Jefferson – and now more and more of them considered her to be a bossy, mannish frump.

She had in her pocket a letter Jefferson had written to Lafayette in reply to the one she'd dictated to the Marquis:

You mention the return of Miss Wright to America. Should her course lead her to a visit of our University which, in its architecture only, is as yet an object, herself and her companion will nowhere find a welcome more hearty than with Mrs Randolph, and all the inhabitants of Monticello. This Athenaeum of our country, the University, is as yet but a promise. But everything has its beginning, its growth, and end; and who knows with what future delicious morsels of philosophy, and by what future Miss Wright raked from its ruins, the world may, someday, be gratified and instructed.

Now as a mere woman, *inculte et inglese*, I get lost in Jefferson's prose, especially the bit about 'raked from its ruins' (What's being raked? How does Miss Wright figure in? Is she a blackened potato?), but this was Fanny's meat. After all, she could read Kant with assurance and in doing so she sincerely believed she was learning something, learning things, word by word, sentence by sentence. Of course even I could detect Jefferson's letter was an invitation and a flattering one.

Now we know that Jefferson was ruined and that to pay his debts he had had to offer everything – his house and grounds, his slaves and books, his farms and ploughs, his wines and table linens – in a public auction, authorized by the State of Virginia, though it was agreed that no matter whose the winning bid, Jefferson himself would have the right to live on there until his death (he was already over eighty). But Fanny certainly did not scruple to drink from his French cellar and eat the delicacies prepared by his French chef nor to be waited on by his slaves, many of whom bore a curious resemblance to Jefferson himself. She and Camilla travelled by diligence from Washington since they couldn't be part of Lafayette's party. Only when the conveyance she hired on the post road to haul her and Camilla up the hill struggled around its narrowing spiralling circumference, the horses foaming, did it occur to her that slaves had transported up the same slope every brick and Persian carpet, the *pendules* chiming softly in every room and the thousands of books. Every bottle of Bordeaux. (By the way, I heard later that Fanny and Cam and Lafayette and his son and Levasseur drank so much that Jefferson had to order a new stock of red wine as soon as they left).

Everyone was *en pleine forme*. Jefferson because he was receiving the Hero of Two Worlds and 'this flirtatious *man*,' as he called the none too feminine Miss Wright with a mixture of revulsion and perverse pleasure. Lafayette because for the moment he was amongst a few of his civilized equals and because he was far from Nellie's irresistible bullying. And Fanny because she had not one but two old men dancing attendance on her, albeit with a rictus in their step. Jefferson was happy but ill; he'd just had an abscess removed from his jaw (he called it an 'impostume') and had to drink his meals through a straw. And Cam was happy but ill with an intermittent fever and great weakness; she hated going up one of Jefferson's narrow staircases (he didn't like to waste space, but the ladies complained they couldn't squeeze their skirts up and down the paltry steps).

After an early supper in the hexagonal dining-room with its *baies vitrées* looking out on Mr Jefferson's trees, imported from every clime and continent, their party (which the tall, rickety old host had kept small despite the clamour of neighbours to be introduced to the Nation's Guest) migrated next door to the high-ceilinged salon. There, as Fanny told me, she would sit on the carpet at Jefferson's feet near the fire and gaze up at him with rapture, her face dreamy and a bit stunned from the nearly opaque red wine; her expressions were not reflecting any of the nuances of the conversation that was, quite literally, going over her head.

Lafayette, recalled to order by the gallantry Jefferson was showing the Miss Wrights, became tender and amusing with them once again and called them '*mes filles adorées*' as he'd done back in France. Fanny wasn't taken in. She looked coldly on his efforts. Lafayette was embarrassed to be snubbed in front of another fine old man. Jefferson, though he winced with almost every step he took, as if he'd been pulled out of working order by the same torture that stretched him so tall, insisted on showing the bare-shouldered Fanny every gadget in his house – the double doors that opened perfectly symmetrically when just one side was pushed; his own cosy bed under a lowered ceiling that concealed a storage cubbyhole and from which he had immediate access to his library; his wooden chair with the arm hypertrophied into a desk; the dumbwaiters concealed in the dining-room mantel – all products of his American ingenuity that no English lord would have condescended to invent, more's the pity. Fanny followed his tall, rickety body, as teetering and fragile as an automaton winding down; she was guided along with a passive delight quite new to her, as if she'd been mesmerized.

The third night they were there Fanny drew Jefferson out on the subject of slavery. Lafayette, who had once owned slaves in Guiana before the French Revolution and who back then had attempted their gradual emancipation, spoke with self-righteousness and some vehemence on the subject, but Jefferson measured his words. He said, 'At the time of *our* Revolution I attempted to pass a law to prevent slavery from ever being introduced into any *new* state, and I lost by just one vote. Even *before* the Revolution I proposed the manumission of my own slaves but our Virginia House of Burgesses refused me permission.' He poured more brandy. 'I now think that only gradual emancipation would work. And there must be found some way for compensating the planters, since half the wealth of the entire South has been sunk into black flesh. They are what we own. They are our real estate and our ambulatory savings accounts.'

Fanny was disturbed by this harsh and queerly pictorial way of talking, which seemed so at odds with Jefferson's usual equanimity. She attributed the change in tone to the slow moral malady of owning slaves a whole long life, his pale body pummelled and kneaded by manacled black hands. Despite his tone she was struck by his idea that slaves must be prepared for freedom slowly and methodically and that their owners must be compensated for the loss of property. This notion would become central to the Utopian experiment she herself was slowly formulating.

Fanny remarked with her usual wide-eyed insensitivity, 'Perhaps miscegenation is the solution. Maybe if blacks and whites interbred and produced a nice *café-au-lait* new race of humanity, all differences would dissolve.'

Alarmed, Jefferson raised one shaggy white eyebrow in his deathly pale face. His pallor suggested he'd seen the future and it was a frightening phantom. He said, 'The amalgamation of whites with blacks produces a moral and intellectual degradation to which no lover of his country, no lover of excellence in the human character, can innocently consent. Don't forget, Miss Wright, we have four million slaves in America.' Fanny could tell he must be quoting himself, so solemn and perfect was his phrasing, though he delivered his reply in his shaking, old man's goat voice. The November night was only slightly chilly but Jefferson's hands were arctic to the touch. The odd thing was that his slave Sally Hemings now came to the door and stood there, her eyes lowered but her posture somehow full and commanding, and Jefferson obediently rose to his inconvenient height and bade them all good-night and creaked off, as if he were badly in need of an oiling, taking Sally's arm just beyond the door, as an exhausted actor waits to collapse until he's in the wings. He was led off to bed by two brown young men who were quite obviously his sons, both tall mulattos with Ciceronian noses, domed brows and deep-set eyes.

The next day Jefferson spent the morning in bed, which was apparently so out of character that the whole anxious house was set to murmuring. But when he appeared at the early afternoon dinner table he seemed to have been patched back together. He even accompanied Fanny on a post-prandial walk to the estate workshops below the vegetable gardens and all the way back to the cemetery where soon enough he himself would be buried in palisaded splendour. Ordinarily he would feel exhausted if he walked more than a hundred paces, but today he had unusual stores of energy. He looked carefully where he stepped so afraid was he of falling and breaking one of those long, fragile femurs. He was like a horse that would have to be put down if it fell. The air was thick with the smell of burning leaves as if his pyre was already heating up. He took frequent exercise on horseback without tiring. And his figure remained as slim and erect as it must have been when he was twenty.

85

The next day he accompanied his guests to the University of Virginia, all red bricks and squat white columns. 'This will be the first institution of higher learning in America', he said, 'unassociated with religion.'

'A division essential to genuine learning,' Fanny interjected. She gave him a potted lecture on Rousseau and the Swiss educator Pestalozzi. Never for a moment did she imagine the two old men might have been studying these thinkers for decades. Although both Jefferson and Lafayette no doubt agreed with her heathenish sentiments, they were a bit shocked by her vehemence – Jefferson, in particular, had learned to avoid conflict over lost causes. It was raining lightly but Fanny appreciated the noble proportions of the Rotunda, the shape of the Pantheon in Rome but exactly half its size, and she admired its covered walkway and the sheltered paths linking it to the dormitory wings. There were ten partially completed pavilions to house the ten professors, only one of whom, a German, had already arrived. He'd been lured away from Oxford, but he looked slightly startled in his room, which still smelled of shaved wood, as if he'd been captured and forced to abandon the veld for a zoo. Fanny peeked in through his open door and asked Jefferson why the bed was so high. 'So that a slave can sleep under it,' Jefferson said.

'Doesn't that strike you as barbarous?' Fanny asked. 'The poor German.'

Jefferson laughed. 'My father used to say that when I was a boy I couldn't go to sleep if there weren't a smell of Negro in the same room.'

'I know you disapprove of miscegenation. But do you think the two races, once the blacks are liberated, will be able to live together in harmony?'

'No,' Jefferson said with a sigh and a visible stiffening of the joints, as if she'd sapped all social gaiety out of his bones by bringing them back to the insoluble problem. 'I'm a proponent of colonization. Blacks must be sent somewhere – back to Africa or to California or Haiti or Texas. Somewhere. The races were not meant to live together. I'm a member of a National Society for the Colonization of Blacks.' He smiled, then said, 'But I'm not at all consistent. I've petitioned the House of Burgesses to permit a few of my slaves, after they are freed, to be allowed to go on living at Monticello. The state law rules that a freed slave must leave Virginia within the year.' He laughed. 'Of course I am on record as saying that the vote will never be extended to children nor to Negroes nor to women, who to prevent degradation of morals and ambiguity of issue, should not be allowed to mix in public meetings with men.'

'Oh,' Fanny called out in a rare moment of coquetry, 'do you find us as tempting as all *that*?' Jefferson looked startled and finally said, with a chuckle of honest confession, 'Yes! Yes. I do.' And Fanny, though she did not agree with him about women not voting nor about the impossibility of the races coexisting, since she was, at least theoretically, quite prepared to live with a black man herself, provided he loved her at night and listened to her by day, nevertheless squirrelled away this new datum.

In the future she would never slap the old planters in the face with her progressive schemes. Perhaps out of respect to Jefferson, she was always alert to the susceptibilities of his tribe. As she came to believe in gradual emancipation and full compensation, she recognized the legal right of one human being to own another, which seemed a major concession to the planters simply out of friendship for Jefferson.

Wherever they walked she took Jefferson's arm and Lafayette was left with poor pale Camilla. Since both Lafayette and Cam were in love with Fanny and thoroughly intimidated by her, they seemed like puppies trotting along behind her, eyes unblinking with fixed rapture. At table Fanny sat on Jefferson's right, served him her own orangeade through a straw and asked him more and more questions about the University, which was obviously the dearest project of his old age. At the end of each evening Fanny would extend her hand for Lafayette to kiss while she looked at Jefferson and addressed a last remark to him.

If she had set out with all due calculation to revive Lafayette's passion for her, she could not have succeeded better. On the warm November morning when they bade farewell to Jefferson and headed for Madison's estate, Fanny and Lafayette rode ahead on two sleek borrowed bays while Cam came jogging along behind in a hired carriage with M. Levasseur and all the baggage. The Nation's Guest drew up beside Fanny. Their mounts walked. He said, 'Here I am, *me voici*, acclaimed by an entire country and scorned by the only woman in it I truly esteem.'

'Marquis, are you referring to me?' she asked without any obvious sign of flirtatiousness.

'Oh, Fanny,' he groaned. The horses' hooves kicked up fragrant fallen chestnut leaves and the two riders looked out over the valley veiled in a blue haze.

'It's odd,' she said, 'when I hear you, if I close my eyes, Marquis, I forget you could be my grandfather and I imagine an ardent young man.'

'Youth I no longer can lay claim to,' he said, 'but ardour has laid claim to me.'

'Neatly put,' she said, as if she were judging a performance of an art to which she was indifferent.

'Did you not hear me pacing up and down in the hall outside your bedroom door the last three nights?'

'But, Gilbert,' she said, and he clutched his heart, to show he was *bouleversé* that she'd employed his first name once again, after addressing him for so long and mockingly by his title. 'You're the one who pushed me aside, though now your romantic rhetoric would have it otherwise.'

'Oh, Fanny, how I've suffered over this dreadful *malentendu*. My children, much as I love them, have tortured me – and you, Fanny, you have said such cold, hateful things to me. I'll never forget that terrible moment in Washington.'

'I think it best we no longer see each other, for our love takes such different forms. You are the Nation's Guest and France's Host and your children's hostage and Nobody's Man, whereas I'm –'

'Fanny, *ma chérie*, you're starting again.'

They rode in silence through the forest in which the darkness was already thickening. Fanny didn't like to quibble with this man. If she had chosen to love a man the age of her grandfather it was because she wanted to count every hour with him as sacred, unique; she wanted a love with no future. In personal if not political terms, she hated the future. In order to thrive, the dead hand of convention needed to grab onto the future, the many, many years to come, the house to live in, the career to build, the children to raise, the reputation to defend. But they would have no children, no house, his several careers were in the past and they were, as a couple, going nowhere. Their goal was here, their destiny now.

But even in this intensely focused present they had still managed to quarrel. His children wanted their father's name unclouded by scandal, he himself wanted to honour his pact with his long-dead wife – and America wanted its French great-uncle neutered (old people in America, Fanny had noticed, were treated as lovable, half-comic eunuchs).

The thought flashed through Fanny's mind that now, just before another long visit with another ex-President, was not the right moment for a definitive break with Lafayette. It would be awkward, chatting and laughing with him constantly during their weekend at Madison's, and Fanny did not subscribe to such social hypocrisy.

But there were no right moments for a rupture, Fanny thought in her serious, reflective manner. Every element in a human union – the proprieties, habit, shared projects – was designed to perpetuate it. A rupture was always a catastrophe.

Now they could hear the carriage rumbling behind them, bearing along poor frail Cam and the argus-eyed Levasseur, frustrated that he was separated from his hero even for an hour. Fanny knew that she and the General had only another moment together unobserved and unlistened to.

She touched his sleeve with her small gloved hand. 'Adieu,' she said.

'But, Fanny,' the General exploded, 'you don't know what you're saying. You Anglo-Saxons are so unfeeling. One cannot end a great love like that . . .' He always said 'like that' in English as a translation of *comme ça*.

Fanny did not argue. She just looked off at the horizon, blending in darkness with the trees and the sky. She frowned and her big tragic mouth turned downward; someone who didn't know her might have imagined she was fighting off tears. But no, it was as if she was smelling something cool and threatening. She looked at him with a start, as though she'd momentarily forgotten him. She said again, but this time tonelessly, 'Adieu.'

Nine

This is where I come back into the tale, as a witness and even as a participant. Soon I'll be telling the tale of my own trip to America with Fanny.

Fanny had passed nearly three years in America on her second trip. After she parted ways with Lafayette, who had been unwilling either to marry her or to adopt her, she returned to Washington where she attended a thrilling lecture delivered to the Congress by Robert Owen, the Scottish philanthropist. He spoke of many things (I'm afraid he was fiercely opposed to God, whom he had proposed to replace with Community Spirit, and to Holy Services, for which he wanted to substitute Polite Conversation and Recreational Dancing). Oh, that was another world, less cynical than ours, more inspired, more philosophical – and infinitely more silly. It was all based on the idea that anything could be improved through System and 'I-know-what-you-want-better-than-you-do'.

From Mr Owen Fanny acquired the idea of Utopia. He had already successfully reformed Scottish work life in a cotton mill town that he owned outside Glasgow. He had abolished child labour (youngsters could not take their place in the factory until aged ten) and had reduced the workday from thirteen to just ten hours. He had built clean new cottages of two rooms for the labourers and insisted each domicile be maintained in the highest degree of hygiene. He arranged for the workers to appoint their own health visitors who would inspect each house and instruct the occupants in domestic economy and cleanliness. To improve the workers' conduct in the factory he had the foremen hand out daily grades. A 'silent monitor,' colour-coded for the illiterate, hung over each work station and read black for bad, blue for indifferent, yellow for good and white for excellent. He was against all punishment and operated only by a system of such marks. Not that I want to ridicule his humane methods, for in my novel *Michael Armstrong, the Factory Boy* I painted a shocking portrait of the youngsters in an ordinary mill – set to work at five, worked so hard and long they fell asleep standing at the looms and were beaten awake by foremen wielding long sticks called 'billy-rollers,' their pitiful wages drunk up by their bullying alcoholic fathers . . . In England in the 1830s 200,000 children were working the looms till midnight in steam-filled rooms deprived of light – and so malnourished they resembled dwarves.

At Mr Owen's factory the grog shop was banned or rather upgraded: the best Scotch replaced raw spirits. It was all sweet sobriety, bells on the leggings and endless precepts of an atheistical, self-improving sort.

Fanny, I suppose, was aching from her failure with the Marquis. She had embraced him as a liberated spirit and assumed that he, like herself, was above mendacity and ready to soar on the cool updraft of freedom. Fanny truly was an unfettered being. She belonged to no society except the extremely liberated one of her intellectual Glaswegian uncle and aunt and the fearfully philosophical salon of the ancient Bentham, deaf (both literally and figuratively) to all human claims. Bentham, it seems, could not endure to be in contact with another person's flesh and would scream if he was accidentally touched. A fine model for a young woman . . .

Fanny had money. She was healthy, her beauty, though already worn, was commanding: I saw her as Athena in helm and robe, leaning slightly on her spear, though others said she was Mercury, so manly were her lineaments. Camilla offered no objections to her plans, only loyalty and love and applause, and Fanny was never sensible to Cam's claims on her sisterly care. It was obvious to anyone who saw Cam that she was a frail child, pale and blue-veined as old Willow-ware and already *poitrinaire*.

Fanny was done with Lafayette – with his intolerable American triumphal parade, these bumpkinish honours handed out to an old Tartuffe of the Left. They were not consistent with her ideas of Republican simplicity and equality.

Done with Lafayette – but not with America. It was then that she heard Mr Owen's discourse; he had been born Welsh but now was a Scot like herself from Glasgow and even surer of his good opinion of himself than she was of hers. His own father-in-law, Mr Dale, had reputedly said to him, 'Thou needest to be very right, for thou art very positive.' Mr Owen was already well known in America, for many of its leaders had visited his New Lanark in Scotland and become aware of his 'new social system.' A Society for Promoting Communities had already been founded in New-York in 1822, based on Owenite principles. Thus when he addressed the Hall of Representatives at Washington he called out, 'By a hard struggle you have attained political liberty, but you have yet to acquire real mental liberty, and, if you cannot possess yourselves of it, your political liberty will be precarious and of much less value.'

Now what Mr Owen objected to was competition, which he thought led to senseless struggle, redundancy of effort and grave lacunae in the services and products society truly needed. He wanted everyone to be assigned jobs that would benefit the entire group. He wanted prices for goods to be fixed by the number of hours that went into their manufacture (by those standards my vast *oeuvre* would come very dear to you, greedy old reader). What he'd learned as an industrialist he was certain he could apply to agriculture. He had everything worked out – he even knew how the workers' dormitories would be laid out in parallelograms, which his critics called 'parallelograms of poverty.' He exhibited to Congress a model of all the communities he was going to build. Within each parallelogram were the culinary, dining- and washing-departments. At each corner would be lecture rooms, laboratories, chapel, ball, concert, committee and conversation rooms. Between the corners were dwelling-rooms on the first and second storeys. On the third floor were rooms for the unmarried and for children over two years old – for only infants were to be allowed to live with their parents. After the age of two children were to be guided by the entire community and raised in common quarters.

He even told Congress that the United States should (and surely *would*) soon be organized entirely into Owenite communities and that the word should be broadcast as quickly and as widely as possible so that no one would waste time and money pursuing any less advantageous scheme. He invited 'the industrious and well-disposed of all nations' to come to New Harmony, his Indiana Utopia that he was building on the banks of the Wabash. He spoke of a 'new empire of peace and goodwill to men.'

There, in New Harmony, he had just paid £30,000 for some 30,000 acres of the richest farmland and for the village and the equipment that had belonged to the followers of George Rapp, German Pietist peasants who sang while they worked and were forbidden to copulate [find a nicer word] lest they bring more sinners into the world. Since they couldn't reproduce they depended on fresh converts from Swabia or wherever it was. Father Rapp was a tall man with a beard like a black spade and the odour of cloves and a sepulchral voice who had burrowed a secret tunnel from his house out into the livestock barn so that he could suddenly materialize as if by miracle in the midst of his farmhands and catch the poor astonished Hansels and Gretels idling, gossiping or ogling each other. Apparently he'd decided – or rather learned during a heavenly vision – that Adam had at first been both male and female but had forgone this blissful

94

hermaphrodite's state through lust, which had caused Eve to split off as a separate being, curvaceous and disruptive. Now he learned that celibacy was more pleasing to God from his reading of Matthew XXII:30: 'For in the Resurrection they neither marry, nor are given in marriage, but are as the angels of God in heaven'. Father Rapp was so convinced that he personally would soon be introducing his followers to God that when he was dying he said with a look of astonishment, 'I'd esteem I was dying did I not know that I shall have to conduct my people to heaven.' He kept a fund of a million dollars under the floorboards so that he could pay to convey his followers to Jerusalem for the Second Coming as soon as it was announced.

What Mr Owen did not tell Congress – but which subsequently developed in debates in Cincinnati, that I chanced to attend – was that he was a militant atheist. By the time he was just nine years old he'd already seen through all the competing claims of the various religions. What had clinched his atheism was the discovery that Mahometans were more numerous than Protestants and were just as convinced in the truth of their beliefs.

He was a persuasive man. The gentle tone of his voice, his sometimes playful, but never ironical manner, the absence of every vehement or harsh expression, the affectionate interest expressed for the whole human family, his candour, his kind smile, his mildness – in short, his whole manner disarmed zeal. Fanny told me it was strange to see the mild, sonorous and wonderfully respectable Mr Owen intoning before the House of Representatives where most of the men sat at unmatched school desks in unmatched straight-back chairs, every last one of them incapable of sitting calmly and neatly upright. They read magazines, chatted loudly with one another, even ate, and of course everyone spat all the time into spitting boxes beside their small, children's desks. Big, over-ripe boys talking and spitting – that's the image I received, in such contrast to the dignified comportment of the Senators.

Fanny had visited New Harmony and came back with glowing reports, of Rapp and also of the new Owenite community. Owen's

New Harmony was the first and only place in America to declare that women were the equal to men. Mr Owen – and many of his followers – believed that 'natural marriage,' that is, a marriage between equals, was impossible given the present inferior level of women's education. He did not approve of the pledge to love one another till death us do part, since, as he argued, men and women are conscious that their affections do not depend upon themselves. At any moment, love can vanish. The old form of marriage, Mr Owen said, is 'irrational, because it obligates us to do what we may not be able to perform, and because it marks a disposition to enslave one half of our fellow creatures.'

Not that Mr Owen was a great champion of the fairer sex. He thought us jealous, undisciplined chatterboxes but said that 'education begun at the age of three years would eradicate these evil passions from our coming generation.' Apparently Mr Owen had rejected the stern God of his Protestant ancestors and their sterner doctrine of predestination, but he had retained all of their dourness. The milieu made the woman, woman's nature could be infinitely ameliorated, but the improvements all lay in the distant future. Men and women needed to overcome the evil ideas and associations of the selfish individual system in which they'd been raised. He foresaw the time when a morning's efficient labour would suffice and the citizen of Utopia could devote his afternoons and evenings to lectures, dancing, hobbies and horticulture. He was very keen about dancing.

I heard about Owen and Rapp when Fanny visited me unannounced in Harrow in October 1827. Fanny, who had always seemed so radiant and calm to me before, now appeared rushed, almost hysterical. Her hair was turning white, though she was only thirty-two. Her pale skin, concealing its bloom discreetly, was sallow and shrunken, as if she'd been hung from a rafter and cured in some ghastly jibaro ritual. She came unannounced into our house, Julians, at exactly the moment when it was most menaced.

Only that morning a bailiff had knocked solemnly at our door.

'I know you are in there; it's childish to hide from the law,' he'd said in his high, nasal, Cockney voice. He'd pounded and pounded on the door until the dust jumped off the wood panels like motes from a beat carpet. He'd peeked in through two of the windows, but luckily my husband was upstairs, prostrate from one of his bilious headaches and an over-liberal dose of calomel (I now think that he, poor thing, was suffering from a brain growth, which was eating into his judgement and unsnapping all his faculties, one by one, but we had no way of knowing that and judged him as a spoilsport and a malingerer, at least in our unchristian moments). My two girls and I were hiding behind the curtain we'd strung across the room in anticipation of that evening's play, Molière's *Imaginary Invalid* (which I now see had been badly chosen, given Mr Trollope's very real illness).

Thomas and Anthony were both at Winchester and Henry, back from Paris, was in London searching out a dancing and a fencing master, for Auguste had put it into his head that if he was to acquire no more in the way of Greek or Latin he should at least pick up the arts of a gentleman. Auguste had fashioned a mock sword out of a stick he had found in the woods and had carefully positioned Henry's limbs with his hands, teaching him how best to hold himself, to lunge and parry and trot across the room half-crouched. I can still see Auguste's slender, nervous hands stroking and adjusting and repositioning Henry's *attitude*, his *plastique*, exactly as if Henry were a still-wet clay statue under a damp cloth whom the sculptor exposes for a moment in order to pat and pinch, to dimple and extrude, before covering again.

Henry, I suspect, was a bit ashamed of his own girlishness – his pretty skin and silky hair, his downy cheeks and beardless chin, the soft layer of baby fat, with which his limbs were still *enrobé*, and he evidently welcomed the prospect of this physical *entraînement* which might hasten his growth, toughen his fibre and tune his movements.

Thus, as it happened, I was alone with my girls when the servant warned us of the bailiff's approach. All four of us shrouded ourselves in our makeshift theatrical curtain. We waited and waited until the bailiff finally shouted, 'It's just a matter of time before I serve you, my lords and ladies; Lord Northwick's agent has issued a distress against you.' He was not speaking of any kindly service, I can assure you. At last he trudged off, but we waited until we were certain he wasn't going to sneak back to a window and catch us. When we were sure he was gone for good we laughed and made light of it gallantly, but I felt bruised, as if someone had damaged me in some intimate, insulting way – indeed, as if a stranger had drugged me and pulled my two prettiest teeth. The girls quarrelled with each other with gnat-like buzzings of irritation, which was only to be expected, I suppose.

When Mr Trollope came down, unshaved and smelling of his medicament, his costume in disarray though I'd done everything to convince him to repair it on the principle that a smart appearance promotes an inner optimism, he groaned with despair. 'It's revenge,' he said. 'Lord Northwick knows he must lower all his rents since every last tenant is in arrears. He's singled me out for punishment because I got up the petition asking for a fifteen per cent reduction. He's agreed to our demands – or rather to *their* demands, since he's reduced their rents but not mine, all by way of punishing me.'

He sat down and lifted his grey-skinned hand from the table, stretched out his fingers and then laced his other hand over it, as if he were pushing a tight glove into place. Then he let his hand flop heavily back onto the table, lifted it and let it fall repeatedly in witless despair. He groaned audibly, as if responding to an inner harangue. At last he smacked his lips in cheerless *dégustation* and said, 'We'll have to move over to Harrow Weald and let out this place.'

I felt a constriction around my chest and was afraid my voice would come out odd, but it sounded just hoarse and defeated. 'When?' I asked. 'When shall we remove to Harrow Weald?' forcing myself to name that little farmhouse, miles away, far from all our friends, from everyone and everything. My heart sickened when I thought of the shabby little rooms of Harrow Weald where we would no longer be able to receive, where – worse! –

we'd have no rooms to which we might retire in search of peace. There I'd live and eat and read in the same room in which Mr Trollope would lie failing, for he seemed dedicated to nothing but failure. [I must omit all this – do I sound as if I'm whining?]

In the midst of this, the latest domestic emergency, Miss Wright descended on us. Later, when I told Harriet Garnett that I'd seen Miss Wright, I bubbled over with *such* enthusiasm (Harriet, now an old lady, only recently returned my letters to me here in Florence):

Never [I wrote at this time] was there I am persuaded such a being as Fanny Wright – if worship may be offered, it must be to her – That she is at once all that women should be – and something more than woman ever was – and I know not what beside . . . Will it be possible to let her depart without vowing to follow her? I think not. I feel greatly inclined to say 'where her country is, there shall be my country.' The more I see of her, the more I listen to her, the more I feel convinced that *all* her notions are right – she is pointing out to man a short road to that goal which for ages he has been in vain endeavouring to reach. Does poor dear Henry still continue to dream of Fanny Wright and settling in her Utopia? More improbable things have happened than that his wish should be listened to – but I dare not tell him so as yet – as his father has by no means made up his mind on the subject.

I cite all of this to remind myself how unqualified was my admiration for Fanny at this point. After that trip to America with Lafayette, she came sweeping back into my house that October and I sailed across the Atlantic with her and Henry and my girls and Monsieur Hervieu on the fourth of November, less than a month later, leaving all Harrow in amaze.

Fanny worked on me with effective guile (or was she truly hesitant?). She definitely looked drawn, all the more because she refused to paint her face and because she'd adopted the baggy tunic and outsize bloomers that were worn as a uniform at New

Harmony, garments the colour of oatmeal that floated about her emaciated body like a flag drifting around a pole. But when I asked her if she'd been ill she shrugged and smiled sweetly, a bit *wildly*, as if I had mentioned an embarrassing failing.

'Yes, I caught something – that's why I am back here in Europe,' she said. 'But dear Mrs Trollope, my real reason to be here, in this dismal Old World, is to *recruit*.'

I raised an eyebrow at the bold word.

'Yes, *recruit*,' she emphasized. She hadn't even removed her gloves, poor cotton things with baggy fingers and a loose fit around the wrists. 'I especially want a woman, a bosom friend, to go with me back to Nashoba, where I have left Camilla.'

My heart started pounding and once again I wanted to be her special friend, her only friend. 'Nah? Nahtoe?' I struggled with the odd Choctaw name.

That convinced her to start at the beginning. After her break with Lafayette she had spent the season in the city of Washington where she had been so popular that President Washington's spiteful granddaughter Nellie had stayed away in *droves* (if an individual, multiplied by rue, can be said to constitute a herd). There Fanny had studied laws relating to the Negro. She gave private readings of her work and attended the vote at the Hall of Representatives, which determined that John Quincy Adams would win as President over the raging Populist Andrew Jackson, even though Jackson had clearly garnered the popular vote. Miss Wright was shocked by this chicanery, divorced from the spirit of true democracy; the American voters were even more out-raged and suspected foul play.

After Fanny met Robert Owen she and Cam travelled a thou-sand miles overland to Indiana and New Harmony by stage, horseback, boat and foot, a frantic pell-mell journey that left them both exhausted. They arrived just as the Rappites were departing, like so many capable cows. Father Rapp was rounding them all up and herding them onto a boat that would convey them toward their next destination, the colony of Economy in Pennsylvania outside Pittsburgh.

Miss Wright was passionate about them. She even followed them to Pennsylvania and observed with focused admiration their way of efficiently (if always placidly) clearing the land, building log cabins in which the sexes could be segregated, raising their church, trapping and hunting game, ensuring the safety and purity of the grain they'd brought with them and so on. She would have insulted George Rapp, who had been trained as a vine-dresser in Württemberg, if she'd told him that she saw little difference between his followers and the black slaves of the South she meant to acquire, but the analogy wasn't strained, since Father Rapp completely controlled the minds and bodies of the Rappites. She said to me, 'I observed at New Harmony and even, in embryonic form, at Economy, well-cultivated fields and gardens and well-conducted manufactures, for the Rappites made an excellent whisky though they imbibed not a drop of it. They interrupted their work only for psalm-singing and other tedious and sometimes ludicrous ceremonies, but I couldn't help but ask myself, Where were the great and beautiful works of art, or libraries, or laboratories or scientific workshops devoted to aid the progress of invention and the sublime conquest of matter by mind?'

The slow but sure fashion with which the Rappites prepared their new colony reassured Fanny that it could be done, even if their cultural achievements were primitive.

For it was exactly at this moment, during her visit to Harmony and Economy, that after long discussions with George Rapp's son Becker, a placid youth with golden peach fuzz, the smell of new-mown hay in his linen and his whole body well anchored by his enormous jiggling bum [better word?] – it was during discussions with Becker that Fanny finally decided to start her own colony, one that would do two rather startlingly diverse things: liberate the Negro; and show that white men and women could live together without God, money, marriage or even occupation, for at Nashoba it turned out that most of the whites wouldn't work despite their professed principles. They would pay out two hundred dollars a year for provisions and have the slaves perform every last task for them.

'Mrs Trollope,' she said, inching closer to the fire and taking my hands in hers and staring into my eyes steadily, as a man proposing marriage might do if he was very sure of himself – 'Mrs Trollope – Fanny!' And here she smiled slowly, thrillingly. 'Listen to me. It was then that I made my way back to Mississippi with Cam and a certain Mr George Flower, an easygoing ex-Quaker who arranged for Mr Owen's purchase of Harmony from the Rappites. Oh, Mr Flower was one of the main settlers of the English Plain in Ohio as well. He is very experienced. He knows everything about land and agriculture and the American seasons and American customs – an invaluable man! He and I had been drawn together by a spark of instant sympathy and a shared love of the Negro. A love of all humanity, in *his* magnanimous case. We would whisper our plans to each other all night long, forgetting to eat, forgetting to sleep, seized by a visionary paroxysm.'

I rolled my eyes, slightly shocked by the idea of an unescorted paroxysm between a man and a woman, but Fanny's ardour made all moral tsk-tsking seem stupid, certainly futile.

'The upshot', she said, 'was that in heading down the Mississippi toward New Orleans we stopped in Memphis and then made our way fifteen miles up the Wolf River to a lovely spot we were both enchanted by. I remember we were travelling on a steamer quaintly named *Walk in the Water*, on which one paid fifty cents to have the first turn at a clean towel. The men were all swearing ferociously, the execrations appearing as often in conversation as commas in a book. An old woman sat on deck and smoked her pipe with relentless application. The banks of the Wolf were thick with the primeval forest save for the occasional cabin where a settler sold game to the steamers or fuel in exchange for bread. It was September 1825 – just two years ago – and with Mr Flower's approval I bought 2,000 acres of land for my colony. My great idea, Fanny, is to establish a colony where slaves can work to earn money to buy their own freedom and the cost of transporting themselves eventually to Haiti.'

'Why Haiti?' I asked, startled by this turn in the conversation. 'Why not let them stay in the United States, where they know

102

the language and where they've worked the soil for generations? Where their fathers and grandfathers are buried?'

'Oh, no,' she said, smirking a bit condescendingly at my naïveté and touching my shoulder, 'Mr Jefferson and Mr Madison have both convinced me that whites and Negroes will never be able to live together peacefully in freedom and equality. The races are just too different. Slavery has degraded blacks to such a degree that they're like wily, corrupt children, lazy and sly. The Master Race is no better and no less in need of instruction, for I tell you that soon the *machine* will replace human labour. Soon man is to exchange dominion over his fellow man for dominion over nature. At Nashoba – for that's the name of my colony, the old Indian place-name – my slaves (for I have fifteen slaves now) spend half their time working the fields and half receiving instruction in preparation for a life of independence. There are firebrands in America such as Mr Garrison who believe slaves should be emancipated fully and at once, that no compensation should be paid their owners and that no preparation should be given these sable children for the eventual burdens of freedom. But I'm not of their persuasion. I think that some of the money the slaves earn should be set aside to buy their liberty in five or ten years, that they should be taught to read and write and do sums and distrust all forms of superstition including Christianity –'

I sat bolt upright. After all, I was a minister's daughter and impiety still shocked me. Worse, it struck me as pure folly to inculcate scepticism in an oppressed race who needed the prospect of heaven to compensate them for all their present suffering in this world.

But I said nothing. Fanny was in full flow, telling me how they had already cleared fifteen acres and planted it with corn and devoted two acres of old ground to cotton. She said they'd fenced in an apple orchard of five acres and an adjoining garden of potatoes and vegetables. (She was strongly opposed to a one-crop plantation – sugar or cotton – since she longed most for self-sufficiency.) They'd erected two double cabins, one for the white settlers and the other for the Negro slaves – 'Although', Fanny threw in, 'I can

103

foresee the day when the races will be intermingled, and a good thing, too. Why, oh why do Americans prize their white skin so, which is usually spotted and darkened anyway by the violent sunlight at the early age of twenty-five?'

I was so outraged by this prospect of miscegenation (then, though later I understood its appeal perfectly) that I scarcely registered at the time how violently she was contradicting herself. If Negroes weren't suited to live amongst the Master Race, as she called us, then how should they interbreed – and *why*? 'You can't be serious,' I murmured.

'Oh, Mrs Trollope,' said Fanny, an intense look crossing her jaundiced face, her lip curling, 'you can't imagine how society is *galloping* along at Nashoba. I left last May to return to Europe to regain my health, a measure that reveals how tired and overexcited I'd become since no climate could be more salubrious than that of Memphis. (That's the new, pretentious name: *Memphis*. I far prefer the old name of the Indian trading post, Chickasaw Bluffs.) One month after I left, James Richardson, a forward-looking Scot lately from Memphis, began to cohabit with our charming little quadroon Mamselle Joseph. Mr Richardson saw fit to publish the minutes of a Nashoba meeting in which he promulgated miscegenation – he put all that in the *Genius of Universal Emancipation*. Here it is!' And she opened a review she'd obviously brought with her out of sheer provocation: '"June 17, 1827 – Met the slaves. James Richardson informed them that last night Mamselle Joseph and he began to live together; and he took this occasion of repeating to them our views on color, and on the sexual relation." Well, I am afraid he stirred up a great deal of controversy amongst the readers of that journal – all abolitionists are pious Christians, it seems, for in the August issue he and his views were denounced: "What is all this but the creation of one great brothel, disgraceful to its institutions, and most reprehensible, as an example, to the vicinity?" some old imbecile dared to ask. See, here it is! I suppose the affront, if that is what we are to call this progressive act of courage, was compounded when Camilla announced that marriage is one of the most subtle inventions of priestcraft –'

104

'Priestcraft!' I exclaimed. 'Why, she makes it sound like *witch-craft.*'

Fanny folded her hands in her lap. She smiled. She said, 'Precisely. Camilla added that marriage only poisons the purest source of human felicity.'

'What on earth could she mean by that?' I asked, genuinely alarmed.

'Why, *sex*, of course. Sensuality. The pleasures of the body.'

I was horrified. Of course as a girl I'd enjoyed it when young men had pushed me vigorously on the swing or held me too tightly when we performed a figure in a quadrille, and Mr Trollope had delighted me, I seemed to recall, when he pretended to be a little squirrel nibbling invisible nuts he fancied I was holding in my palm, but all that was long ago and mere foolishness and the only images that Fanny's words summoned up for me were monstrous, hairy, sweating, bug-eyed, sticky – nothing, nothing a lady could desire or even contemplate and would accept only in order to come into the family way. Later, of course, I changed my tune.

Fanny stayed with us a few days and managed to back away from all that was alarming. She calmed down. Like someone given to apoplexy and practised in combating it, she inhaled deeply, dropped her shoulders, unknotted her hands. She played whist with us and pleased Mr Trollope with her newly calm sociability. He was badly in need of company but his nerves could not endure women's voices if pitched too high; Miss Wright's sibylline tones were exquisitely judged. She cast a spell as of old over Henry, who was now taking tuition as a dancer and fencer; after our miserable little supper of sausage and mash, so different from our once habitual feasts of oysters, venison and beef back at Kepple Street, she would ask Henry to show us his turn-out and *port de bras*. For these demonstrations Monsieur Hervieu would suddenly materialize and, drawing on his profound sense of plastic decorum, mould and pat Henry's limbs into the correct poses, true to the gestuary of ancient Greek sculpture he alone understood.

'You should all come to Nashoba,' Miss Wright said one evening after Mr Trollope had retired. 'We're quite settled there now and my latest letter from my sister reveals that our little village is flourishing.' Her feverish, weirdly amused way of talking about miscegenation and the galloping morals of Nashoba had given way to a warm, sweet, relaxed composure. Now she was looking at us as if she were seeking approval. Now she was back to touching me and replacing a comb in my hair or a shawl on my shoulders.

'Could you tell us, Miss Wright,' Henry asked, sitting at her feet on a velvet cushion near the fire, 'what it was like for you to *buy* slaves?'

'An excellent question,' Fanny said, 'since it reveals the vividness and humanity of your imagination.' She leaned back and let the firelight travel over her features, softened after several days of English country life. 'Oh, Henry, if you could only have been there and seen the human beings in chains, led to the market in the centre of town where they were sold not far from the sheep and the horse auctions, for in that part of the world the settlers are as proud of their livestock as they are of their slaves. The slave is chattel. He is property and has no right to hold property. He cannot be married legally nor does he possess political rights. His movements, his time and labour – *all* belong to his master. He has no control over his children. He is punished by whippings. He is subject to sale, as is any other piece of property. It's an abominable world where all the work is done by slaves and all but the poorest whites despise labour of any sort and are so idle that if the mayor rings the town-hall bell he can assemble the entire population of white men, women and children, all turned out in their Sunday best, within just half an hour. They have nothing to do! Work, which should be the most sacred mission in life, they know nothing of.'

I noticed that like so many atheists of the *hectic* sort, Miss Wright made inordinate use of such words as 'spiritual' and 'sacred', but her rhetoric excited Henry and Auguste, who very kindly was massaging the strained muscles in Henry's legs,

106

working out the damage the boy had done himself through overexertion. I only wished he could speed up Henry's growth too for next to Auguste's long thin body Henry looked like a child, a female child at that.

'Well,' Miss Wright continued, 'I knew I needed a handful of slaves for the Nashoba experiment. I was torn by an urge to buy the most pitiful and abject specimens since I knew I would administer to their broken health and never harm them, but I was just as determined to purchase strong, healthy workers who would strive for their own emancipation and in the process help us build our New Jerusalem. I needed to show planters everywhere – those who are moved by their conscience to seek their slaves' liberty – that my system could work. There was a frightful din as all around us in the market-place, which is covered but open on the sides, farmers were crying out the prices of their onions and grain, of their poultry and human beings, and there each slave mounted the block after he'd been stripped down to just a few rags in order to show how solid was his musculature, how steady his frame. They smell bad because they are never allowed to bathe and their clothes are filthy. Often their teeth are rotting out and on the back a big man will be engraved with a whole *tree* of welts and scars, if you will, roots, trunk and branches, weirdly impressive, as if custom had engraved them at birth with royal insignia, pink if still fresh and glossy black if old. Sometimes they manage against all odds to lend a bit of insolence to a moment's hesitation before they mount the block or respond to orders to turn around, something like a dancer's fractional pause or lingering glance by which a member of a well-drilled *corps de ballet* will demonstrate her individuality. Many of these slaves come from Old Virginia where they are raised as cattle are bred in the West, along the Mississippi. Slaves are the main export from Virginia. In Washington, which is just beside Virginia, I saw a prison where runaway slaves were punished. As if the whites fear taking responsibility for beating them personally, the Negroes were bound to a board and their backs exposed and submitted to nineteen lashes from a flogging machine. They were then put inside a treadmill where they walked for twelve hours at a stretch; the action of the machine ground grain.'

Henry, however, didn't want sad stories or useful statistics. 'How did you feel when you bid for them? When they were handed over to you? Did you have them delivered to your door? Did you bathe them? Dress them in proper attire? Remove their chains? What did you feed them?'

Fanny, who seldom smiled, now laughed hugely and flooded us all with the warmth of her good spirits. 'Oh, Henry, for some reason you make me recall that once as a girl, here in England, I won a duck at a county fair and suddenly someone thrust it in my hands. He'd pulled the wings back and held them raised and pressed together and gave the bird to me and there I was, holding the wings – I could feel the pulse and the heat. I wanted to scream and release it but I somehow wrestled it into our buggy and had the driver speed me back to my aunt's house.'

'Yes,' Henry said, 'exactly!'

I was a bit dazzled by the way Fanny had side-stepped answering Henry's questions, which were so interesting and probing, by telling a rare personal anecdote. It was typical of her manner, as I was to discover: apparently confiding, profoundly private. She had a warm, easygoing way of talking when she wasn't exalted by romantic urges or didacticism, but both the ease and the exaltation concealed a will of iron and a lock-safe discretion.

I'm not sure Auguste could follow everything she was saying but he nodded, smiling, and continued kneading Henry's thighs. Auguste was the sort of man who falls in love with a whole family (he was painting a large group portrait of us all). Perhaps it was the warmth of that fireside chat that inspired me, or the dread prospect of coming down in the world and nursing Mr Trollope day and night at Harrow Weald – or most probably the idea that I could finally find a useful occupation for Henry in the New World that might allow him to rebuild the family fortunes – but in any event that night was the first time I thought seriously about emigrating. After the death of my little Arthur I'd decided to put aside a too exclusive devotion to my children. I couldn't bear it if I remained so maternal and vulnerable and attached were I to lose another child. Perhaps my heart had already broken – or been ripped out. No, no! That's absurd. I loved Henry as much as Auguste (secretly) loved me, but I couldn't wallow in that affection. I had to *do* something – for him, for myself, for my girls. *Allez toujours!* became my motto at that time: Ever onward!

I went to sleep that night and dreamed of a Nashoba that resembled Marie Antoinette's village at Versailles, *le hameau de la reine*, where she played milkmaid. There were half-timbered houses gay with rose trellises. An ornamental lake with swans devolved into a stream that flowed just under the balconies and, further along, pushed a mill around at a merry clip. In a class-room students called out their Latin verbs; the teacher, strangely enough, was a woman. Even stranger, under her glossy chignon and over her brooch-fastened, high-necked dress, her face was black – but most becomingly so, since her cheeks were as ruddy as cherries swimming in chocolate. I could feel Fanny's sustaining spirit everywhere around and under me, buoying me up. I knew I'd be very free of care at Nashoba.

Ten

Onward we went. I told Fanny that I would go to America – to Nashoba – with Henry and possibly Auguste (who was terribly undecided and highly agitated), with my daughters Cecilia and Emily and our maid Esther Rust and a young farmer, William Abbott. Miss Wright protested, grabbing my hands and turning them palm up and saying, 'Look at these ladylike hands! Will you be suited for living in the wilderness?'

'*Allez toujours!*' I called out recklessly, and she grinned at my gaiety. I knew she was terribly pleased. I was the confidante she'd so badly wanted to recruit.

My husband opposed the voyage to the last and finally, broken on the wheel of my wheedling, gave in only five days before our departure. Since I was so unsure whether our darling Pater would ever let me go I told no one of our plans. Then at last he said, 'Our situation is so desperate that I can see many good reasons but none definitive for opposing your heartfelt wish' – a pronouncement so characteristically elaborate that at first I wasn't sure if he'd said yea or nay.

Then I became a whirlwind. I installed my husband in two rooms at Harrow Weald with some of our furniture; he was determined to keep his law chambers at the Inns of Court. The rest of the furniture I had carefully packed to be brought along with us to Nashoba – that was my best way of demonstrating to Miss Wright how serious I was.

Henry was very eager to go to the New World and had received an appointment from Miss Wright to teach Latin, dancing and fencing at Nashoba. Auguste was given a job as professor of art. I'd catch Henry up under the eaves finding different intonations (severe, kindly, wry, impatient) with which to say, 'Now, children, let us begin again.' He and I were living intensely in those few moments before the great departure, trying on our future as if it were a new costume that needed to be let out or taken in. For if Henry complained about virtually any reality handed him (or so, with dread, I'd begun to suspect), almost any future prospect was capable of delighting him so long as it remained vague. He could infuse any plan with an absence of struggle and an abundance of reward. He could now picture himself teaching big-eyed, white-toothed, nappy-haired students somewhere west of New-York and not far from Niagara Falls.

We sailed out of Gravesend on the *Edward*. It was a cold, cramped, rainy day that later gave way to a spacious afternoon in which grey weather was replaced with distant white clouds adrift in pale blue skies right out of Poussin. All that was lacking were classical figures draped in smouldering red or cadmium yellow gowns. Instead there were nothing but colourless bonnets and black cloaks, monochromatic figures thrown, however, into heroic relief by the cold, circumambient light. [Oh, if only I had more time I'd write many more lovely descriptions like this one.]

A ship voyage is a long tedium stretched out between two panics – departure and arrival. Our departure was all the more anguished since until the very last moment Monsieur Hervieu had not decided whether he was joining us or not. Henry and he had come to blows over Auguste's indecision, though privately I realized that Auguste couldn't be sure if he wanted to live so close to me during the eight or nine weeks of the voyage and then indefinitely in the wilderness. Perhaps he hoped that in Tennessee, far from civilization, I might forget my duty to Mr Trollope and surrender to desire – but if so he had judged me poorly. Or perhaps he feared I'd remain virtuous and that proximity and hopelessness would make him all the more lovesick and melancholy. I read Chateaubriand's posthumous memoirs which came out just a few years ago. I smiled at his description of the French *petit maître* in silk hose and powdered wig scraping his violin and teaching the Indians how to dance the minuet in a clearing in the American forest – that was *exactly* my image of dear Auguste at Nashoba.

The *Edward* looked like a bonny vessel but we could afford nothing except steerage and soon enough we were thrown into the entrails of the ship with fifty other people, only the thinnest pretence of a wall serving to protect us from an intimate acquaintance with all their vilest animal realities. [Soften this passage, my daughter-in-law tells me. I wonder how many women of my generation have been corrected and curbed by girls of *hers*?]

We paid £15 each and for that princely sum received twelve square feet to stretch out on at night and meagre, tasteless provisions, cooking privileges and water (rather dirty); we brought with us tea and sugar. The tea, however, was undrinkable, since the cook would not infuse it but boiled it vigorously until it became black enough to compromise the digestion of a rhinoceros. For a treat we occasionally ate neat's tongue, recently salted, little cakes of bread baked by the cook and now and then an egg. For the sixty-day trip we brought along fifteen pounds of butter, three pounds of coffee, half a dozen codfish cut and dried for keeping, plenty of carrots, turnips and onions for broth, forty pounds of beef in brine, a few oranges and pickles as antiscorbutics (against scurvy) and eighteen pecks of potatoes in a barrel with a lock on it. We carried flour and oatmeal with us and lots of vinegar, for we'd been told that vinegar and lemons counteracted the sickening effect of brine and seasickness.

We'd paid an additional £2 to put up that partition of inch boards and a door to lock, which separated us from the belching, wind-passing, vomiting, mewling mass of our fellow passengers. There was a smell from hides being shipped with us; the *Edward* carried, moreover, a heavy load of pig-iron that made the ship roll in heavy weather though it gave us ballast in fair. Fanny was spared all this creaturely closeness since she had paid handsomely for a first-class cabin of her own.

My daughters and Henry were almost constantly ill for at least a month. They vomited so much [I wonder how you convey *that* in this new age of dainty propriety?] that I put them to bed on old newspapers which I threw overboard, thoroughly soiled, every morning. Like all people afflicted with seasickness they slept constantly if fitfully. I had heard from a sailor that perpetual activity was the best antidote, but my girls had no interest in exercise and groaned loudly if I attempted to stir them.

Fanny ignored us and I was deeply wounded by her indifference. I kept feeling that this was an ideal time for us to be discussing our new lives – the curriculum Henry would offer the students at Nashoba, the art lessons Auguste should devise, my travels to scenic spots, my daughters' prospects of improving themselves (and eventually of finding suitable husbands) – but Fanny seldom emerged from her cabin.

I couldn't help but observe the other passengers in steerage who had been so animated during the cheerful confusion of departure but who now, two or three days out, wept in mute despair, remembering, perhaps, all the dear people and places they were leaving behind. Rather cruelly the Captain sailed close to the English shore and we could see the thatched cottages and hedgerows and stiles and pale brown fields and still-green trees and meadows of sheep cropping the autumn stubble beside small grazing flocks of crows and a ruined chapel filling up with fog – all the heartbreaking beauties of the England we were putting behind us. I suppose the ideal immigrant is young, unattached, eager for adventure, lean, healthy, not too imaginative, but I was surrounded by family men, unbearably mild and already half-effaced by adversity, ignorance depriving their features of any stamp of character, and by mothers so worn they could be mistaken for their own mothers. To be sure, there was a party of young people who danced day in and day out with hysterical, driven excitement; I could hear their thumping through the decking just above our heads. Since there was no room for a galloping polka or quadrille, the dancers were reduced to the monotonous reel and jig. The surgeon played the fiddle and the barber acted as the master of ceremonies, calling out the steps.

We'd been provided with berths screwed into the floor and a table between them that was similarly secured. Water-closets for women were on either side of the steerage deck, but for men they were up above. What light and ventilation there were came down through the open hatches; in a storm they were, of course, closed, and we nearly suffocated. The decks were swept daily by two or three of the male passengers over the age of fourteen; they were selected on a rotating basis. On our ship, alas, there were three long-faced Presbyterian ministers amongst the passengers who held a service every day for their few adherents. I confined my worship to the Captain's hour of Bible-reading on Sundays.

We were not allowed to bathe more than once a week or to wash our clothes more than once a fortnight, since water was so restricted. Soon everyone began to smell and (I hate to admit it) we were all infested with lice. [Strike all this?]

Naturally I had brought many books with me, mostly novels, I confess, but a few serious works as well, including a volume of my father's sermons, which I found comforting during the most trying days when the girls were vomiting and scratching themselves and cursing Columbus that he'd ever discovered America, and when Henry was spending his time with the sailors on the deck between foremast and bowsprit where they slept.

Auguste was brooding in heavy vestments of resentment and my servant girl was fomenting a flirt of major proportions with a Bristol shopkeeper's assistant. Then it was that the Reverend Milton's words, so calm and reassuring, applied balm to my agitated soul. Miss Wright appeared exasperated with us all – with me because I worried about the proprieties, bodily and spiritual.

114

With Auguste, who she had decided – on what basis I'll never know – might be a fine artist but was seriously limited as a human being or as an intellect. And with my children because they all whined incessantly and hated me for separating them from their friends and occupations back in Harrow. I couldn't think of a way to explain to them that their happiness at home was about to run out anyway, since any explanation would have sounded like an unpardonable attack on their father.

We had a terrible storm at sea when a mizzen mast was snapped off as if it were a match in a giant's calloused hand. The ship's timbers creaked and groaned around us as if they'd give way, waves pounded on the deck above and leaked in rivulets down on us and our mouldering stores. We could hear the Captain shouting orders through his trumpet and the sailors wailed their responses wrapped in the sodden shrouds, all as in some devil's parody of a midnight mass. Henry reported to us that the universal darkness was suddenly illuminated by a magnificent display of lightning. A heave of the ship would dislodge us all from our berths and cast us on the floor. Auguste's popish muttering in Latin I found particularly irritating, since in fair weather he was a militant atheist. We had fresh, beautiful days when our ship sliced through the surf and led a school of enchanting dolphins. We had windless, utterly becalmed days that seemed like the headachy prelude to tornadoes that never materialized, thanks be. The cloudless sky was reflected in a sea as smooth as a pane of glass. I can remember a tiny land bird that was so exhausted from its flight that it was easily captured by a sailor and caged.We had slow, rolling days when the Captain seemed deliberately to plough the long furrows between waves and the pig-iron slammed from side to side in the hull, like thundering horses trapped in a box and kicking to get out – these were the days when my girls became green and turned themselves inside out. I walked the upper decks and patted cologne on my temples and rearranged my scarves for the five-thousandth time and if I found her I tried to lead Fanny into a discussion about Nashoba, of Bentham, of her detested aunt, of our revered

115

Lafayette – but she wouldn't swallow any of the bright bait I trailed under her nose. She was determined to finish reading a treatise by Hume to an old sailor repairing the rigging. At one point she tried to get up a debating club amongst the other passengers, but they all stared at her as if she were mad.

During our crossing two babies were born and one child died. Much later, when we approached the shore below New Orleans, a bucket of sand was hauled up and the feet of one of the newborn were bathed in it so that she might be the first to 'land' in America. I remember the nautical funeral. Little notices had been posted in different places on board telling us the time of burial. As the hour approached the ship's bells tolled and a solemn crowd gathered on deck. Two sailors, marching slowly to the knell, carried the tiny body between them. It was wrapped in sail with a bit of pig-iron sewn to the lower part below the feet so that it might sink directly. The child was placed on a board resting on a trestle and the Captain read out those ringing words, 'We therefore commit his body to the deep . . . in sure and certain hope of the resurrection to eternal life.' At that, the board was tilted and the body slid down it, splashed and was swallowed by the waves. Idiotically we stared at the water as if by miracle the resurrection might occur now, before our very eyes. A fife was played, sails were let out and the *Edward* sped away.

I wept as I thought of my little Arthur, peeking down from heaven above, a translucent finger pressed to lips as red as fruit jelly. One day Fanny Wright (whose cabin she said was just big enough for two people to turn around in, 'begging room for their elbows') confessed to me she'd been writing an essay, 'Explanatory Notes Respecting the Nature and Object of the Institution at Nashoba and the Principles Upon Which It Is Founded: Addressed to the Friends of Human Improvement in All Countries and All Nations'. In that one title everything is contained. Fanny's grandiosity, her mind-numbing style and the impracticality of her ambitions. What I admired in her, however, was her energy, despite her bad health, for now, in the cold light, I could see the fever was eating away at her.

116

And I felt that with every passing day our grasp on respectability was slipping away. Young mothers nursed their infants openly without attempting to hide the act or conceal their breasts. The stench of the water-closets poisoned the atmosphere below decks, all the more noticeable when one came down from the open air above. One family in steerage had bought supplies from an unscrupulous merchant who had sold them rotten beef and stale biscuit covered with mould; they'd had to throw all their food overboard and now they were openly begging from the more fortunate others. Doubtless we had much to be grateful for, since no cases of Asiatic cholera had broken out but the decks were slippery from the effluvia of banal seasickness.

When I thought I could bear no more we had ten more days to travel. I dreamed every night of apricots. I could enter into the sweetest reverie imagining roast beef and Yorkshire pudding or just mushy peas and a tepid glass of stout. I had not a moment of seasickness and I constantly fought against the temptation to regard my immunity as moral superiority.

At last we were approaching land. Though we were arriving in America just before Christmas the air off Florida was growing warmer and sweeter every day and on the coast we could see palm trees waving in the wind and, as we skimmed past unpeopled islands, we observed white sand beaches and clear green waters thick with gleaming, golden tropical fish. Through a telescope we could make out macaws flying from one gnarled tree to another ('Mangroves,' a sailor told me). At the very tip of Florida, as we turned and headed west, I saw the dark clouded waters of the Gulf meet the clear aquamarine current of the Atlantic. We were accompanied by a fairy-tale band of delicate flying fish.

Somehow I'd never imagined that the access to New Orleans would be so slow and tedious. I'd imagined a joyous *débarquement* on a levee lively with banjo-strumming, high-stepping Negroes and apricot vendors. Instead I saw the murky, muddy rush of clay-coloured water where the Mississippi debouched into the Gulf some twenty miles south of the bar and I beheld the

117

sandy, grassy but inhabited island of Balize – a sight that instead of cheering me as promise of the imminent appearance of civilization tore at me as if it were an omen of disaster. We needed two full days before we were led upstream by a smaller boat past some ninety miles of reeds and muddy shores, littered with hundreds of tree-trunks that had floated down from the North.

Here and there slaves were sawing the felled trees into boards or splitting them into firewood. Huge bulrushes lined the river and pelicans stood on the mud flats. We even saw a crocodile sleeping on the shore, a vile monster of habitual indolence and occasional deadly rapidity. Poplars and sycamores, wild vines and tall cane formed an unbroken wall of vegetation. Most of the trees were festooned with a grey parasite that hangs down in graceful swags. It's called 'Spanish Moss,' I believe. We slipped between two American fortresses, one on either bank of the river, Fort Jackson and Fort Philip, and just above them was the battlefield where General Jackson had defeated the British ten or fifteen years earlier (the Americans are welcome to these malarial swamps, I thought). At last we saw a cathedral spire and the high-masted ships. We arrived in New Orleans itself on Christmas Day.

There were fifty steamboats, which ply the Mississippi, as well as those ocean-sailing vessels flying the flags of every nationality (no steamships crossed the Atlantic till a decade later). Amongst and beyond the big ships are literally *thousands* of flatboats, low narrow rafts outfitted with a roof to protect their cargoes. I was told these light craft are extremely dangerous and are often turned over by sudden squalls. They do the real work of conveying goods up and down the Mississippi. We descended at the Levee, an immense quay some four miles long and a hundred feet wide, loud with shouts in Spanish, French (or patois), German and English, despite the holiness of the day. The steamboats had names like the *Washington*, the *Feliciana*, the *Providence*, the *Fashion* and the *Henry Clay* (a local politician).

We were so pleased to touch land, even if it was beside this half-mile-wide, charmless turbid river with its slimy shore, into which an entire nation had dumped its dirt. At first we had trouble keeping our balance on solid land, so habituated had we become to the ever-shifting deck. We rushed into the first café, where the sole servant was strumming a guitar and singing softly to himself in Spanish. At last he was convinced to prepare us coffee; how delightful it was to drink a good, savoury, freshly roasted and ground coffee with *milk* in it after weeks of a stale, lean brew, even if this New Orleans coffee tasted of chicory.

Despite the season the market-place was piled high with red peppers and baskets of tiny pineapples, bananas, pecans and hairy coconuts, sacks of coffee beans and hogsheads of apples. Big fragrant bundles of tobacco from Kentucky (the origin was plainly printed in faded blue on the hemp bags) and mammoth jugs of whisky were flung about recklessly on the quayside. At harvest time, apparently, every inch of wharf is covered with cotton, for more cotton is shipped from here than from any other port in America (or possibly the world). On the day of our arrival vendors were constantly shouting what sounded like 'Unpicalion, unpicalion.' Only a few hours later did I discover they meant a 'picayune,' a local coin of so little value that a mean person is called 'picayunish.' For a picayune one can buy a burnt-sugar wafer called a 'praline' or tiny, heart-shaped cheeses or a cornet of something called gumbo filé which was so spicy we spat it out, although here it's considered a great delicacy. A Negro wench sold us warm potatoes and sausage. She kept muttering, '*Sacré nom de Dieu*,' which seemed excessive on Christmas Day.

We were fascinated by the sight of so many Negroes and their colourful costumes. In England we'd read so many accounts of the horrors of slavery that we looked at each passing coloured man, woman and child as at a tortured victim. Our faces were creased into a constant frown of gentleness and sympathy – which the 'victims' took no notice of and discountenanced by constantly laughing. What we found the most unbelievable was that slaves ran unshackled about this large city of a hundred thousand cit-izens performing errands and even socializing with one another; they are obliged to return home only when a bell rings out their curfew at fifteen minutes after nine in the evening.

119

In the covered market we heard a hundred tongues spoken at once. 'My eyes!' 'Foutre!' 'Schweinhund, trois scalins!' 'Only a dollar.' 'Ein thaler?' 'Salope!' 'Real habañeros, two for a picayune.' My nine-year-old daughter Emily fell in love with a 'picayune doll,' a poor thing of wooden joints and a round head on which face, hair and yellow earrings had been painted. She had to have one, though it looked pathetically crude next to her lovely English doll with its porcelain face and weighted eyelids. It was so cheap I bought the picayune doll just to silence her mewling.

We stayed in a hotel in the French Quarter that had but four rooms upstairs even though downstairs it offered a big three o'clock dinner to many neighbourhood men. We were so happy to bathe in a tub of hot water at last and [but I must eliminate this] disinfect ourselves of lice. I felt a new woman, lighter and prettier and 'gooder' as Emily would have said when she was a baby. I had hoped that Fanny would stay with us but she had disappeared soon after our landing. I was cut to the quick by her coldness. Did she think of us now as mere colonists, *her* colonists? Was she afraid to associate with us lest she lose authority over us? Or did I chatter too much and had she lost patience with me? But she had known my defects back in England; if she wanted to avoid my company why had she invited me to the New World? Or did she have work to do here in New Orleans? But surely not on Christmas. Or had she a secret rendezvous with her Mr Flower? If so, I was wounded she hadn't taken me into her confidence.

At the dinner many delicious dishes were served, it being Christmas, for the French tradition in New Orleans remains strong, but that legacy did not include the art of conversation. The men (for there were no other women present save the pro-prietress) rushed into the room, scraping and shoving into their chairs, sticking their knives into communal dishes and into their mouths and back again, never uttering a word. Within five min-utes most of them had finished a copious meal of many plates, including a loathsome scavenger called a 'catfish' and succulent *écrevisses* called 'crawfish.' Not to mention a goose stuffed with prunes and bacon and a duck roasted with green olives, doubtlessly imported, for I never saw an olive in the New World again, more's the pity. For pudding we had a whisky-soaked fruit-cake as well as many ingenious *mignardises*, all prettily presented to these gobbling vulgarians. Only then did the conversation begin, which was entirely about commerce and money.

'Beans!' said one.

'Sugar!' cried another.

'Lead –'

'Five thousand sacks of corn –'

'Furs –'

'I trust that molasses was not sour.'

'I knocked the hides down at twenty cents.'

'The rope was good, but don't touch beeswax.'

'Colonel, suppose we exchange: my lime for your shingles.'

'Can't do it, General, unless you take the staves.'

'Lost a thousand on butter, but oats are quick.'

'Pickles –'

'Cheese, Captain –'

'Hay and vinegar. The first musty and the other as flat as my hand.'

'Twine –'

'Iron, Lieutenant . . .'

I was astonished by their manners, their speed, the absence of polite smiles and softening qualifiers, their brutal ejaculations. And by their naked greed. And by their loud voices. And by the number of officers of the highest rank who had graced this one table. Only later did I discover that Americans all confer military titles on one another, whether earned or not, and that there are more colonels in the South than privates.

The next day we spied something called the 'Big Bone Museum' and couldn't resist entering, imagining it might be a palaeontological display, but in fact it was but one creature, fantastically large, with a long jointed tail, huge rear legs and atrophied fore-paws, a small head with many lethal teeth, the whole as immense as the largest whale but resembling nothing I had ever seen or heard of. It was clearly a lizard, but at least 150 feet long.

We went for a walk into the swamps (called *bayous*) beside the river and marvelled at the pawpaw, splendid shrub, and the palmetto, loveliest plant I know. The mosquitoes, however, were as large as Father Long-legs and as numerous as Pharaoh's lice [that word again!]. But we ignored the pests, so charmed were we by the sight of oranges and red pepper growing in gardens in midwinter. Exotic and ravishing as the *bayous* were, unfortunately until they are drained the city will be beset by yellow fever once or twice a year between June and the end of October, or so I've been told. Yellow fever is called here 'Jack' or 'Danza' or 'the cholera.'

We slipped into the Cathedral, a crude, ugly building unworthy of its important role in a large, rich Catholic city, and admired the *beau monde*. On ordinary days whites never attend mass and one finds only Negroes loitering about. Auguste, I noticed with derision, crossed himself languidly and with large, sloppy gestures, designed to be highly conspicuous. The frivolous, theatrical spirit of Louisiana piety was best captured for me by the fact I later heard that the silk and gold cape worn by Miss Adizé to the Mardi Gras Ball last year was refashioned *this* year into a cope for the Bishop.

Auguste had called on some distant relatives on his mother's side and they invited us to move in for the two days that remained to us in New Orleans.We had finally run into Miss Wright on the street. I asked her to join us but she said she preferred to stay at her hotel and see her friends. (I had thought we were her friends!) She was eager to return to her plantation of Nashoba and we to discover our future home; I was certain that once there my friendship with Fanny would flourish again and all my burdens would be lifted. After all, every practical task (or chore, as the Americans call it) would be assumed by the slaves. In return for their labour I was determined to be very, very polite and considerate; if they observed a real lady in action, I reasoned, that would constitute an educational, indeed a priceless and essential part of their preparation for freedom back in Africa.

Auguste's cousins were called Huger, a normal French name but pronounced in New Orleans as You Gee, accent on the You, which made no sense though they clung to it (provincial snobbishness, I suppose).

I was fascinated to see what their house and manners and clothes resembled, for this old Creole family had been in New Orleans half a century, although their long residence had not temporized their scorn for the 'Anglos,' whom they called *animals* (*les animaux*)! The house was very small – they could never have received more than ten people at a time in their salon, or 'parlour,' as the Anglos called it. Indeed, they were excitedly discussing their preparations for New Year's Day, when apparently men in stovepipe hats and women who were 'prinked up, pometumed up and powdered up' (as one of the daughters who spoke English – approximately – told me) would arrive in twos and threes for cake and eggnog and in order to drop their cards on their friends. This card-dropping and eggnog-sipping were absolutely obligatory, it seemed.

The men wore skin-tight pantaloons of light colours, which were pulled so tight over the shoe that they all had a stiff, mincing gait. To add to the general stiffness they wore a rigid stock around the neck. Their tall silk hats shone like patent leather. These had been the fashions of England twenty years earlier, in my youth, the Regency.

The women wore the latest French *nouveautés* made out of organdies (indigo blue and cochineal red) and gowns of light blue crêpe shirred crosswise. Over their frocks they wore a *visite* of the thinnest muslin, heavily embroidered and, if they were going out to shop by day, a green barège veil. All the shops were clustered on Chartres (pronounced 'Charters' by the *animaux*) and Royal Streets, which were also the only paved streets.

Very few people had carriages and there was no public transportation. As a result people walked everywhere, even through the rain. Our hosts, *les Hugers*, invited us to the opera and we dutifully ran through a downpour and sat in two adjoining boxes, drenched to the bone (each box held four people). We saw a grand opera with many set changes and passable voices – *La Dame Blanche* was the name, I believe. The English speakers could scarcely follow the plot and whispered loudly amongst themselves out of bored tomfoolery.

Again, the ladies wore the most elegant French *toilettes* with so much bare breast they would have been dismissed as tarts in London. Our hostess, Hortensie, pointed out the latticed boxes in the rear, reserved for those in mourning (or for indecent couples, I divined, for I'd been told that many men in New Orleans *prostituted* their own wives, then pretended to discover the infidelity and threatened to create a scandal unless the hapless lover paid off). Up above were seated quadroons (freemen with one Negro grandparent) and octoroons (one Negro great-grandparent). The octoroon girls were swooningly lovely, with big dark eyes, features *petits* and perfect as ours, their *teint* a honey-gold. They, too, were dressed lavishly and stirred the perfumed air with great painted fans that snapped shut into ivory staves, a stroke of dull cream in the darkness. On the very top rung were two rows of slaves. I suppose they had to stay to light their masters home. Maybe they enjoyed the music (many of the slaves spoke French or patois).

I observed that the French could be crueller and more capricious than the Animals in the treatment of their slaves, but at the same time they had a keener sense of them as individuals, as flirts or dullards or sly boots (*les malicieux*), and this perceptiveness struck me as, ultimately, more humane. And of course there were many, many freedmen living in New Orleans and plying their trades. Some of them even had slaves of their own, which made the Anglo-Americans very uncomfortable.

We hurried home through the last of the winter drizzle, but once there half our youngsters set out for a ball, though it was nearly midnight. The Hugers' house would have seemed poor and uncomfortable to a Londoner, nevertheless our hosts were clearly part of society. Indoors there was no running water, nothing but a hydrant in the courtyard behind. The women wore garish calico gowns at home and the curtains, all of Turkey red, were equally gaudy. Rainwater was collected in a huge cistern and stored in Ali Baba jars. If there wasn't enough rain, muddy river water was allowed to settle in vats over almond shells or white pebbles.

There was little illumination – just a girandole of crystal drops on the dining-room table to hold a single candle and an oil lamp carried by a slave who showed me up the narrow steps to bed. I passed an open door and saw the young daughter of the house being dressed by the feeble light of two candles, each held by a dusky maid. The girl, bare-shouldered with brilliants choking her thin neck, was urging her slaves to hurry up. They were smiling hugely and pulling at her hem, her hair, her corset strings and the gauze they'd draped over her shoulders. The big slave girls, who were truly obese, and their fragile white mistress in her voluminous skirts, filled the entire dim room. The slaves were dressed in crude osnaburg linen and linsey-woolsey.

For me New Orleans seemed compounded of nothing but slang, mud and mosquitoes, yet Henry and Auguste found it delightful. They went to the masked ball with the Huger family; Henry was given a simple black mask and looked most elegant with his thick shock of flaxen hair and dramatically pale face – rather like an aristocratic thief, I thought, or a girl in trousers. At dawn he and Auguste came stumbling into the room where I was dozing in a not very wide bed with my daughters, all of us warm and muzzy with sleep. The boys weren't particularly sober but they had to tell us all about it. Henry said, 'We stayed just a while at the masked ball and then Auguste was told about an octoroon ball right next to the French Theatre. We rushed over there – oh, Mother, you can't imagine how beautiful those girls are! At these balls all the men are white and all the girls are octoroons, most of them tall and elegant. Their petticoats are ornamented at the bottom with gold lace or gold fringe and their slippers are composed of gold embroidery and their stockings –'

'Stop!' I pleaded, laughing. 'You're not going to tell your sisters and mother about the nether parts of these charming savages, I trust. You're obviously bewitched – they say these women are all sorceresses who possess the black arts of Africa.'

Henry smiled his lopsided little smile that reminded me he was still half a small boy, even if he did have to shave once a week, since as a child it was with this frown and smile he would greet in mild indignation the teasing foolishness perpetrated by the adult world.

'No, it was divine,' said Auguste, who usually started a simple declaration with the word *no*, since he could never grasp exactly what had just been said in English, which he always regarded as a deliberately slippery betrayal that had taken the guise of a language. 'We *had* to return to our hosts the Huger at the masked ball, but we far preferred the little octoroons, who were delicious. I would even say they were more modest since they exposed – do you say *exposed*? – much less bosom than the masked women, who think a mask permits them every licentiousness. No, the little octoroons are carefully chaperoned by their mothers, who are on the outlook for a rich man to become their daughter's protector. The octoroons despise the men of their own colour – "*Ils sont si dégoutants*," I heard one say. It is very, very French, of course.'

'Hmnn . . .' I said. 'No doubt. But now you must let us sleep and entertain us no more with your wickedness.'

Again Henry wore his cock-eyed little smile, half-suspicious and half-put-upon – how it breaks my heart to remember his last words before they slipped away. 'Oh, Mother, I've never been so happy as tonight, never in my whole long life.' I'm glad that just then, when he was so happy, his life seemed long to him.

Once they'd banged and ssh-h-h-d their way to their room (for they were quite, quite merry), my daughters said it wasn't fair that men could go out exploring all this exciting immorality whereas they were allowed only to see a boring old opera and walk around in the rain. 'Good old Heirview,' Emily grumbled, though a second later she was breathing heavily; that was her name for Monsieur Hervieu, as though she suspected him of manoeuvring after my fortune, absurd notion, an impossibility in pursuit of a chimera, though the truth would soon turn out to be quite ruefully the contrary. Without Hervieu we would never have survived in the New World.

The following day we went around the shops, though we could afford nothing. Fanny for once had agreed to accompany us and I kept watching her anxiously, for now I worried that in some small way I was irritating her. I longed for a new hat to replace my old bonnet, which I could pull up and forward like the convertible roof of a hansom cab in the rain – and which was also about as greasy and faded as the outfittings of a public conveyance. But we had not a penny to spare – and if we would have had, any profligacy would have been humbled into self-denial by the thought of our poor Pater attempting to farm back at Harrow Weald. I also thought of poor Anthony walking in the rain, wearing nothing but rags. Too poor to buy even a bun for his lunch. I remember years later an old Harrovian – who was visiting us in Brussels – laughed fondly as he recalled so many little things: a favourite pudding of raisins in heavy batter the boys called 'Stick-jaw,' the visits to the tuck shop for large tumblers of hot rum punch, the unctuousness of the servants at Christmas-time when they lined up for their *douceurs* or gratuities, the nicknames for the pretty boys with fair complexions ('Polly,' 'Fanny,' 'Dolly'). Tony became sadder and sadder – he had not been able to afford any of those jolly memories.

Even if I was too poor to buy a bonnet I could visit a fashionable *modiste*, Miss Mary Carroll, who promoted Miss Wright's ideas in her millinery shop. She was truly very graceful and clever in her way of discussing fashions in French with her customers and revolutionary philosophy in English with her friends. As a mere English lady, of course, I was astounded that a hat maker in America dared to lead the conversation and conduct a political *salon*, but the humbling experience no doubt *democratized* me. Later I heard that she opened a radical bookshop in New Orleans to sell inflammatory pamphlets but, as seemed inevitably the case in America, all intellectual endeavours were doomed to be praised but not patronized; she died in 1832, friendless and impoverished.

On that sunny winter day, however, she seemed wonderfully alive and buoyant and sophisticated and I felt like the awkward country cousin. She was asking Miss Wright about marriage at Nashoba. I was stung by the very question, which suggested an opening for impropriety, and I was about to say something to the immodest *modiste* to put her in her place when Fanny Wright took my breath away with *her* answer: 'Whatever legal ties of union shall have been performed outside Nashoba will not be recognized within,' she said. 'No woman at Nashoba can forfeit her individual rights or her independent existence – and marriage as we know it is a rude diminishment of a woman's integrity. I shall dissolve all marriages the moment new colonists arrive at Nashoba.'

'Does that mean', asked Miss Carroll, 'that you reject conventional morality and would have your colonists at Nashoba live in sin?' She gave such a mildly splendid smile that I had no doubt she hoped we were all damned.

Fanny lifted a bit of fancy passementerie without looking at it, then noticed it and placed it back on the table, even nudged it further away as if it were the very idea she was rejecting. 'I cannot subscribe to an ignorant code of morals which condemns one part of the female sex to vicious excess (by which I mean prostitution), another to an equally vicious restraint (by which I mean virtuous spinsterhood) and condemns all to defenceless helplessness and slavery (by which I mean girlhood and then marriage); I detest a code that trains generally the whole of the male sex to debasing licentiousness if not outright brutality.' As if in such a long, vehement speech she'd exhausted the passementerie's power to inflict harm, she now lifted it and patted it distractedly.

I found this speech disquieting and was grateful that my daughters weren't paying attention. Like many girls who have busy, confident mothers, they spent their whole time whispering to each other and worrying about minute questions of schedule and privilege, a small-mindedness for which I felt grateful in this instance though usually it maddened me. Did Fanny despise my daughters? I suddenly wondered.

'And do you worry about the mixing of the races, white and black, in so liberal a society, one where they live in such close proximity?' Miss Carroll was now quite free of clients and prepared to ask questions that could never normally be framed in New Orleans, despite its mestizos and quadroons and octoroons. The whites of New Orleans lived in a constant fear of a slave uprising like the one that had broken out in Haiti. Almost equally they dreaded the gradual, generational *darkening* of their own skins.

'Worry?' Miss Wright asked. 'Why should I worry about such a happy eventuality? I regard the blending of the races as only natural. Negroes and whites all must be educated side by side, for if they enjoy a pedagogical intimacy, then other kinds of closeness will inevitably follow. And mixed-race children will be more suited to the Southern climate of America than whites are. Of course here in New Orleans we see the children of so many forced interracial couplings – let's call it *rape* if we must. The octoroons acquire the blood and colour of their masters through births caused by rape without receiving their protection or their privileges. As a result every mestizo scorns his mother and hates his father.'

There was a strange, grumbling man in the corner who was puffing his pipe and humming to himself as if he were a leaking Franklin stove, glowing with rage within and emitting fumes with ever more alarming efficiency. He exploded when Miss Wright began to speak next, this time vehemently ranting against competition, which she hoped to eradicate from Nashoba as well. 'It is a vile impulse,' she said, 'which makes of one man's loss another man's gain and which inspires an infernal spirit of accumulation that crushes every noble sentiment and fosters every degrading one.' Perhaps she'd picked up this idea from Robert Owen and his son.

At this comment the Franklin stove in the corner erupted, but with joy and cries of accord rather than with indignation. 'Bravo! Bravo! Dear Madam,' he shouted, though even his exuberance could not distract my daughters from their rapt comparison of two nearly identical hats.

'You are the woman I have waited for half a life, nay, an entire existence, for your ideas echo or indeed expand on my own.'

'Yes,' Miss Carroll said languidly, 'I rather thought you two would like each other, but I preferred you meet on an intellectual plane rather than on the crude *trottoir* of ordinary polite conversation. Mr William Maclure, Miss Wright, a Scot like yourself. Mr Maclure is a great scientist known as the Father of American Geology.'

Whereas a more conventional woman might have gushed or lowered her eyes or extended her hand, Fanny folded hers, stared at him and merely smiled. She said, 'I have heard of you from Robert Owen and his son, Robert Dale Owen. I visited their colony at New Harmony in the Indiana.'

'Yes, yes,' Mr Maclure said as if the reality of New Harmony – or *any* reality – were just a plaguey detail and would always be disappointing after the exhilaration of pure theory. 'I am one of the founders and I dare say co-owners of New Harmony. To the tune of 86,000 dollars,' he added with an air of defiance, petulance and self-importance.

We drew a bit closer to his smoking corner and listened attentively to his nasal burr, so metallic that we thought he must have eaten brass bolts with his morning oatmeal. He said that his health had given out and that now he was heading for Mexico, where he hoped to regain it. He was leaving his interests in the hands of a Frenchwoman, Madame Frétageot. I had to repress the urge to say, 'Of course your health is bad since you eat metal for breakfast and you spend your mornings impersonating an overheated stove.'

Though he had as much charm as a machine, Fanny seemed drawn to him and quizzed him closely. I was even a tiny bit jealous. It turned out that when he was just nineteen he'd been posted by his firm to New-York and later Richmond and had so liked America he'd quickly taken out citizenship. Between 1799 and 1803 he'd lived in Paris, where Mr Jefferson had sent him to sort out French and American naval disputes. While there, he'd studied everything scientific. He was, of course, entirely self-taught. He collected minerals and he stuffed animals and he dried leaves for American museums. He travelled as far as Russia. And he decided to undertake his life's work, the geological survey of the United States, which he did all on his own and with tireless energy over the next few years. He believed that the world was tens of thousands of years old – which obviously contradicted the Bible and set every theologian against him. He'd become so successful as a merchant in Philadelphia and had accumulated such a great fortune that he had retired in order to devote himself entirely to his intellectual pursuits.

One of the oddest of those pursuits was collecting French revolutionary publications. He possessed some 25,000 items of this incendiary sort (of course he and Miss Wright regarded the French Revolution as one of the highest moments in the Human Narrative). These documents he'd only recently bestowed on the Philadelphia Academy of Natural Sciences, an institution he'd helped to found and had largely funded.

He had many strange ideas. He advocated (and I place these enthusiasms in an order as random as his fashion of relating them to us) direct taxes on all property, national banking under governmental control, vocational training, the universal establishment of the Code Napoléon ('It's easier to learn and more rational,' he said), freedom for all of Spain's colonies in the New World, the co-operative publishing of books and an end to standing armies. He expected the eventual triumph of the Indians over the whites in Mexico, he approved of national revolutions at infrequent intervals as a purgative for the body politic and a way of levelling social classes, and he believed education would someday make all men good.

Such a hodgepodge of ideas did nothing to conceal that he was a querulous, confused and forgetful old man who spoke with impersonal zeal on all subjects.

'My special mission at New Harmony', he said, 'is education. The education of children in accord with the principles of the great Pestalozzi.'

'Who is he?' I asked.

The question might have been the silliest ever posed judging from Mr Maclure's sputtering. 'Why, he-he-he is the greatest educator who ever lived, greater than Rousseau himself!' I thought the comparison not very convincing, since I regarded Rousseau as an inadvertent author of the bloody French Revolution and a complete hypocrite who while preaching progressive education abandoned his own children before sinking into lunacy. With surprise I noticed that the subject interested Henry, who'd been teasing and poking his sisters but now calmed down and came closer to the great – well, I won't say *man*, but the great *stove*.

'Pestalozzi', the old man said, 'is Swiss and that's where I've visited him over the years. I am someone who has travelled extensively – I've crossed the Alleghenies fifty times and the Atlantic almost as often – but I've never met a man so revolutionary.' Apparently this last word (he rolled the opening and closing *r*s in *revolutionary* as if they were snare drums in a marching band) was Mr Maclure's highest accolade.

'Herr Pestalozzi does not start children out with books but rather with the direct observation of things in their environment, just as he has them add and subtract walnuts rather than numbers on a slate. Nor does he bore everyone with ornamental subjects such as Latin or Greek or literature in the ancient or modern languages. He is opposed to rhetoric in any form, since it serves only to disguise the truth and puzzle all who want to convert it into common sense. No, Pestalozzi is the founder of physical education – in 1806 or '7 he wrote *On the Training of the Body: An Introduction to Elementary Gymnastics*. And he also founded vocational training; poor students learn carpentry and agricultural science, and the girls how to cook and sew, though that is the *only* concession to male-female differences. I mean the *only*. In all other ways the girls are raised *exactly*, but *exactly*, as the boys are.'

Miss Wright nodded vigorously. I kept wishing I could elicit her approval to a similar degree, but when I spoke she usually turned away or the interest in her eyes faded. I wondered if she had adopted a deliberate policy of emotional undernourishment of our friendship. If so, had she done so to improve me (for she

132

wanted to improve people, even her friends)? Or was she feeling a simple aversion to me – was she, for instance, ashamed of me?

'If Pestalozzi had his way they'd study nothing but tobogganing, skating, woodwork, nature and gymnastics, but he's been forced to add the natural sciences, geography and history. If he enters a classroom and finds the students silent and the teacher instructing them from a book, he becomes very cross and storms out, slamming the door behind him. In America we, too, give children as much freedom as possible. We do not punish them or silence them. We listen to the little people – children are the *guests* of humanity, we believe.'

At this point Henry spoke up. 'That sounds like a capital system! In England, at Harrow, all we studied was Latin and Greek, just enough to make silly jokes in it. And of course we were flogged every day. We also played rugby and got bones broken. The younger boys – pardon, ladies – were regularly and royally buggered by the older ones. As their fags we had to put out their breakfast things and come running if they shouted, 'Boy-*hoy!*' Other than that we learned nothing but snobbism and arrogance – how to mistreat servants and the townsmen. What a mean-spirited little world. Better physical education –'

'And *no* snobbery!' cried Mr Maclure, whose bony face had broken into a ghastly smile, so delighted was he by Henry's testimony. 'And no corporeal punishment. Our Pestalozzi teacher at New Harmony, Joseph Neef, has declared, 'I shall be nothing but my students' friend and guide, their school-fellow, playfellow and messmate.' No, no, in Switzerland the children loved studying and made no distinction between it and play. Or *work*, for that matter. At New Harmony the boys learn crafts and the girls work in the cotton mills. I am convinced that under proper management children can feed and clothe themselves by the practice of the best and most useful part of their instruction. No more Latin and Greek! And most especially no more religion. That's where I most differ with Herr Pestalozzi, who prays with his students every morning and night. Here in the New World we've surely earned the right to escape from religious obscurantism!'

The lava and hissing gas erupted yet again and Henry applauded, as if he were saluting a natural wonder. In a final gurgle and ooze Mr Maclure added, 'No, no, we don't train children as you'd train a dog. We believe in freedom. The Pestalozzi system is without precedent. The truest thing one can say of Pestalozzi is: "His intellect has no history."'

I looked around with a satirical smile, hoping to catch an echo of derision, but Fanny was nodding as solemnly as a Chinese sage and Miss Carroll was impenetrable as she curled a bit of blue ribbon by running it rapidly across the open blade of her shears. Later I discovered that Americans are – what? – *afraid* of laughing at others. They're such a violent people that a punch in the face is never far away and the gentlest teasing can elicit the most barbarous fisticuffs. Then again, in an old civilized nation such as England, we all have a fairly clear notion as to what's unacceptable licence and we're all quick to lampoon it, but in such a vague, unformed place as America no one really knows what is *infra dignitate* (since no one has much dignity to start with). In any event Americans are painfully afraid of offending public opinion. They will contradict themselves three times in three minutes rather than be caught out espousing something other than the prevailing opinion. What American would dare to be independent at the risk of being considered bad company?

Henry remained fascinated by Mr Maclure and talked to him so long that Auguste came up behind him and started kneading his shoulders. Rather annoyed, Henry shrugged off his attentions. Henry said, 'I hope, Mr Maclure, I can study at your school some day.'

Eleven

And then we were off! The next morning Fanny routed us out of our kindly French hosts' house. The *Hugers* had ordered their big black maids to feed us hot milk and coffee and hot sugary beignets, to wash and dress us – and we all felt excited and ready for our adventure in the wilderness. Rather quickly I had become used to the attendance of slaves, though a nagging doubt about the propriety of slavery continued to plague me. I could see that slaves were slow and inefficient, that they shuffled about like big children and needed constant prodding, and I recognized that the whole institution was rather unfair, though Madame Huger assured me *she* would, quite honestly, *prefer* slavery if she were poor, since slaves had no taxes to pay or clothes to buy or mouths to feed. 'Everything is handed to them,' she said, 'on a *plateau d'argent*! Oh, we're so indulgent with them. And they repay us with such insolence and slovenliness. I defy any English man or woman, or any Yankee, to sit calmly and wait uncomplainingly as long as *half an hour* between courses at table! And yet we do so nearly every day, smiling, our hands in our laps, listening to all the banging and slamming coming out of the kitchen. They're really good-for-nothing, but on purpose, just to spite us. My, I suppose it's God's test of our patience. God has made us patient, lord knows, thanks to our lazy, no-count slaves.'

I asked if Caesar and Antoinette, a slave couple they owned, were married. 'No,' Madame Huger said, 'my husband won't let them marry, because he keeps thinking he'll sell Caesar and he can't bear to separate a married couple.'

'How many children do Caesar and Antoinette have?' I asked. 'Four,' she said.

We boarded a great steamboat, the *Belvidere*, which would be our home for the next week. There was a Babel of languages on the docks around us – 'une picayune!' 'Grosse teufel!' 'Here, porter, here!' 'Claro, signor!' – as we were jostled by a crowd that seemed as exhilarated as we were.

There was a rank of steamboats in New Orleans nearly two miles long, all of them belching black smoke into the air and each flying its own flag at the jack staff. Freight barrels were rolled down the levee and one had to step nimbly to avoid the teams of cursing mates, the wheelbarrows and carriages streaming past, the last-minute passengers carrying reticules, carpet-bags and screaming, frightened babies.

Looming up beside us were the steamboats themselves, the size of stately homes, each two or three storeys tall, each darkening the sky with the soot rising out of the twin smokestacks fore and with the white clouds of steam released through a third, shorter escape stack a bit aft. Black navvies, stripped to the waist, were lowering the cargo into the hatches; even though the weather was mild they were perspiring profusely and crooning, 'De las' sack! De las' sack!' It was almost a song, certainly chanted in chorus. I thought they were lovely, though of course they were savages. And the white Americans would have been horrified by my admiration, since for them the blacks weren't even human.

Up ahead the water was thick with a fleet of flatboats extending as far as I could see, as if a road were paved with cobblestones, but all bubbling and undulating.

The water-level deck and the one above were surrounded on every side with wide galleries (or 'guards' as the Americans called

136

them) graced every four feet with white wood *colonettes* except midway back where a giant paddle-wheel, two storeys tall, was trapped inside a white wood shed. I could hear it churning in its house like a rabid dog.

We were led past a charming room, neatly furnished with well-made cots under each window, the beds outfitted in flowing clothes tucked here and there with shipshape ingenuity, the windows covered with freshly painted green shutters and tidily framed in wood – but, alas, that was the men's dormitory, by far the finest on board but in this strange country it was an apartment denied the ladies, though we were permitted to enter it for our meals. We found the room destined for the ladies dismal enough, since its only windows were below the stern gallery. At least we enjoyed one blessing there – we didn't have to worry about trailing our skirts through tobacco spit, as we did everywhere else in American public rooms. We soon found chairs on the galleries where we looked out on the banks (or 'coasts,' as the people of Louisiana insist on calling them, as if the Mississippi were an ocean). For a hundred miles north of New Orleans the plantations are protected from flooding by raised earthworks, the famous levee, and behind them are the graceful manor houses at the end of allees of trees and beside or behind them the sugar refineries and slave quarters and, further still, the fields. The band of cultivation and habitation is about two miles wide on either side of the river. Behind it looms the primeval forest, as sombre as the promise of a highly moral afterlife.

In the clear December evening light we could see children, black and white, playing together on spacious green lawns, every ribbon distinct in the fogless air, and we watched flatboats, burdened with stacked loaves of white sugar, drifting down to New Orleans. The boats heading upstream clung close to the shore, whereas those going down moved out to the centre. Every once in a while our smokestacks streaked the darkening sky with showers of red sparks. We could hear the paddle-wheel lashing the river. Fanny kept to herself as was her wont. I wondered idly if she were seasick and solitude was her way of disguising her condition . . . Did she think that once we arrived at Nashoba we would have abundant time for talk of the most intimate sort and therefore we shouldn't chatter now? I could not be angry with her for being aloof – after all, she was providing us with a wonderful new home in the wilderness.

There was a talkative man seated next to me, at least he became talkative when he saw me slapping at mosquitoes, which were swarming in lethal clouds around us. 'Pardon me, ma'am,' he said in a big, unvarnished voice, as inoffensive as it proved to be inexhaustible, 'but did you know we have some forty-two varieties of mosquito? We have the spring mosquito, a little feller, and then the greyback, that's the classic one, then you have your specklebacks, relatively inoffensive –' he laughed weirdly at that *relatively* – 'and the gallisnippers, most noxious, and worst of all, the black skeeters . . . And if you ask me they spread the dengue and the yaller fever and paludial fever, better known as malaria. Why, when a lady told me she was planning to settle in Memphis I told her, yassir I did, I told her she should take along enough plank to make coffins for the *whole* family.' He laughed at his grim expression and I hugged myself, either from the ghastly image he summoned up or from the cold suddenly exhaled by the dark water.

'There don't seem to be as many lights now,' I said, awed by the melancholy greys flowing past though I was still unpoetically slapping at various parts of my person.

'No, ma'am, you're right,' he said, though an American will always agree initially no matter how much he'll eventually object. 'You can go two miles or more along the Father of all Waters (that's what we call this river) without seeing a single human habitation, though someday – and soon! – it will be as densely settled here as the Thames River' (that's what they call the River Thames).

'Doubtless,' I said dubiously. 'And who are all those men down there?' I nodded towards a group of men in work clothes, many of them barefoot, sprawling on the foredeck, talking loudly and laughing, passing a bottle of whisky back and forth.

'Oh,' he said. 'They're the real men, the River Men. They pole their broadhorns, what you call flatboats, loaded with goods down the Mississippi, discharge them and break them up for firewood and then hop on a steamboat going up to St Louis and sleep on the deck and brawl and drink away or gamble away whatever money they have left after they've paid their five dollars for passage up to Louisville.'

'Five?'

'Yes, ma'am, not the twenty-five you're paying for a bed and sheets and shelter from the rain, though they have to work for the difference. You'll see – the boat will pull into shore and be loaded up with considerable firewood. The River Men will scurry back and forth so fast we'll be reprovisioned in five minutes flat. That happens two or three times a day.'

In England, of course, I'd never have talked to a man without being introduced, and even then never to a stranger except in the presence of one of my servants, but with my usual powers of mimicry I'd already assimilated American manners. I was decidedly enjoying this calm male voice stroking the back of the night, and I only hoped I wasn't sending him a misleading signal [my daughter-in-law, reading over my shoulder, says I must rewrite this so that it will sound as if we had been properly introduced. She's right, of course]. This gentleman, whom Miss Wright had presented to me as one of her very particular friends [there! that should do it], was perhaps about forty, long and skinny, with shaggy hair and a shaggier brown beard flecked with white. Of course he was spitting, but into a cuspidor on the side away from me, which already counted as an improvement. There were streaks of tobacco yellow stained into his beard. He had the most original way of talking and I took notes that very evening, for already I must have been planning on writing about my trip.

He told me that the River Men down below were half-horse and half-alligator and a little touched with the snapping turtle. 'Why,' he told me, 'a good River Man can wade the Mississippi, leap the Ohio in one stride, ride upon a streak of lightning and slip without a scratch down a honey locust. He can whip his weight in wild cats – and if any gentleman pleases, for a ten-dollar

139

bill he may throw in a panther or hug a bear too close for comfort, and eat any man opposed to Jackson.'

He told me the River Women were equally wild, that they gathered in the woods like Bacchantes and danced barefoot all night, shouting and stomping. 'You may think they don't go their death on a jig, but they do, for I have frequently sneaked in there the next morning and scooped up my two hands full of toenails.'

I asked him if he was married and would I have the pleasure of meeting his wife. He said, 'I loved a woman, and it was the worst case of hard love this world has ever known. Hard love. When I first saw this pretty little gal I got in a considerable of a narl. I just stared and stared at her – I was like a nighthawk swooping down on a June bug. When she would speak my heart would flutter and when I'd try to reply my heart would choke me like a cold potato. I imagined she was in love, too, but one day I discovered she had a fiancé – I saw my cake was dough. Not that my disappointment cooled off my love. I had hardly safety pipes enough; my love was so hot as mighty nigh to burst my boilers.' (He pronounced it 'berlers'.)

'Did you woo her with sweet speeches?' I asked sceptically, wondering how one could make love in such a rough dialect.

He laughed ruefully. 'Now I talk all the time but then I was a quiet boy; I thought I didn't have much to say and should hide my ignorance. After all, I reckoned a short horse is soon curried. Love made me monstrous solemn.'

'And did you ingratiate yourself to her parents?'

He let out a whoop of laughter and said, 'Well, what I wanted to do was kick her mother into next week. That's what I wanted to do. Her mother disliked me something awful, I don't know why. Every time she spoke to me it was hot as fresh mustard on a sore shin. Like most women, beggin' yer pardon, she had entirely too much tongue. I'd try to mollify her, but ever time I gits near her, her Irish was too high to do anything with her. She thought her and her kin were too good for me, which was nothing but a piece of pride. I wooed her, though, God knows, on the principle that you must salt the cow to catch the calf. I'd go over there all washed and combed, wearing my best bib and tucker. The funny thing is I knew the daughter liked me more than her fiancé – why, ma'am, she preferred me all holler. But that old mother of hers forced her into the other man's arms.'

'And that was the one great love of your life?' I asked wistfully. The River Men down below were now clapping their hands and dancing a square dance, all laughing and falling down. There was no light and the December cold was penetrating up off the water (slap, slap, slap, the paddle-wheel recounted, adding its rapid rhythm to the River Men's clapping). The sky would light up with a sudden rain of brilliant red and gold sparks flying up out of our twin smokestacks (they looked dangerous to me).

'The one great and only love,' he said. 'Nigh on twenty long years ago. I saw that in making me the good Lord forgot to make my mate. I was born odd, and would always remain so, and nobody would ever have me.'

And now, as if the tenor had just finished his great lovelorn aria and the chorus of montagnards rushed in, gaily prancing, the River Men began to dance so hard and turn so wildly I feared one would fall in. They were moving most curiously, and the master of ceremonies was calling out, 'We are on our way to Baltimore,' which was the name of the dance, I suppose, for we were heading to Memphis. When the men became the most agitated he instructed them, 'Now, weed corn, kiver taters, an' double shuffle.' I transcribed all as if I were watching and listening to the Hindoo, so little did I comprehend. A wizened old black man was playing the banjo. I'd been told he was a free man, though the other blacks on board were slaves, even if they weren't in chains. Some of them, it seems, had been hired out to the ship captain by their masters (who received all their wages, of course).

My companion's tale made me so sad. I thought, America is an astounding country if people can become so intimate so quickly without even knowing each other's names. He stood and said, 'Well, ma'am, I hope you like our beautiful country, which is the greatest one on earth. It's been mighty agreeable jawing with you. I'm off to work. I hope you don't think I was putting on

141

poetical airs. I don't want to be like the foolish jackdaw who borrows a tail to play the peacock.'

I started to reassure him as to how touched I'd been by his story, but he'd already glided away, becoming one with the night.

Much later, as I was about to retire to the ladies' dormitory, I saw through an open door my elusive companion playing cards with three men in silk waistcoats. The others had gold chains stretched across their prosperous forms, but my friend was in nothing but his buckskins. His hat was pushed to the back of his head. He had a big pile of money in front of him. The next morning I was told he'd cleaned everyone out and had slipped to shore during a refuelling stop; apparently he got away just in time, since someone had identified him as a notorious gambling man who fooled the unsuspecting with his airs of back-country naïveté.

*   *   *

As we sailed up the American Nile, a metal band of anxious melancholy was tightening around my heart every day. I kept wondering how Nashoba, constructed as it was beside a tributary of the vast river – how Nashoba could be the delicious little paradise, the calm retreat, that Fanny Wright had advertised to us, when every other habitation along the way seemed so desolate. There were few houses, maybe only one or two every three miles or so, and many of them were just cabins open at the sides – 'dog-trot cabins,' as someone said. And the habitants, who exchanged their firewood or game for our bread and money, all looked sickly and yellow from fever. Fanny herself had lost weight and yellowed. Her old optimism and energy and gift for friendship seemed reduced by whatever had transpired in the wilderness.

I became the sort of foreign traveller the Americans like most: a listener. Everyone on the ship, it seemed, eventually had his or her turn of sitting next to me and talking. They registered I was English and therefore in need of instruction about the richest, most progressive and beautiful land on earth. By the time I was to leave America four years later I was ready to agree if wealth

142

meant millions of acres of wasted timber, filthy huts and impertinent children, if progress meant an absence of all deference and if beauty was nothing but such natural monstrosities as the Niagara Cataract and the Mighty Muddy Mississippi.

As I listened to all these fellow passengers (I felt like a priest hearing confession, never required to say anything beyond a general absolution) I learned a hundred little things. One man told me the Mississippi is the 'crookedest' river in the world after the Jordan. He also opined that it was a 'proven fact' that ill luck would attend any boat whose name began with the letter M and that the *Midas*, the *Mayflower* and the *Magnolia* had all duly sunk.

An old woman who mumbled her sentences through toothless gums told me she had 'knocked about' Kentucky and that she lived on a hill from which she could see eighty 'bee trees,' so great was the local quantity of honey. Her old man said he'd 'walked jawbone from Tennessee,' whatever that means, and that he was so 'backward' that the first time he'd ever seen a carpet he thought it was the 'folks" best bed-quilt. An English peasant would have been ashamed of his ignorance, but this man laughed and invited me to share his merriment. His mother, he said, was from the eastern part of Mississippi, a region called 'the Shakes' ever since the big earthquake.

The old couple started exchanging stories between them about all the corrupt and lazy circuit judges they'd known, as if we had no judicial incompetents of our own back in England and I'd be astonished by these tall tales of local lapses. He told a story about a judge in Tennessee who kept slipping off the bench and ducking out back to eat water-melon, leaving the court to get on as best it could without him. The lady, mumbling in her faint, drooling way, slapped her thigh when she remembered how in a disputed farm sale the cocky East Coast judge had ruled that the new buyer had no right to the feed corn in the mangers because it was personal property but could justifiably claim the manure in the stable – at which the plaintiff, a sly old woodsman, asked, 'Well, can you tell us, your honour, how can a mule eat personal property and discharge real estate?'

143

She laughed and shook all over and revealed her terrifying gums and he kept up a regular drumbeat of thigh-slapping. 'That right funny, don't you think, Missy?' she asked. She kept coming back to the chute of her story over and over again, repeating it like a highly spiced, indigestible meal. 'Personal property,' she said and laughed mildly. 'Real estate,' she whispered and sighed.

I found her to be a treasure of local idiom. She talked about the old days and the Indians – their ghastly killing sorties, their half-breed offspring called 'White Indians,' their expressionless faces ('like graven images,' she said) when they were wounded or ailing, the foul-smelling blend of tobacco and sumac they smoked (called 'killikinick'), her first glimpse, so memorable, some thirty years earlier, of the Chickasaws, a 'very wealthy' tribe. 'I never will forget those old warriors wearing their chintz head rags and heavy shiny silver bracelets with their short chintz tops above lustrous shiny buckskin leggings. And the women! Those old women, all tan as good shoes, proud of a big gold tooth in the middle, their pride in the gold their only reason for smiling, don't you just know, wearing their long tops and solid silver arm-lets, and their big ol' broad scalping knives worked into intricate wampum belts – those knives gave me some real cold chicken flesh, I'll tell you, Missy.' Her way of saying 'lustrous shiny' was typical of backwoods speech, for the 'Kaintucks,' the old people of Kentucky, double their nouns in the Elizabethan way and refer to 'sulphur matches,' 'bacon meat' and 'eatin' vittles.'

The next day – or was it two days later? (time blended together as the dark, gloomy woods floated past and as dead logs slid under our hull, logs called 'sawyers' if they were nearly uprooted, 'snags' if they were still firmly anchored) – we longed to sleep even longer in order to reduce the boredom of staring at those trees. Now that we were further north there were no more pal-mettos or crocodiles to amuse us and only the odd parrot to sew a stitch of red or green through the morose tapestry. Often the forests were on fire and the air became thick with smoke. Birds hidden in the straggly branches tutted, for the dying foliage seemed to prove Miss Wright's dim view of competition; since

144

no trees had been trimmed back they all had o'erreached themselves in sickly excess.

I met a few genuine peasants except we're not allowed to use that word in America. They have such a curious way of talking that I transcribed their speech directly, which made them feel sulky and flattered, like a cat that both enjoys and suspects a stroke behind the ears, that both purrs and bites. One such peasant girl, from Ohio, had dreadful freckles and enormous teeth and a vulgar way of spreading her legs under her full skirts and leaning her elbows on them, so that she was sometimes doubled over.

We discussed men. When I asked her if she had any sweethearts she replied, 'Well, now, I can't exactly say: I bees a sorter courted, and a sorter not; reckon more a sorter yes than a sorter no.'

When I said I found something imposing but eerie about the banks of the Mississippi she snapped, 'That's catamount to a criticism.'

'Do you mean tantamount?' I asked patiently.

'I am not so ignorant not to be aware that catamount and tantamount are anonymous.'

I let the subject drop, but with aggressive unpleasantness she said after a long silence, 'I suspicion you're looking down on us. You may think America a minor country, but I opinion quite the contrary and I've heard other foreigners praise it considerable. I reckon that's just the way you calculate.'

I reckon you're right, I conceded, almost bursting with derision, so eager was I to repeat this fantastic conversation to Henry and the girls before I forgot it.

The amazing thing is that a poet attacked me soon after the publication of my travel book about America and my novel, *Refugee in America*, for not noticing that the English spoken in America was the purest that exists. He wrote:

While 'tis well known, of numerous sorts, the mixture
Has made the purest English there a fixture;
Each dialect the other has corrected,
And thus a perfect model is collected.

145

The lowest cockney-slang she has imputed
To one of New-York's magistrates! (well-suited
To her weak-bred and mode-empoisoned mind);
Her gross perversions (tending but to blind
Great Britain to Columbia's real worth)
May serve the proud and ignorant for mirth,
But sadly prove her twofold publication
Disgraceful to her age, her sex and nation!

Although I felt properly chastened, I thought it a pity that his indignation had not improved his prosody. Of course he was a Whig. All my enemies were Whigs. They thought I'd published my book to defeat the Reform Bill of 1832. And indeed the Tories did bruit it about that my book showed that if the Reform Bill passed and the franchise to vote were extended we'd all behave like Mrs Trollope's Americans.

After so much travel, across the Atlantic from Gravesend to New Orleans and now up the Mississippi, my children were sad and silent. They no longer complained. Like orphans they'd stopped grieving openly and had become dry-eyed and remote. They preoccupied my thoughts but I had no idea what to do for them. I, too, was in a new land where even peasants snapped at one if one weren't lavish enough with praise for everything American, a country (as I observed on the boat) where women flirted but leadenly, with no grace nor vivacity. They were all too visibly running after husbands – they were *coquettes à froid* – and they didn't even bother to pretend that they hoped to encounter in a man something more than just another agreeable fellow much like themselves. They had no winning ways and treated men and women in the same bluff fashion, unsmiling, their shrill tones unmodulated. After two years of marriage the women are faded, lined and used up, even if they're barely twenty. Of course a climate that's arctic in the winter and tropical in the summer dries out a woman's skin and flays it alternately with chilblains and insect bites. (Is this only more of my mode-empoisoned mind speaking?) I wondered if my little

Emily's roses would soon fade; after all, they'd been nourished by London fogs.

A few years later, in 1834 I'd hazard, I saw a panorama of the Mississippi exposed in London, a great scroll meticulously painted by a Mr J. R. Smith. It was four miles in length and took two hours and a half to revolve past the spectator. It recorded every town, every bend in the river, every last habitation and was much studied by future immigrants. It pictured slaves at work in the sugar fields, it depicted a burning steamboat, the *Ben Sherrod*, it gave us orange plantations, it rendered in minutest detail every house and warehouse in New Orleans, Vicksburg and Memphis.

But what it didn't capture was the tedium of the passage, the opacity of the brown water, the listless plight of the people living in huts on stilts and piles, nor did it record my growing fear. As the reader knows by now, I was a doughty old thing, ever gay and gallant, full of amusing ways and spiritual resources, but I was also a mother in a strange land surrounded by her babies, who were solemn as owls by now as they watched another 10,000 trees brush past, another five hundred miles annihilate themselves in this American Ganges – and we were being pulled towards a destination, Memphis, where yellow fever had reportedly killed fifty-three people the year before and buffalo gnats (whatever they were) had destroyed all the cattle, where dengue or 'breakbone' fever plagued the children and homesickness sapped the marrow out of the adults.

All my peasant girls and toothless backwoods grandmothers and dashing gamblers – they all praised their country and took umbrage at the slightest reservation, but I was more and more convinced that they feared America as much as I did with its bears and alligators and scalping knives and intemperate climate and mortal fevers and its untracked wastes, its emptiness. Their only recourse in the face of so much sadness and emptiness was a certain thin-skinned irritability.

147

Twelve

We arrived at Memphis at midnight and in the rain. Memphis stands on a high bluff, and at the time of our arrival was nearly inaccessible. The heavy rain, which had been falling for many hours, would have made any steep ascent difficult, but unfortunately a new road, what they call a 'corduroy' road of logs sunk crosswise into a mud ascent, had been recently marked out, which beguiled us into its almost bottomless mud. Shoes and gloves were lost in the mire, and we reached the Grand Hotel in a most deplorable state.

Once we were in the hotel, a mortar-smelling tavern at the Gayoso Bayou Bridge, we bathed rather approximately and fell into a swoon of sleep. The next morning we looked out our windows on a desolation of mud and winter rain, crystallizing here and there into ice. I called for tea and breakfast in the room, and the maid, with a smirk, said, 'I'll oblige you, seeing you're from the Old Country, and used to backward ways.' But a minute later the owner of the inn was standing, red-faced, in my door and shouting, 'You'll take your tea with my wife and me and the other guests, or you'll not have any at all. We are not subscribing to your arrogant English ways here!'

Memphis is the largest town now between New Orleans and St Louis but back then, in 1827, it had but two or three hundred houses perched on the Fort Chickasaw Bluff some eighty feet above the murky Mississippi. Most people called it the 'Bluff City,' though a few boosters were pushing forward the fancy Egyptian name. As Fanny Wright said, 'Ancient Memphis was probably just as dreary and dull.'

There were but two eminent personages in the town, Fanny's friend Marcus Winchester and Isaac Rawlings ('Old Ike') who'd arrived in Mississippi as a sutler in General Jackson's army in 1813, though some detractors said he was lying and had arrived only in 1820 and then as a simple, needy citizen. The remarkable thing was that there were so few 'old-timers' that no one could verify or disprove the competing versions. Ike owned the store, a big log house we visited, where he traded with the Creeks and the Chickasaws. They gave him wondrous, rich pelts from the beaver, otter, raccoon, deer and wildcat and he paid them off in gewgaws and bolts of worthless starchy cloth they draped around themselves, those famous chintz tunics the old woman in the steamboat had told me about.

Winchester, who was the mayor, postmaster and justice of the peace, owned the newspaper and a four-horse coach that transported the mail once a week back and forth to Jackson, Tennessee.

He came by to call on us and walk us through the town which, in typical American fashion, had been laid out in squares on a grid. He was a tall man – 'lanky,' if you will forgive the vulgar new expression – who had red hair sprouting from his ears and nostrils and knuckles and creeping up his neck out of his shirt collar, as if an explosion of rust had occurred somewhere within. Despite all of this bristling extrusion he had beautiful, regular features and a large bump of Sympathy on his forehead, as the phrenologists would say. His speech was better (more grammatical and less picturesque) than that of all the strange people who'd addressed me on the *Belvidere*.

When I commented on it he said his father had been a rather self-important general who'd maintained an Old World courtliness

149

that had somewhat estranged his buckskin-wearing backwoods neighbours. 'He built the biggest stone house back of the Alleghenies,' he said, 'and he named it Cragfont. His children he gave very grand names – mine is Marcus Brutus Winchester. He's the one who named one town Cairo, pronounced Kay-roh by the locals, but he hadn't had Egypt in mind. No, he was thinking of the French Revolution and their battle cry, *Ça ira*, but no one could say *that*!' He laughed.

He gave me his arm but seemed totally uninterested in me as a physical being. (A woman, no matter how old, remarks on something like that.) Soon enough I found out why. He said to Fanny, 'You know everyone in this town is turning against me.'

'Against you?' Fanny asked. 'How could that be?'

'It's this damn matter of race which plagues and scares everyone in our Republic but most especially in a slave state like Tennessee. The funny thing is that most folks here don't even like slavery, since they think it discourages settlement.'

Fanny instantly seized the opening for a homily: 'I have always thought that if the slave question could once be settled our free coloured population would become gradually and easily incorporated with the white.' She smiled, pleased with the point she'd scored, but I was most impatient to know what had happened to our Marcus Brutus.

Eventually I put the pieces together. Apparently years ago he'd met a lovely quadroon named Mary Loiselle whom he'd married and with whom he'd had eight children – one daughter named after Frances Wright and the oldest boy after Robert Owen. Robert, a sprightly lad, would sit by the fire and though only ten years old make comments on the newspaper and current events in a manner that would have been creditable to a mature man. He was already the most expert cotton weigher and marker on the Bluff, witty and winsome – *but* (and this is always the mighty, damning copula in America) his complexion was tinged with copper.

Winchester confided to me that Frances Wright was the most superb and superior woman he'd ever encountered. I was quick

150

to agree, since she was my one hope in this new world and I needed to believe she merited our trust. It reassured me that such an intelligent man had such high esteem for her.

He, too, was a slave owner but he was encouraging his slaves to follow Miss Wright's plan and work to buy their freedom. He too kept a little store, which also served as a local bank for the savings of all the slaves in West Tennessee. He spoke vehemently against the unreconstructed slave owners, those men he called the 'timid and indolent lovers of slavery,' for Winchester contended that only those whites too lazy to work or too hamstrung to defy convention could possibly envision a future for slavery.

Marcus told us that even though Mary was a splendid Christian who nursed the ill and aided the poor, even though she was a devoted sister to the lovely Amirante Loiselle and had provided *her* with three slaves of her own, even though Mary was a beautiful, charming hostess and many a desperate family of new arrivals had greedily accepted her hospitality – *nevertheless* (in America, when it comes to race, there is always this *but* or *nevertheless*), nevertheless, once a family had taken hold, the first sign of their new respectability was a rejection of the very woman who had received and helped them. People were so enraged that Marcus Winchester had legally married his lovely Mary in 1820, that in 1822 the Tennessee Legislature had enacted a new law against mixed marriage. Soon after I left Tennessee a local ordinance forbade Mary Winchester specifically to enter Memphis, the city her husband had founded. Travellers coming back from the United States now inform me that racial tensions in America are only worsening and may soon lead to war, though I doubt it, since most Americans love money and money alone and a war would strike them as unprofitable. [*Editor's note*: Here, of course, Mrs Trollope was wrong on every count. The American Civil War was to break out only a few years after her penning these lines, and it proved to be the deadliest of all modern conflicts – *and* it was ultimately profitable for the North.]

In later years I discovered that poor Mr Winchester suffered terribly for his love marriage to the quadroon. He was driven

151

out of office, no one would trade with him, he lost Mary to an early death and even after his second marriage, this time to a wife as white as meringue, he still couldn't make his neighbours forget the 'stain' of his earlier indiscretion. Nor would they forgive the copper tinging the cheeks of his exceptional children. (What made it all the more hypocritical and maddening is that his great rival, Ike Rawlings, also lived with a black woman, but he'd been 'moral' enough not to marry her!)

Miss Wright was wildly impatient to set off for her plantation, despite the rain and cold and freezing mud. She engaged a big wagon, called a Deerborn, a driver and two horses to convey us the fifteen miles to Nashoba, since the Wolf River is navigable only during two short periods a year. ('Nashoba', she told me, 'is the Choctaw word for the Wolf.') The driver, a lugubrious black man called Linus, drove us all – Miss Wright, my two girls, my maid, my farmer, and of course my son and Auguste Hervieu as well as our shipment of furniture – he drove all of us and our possessions right into a river, where the axle broke and we were forced to stagger back to Memphis and to Mrs Anderson's fireside. Miss Wright, however, grabbed one of the dray horses and darted off through the forest toward Nashoba. Linus told us that she was famous in the vicinity for riding forty miles a day and sleeping in a ruined, roofless house on a bear-skin with her saddle for a pillow. If she fell ill and feverish, he said, she thought the best cure was an even longer horseback ride through the unmarked terrain, the wetter and colder the elements the better. I found her desertion, however, disquieting at first though later I convinced myself she had raced ahead to make sure everything at the plantation would be in impressive order for our arrival.

That night we asked our hostess why only men came to her hotel to eat. She said that the men demanded a hot meal of hard venison in peach sauce but that the women preferred mush and milk at home. No wonder, since the men were as silent and unsmiling as executioners testing a blade. There was no hint at sociability; they were merely animals submitting to the necessity of feeding. Only they weren't as clean as animals; the general slovenliness of the people, as well as the emptiness and haphaz-ardness of their houses, struck me everywhere in America. Just as they haven't existed long enough as a culture to acquire the graces, in the same way they haven't had time to pick up many *things*. In America there is an absence of things, of pincushions, dishes, andirons, pictures, tea cosies, books. Everything is stark, empty, uncomfortable, even the people's minds are seriously underfurnished. Maybe civilization, after all, amounts to nothing more than a sufficient quantity of *clutter*.

The next morning was crisp but sunny and we rode off in a new high-sprung carriage into the forest, our furniture having been retrieved from the submerged Deerborn and loaded onto the new conveyance. We were in an excellent mood because blue jays were darting through the forest like falling flowers and a single green parrot kept haunting our movements with its concentration of verdure and sunlight, for its beak was bright yellow. After two or three miles the road, which at its best was never more than a few ruts and hacked trees, gave out altogether and we were forced to plunge ahead into the swaying, creaking foliage, as if we were riding a water buffalo that had broken free. The knocking about we got only added to our amusement.

As the sun was setting our driver told us we were approaching Nashoba, which to my imagination had now metamorphosed into a tidy English village – steeple, stile and well, sheep grazing on the common and the manor house beckoning us with its thread of chimney smoke to its closely laid brick floor, low-beamed ceiling, walk-in fireplaces and maids in caps and aprons.

What we saw, in fact, was a rough clearing in the gloomy woods, three roofless cabins, a serpentine fence of piled wood chevrons and two yellow children, too feeble even to look up from their listless game of slapping a stick into the cold mud. Miss Wright came plunging out, her hair electric, her bodice half undone, a rictus of a smile freezing her face as if she'd just seen the awful glory that lies beyond the Veil. Her sister Camilla, emaciated and the colour of old piano keys, tottered unsteadily in her wake.

I was devastated. What lay before me was a devastation. My

153

first instinct was to stop Linus, the driver, and to tell him not to unload the furniture. To take us. To return. To return. To take. To hasten. Not to. Don't hurry off – I listened to that curious bird, the woodpecker, tap out what sounded like pegs driven into a well-made, hermetically sealed coffin.

Thirteen

Our things were unloaded and carried with the help of Linus, Auguste and a complaining Henry into Miss Wright's cabin. I suggested the bits of furniture could remain in their packing cases until we'd sorted out our living situation. My voice quavered; I was trying to be brave, I was also buying time to think out a new plan. Night was coming down on us rapidly. Linus said, 'Why, Miss Wright, this here's no place for white ladies to live ins. You don't have no roofs over yo' *haid*!' We all laughed. I was immensely relieved that someone had pointed out the emperor's nudity.

Miss Wright said, 'Things got a bit disorganized in my absence. An unscrupulous member of the community sought to spread dissension but he's now been voted out and has taken his departure. Though I have advertised in *The Genius of Universal Emancipation* for carpenters and bricklayers, either white or black, none has responded. We're expecting Mr Flower to return any day. He's the leader of the English community in Illinois and has promised to bring us back several animals – cows, chickens, sheep – as well as grain and salt meat for us and feed for the cattle. We've already built two double cabins, one for whites and one for Negroes. We've raised other farm buildings for immediate use, cleared and fenced the area around them, planted a vegetable garden, set out potatoes, opened fifteen acres for corn and two for cotton –'

'Fanny,' I said, 'you haven't done all that. You *wish* you had. You've told all the world that's what you've done. But it hasn't happened.'

'Not yet, not exactly,' Camilla said in her frail voice. She was cooking up a pot of beans though she looked as if she hadn't eaten anything in weeks and was unlikely ever to eat again. I could see the blue veins ticking in the back of her delicate hand and her fingers had become as *effilés* as a swan's quills.

There was a rustling of leaves and suddenly a man was standing there, who was introduced as Richeson Whitby. He was a young, thin man wearing braces, a coarse-spun jacket and a round hat held up on his two protruding ears, which were small and red. That round flat hat resting on the blood-red ears reminded me of a soup bowl with handles on either side, the shallow elegant sort you see at banquets where the food is more symbolic than real. He, too, was insubstantial, undernourished, more a symbol of a man than a flesh-and-blood instance of humanity.

There was no bread, no tea, no milk. We ate the beans in silence sitting on the cold, damp ground. My daughter, Emily, said to me, 'Mother, why are we stopping here? When are we going to get on to Nashoba?'

I looked at Fanny to see if she'd heard the question. I said, 'Darling, we're here. This is Nashoba.' Emily looked frightened. She and her sister were allotted but one spoon between them and ate their beans in silence.

Henry said, 'But are there no blankets? Mother, we'll freeze tonight,' for none of us, in our despair, could contemplate staying here longer than overnight. I didn't think it very enlightened to petition God to solve daily problems; He had enough to think about in winding up the crystal spheres and circulating them through the Ether. But all intelligent resolve melted away in the face of our plight. I began to pray furiously to the Deity though

156

I knew He could scarcely be decoding every mental message wafting up to him from Tennessee.

When Fanny said, 'Shall we take a torch, Mrs Trollope, and visit the slave quarters?' I replied, 'Yes. Yes. I must see everything.'

I followed the mad Fanny and the frail Camilla and her theoretical Mr Whitby to the equally implausible slave cabin. By the flare of the burning stick we crossed the stretch of level land to the next cabin but even though it had no door or roof we could hear nothing, neither the murmur of voices nor the strum of a banjo nor the sizzle of a skillet. Miss Wright held up the torch and we entered the shelter and there, sitting on the ground and shivering, was a family of slaves, their bodies so emaciated that they were nothing but large white eyes trained on us with reproach.

'Good evening,' Miss Wright called out, but the slaves only blinked. I think they'd gone beyond fear and resentment into a state that was dull, stunned. I'd feared unpleasant smells and signs of vile voodoo practices, but their energy had been sapped by hunger and the cold and they'd entered into spiritual hibernation.

That night I spread my scarves on the ground and drew my brood around me, and for once they were too frightened to complain. Miss Wright made cheery, positive sounds like a hearty old nanny, but we just sat there like sick birds retracting their heads into their ruffs and clinging tenuously to the rungs with bloodless claws.

I couldn't sleep. My mind was racing but in no useful, directed way. Rather, I darted mentally, rehearsing hateful scenes in which I denounced Fanny for egotism, irresponsibility, even madness, but then a minute later in my fantasies Auguste was attacking me for my arrogance and folly in leading them all to the wilderness without having first gathered any information about the place, the climate and the salubriousness of the location. He was especially furious at Fanny for having misled us all. Where was the studio she had promised him? The school? Fanny had said the black children

157

were being carefully educated by Camilla and Mamselle Joseph, but Camilla was too ill to stand up, much less to instruct, and the other lady was nowhere in sight. In the whispering, crepitating leaves I thought I could hear raindrops, which would soon be falling on us, but then I remembered the trees were denuded, that it was winter here and that snow could fall just as easily as rain could. I pictured Henry, so full of energy and attitude but weak in the lungs, succumbing to the dreadful local fevers.

At last I fell asleep and dreamed that our plantation was like one of those we'd seen just above New Orleans, the black and white children playing hoops together on the mint-sauce lawn in front of a white mansion with columns . . . A black nanny in a starched white apron and red kerchief was coming toward me with a glowing dish – was it molten gold or hot cornbread?

When I awakened I was hungry and aguey. The slaves were in their cabin like birds that refused to fly out of the cage but rocked mournfully on their swing, still hoping for seed. Camilla was coughing.

I hated Fanny. She had wooed me and courted me and convinced me to move my family to this wasteland, which she had entirely misrepresented. She could sacrifice her health to her bizarre Utopianism, but I was a mother responsible for children. Fanny had money to ease her way out of any disaster, but I was destitute. I had only one or two choices to make – and I could scarcely afford them. Until now I had always felt that Fanny was my friend, someone who had my best interests at heart. I had made a hundred excuses for her remoteness during our long journey here, but now I understood that I was just another warm body she had 'recruited'.

Auguste was dressed and resolved. He said, 'Madame Trollope, I am heading back to Memphis. I've decided I will paint all the local notables and bring you money so we can leave.'

I sank to my knees in the mud before him – I felt like Cora in *The Last of the Mohicans* – and I kissed his hand. Henry smirked and Auguste raised me – I could tell how moved he was by the gratitude of the woman he loved most.

Fourteen

And then we decided to leave. We had to leave or sink into a state of disease or debasement. We had spent all our available money getting here and we had no idea how to finance our next move. While we stayed on at Nashoba for another ten days, conjuring a plan, Auguste headed back for Memphis. Within a week he had painted the few notables of the place (Ike Rawlings and Marcus Winchester and Mrs Winchester and her sister Amirante and their various *café-au-lait* children). Later, when illustrating my 1836 anti-slavery novel, *The Life and Adventures of Jonathan Jefferson Whitlaw*, Auguste became highly efficient in depicting Negroes – the frightening voodoo sorceress Juno, the frightened child Phebe, the fierce Negro revenge against their cruel white owner – but in 1828 their features and colouring and hair texture were all new to him.

He then worked his way a few miles up and down the Mississippi and painted another four or five local leaders for twenty dollars each. Some people had the temerity to declare he wasn't much of a painter, but Auguste gave them one of his best French sneers and soldiered on.

Fanny Wright accepted that we weren't cut out for her noble experiment in communal living. I told her that Henry's constitution was too weak – I could never bear to lose him as I'd lost Arthur. Fanny nodded and said, 'The cemetery in Memphis is filling up fast with yellow fever deaths,' but she said it as if this information were something that had just occurred to her.

We'd come to America and Nashoba because Miss Wright had promised us that Henry could teach Latin and Greek to the black and white children and Auguste could instruct them in drawing and painting, but we had discovered that the children were hungry and there was nothing to drink but rainwater, no butter or cheese to eat and no meat but pork. The forest was too dense to penetrate. Whereas I'd expected something like a bigger, grander Windsor Forest, the Nashoba trees were etiolated and half fallen – tall, feeble things that had no shape and no living branches except at the very top, though the underbrush was thick and kept us from taking the sort of walk we so enjoyed. Day after day we were confined to the cabin, in which the daubed and wattled chimney frequently caught fire. We'd all have to rouse ourselves and beat out the flames with branches.

As a mother what frightened me the most was to see the sickly state Camilla had fallen into. Richeson Whitby, the man with the round blood-red ears, was also obviously suffering from the ague or swamp fever. They slept all the time and shook and woke up drenched through. They didn't seem very affectionate with each other. Miss Wright, putting a great masculine hand with trimmed-back nails on the young man's shoulder, said, 'Mrs Trollope, meet the bridegroom! Yes, they had a big surprise waiting for me when I arrived at Nashoba. They've married, despite Cam's brave, theoretical pronouncements against marriage. Yes, they were married 15 December, just ten days before we landed in New Orleans.'

Cam and Richeson smiled as children do when adults ask them inappropriately mature questions. ('And would that be your doll or your baby, for I think I heard her cry.' '*Doll*, she's my *doll*. I don't have a *baby*,' the child protests with a shy smile.)

'Yes,' Cam rattled off, 'the heart has its reasons that the reason knows not.'

160

I simply embraced her, as if overcome with emotion, which was true enough though what I felt wasn't joy but foreboding. I was certain they were both dying. Poor Richeson, who'd been a Quaker and then lived at New Harmony, seemed sexless and subdued, a capon except the neutering hadn't made him plump. He put an arm around Cam's waist, which was as small as my wrist, but the gesture seemed fraternal and infertile, the unconscious linking up of baby bodies, the same urge that makes puppies sleep in a pile.

When I first hinted to Fanny that we might not stay at Nashoba, she immediately assumed that I'd heard rumours about James Richardson, the other white man who had been living – I won't say 'under the same roof' with a black woman, since the truth forbids such a locution. We had no ceiling and only the crudest, half-finished, uncaulked roof.

It took some time to decipher her meaning, for Miss Wright always assumed I was much more prudish than I was and in any event I had never dreamed of assigning conventionality to her – not even a tenderness toward other women's more delicate feelings. At last I learned that Mr Richardson had left Nashoba with his mistress, the mulatto Mamselle Joseph. They'd headed off for New Orleans (we must have crossed them on the way). His idea was to establish eventually his mulatto wife and children in Haiti and to earn money for them in New Orleans; after he'd saved enough he'd join them in Port au Prince. He'd left behind a very nasty reputation of having beaten the fifteen slaves at Nashoba, who he was convinced were 'no-count.' He'd become angry when he saw that they wouldn't work hard, not even for their own liberation. Of course no one – neither Fan nor Cam nor the white men – was enterprising in the least. After only a very brief exposure to the slaves I'd learned that Fanny's great idea of freeing them only to send them all back to Africa terrified them. No wonder they wouldn't work! They spoke no African languages and their white masters had mixed them systematically for generations so that they would not be able to preserve either their African religion or their native customs. Obviously they were in no hurry to buy their freedom if that meant exile.

I could scarcely understand the slaves when they spoke, but I *think* I heard them discussing how Mr Richardson had *raped* poor Camilla. Apparently she was pregnant, and the unruly, violent Mr Richardson might have been the instigator instead of the castrato-like Mr Whitby. It was hard to imagine Mr Whitby at his conjugal labours.

[*Editor's note*: And yet Mrs Trollope was obviously busy imagining them! I find her whole report on Nashoba highly suspect. Like many Tories she is intent on denigrating every experiment in human improvement. I myself have suffered tremendously at the hands of the forces of reaction, but that is another tale.]

The day I was leaving I came across a letter Fanny was finishing up so that I could convey it to Memphis and Mr Winchester's postal service. Since it was addressed to Julia Garnett, I couldn't resist glancing at it: 'Our land is gently undulating & hilly what is called thro'out the great western valley *rolling* – our houses are placed within a quarter of a mile from the pretty little Wolf river on the bank of which we have raised our washing house bathing house & dairy & where we have opened some beautiful wooded pastures and retired walks extending our meadows . . .' Lies! I thought. Self-delusion! False, deliberately misleading propaganda meant to lure the Garnetts to Tennessee and to read out loud to all their visitors. I looked out reproachfully on the muddy swamps around our crude cabins.

When Fanny handed me the draft on her bank she said, musingly, 'Sometime hence, but I fear not in this generation, *money* may be done away.'

I looked at her with real hatred while I smiled and humbly accepted the life-saving slip of paper. I thought that her inherited fortune had given her the freedom to muse about first principles and ultimate values. If I was so avid, so vulgar, a terrier sniffing in circles in pursuit of the quarry's scent, that was because I was always hungry, usually just a few hours away from disaster. As Miss Wright contemplated the future of humanity I was worrying about our next meal. Only *money* could buy the higher morality. Oh, I was good enough, but not so good as to turn down a hot dinner.

While we were about to leave Nashoba George Flower and his wife and children arrived from Albion, Illinois to live there. Mrs Flower was ill with milk fever since she'd just weaned a baby. In New Orleans I'd heard that Fanny and George had become lovers two years previously, which of course I'd instantly dismissed as ignoble twaddle, but my interlocutor, a female friend of the Huger family who was well connected in progressive and abolitionist circles, swore to me that Mr Flower was a known bigamist. He'd left a much-hated wife behind in England and married Eliza Andrews in Philadelphia before they moved west to English Prairie, or Albion, in Illinois. Apparently George Flower had wooed Eliza away from a rival, a certain Mr Birbeck, who was their neighbour in Albion. By the time the Flowers had moved to Albion, Birbeck had come to hate them. He refused to speak to them. That first summer Flower and Eliza fell ill, but Birbeck would not help them in any way. They had almost died.

At first, according to my loquacious informant, Eliza Flower accepted Fanny and Camilla, and Cam even lived with Eliza and her children for long stretches while Fanny and George Flower ran about the West. They were looking for land together and George, by now an experienced pioneer, helped Fanny choose the Nashoba property. He floated a few cows and horses and seed and a plough downstream from Illinois. Back in Albion life became more and more unpleasant as his neighbours whispered with increasing fury about his two wives, his many children, his insulting behaviour to the venerable Mr Birbeck and now his affair with the passionate, masculine, wealthy Fanny Wright, the Apostle of Free Love.

Of course I'd been careful to set this 'progressive' chatterbox straight. I told her that Fanny was the soul of modesty, etc. 'She's so innocent she can't even *imagine* how others will interpret her behaviour,' I said, and here I peeped out over the tops of imaginary glasses at Fanny's indiscretions.

Now I was meeting the Flowers for myself. Eliza was still young,

163

no more than thirty, but the roses in her cheeks were faded after so many disastrous New World winters – and summers! She had three children (two others had died); her youngest was still almost an infant. She had been reluctant to sell their farm and leave a world she knew, even if it was hostile to her, for a place further south, wilder and even more tormented by mosquitoes. She scarcely spoke. She seemed like a woman who prayed for nothing but an early death.

Her husband made up for her silence. He was a big brute with long black hair he parted down the middle, a clean-shaven chin that reminded you of its suppressed beard by sprouting visibly while you looked on, and facial skin that was the blue of a factory worker's knee. He loped around the plantation, looking back over his shoulder like a wolf roused out of his lair during the day.

Over our dinner, which was richer thanks to the butter and bread the Flowers had brought with them, Fanny stared at George with open-mouthed hunger, and he, with his black wolf's eyes, took in her whole body every time she stood or crossed the room. Mrs Flower guarded her silence and her inner solitude.

That night I had a moment alone with Fanny. I whispered to her, 'It's so obvious you're in love with George.'

She feigned surprise but I could see I'd hit the mark. 'Love? We're comrades in arms. And when he decided to bring Eliza and the children to Nashoba, he and I solemnly vowed to give up all further intimacies.'

I felt that Fanny was capable of keeping such a vow but I wondered if a man like Mr Flower, already a bigamist and obviously cursed or blessed with *un goût sensuel*, would ever be able to comply here in the amoral forest.

Its amorality did not exclude tenderness. One afternoon I saw a Negro couple, man and woman, returning from the fields. She was limping and he was letting her lean on his shoulder. Once home she sat on a freshly cut stump, which was still oozing sap, and he knelt before her and looked at her foot from many angles. He washed it and bound it in a piece of cotton fabric he tore

164

from his own shirt. I watched the whole operation with such absorption I forgot I existed. It occurred to me that Negroes were kinder amongst themselves than we whites were with one another. I almost envied the poor woman, so loving was her partner.

Richeson Whitby was the only director other than Fanny who was present, and they both voted to advance me and mine some three hundred dollars that we might relocate to Cincinnati. We had to draw the sum from Mr Winchester's little bank in Memphis, so ten days after we'd arrived in Nashoba we headed back to the bluffs overlooking the Mississippi, withdrew our fortune, made plans with Monsieur Hervieu and awaited the next steamboat sailing north.

A day after we arrived in Memphis Henry was sent off to New Harmony, which was now operating a work and study programme for students on the banks of the Wabash. Fanny, who was so visibly disappointed with me and my daughters, though she treated us with long-suffering civility, took a quite obvious delight in Henry's enthusiasm for Mr Maclure and the Pestalozzi system. She assured us that though Mr Maclure himself was in Mexico seeking renewed health (a pursuit that came to naught), he'd left his school under the direction of Madame Frétageot, who'd run a Pestalozzi school in Switzerland, I believe, and most certainly in Philadelphia, where Mr Maclure had *known* her, I fear, in all senses of the word.

The voyage from Memphis to New Harmony, on the Wabash (a tributary of the Ohio) took just thirty-six hours by steamboat, and New Harmony wasn't far from Cincinnati, our destination. I can still see Henry's lean, handsome face with the big eyes as he looked down from the deck of the fine steamboat and waved at us. I'd tried to convince him to wear a jumper, but he'd do nothing more than drape a scarf around his neck, since the boys back at Harrow refused to take any greater precaution against the cold. I can still see his breath issuing from his sweet, girlish mouth. I noticed that no one else's breath was as dense or white and for an instant I feared Henry was breathing too hard and I wanted to rush up to the deck and hold him to my healing breast and bring him back to the quay with me. Oh, this boy, I thought, and I grabbed Monsieur Hervieu's arm, for he, too, I noticed, had tears in his eyes. It was odd but I felt for a second as if we were Henry's parents.

After three days in Memphis, Auguste and my girls and my maid and my farmer all boarded a steamer bound for Cincinnati. We had decided to leave my furniture behind at Nashoba – in Cincinnati we would rent a furnished house. Everyone told us that Cincinnati was the capital of the land of plenty, that two decades earlier Cincinnati had been just a frontier settlement yet now it was a thriving metropolis of 20,000.

'Anyone with the least gumption,' Marcus Winchester told me, 'can make a fortune in Cincinnati.'

'Oh, Mr Winchester, I know I have an excess of gumption,' I said, so moved was I by optimism that I resorted to this curious new word, and I clung to his arm so tightly he pulled away with a laugh and a frown, as if a violent child had just kicked him in the shins. 'Sorry,' I said, 'it's just I can feel the gumption throbbing through my whole body!'

[My daughter-in-law Theodosia has discreetly drawn a line through the last four words and has put a question mark next to 'throbbing.']

Our steamboat soon entered the Ohio River which the French have for good reason named 'La Belle Rivière.' The sun was out, for in America the sun shines even in winter and there is less drizzle. Mind you, I find our English fogs and rains comfortable, perfect weather for thinking, as if the sky had lowered a woolly tea cosy on a pot that was steeping meditatively.

Whereas the Mississippi had been so desolate, muddy and treacherous, shifting its course so often that it engulfed whole forests on one bank or the other, leaving them to rot and tumble, the Ohio had many cheerful cottages on either bank, tidy docks and well-tilled fields stretching up to the hill-tops. The month was February and our vessel had to pick its way carefully past

166

floating blocks of ice like a nanny through a darkened nursery littered with toys. The ice blocks thudded against and shocked the hull of our boat, but still we advanced, the vapour trails issuing from our chimneystacks drawing self-erasing lines on the palpitating blue of the sky. [Here I've written a truly lovely description, one of my best, worthy of an anthology.]

We'd heard so much about Cincinnati – the city where everyone was busy and where the population doubled every ten years – that we were eager to see it. We thought that at last we'd be able to put down roots in this rich American soil and draw sustenance from it. The people we talked to on board the ship were typically American in vaunting the virtues of their city. 'It rivals Rome!' one fat-lipped man exclaimed in a perfect spray of rapture. A cloud of scepticism must have passed over my brow, for he said, 'It *has* seven hills,' as if that sealed the argument.

Someone else told us the city boasted of an Asylum provided with thirty-four lunatic cells and also a museum that displayed a hundred elephant bones, fifty bones of the megalonix, thirty-five hundred samples of minerals and the tattooed head of a New Zealand chief. The finest artists in town, added a woman who squinted, were Mr Eckstein and H. H. Corwine. Auguste lifted a sceptical eyebrow while carefully noting these difficult foreign names.

'Is this young man your butler, Old Woman?' the thick-lipped man asked me, nodding at Hervieu.

I was rather staggered by the multiple impact of his insulting question since I'd never before been called by that hideous epithet and at first looked around to see whom he might be addressing. After all, I was scarcely more than fifty at the time and Auguste was way up somewhere in his thirties. And he and I were such friends and he was so distinguished in his manner that one could never have seen him as my servant or as anyone's. If for no other reason, servants don't wear beards. Hervieu was so obviously a gentleman and an artist, but one couldn't expect a Cincinnati pig butcher to be a physiognomist.

To change the subject I leaned further over the rail and called out recklessly, 'Oh, look! Cincinnati!' though there were no signs anywhere of a city and the squinting woman and the lip-smacking man exchanged a knowing glance, as if I had provided proof positive of senility. Fortunately, Auguste seldom listened to what people said in English unless it concerned him narrowly. Then he'd furrow his brow, hunch his shoulders forward and lean closer as if someone very feeble were whispering a death-bed message – or as if a microscopic insect were addressing him.

My heart pounded. I'd been slapped in the face with the horrid fact of my advanced age, all the more nakedly evident and exposed in this land of youth, for one saw young people everywhere, everywhere in America, great jostling crowds of the young, male and female, their faces as blank as unaddressed, unfranked envelopes. Whereas I came with layers and layers of gummy stamps, a struck-out street, a red hand indicating the new forwarding address, a tear and smudges and a scalding puddle of sealing wax!

No, it was intolerable. In England, and even more so in France, people were connoisseurs of the whole life and they saw beyond the envelope into the varied, accumulated contents. In London a man of the world would take my measure, decipher my class and region from my accent, deduce from a few words the members of my circle, decode from my laugh and glances the extent of my gallant adventures [Theodosia has drawn an angry X through all this] – in England a past is a rich compost as intriguing to a scholar of the spirit as a lamp-post is to a dog. Only in America do people judge by the most superficial of appearances.

At last our ship blew its whistle and we all rushed to the guard on one side and looked down on the large city which had suddenly swung into view. It was the tenth of February. There it all was: thatched cottages, trim brick houses, toward the west the sordid shanties of the free Negroes in 'Little Africa,' streets overflowing with debris, houses under construction – and everywhere people running about or whipping their horses and speeding their carts through the plumb-straight streets. What the city lacked were domes and towers, a romantic ruin or a poetic castle.

Here everything was workaday, as unfanciful and utilitarian as a wedding supper without champagne. Just row after row of brick houses, two storeys tall and all exactly the same width.

A vast amphitheatre of hills surrounded a town in which American individualism (or anarchy) permitted a church to push its spire up beside a small factory or a boarding-house. Empty lots pocked the otherwise smooth row of city blocks, as if the city had been subjected to bombardment rather than left incomplete.

Nowhere had we seen fine mansions in the Ohio Valley, although here we eventually discovered a few in the highest, remotest hills and there was one gleaming new one in the centre city we could spot now. It was white with green shutters, only one storey high though the central entrance was framed by white pillars and looked rather noble. My fat-lipped booster said, 'That's Martin Baum's house on Pike Street, the most elegant house in town. He's our leading citizen, owns the woollen mill, flour mill, iron foundry, sugar refinery and exporting firm.' The *p* in 'exporting' drew a particularly explosive tribute of spray. 'And he's organized a library, a school, the museum, a literary society, an agriculture society and several musical groups. Music, of course, since he's German. He sings old German folk songs with his cronies at Frederick Amelung's house once a week over on Sycamore. If you want to rise in Cincinnati society, Old Woman, you better oil those vocal pipes or learn to scrape a fiddle, though I suspect dressed that way you'd rather stay nice and cosy at home.'

We headed toward the Washington Hotel where some seventy men were sitting down to the midday meal. We joined them and once again sat through a repast nearly devoid of conversation, though we did hear one man extol a local invention, a dog-powered machine to churn milk, if you please. My girls and I had of course been assigned to a table with the few ladies – the proprietress and two women friends who'd come from Kentucky to do some marketing. They were inquisitive about us to the point of impertinence, but we gave them little satisfaction. The proprietress, perhaps to find a topic, said she hoped her girls would eventually go to school.

'What fer?' the bonneted old lady asked pugnaciously.

'To learn to read and write, if nothing more,' the proprietress said, shrugging her shoulders.

'That way leads to damnation. Ain't so bad for mens, our farmer mens, to read, for there's a heap of time when they can't work outdoors and can jest sit by the fire; and if a man had books and kerred to read he mought; but women have no business to hurtle away their time, cause they can allus find something to do, and don't you know there was a heap of trouble in old Kaintuck with some rich men's gals that had learned to write. They were sent to school and were high larnt and cud write letters almost as well as a man, and would write to young fellers, and bless your soul get a match fixed up before their father and mother knowed a hait about it.'

She folded her hands across her little round melon of a belly in the most self-satisfied way I'd ever observed, made all the more grotesque by the set but soft line of her mouth, which was tooth-less, and the blaze of her small resentful eyes.

I was so tempted to object, to say that reading was the gateway of the soul, that it was an anti-clock to banish time, that it was a wand to give us the past alive and warm and softly treading in our palm like a kitten, that reading dropped over us a veil and spirited us into a harem or clamped us in chains and put us behind bars, that it fed us on the drugged sherbets of Arabia or the raw meat of the steppes – but I bit my tongue (I could still bite mine, or at least nibble on it) and reflected on the chilling horrors of New World pragmatism.

Esther Rust, my maid, had decided to go back to New Orleans, where she was convinced she could find some fun before old age set in (she was twenty). She'd stayed out all night once in New Orleans. I'd never permitted myself to quiz her about her absence, since I felt my inability to pay her wages had under-mined my authority, but I suspected she'd fallen in love there since afterward she compared every place, even Cincinnati, the

170

so-called Queen City, unfavourably to dirty, chaotic (but oh so poetic!) New Orleans. A few days later she slipped away on a steamboat; she was a girl devoid of guile, someone who turned to love without hesitation in whatever form it presented itself. I can still see her full lips and her eyes, which she screwed up into a suspicious glance because she'd been tricked so often, though the instant a man began to speak to her in a low voice her squint melted away and she forgot herself and drank in his words. She had an uncouth but musical Devonshire accent and such a full figure I feared she'd start running to flesh in a few years. Our shared travails during the Atlantic voyage and at the desolate, malarial outpost of Nashoba had brought us together, no longer as mistress and servant but now as mother and daughter. We wept when we parted, for travel mimics death; we hoped to see each other again, but an eventual reunion is a question of faith.

America swallowed her whole. I've never heard from her again.

My farmer had also disappeared, but in his case without taking my leave. He must have met an Ohio farmer who'd come up to town to trade, someone who'd lured him back to a forsaken clearing in the woods, where the man lived with a crone for a wife and a tribe of children no more civilized than redskins. I pity my poor farmer, but perhaps he, too, has by now become a wealthy landowner in Ohio or Illinois and he, too, forbids his daughter to read . . . His name is William Abbott. If any Ohio reader should ever encounter him, please let me know Mr Abbott's fate by addressing me at the Villino Trollope, Firenze, Italia – I'm most fearfully curious.

That first day in Cincinnati, after our repast we set out to find ourselves a house. I felt brave but desolate knowing that Fanny was no longer part of my life. Until now I had half-believed that Fanny stood as a guarantor of everything I ventured or lost. I could afford to fail since I had my solid friend beside me. But now I was on my own. Fanny had not been the woman I had thought. No, she was a crank, perilously close to madness. In one of his books Balzac explains to the French reader that in England an 'eccentric' is a mad person who is rich, whose wealth

171

buys forgiveness of his excesses and waywardness. By those lights Fanny was indisputably an 'eccentric.' But I couldn't dismiss her with a definition. Her betrayal had left me feeling like a wronged lover; I was still longing for a person I knew was harmful to my well-being.

A cheeky little ragamuffin accosted us as soon as we emerged from the hotel. His shoes had holes in them, the cuffs of his trousers were ragged and he'd hitched up the waist with a dried-out unravelling bit of rope. He wore a gentleman's frock coat large enough to swallow his bird-like form, but he took pride in it and made a great dumb-show of flicking off bits of imaginary lint from the wide lapels. When we passed a lady in a bright geranium promenade dress dangling a dark sable muff from a tiny, yellow-gloved hand, the ragamuffin made her a deep bow and blew her a kiss with his bunched fingertips – a strange combination of gallantry and licentiousness made all the stranger in that the connoisseur was a Cincinnati beggar boy of ten.

He assured us that he knew all the available houses in town and would 'fix us up nicely.' But soon enough we realized he was just leading us up and down one street after another purely at random. When I dismissed him, saying we could search out a house just as efficaciously without his help, he stuck out a tiny, dirty mitt and demanded a dollar for his pains. I waved him away with a laugh, but eventually I had to pay him off since he followed us everywhere bawling out, 'The old foreign woman is a cheat, she doesn't pay her debts,' and I didn't think that sort of advertisement would inspire confidence in a future landlord.

At last we found a neat, new house that I rented on the spot, though only later, once we were settled in, did I realize that it had no pump, no cistern, no drain and no dustman's cart. When I sent for the landlord and asked him how I was to dispose of the rubbish, he seemed irritated by my summons and snapped, 'You'll have to place them all in the centre of the road for the pigs to eat. Now mind you, Old Woman, neither in the gutter far nor near but exactly in the centre.'

Only the next morning did I get to test his porcine theory. No sooner had the girls and I put our little sack of peels and gristle in the roadway than a big sow advanced on us, snuffling and regal, to make quick work of our humble tribute.

Pigs are omnipresent in Cincinnati and producing pig products of all sorts is so crucial to the local economy that the town is called 'Porkopolis' with less satirical intent than one might expect. I felt safe from brigands and from violent men even at night in Cincinnati, but I rarely traversed the unlit streets without having a cold, wet snout shoved against my person.

When the first warm days of spring came we went to the countryside for a picnic, a form of communion seldom practised in this hard-working, pleasure-shunning city. But no sooner had we spread our damask and brought out our delicacies from their hampers than the little brook beside us ran red with animal blood and the air was filled with frightful squeals so like the cries of human babies!

We walked five minutes upstream and discovered that a new slaughterhouse had just opened for business. The stench was overpowering and discarded pig skulls lay scattered about on every side.

Unfortunately there are ten vast slaughterhouses ringing the city, exactly where one would be tempted to stroll or picnic. Mind you, the Cincinnatians disapprove of picnics anyway, since they are convinced it's sinful for men and women to sit side by side on the grass. Every slaughterhouse is hissing steam, its vents are flapping open or shut according to the temperature outside, for the carcasses must not be allowed to freeze. The streams flowing through the factories are polluted; no wonder Deer Creek is now called Bloody Run. And the whole smells of dead flesh. Picture me with my 'Tintern Abbey' beside this wheezing, stinking mulcher and you'll have an image of Mrs Trollope in Cincinnati. I am sure I should have liked Cincinnati more if the people had not dealt so very largely in hogs.

The three hundred dollars that Nashoba had granted us was quickly running out. All my letters to my husband elicited no response – and posting mail to England cost extremely dear. Mr Trollope made no sign of life, though I wrote him *urgentissime*, begging him to send me more money (or at least comfort for the travails I was suffering). I felt like a pearl diver who assumes the line around his waist will pull him back up to air but discovers it's floating free and he's full fathom deep. Although my husband had been a gloomy boots for years by now, nevertheless I believed he would ultimately sustain me in my hour of crisis. The crisis had come – not an hour but a whole *season* of it – and Mr Trollope was playing dead. Or had he in fact died? Were my letters being delivered? Had he fallen into direst poverty and was he too melancholy to respond? Was he locked up in debtors' prison or a charity madhouse?

My girls and I were entirely dependent on Auguste Hervieu for money to eat. He was now painting the portrait of a Mrs Guest whose husband was a steamboat captain known to Marcus Winchester; Marcus had recommended Auguste for the job. Every morning at ten a maid let Auguste in through the servants' door of the Guests' simple three-storey town house on Vine. The maid in her dirty apron and filthy mobcap would serve Auguste a cup of tea, a beverage he despised, which he called 'spinster's bathwater.' Then Mrs Guest, or 'Eulalie' to give her her Christian name, would enter, a tall, perfectly white woman with a man's head, coarse red hands and a nearly comatose composure. She'd be wearing a walking dress most inappropriate for her solid, tubular body – a white lacy robe topped by a bright green spenser cradling and uplifting her breasts, her whole strange frame surmounted by a plumed hat made of cork and worn over a sort of lace wimple called, I believe, a 'cornette.' To finish her off she was supplied with green shoes and Limerick gloves. Her hair was dressed in tight curls marching across her forehead like stylized Greek meanders.

This stiff pagan idol with her hog-butcher hands and bonneted male head offered her lugubrious person to Auguste's delectation for exactly one hour every day. Eulalie never showed the least bit of curiosity about the painted results, an indifference

174

made up for by the maid's tiresome interest and liberally offered opinions. 'Oh, no, sir, I'd make the fingers much smaller and paler – far more elegant, don't you jes' know? And Madam's mouth is not so severe – well, not usually. How about a little smile, pinker cheeks, wind-tousled curls?'

Eulalie never spoke beyond a sepulchral 'good-day' when she determined the sitting was over. She seemed no more thoughtful than a harnessed horse behind its blinkers flicking flies with its tail.

When at last she saw the finished portrait she gave no sign of approval or displeasure; she accepted it as she accepted herself, as an unalterable fact of the landscape, like pig's blood.

I hired a servant girl named Nancy with some of the money Monsieur Hervieu gave me. She was a tall girl with a gap between her teeth and a constant flush threatening to brighten into a sunburn. She came into our little underfurnished house with a certain disdain, picked up objects here and there as if she were strolling through a jumble shop in search of a bargain, then cast them aside, disappointed.

'Have you ever been a servant before?' I asked, since she looked no more than eighteen.

'Nor am I beginning now!' she exclaimed, as if stung. 'I'm willing to help out a bit if you can't do all the work yourself, but I'd die before I'd become a servant.'

I lowered my head, taking an instant both to show and to master my irritation. 'It's very kind of you to help me,' I said with a dose of irony, but she didn't pay attention, since she was flushed with anger, her eyes were slightly crossed and she was walking off her vexation.

'Servant,' she muttered. 'I think you'll find, Mrs Trollope, servant!, that we don't take kindly to that kind of talk in these United States.' She subsequently always referred to my English brand of condescension as 'that kind of talk,' as if it were a form of cursing.

We discussed our arrangements, but when I offered to engage her for a year and pay her her first month's and last month's wages in advance, she laughed noisily (oh, if only these American women could be trained to speak less loudly, to laugh melodiously, to expose their teeth less often and to make fewer broad gestures their country would be a far finer place). 'A year!' she shouted and fell about laughing all over again. 'I hope to be married within two or three months.'

'Oh,' I said, 'are you *affiancée*?'

'No,' she replied, 'I don't have a fiancé but hope to find one before summer. After all I'm going on seventeen.'

I asked her if she'd be prepared to scrub floors and wash windows and she laughed again and said, 'No, but I'll go over to my mother's in Kentucky and bring back her slave girl and get her to do all the heavy work when we need it.'

I was indignant in many ways – she would be shirking her duties, handing them over to her mother's chattel and compromising my principles by bringing a slave into my house and *not* in order to liberate her, as Miss Wright so fervently wanted to do. 'Aren't you capable of doing the heavy work yourself? I'm not certain I want yet another person in my house.'

'Don't worry, Miss, this girl don't smell nor talk.' She brooded for a moment and said, 'Really heavy work ain't fit for a white woman.'

'And aren't you concerned lest she break away and run free – for surely you can't bring her in chains over into a free state?'

She laughed and said, 'I do declare you sound like an immediatrist.'

Eventually I figured out she'd become confused and taken the name of those who demanded the *immediate* freedom of the slaves and applied it to all abolitionists, even those who were *gradualists* like Miss Wright.

After a pause, Nancy said, 'Anyway, she won't run away. Haven't you ever heard of the laws protecting private property?' Having delivered this pert response, she felt so pleased with herself she screwed a fingertip into her cheek then sketched a humorous half-curtsy. There were so few servants available that I was forced to hire her.

The first day Nancy presented herself for work she was outfitted in a yellow dress parsemé with roses – the sort of gown a superior shop girl in London might wear out for a night at the Vauxhall Gardens. I hinted she might spoil her fine gown and should change into a plain smock but she said, ''Tis just my best and my worst and I've got no other.'

When my daughters and I made her a dress she stared at our efforts with amazed eyes and seemed delighted with the results, but she never thanked us. Nor did she ever thank us for any of our attentions. And when Emily refused to lend her her finest paisley scarf, a furious Nancy said we treated her no better than 'a Negur.' She was possessed of a sore, angry, ever wakeful pride that tormented her as if it were one of the infernal punishments Dante devised for his personal enemies. Within two months she'd quit my service, in a rage that I wouldn't lend her the money to buy a white silk gown for a ball she hoped to attend.

Henry was unhappy in New Harmony. He wrote me a letter begging me to come rescue him. Since the journey there was not long and Monsieur Hervieu seemed especially eager that we all be reunited in Cincinnati, I bent to the boy's will. After all, my only reason for coming to the New World had been to find a lucrative situation for Henry. The other boys, Thomas Adolphus and Anthony, were pursuing their studies in England and would surely find themselves solid positions somewhere. Anthony, as time would prove, would rise quite high in the postal office as a Surveyor, and Thomas Adolphus taught boys Latin and Greek – and caned them incessantly! – in a day school in Birmingham until he wearied of the violence and loneliness and he and I decided he should devote himself to my affairs exclusively. As I laboured through four or five books a year, alternating novels with travel books, Thomas Adolphus voyaged with me, ventured into all-male worlds on my behalf and served as my eyes, my hand and often my brain! There were those who criticized me for preventing my son from entering into a normal profession and for encouraging his 'idleness,' but in fact when I wrote my *Michael Armstrong*, which agitated in favour of a short ten-hour day for child labourers, a novel I penned at the encouragement of the reformer Lord Shaftesbury, my Thomas Adolphus was invaluable. He visited the factories, interviewed the children whenever possible and gathered statistics. Later, when we moved to Florence to economize, Thomas Adolphus would organize intimate evenings and our big monthly routs. In referring to these two kinds of events, he once said I received people '*en ménage*' and '*en ménagerie*.' He was – and is! – always so witty. And like his mother he could speed through an entire novel in under thirty days. I remember once he needed to take his ailing wife to a still warmer, drier climate, and in order to finance the Sicilian trip he wrote six hundred post octavo pages in just twenty-four days.

But I digress . . . It occurs to me that before the scene shifts to New Harmony, where I promise I will return to Fanny Wright, my subject, I should say a bit more about Cincinnati, since it is the city where Miss Wright would eventually settle.

I should remind my English readers that Cincinnati has a climate of long, snowed-in winters and heavy, sweat-soaked summers, something like the Ukraine. In December I was a slipping haystack of garments creeping across uncharted tracts of snow, the latest blizzard fumbling under my scarf and blanching even my eyelashes. In July I sat in total defeat and could think of nothing but the widening beads of perspiration drawing lines down my body from crown to waist. I longed for the privacy of my chamber where I could claw off my clothes which had become heavy wet rags, and sit in a tepid hip bath and stare at the blazing sun outside prying through the closed shutters. One thinks of a stunned nothing. A major project is moving from bed to armchair or, after a long wait, from chair to desk. One must prop one's manuscript up on a lectern or else one drips all over it, the paper buckles and the ink runs. Cincinnati is a hundred degrees in July and in December the ground is frozen six feet deep.

In London, Paris or Vienna I have lived by my wits alone and have been received by reigning and celebrated artists because they knew I would amuse them. I might hobble in in a dubious old bonnet and a worn gown from a forgotten decade, but my chatter has counted more than yet another glinting tiara and lengthy pedigree. I've always been welcomed as the lively mongrel, not the stately, stupid Russian wolfhound.

But in Cincinnati they would have preferred the tiara and the pedigree, certainly a flash new gown. It never occurred to me to seek out letters of introduction to the leading Cincinnati hostesses – the very idea that such anomalies might exist would have brought a smile to my lips. And it's equally true that my dowdiness put them off – they had virtually a Hottentot respect for finery. And then I was living with a bearded Frenchman who, at thirty-three, was fifteen years younger than I, more or less. The fact that I was the daughter of the Reverend Milton, that I had a highly respectable invalid of a husband back in England, that I'd come to the New World to secure my youngest son's future – none of these virtues mitigated my vices in the eyes of Cincinnati's matrons. I wasn't wounded or offended; I shrugged it off as risible effrontery.

Just once did I have a literary conversation with a serious old gentleman. He dismissed, one by one, all the great English writers, and each time he waved a huge white pocket-handkerchief, a gesture worthy of Paul to the offending Jews and signalling, 'I am clean.' He considered Pope 'entirely gone by' and when I demurred and mentioned *The Rape of the Lock* he declared, 'The very title!' In the same vein Shakespeare was 'obscene,' Grey 'had had his day' and Chaucer and Spenser were 'no longer intelligible.' I never heard those civic leaders Martin Baum or Frederick Amelung bawl out their old German songs – I never had access to the penetralia of Cincinnati culture – but after my literary conversation with old Mr Herschede I felt I'd risen high enough after all.

Women in America are so uneducated and witless that at dinners and balls they cluster together, for the men shun them except, one presumes, in nocturnal congress. ['Oh la la!' my daughter-in-law comments. 'You're the imp here!'] The poor women have no general conversation, no knowledge of current

179

events, no gay impertinent spirit of contradiction and can discuss nothing but one another's *toilette* down to the last shred of lace or parasol trim.

In any event we were never socially ambitious and the opposite of pretentious. My girls and I were happy together and after Nancy abandoned us we did our own scrubbing and baking and cooking and washing, though I feared my daughters would ruin their hands before I married them off. We made a game of our drudgery and every noon and evening we fed our honoured – well, guest but also host, since now we were living entirely from the pittance Monsieur Hervieu earned. After such an unstable life in England and the United States, he appreciated the solidity of two hot meals a day and we thought up what we considered to be French ways of serving the eternal ham – on a bed of spinach in a mustard sauce was one of his favourites, though he also liked it sautéed with boiling potatoes. On one of our strolls we once had the satisfaction of finding wild mint, which we sprinkled rather unsuccessfully, I fear, over fried apples and ham cooked in cream.

Auguste never upbraided me for my bad judgement in trusting Fanny and spiriting us all to Nashoba. Although Englishmen were allergic to his Gallic excesses, he was a true gentleman. He accepted our grim situation, never harangued me, worked hard to earn us all a subsistence and seemed happy to be with us. We had become his family. My devotion to him grew more intense now that my heart no longer had a place for the faithless Fanny.

Monsieur Hervieu was working on a wonderfully inspired grand composition, *Lafayette Landing in Cincinnati*, in which the artist inserted local notables on the wharf, embracing the Nation's Guest and bringing forward a silver trophy, which they'd *intended* to bestow on their visitor, though they'd failed to subscribe the necessary funds. Some of the most ecstatic local gentlemen in the painting hadn't even been present for the occasion but Auguste thought he would correct this historical error; he would have added mermaids as well in imitation of Rubens's canvas devoted to Marie de Medici's disembarkation on the shores of France, but he doubted if the Ohioans would catch the allusion or accept the allegorical exposed breasts.

When he'd finished it he arranged to exhibit it to a select group of gentlemen (those he'd placed in the painting), but though they exclaimed over its historical importance and the Frenchman's sublime genius, though they said they were certain he'd captured the most important moment in the Saga of Cincinnati, nevertheless not one of them offered to buy it. And when poor Hervieu, close to tears, offered to do scaled-down versions for their salons, he had no takers. When at last he proposed that they each subscribe a modest sum that would procure this masterpiece for the town hall, they all raised a great cheer and signed the subscription form, but not one, not a single one, ever honoured his debt.

Fifteen

We decided we should go to New Harmony to collect Henry but we had to wait another month until Monsieur Hervieu had done some pastels of a clergyman's daughters. The delay was fruitful for by then Fanny Wright was visiting New Harmony as well. By the end of March we had the funds necessary to set off.

We were enchanted by the early spring that was bubbling up out of the cold dankness of winter. We were drifting downstream in a flatboat and we took a soul-expanding pleasure in the plash of swift waves against the hull, the silent unscrolling of the ever-varying landscape, the skilful manoeuvring of the long pole that kept us on course. Bushes and trees everywhere were in tender blossom – the wedding-veil daintiness of tiny flowered white pear trees in orderly rows, like bridal maids tiptoeing into a wedding. And over there the yellow clamour of a forsythia bush brightening the still-leafless woods like a trumpet playing to itself in an empty chapel. A farmer was sowing seeds with long swinging arcs of his powerful arm. Another mile downstream and we saw a horse, followed by a barefoot boy almost submerged by his father's straw hat, digging one long furrow up a rolling hill. It looked like a dark page inscribed with a single line of darker ink.

Beyond the crest a lazy exhalation of blue smoke suggested the unseen farmhouse. That invisible house struck me as an emblem of all the loneliness in the New World.

At last we came to the point where the Wabash flowed into the Ohio and there we landed in a huzzah of male shouts and creaking carts and stevedores dashing about, a confusion that shocked us after our tranquil voyage. Soon we were installed in a steamboat and heading up to Henry and New Harmony. Our new captain was determined to make the trip with the utmost rapidity and had ordered the engines stoked with so much fuel that we feared they'd explode. An errant spark did land on my lap and singe its way through my skirt until my Emily hurled a dipperful of water at me out of a cistern kept on deck for just such an emergency.

The river-beds were littered with burned-out wrecks of boats or the capsized ships' carcasses that had rammed into floating trees at night. One would have thought that all these nautical casualties would have convinced the River Men to go slower or sail only by day, but Americans believe so blindly in luck and have such a childlike underestimation of danger that no number of previous disasters can persuade them to change their ways. They just laugh and call for more steam – no wonder the men inside were all gambling since the voyage itself was played for the biggest stakes of all.

The prospect of seeing Fanny frightened me. I was worried that she would ignore me now that I no longer figured into her Nashoba plans. Or I feared that in spite of myself I would express my rancour against her and spoil our friendship for ever. When we arrived at New Harmony early the next day, a frowning, visibly thinner Henry was awaiting us. My heart leapt and I rushed down the gangplank to fold him in my arms. With a boy's real delight and feigned vexation, Henry submitted to our affectionate pummellings, but then he pulled away from us and embraced Auguste. I studied the expression on Henry's face and on Auguste's: the same. The very same look of peace and fulfilment, the surprisingly mature look of sailing into a safe haven. Natural, of course, between two spiritual brothers.

183

We'd brought only one cloth valise since we were planning on spending just three nights. Henry said, 'I had to run away from Madame Frétageot's classroom.'

'Surely,' I said, laughing, 'even that magisterial lady must concede a mother and son have a natural right to see each other.'

'Not at all,' Henry said grimly. 'New Harmony regards the family as nefarious, the most conservative of all institutions, and even children of six or seven are permitted to see their parents no more than once or twice a year. And this sustained practice causes children to greet their parents with the greatest indifference.'

'What utter rubbish,' I exclaimed.

Henry looked at Monsieur Hervieu and said in a soft voice as if between intimate parentheses, '*Ça va, mon vieux?*'

'*De mieux en mieux.*'

I had forgotten that the two boys spoke to each other in French; it made them seem all the more separate from us, their ladies – I almost said something about the 'distaff side' except I've never once held a distaff in my hands.

On the far bank a hill rose gently, covered with huge oaks and elms. Here on this side of the water we were walking past a row of log cabins that was being torn down. 'Mr Owen ordered them to be destroyed,' Henry said, 'since he considers them a disgrace to our high level of civilization, though in fact we need more not fewer habitations.'

'How do you happen to know that?' I asked, amused.

'Impossible not to know, since Mr Owen speaks for several hours two or three times a week, and we're all expected to attend. He has been called the most unstoppable monologist of our day.'

'Oh, dear,' I said. 'Henry, you look a bit thinner,' because I couldn't help noticing he'd added two notches to tighten his belt and that his shoulder blades were cutting sharply through his shirt.

'That's because they keep us working here all the time!' Henry exclaimed, a bit exasperated, as if I'd stupidly failed to understand him, though he was telling me this for the first time. Henry informed us that two years ago when Mr Owen had bought this village and everything in it and twenty thousand acres surrounding it, he'd announced in lectures all over the United States that he was initiating a new experiment in communism and welcomed all comers. Within two weeks this village, which could accommodate only about seven hundred people, had attracted more than a thousand and they were sleeping everywhere.

Here Henry exchanged a shy smile with Auguste. He pointed up to a solid three-storey building astoundingly large for this part of the world, with its shuttered windows and dormers piercing a mansard roof and down below its three pairs of double doors. 'The villagers live not only in this dormitory,' Henry went on, 'or in the 180 other buildings the Rappites put up and left behind, but in that big barn over there, too, which they call the Fort, since it was meant to protect the people against marauders, though there's never been an attack and it serves merely as a granary.' He looked decidedly disappointed by the paucity of armed conflicts in this part of the world.

'The thousand newcomers', he went on, 'were some of them sincere, eager to prove Mr Owen's theories of shared labour and shared wealth and shared hostility toward religion, marriage and the family, but I'm afraid half of them are useless layabouts looking for a free ride and without advanced free-thinking principles of any sort.'

'Principles!' I snorted indignantly.

I was dismayed to hear Henry use a crude Americanism such as 'free ride' and I feared he was already picking up a vulgar New World accent with its flat Indiana *a*s and mumbled underarticulation. And he'd even pronounced *dormitory* as '*dawmuhtry*'.

I wondered where Fanny was. Why hadn't she come to greet our arrival?

'There's nothing but wrangling here,' Henry said, pointing out two dirty men on the street corner tapping each other on the chest and quarrelling so vociferously that they'd overexcited a pair of mongrels, which were yapping and dancing in circles. 'Everyone is supposed to be equal and Mr Owen is equally opposed to punishment or encouragement, so each man is his own philosopher, and no one can be told to shut up. Mr Owen has declared, Man is not a fit subject for praise or blame.' And here Henry stopped us in the street since we had already reached the Tavern where we would be staying and he wanted to make his point before we went in. We were standing under a leafless poplar that was about fifteen years old, I would judge, the legacy of the Germans who had built this pretty village and sold it to Mr Owen.

'There are over a hundred paying students here,' Henry said, 'but we charity cases must all work. I've had to work in the fields, the kitchen and the barnyard. I've had to water and feed the livestock. Recently I've been assigned to the vegetable garden and we're supervised by a naturalist, Thomas Say, who is much too ill for the work, though we all like him. He's a nice mild-mannered Philadelphia Quaker with a beautiful wife. He's an entomologist, which is only appropriate, since we're nothing but worker ants.' He told us they were kept busy from five in the morning till eight at night. They worked for two hours in the morning until breakfast at seven. They were back to work from eight to eleven, when their lessons began. They studied till half past two, with half an hour off for luncheon. Then they were back to manual labour till five, when they went in to dinner. Finally they had evening lessons till eight and bedtime. 'As you can see,' Henry said, 'a factory boy might consider this schedule benign –'

'But it's a scandal!' Auguste exclaimed, his face darkening as it did whenever he fell into a regicidal rage. 'They're trying to get rich from you and your . . . transpiration!' (I suppose he didn't know the word *sweat* or was too polite to use it.) Once again Auguste had said what we were all thinking. 'And to think this tyrant, this Frétageot is a Frenchwoman. It doesn't surprise me she was forced to emigrate from France.'

Although some of the people passing us by in the streets were dressed normally, more than half wore the costume of the colony – the men in matching wide pantaloons and collarless little jackets, the women in knee-length coats worn over pantaloons as well. All the costumes were made of plain muslin.

I suddenly thought I saw Fanny up ahead and my heart beat quicker – but it turned out to be someone who in no way resembled her. I prayed that my girls wouldn't take it into their heads to don trousers – then where would we all be? Here, in the wilderness, anything was possible (children raised by the state, corn for dinner, harem pants) but I knew my children's fate lay in England, and for England they must maintain the proprieties and unchapped hands.

'The most scandalous part,' Henry said, 'is that we're taught nothing useful like Latin or Greek or archaeology, because Mr Maclure is opposed to studying the past, which he says will only hold us back.'

Poor Henry. I took his hands and examined them and could see the thick calluses and dirty, ragged nails from all his hoeing and digging. His neck was as burned as a peasant's. 'I'd love to tell Mr Owen what I think of his utopia,' I exclaimed. Henry frantically waved his hands and made an anguished face.

'What would you tell me?' asked a small, neatly dressed man smoking a pipe as long as a Dutchman's. He was just stepping out of the Tavern. He had big fleshy ears that looked like crushed red velvet and a huge prehensile nose with nostrils as big and black as cooked raisins. On his nose were perched fine wire-rimmed spectacles much too small for his massive features.

'Mr Owen!' I exclaimed, flustered, 'I didn't expect you to hear the immoderate remarks of a mother!'

'Well,' he said, 'I live here in the Tavern so you'll have a chance to address remarks moderate and immoderate to me over the next few days.'

'You do!' I nearly shouted, so embarrassed was I by our encounter. 'And why do you not live in that great house over there,' pointing to a gracious woodframe house with a large colonnaded porch and a sloping roof, obviously the sole mansion in town.

'Because I'm utterly indifferent to all signs of material

187

superiority,' Mr Owen said. He was wearing a wide-brimmed hat that cast his face in shadow though his small sharp eyes glittered behind his tiny glasses and his acquisitive nose kept distending. 'That house', he said with disdain, drawing on his pipe, 'is where Mr Maclure lives with Madame Frétageot. It was built by Father Rapp.' His nose retracted. 'I gather your son is complaining about working seven hours a day, but at that rate he is far from earning out the expenses of his room and board or education and clothing. Mr Maclure and I have had to subsidize everything. In tonight's speech' – and here he pulled out of his pocket a long scroll of paper covered with microscopic handwriting – 'I have many important admonitions or rather considerations, including, including . . .' and here his voice trailed off into a hum he maintained lest someone attempt to interrupt him, 'here it is! "There must be no abuse, growling, or loud talking. No grumbling, carping, or murmuring against the work of other individuals; those who shirk their work are deserving of pity . . ."' And still talking and puffing his pipe Mr Owen walked away, his nose working all the while as if it were engrossing every precept.

Henry whispered, 'I should have warned you that he's always creeping around, but it's better, even so, when he's here. When he's gone for long periods the whole community falls apart.' Henry now led us into the Tavern. Just as we were making our arrangements to stay for three nights, Mr Owen strolled back in, still talking. He seized my hand and looked at me with great kindliness. Now that I was less embarrassed, I was free to notice that his voice was gentle and well-pitched, but this very pleasantness made it all the more soporific. I decided on the spot that Henry was right. Mr Owen must be one of the great bores of the nineteenth century, even if his intentions were of the highest.

'Madam,' he said, 'I heard you say that you're staying just three nights, which is far too short a time for you to absorb the principles of the New Moral Order, but if I have a chance I will attempt to instruct you in my plans to remodel the world entirely, to root out all crime, abolish punishment and end warfare by instilling the same, identical wants and views in all people. If everyone thinks alike there will be no more reason for dissension, now, will there? Nor will there be any more competition or even trade, for each man will be able to provide the necessities if he learns a few basic skills and avails himself of the mechanical progress of our era.'

I was used to friendly, lively controversy and said, 'How appalling, Mr Owen! I don't like at all the sound of identical people all banging away at their own shoes.' But at the first sign of disagreement Mr Owen faded away in a cloud of sweet pipe smoke, murmuring all the while.

That evening, after our nap, we had a Spartan supper at the Tavern of hard cheese, brown bread, dried apricots and cider, neither effervescent nor alcoholic. Henry told us that though the colony produced distilled spirits and sold them elsewhere, alcohol of any sort was forbidden at New Harmony. But already a few drunkards had started a rival colony a few miles off where they would be free to stagger about from dawn to dust.

There was a smelly old man at our table who overheard us speaking in French and chose to address us in that language. He had a charming, old-fashioned way of expressing himself but he'd obviously forgotten many words in French and had to fill them in with English substitutions. He told us he was called Constantine Raffinesque and that he'd been born in Constantinople in 1774 and that blended in his veins were French, Turkish, German and Greek blood. 'After a childhood spent in Marseilles,' he said, 'where I became a naturalist and published my first scientific paper before the age of twelve, my parents sent me to Philadelphia once the French Revolution had broken out. In 1805 I returned to the Old World, this time to Sicily, where I helped the impoverished natives by showing them how to extract a medicine from the squill.' (He said 'squill' in English – just as well, since I wouldn't have known the French word.) 'I spent ten years on that island, happily botanizing and studying the fish – in fact in 1810 I published two works on the fish of Sicily. Five years later I sailed back to these United States but oh horror!' – and here Mr Raffinesque held up a hand at arm's length, as if to ward off an appalling sight. 'My ship sank,' and now he lowered his reedy, whistling old man's quaver three octaves, 'and with it all my books and scientific collections.'

'And did anyone drown?' I asked.

Mr Raffinesque shrugged. 'Possibly.' He rubbed his powerful forehead over which the skin was stretched so tight that it wrinkled like the surface of a smooth sea under a sudden squall. 'What a tragedy,' he said. Like all Americans, even an adopted American, Mr Raffinesque was a practised narrator of his own 'story,' but the recounting seemed to have left him exhausted.

Monsieur Hervieu, who could be alarmingly sly, asked with a countenance of total innocence, 'Tell me, good sir, you who are a friend to New Harmony and a frequent visitor here, have you heard people speaking of a certain Miss Fanny Wright, newly arrived?'

'Goodness yes,' Mr Raffinesque said. 'One talks of nothing else.' He revived a bit and opened a tin of chewing tobacco and with the unexpectedly fussy gesture of a connoisseur delicately placed a small wad into his cheek.

'And what do they say about her?' Monsieur Hervieu pursued.

'She is quite an extraordinary woman, it seems. She was raised by Jeremy Bentham in accord with the most advanced views. He had her philosophizing with him when she was no more than five and until the age of ten she never saw an adult woman, since Bentham despises the whole sex. Subsequently Bentham confided her to Lafayette, who adopted her and filled her head with sound republican ideas. She travelled to America with him where she met Jefferson and became his mistress. Jefferson convinced her to take up the cause of the slave. Somewhere in Louisiana she established a plantation and furnished it with slaves she bought. Her idea was that they'd work supplementary hours and earn their freedom, but none of them was too keen on that since freedom would entail being shipped off to Liberia, where they'd surely be enslaved all over again and sold off to even crueller African masters. Worse, Miss Wright and her sister, who preach free love, began to

190

sleep with their chattel, which compromised all sense of discipline. And rather irritated their slave-holding neighbours.' He spat his tobacco as if to demonstrate the neighbours' vexation. 'Folks call it Fanny Wright's Free Love Colony, don't they?'

I was about to erupt in indignation but Monsieur Hervieu, who was enjoying his game, raised a repressive hand and asked, 'And why is she here?'

'It seems she's abandoned her colony as a job well botched. Now she's here editing the *New Harmony Gazette* with Robert Dale Owen, Mr Owen's son; she's his new mistress. He's encouraging her to go on the lecture circuit in order to drum up new subscribers for the paper. "To promote the cause of human improvement," is how *she* puts it. Robert Dale convinced her it would be a poor appropriation of her talents to devote herself to the emancipation of a few slaves, besides its being an employment for which she was altogether and in every respect incompetent.'

'And do the Owens, *père et fils*, have a plan of their own for freeing the slaves? A subject dear to Miss Wright's heart, I presume,' Monsieur Hervieu asked.

'I don't know about the son,' said Mr Raffinesque, 'but the father is utterly indifferent to the fate of the Negro race.'

Perhaps in the past I would have taken in this bit of information with equanimity, as if indifference were a justifiable option. But now I was surprised to discover that hot tears were stinging my eyes. Ever since I'd seen that black man clean and bandage his wife's foot at Nashoba I had a new sense of the patient, undramatic kindness of Negroes and in some ill-defined way I wanted to defend it, participate in it: *know* it.

Auguste, with a deep bow, thanked the good man for his 'objective and scientific account' of Miss Wright and said he only hoped his descriptions of Sicilian fish were equally accurate. The old fool didn't know whether he was being complimented or satirized and made something like a half-curtsy holding his long yellow coat-tail in one hand but with a smile playing across his lips. He resolved his awkwardness in another juicy expectoration of brown liquid.

Once he had waltzed hesitantly out of the room, still smiling,

we all fell about in loud guffaws. But it was that very day, perhaps, when I first conceived of writing Miss Wright's life. I realized that a woman who had been the first to address a mixed
audience of men and women in America, who had been a pioneer of the anti-slavery and women's rights movements, who had
championed universal and free public education and who had
fought God, the family and the marriage contract – that such a
woman, praised as a saviour or denounced as the high priestess
of Beelzebub, required a carefully researched, well-organized,
balanced biography. Now that I was a bit disillusioned by Fanny
I could be more objective about her. My disappointed love was
slowly turning into a cooler, more nuanced admiration. I admit
that I have not always approved of Fanny's positions, but I have
invariably loved her and understood her unique mind. I wish I
had had more time to prepare this book.

That evening we attended the community assembly in the Hall
of New Harmony. I was so anxious about the possibility of seeing
Fanny that I had some difficulty drawing my breath. Over the
lovely double door with its glass fanlight and flanking stone
columns was carved a golden rose, a relic from the Rappite days
(a reference to a passage in the Bible), and inscribed 1822. The
room, so obviously an ex-church, had been stripped of its altar.
It smelled deliciously of river water, as if it were connected directly
to the Wabash. Children were streaking about playing tag and
shouting in a way that would never be permitted in London or
in Boston. Women in their beige pantaloons were rehearsing a
dance step; one of them had a wailing baby strapped to her back
in the best papoose-fashion.

We suddenly saw Frances Wright talking to a tall young man
who could never have been called handsome though he had
something courtly about the way he leaned into Fanny's words.
He had those telltale big crushed-velvet ears and the prominent
acquisitive nose – surely this was Robert Owen's son! His eyebrows curved down at the outer edges and half circled back like
the rims of spectacles.

Fanny and I melted into each other's arms, so overjoyed to be reunited, so overwhelmed to find each other happy and well – although truth be told I always felt that underlying Fanny's protestations of ardour, even her physical attentions, was a certain horror of the flesh, a kind of physical Puritanism that made her shrink slightly away from even her dearest friend. To be sure she was famous for her numerous lovers; some, like Lafayette, were no longer in their first youth. But I say that the very fact that she could make love to all these wrecks *proves*, doesn't it, that she was, on the mineral and vegetative planes of the body, as fastidious as a virgin. I mean, fundamentally she was not responding to a man's caress, not in the way metal filaments fly to a magnet or a sunflower turns to the light. No, it was all pure, willed choice, a decision to be the consort to the greatest man of her day. Though she was among the first defenders of female rights she'd become so not in hoping to overthrow male authority. No, she wanted to be the co-ruler, the sharing monarch of a double throne.

'Fanny!' I exclaimed.

'Fanny!' she echoed more softly, almost as if mocking my feminine excitement. Perhaps in fact she no longer liked me overmuch, since I had quit Nashoba. I was a witness to her failure or at least her fraudulence, and she probably did not like such a voluble, honest witness as me at New Harmony. Here she could still pass herself off as a pioneer of social justice, but I knew the shameful reality.

She introduced me to Robert Dale Owen who on closer inspection turned out to be a flagrantly ugly young man. I remember that a few years later, when he'd tired of Fanny Wright's intensity, as so many men did, he fell in love with a thoughtful, pretty girl named Mary Jane Robinson. The story has it that Mary declared to her mother the evening of their first encounter, 'I have just seen the homeliest young man of my experience. And he is the man I want for my husband.' I should point out that *homely* in American does not mean 'domestic' but rather 'ugly'.

That night he seemed completely enamoured of Frances

Wright. He blinked at her his pale blue eyes with their sandy lashes. His childish weak mouth wobbled indefinitely above an even more indeterminate chin. He kept bowing and smiling and if his severely egalitarian manners would have permitted it he would surely have kissed her hand repeatedly and even nibbled it like the big affectionate rabbit he was.

'Darling Fanny,' I said, 'how goes Nashoba?'

'I love it so!' she exclaimed with no irony and genuine enthusiasm. 'Nowhere do I feel more peaceful than in my forest beside my stream, far from the wrangling and scheming of the so-called civilized world.'

'No one would dispute that it's far from civilized – I mean, civilization,' I said, but I didn't want to sound as if I bore a grudge, so I instantly added, 'New Harmony strikes me as a perfect balance between the charms of society and the beauties of nature.'

She suddenly looked sorrowful. 'I'm afraid Nashoba is increasingly beyond my means, spiritual and material.'

'I'm sorry to hear it,' I said, secretly delighted she was admitting as much.

'The slaves, corrupted by servitude itself, are always scheming to get out of work rather than recognizing that they are labouring for their own liberation. Nor do the black mothers like it that we've removed their children from their influence entirely. Of course we can never hope to shape a new generation possessed of healthy views and sound values unless we quarantine the children categorically from their parents.'

'And yet . . . ' I demurred.

'Recently there's been a bit of intergenerational contamination,' she said. 'Children and mothers have been arranging to see each other behind our backs, whereas I want them to be exposed only to Camilla and eventually to Mr Jennings, with whom they will enter on a regular system of instruction.'

'How dreadful,' I murmured. She could apply my lament as she pleased.

'And yet there are reasons for rejoicing,' she said. 'Mr Flower

194

has vastly improved the amenities of everyday life, laid out new walks down to the Wolf and finished roofing our houses. Our tavern is now open and serving healthful if simple fare. All are cheerful and contented and a fiddle which we procured for one of the men who knows how to turn some merry tunes strikes up regularly every evening. But Mrs Flower is disgruntled and a force for discontent. She is not in any way suited to fill any situation in this establishment nor does she possess a mind calculated to enter into the views connected with it. We are going to have to ask her to leave.'

'What?!' I exclaimed. 'But if you value her husband so much?'

'I'm speaking of her, not him. As you know, Mrs Trollope, Nashoba does not recognize the institution of marriage. I dissolved the Flowers' marriage when they arrived.'

I had no heart to pursue the matter. I wanted to ask what would become of the Flower children, and whether the laws of Tennessee might not condemn Mrs Flower's banishment, but I dared not stir up further discussion. Had Fanny been just as callous and indifferent about my departure from Nashoba?

I couldn't help but notice how ardently Mr Owen followed every one of Fanny's sallies.

But Fanny had had another Nashoba thought. She said, 'I've spent 10,000 dollars on my slaves, more than a third of my remaining fortune. I thought our farm and tavern and store would be thriving by now, but I've received no money from the subscribers I hoped would help me, I suppose because most abolitionists are religious and conservative people and the notes published in *The Genius of Emancipation* suggested we are all free love apologists. To be sure we have received one donation from a wealthy Quaker merchant in New-York, a certain Jeremiah Thompson, who gave us goods worth 550 dollars to help outfit our store. And of course Lafayette keeps wanting to contribute – but I can't accept his money.'

When Fanny spoke of Nashoba with its tavern and store and farm with paths wending through the forest, one would never have suspected she was referring to a swamp where two children slapped mud with sticks and every fire threatened to burn down the chimney.

I may sound independent and satirical, but it is crucial for the reader to remember that I had but five pounds in my reticule and little hope of finding more. Mine is not a resentful nature and I do, I really *do* trust in omniscient and generous Providence, but the pauper is always aware that she's consorting with the prince (or princess) whose freedom is less constrained, whose perspective is decidedly broader, and whose gift is virtually unlimited. I'd learned through circumstances how to court my masters and profit from their caprices.

My Emily kept clinging to my waist. She was bored, perhaps, or intimidated by the many eccentrics we'd chanced upon at New Harmony. But her childish dependence made a bad impression, especially in this place that despised the family and sneered at its very right to exist. At least Henry and Hervieu were wholly independent of me, I observed gratefully. In fact they seemed absorbed in each other, speaking in French off in a corner and bumping into each other with coltish delight.

The Hall was lit by a great gas chandelier above us, which cast a shadow-free light. It was nearly as bright as daylight and allowed me to gaze into even the most distant corners. The factionalism and lawlessness of New Harmony were obvious no matter where we looked. One man with the bright red nose of the tippler and the rags of a vagabond was stretched out full-length on a bench awaiting the evening's entertainment with a smile on his lips – a smile that eventually faded into a slack little snore. Americans, I'd noticed, seldom hold themselves upright in a neat, contained way. They sprawl all over, think nothing of crossing their legs so that passers-by have to squeeze over a big, dangling boot, and are equally prone to putting their feet onto a facing chair, even daubing the upholstery with the mud on their shoes. They never creep about with the tidy discretion of an Englishman but yawn constantly and stretch everywhere as if about to go to bed.

There was one well-behaved group of young ladies clustered around Madame Frétageot in the corner. Later I joined their company; they sneered at nearly everything, which prejudiced my view of New Harmony. They represented the anti-democratic party. Whereas the Owens, father and son, were by instinct such patriarchs if by policy such *levellers*, Madame Frétageot had once been a communist but had now repented of her ways and become aristocratic. She wore an ancient black dress that had turned green and detachable lace cuffs that had turned yellow. Her 'girls' were all neatly dressed and coiffed in conventional frocks that looked nearly luxurious in contrast with the homespun Turkish trousers and vests every other woman wore.

In their midst was Camilla, who seemed strangely transformed. She scarcely rose to greet me and extended a hand to deflect my embrace. She had painted her pale cheeks with bright red spots like a ballerina. She mumbled answers to my detailed questions. When the other girls said malicious things about one of the many eccentrics in the assembly, she beat her hands together in excited applause. Almost as if someone had cut a nerve in her face, her expression sagged to one side in an unpleasant grimace. Though I saw her and Fanny separately several times during our three-day stay, I never once perceived the sisters together, though in the past they'd been inseparable. When I mentioned Nashoba to Camilla and inquired after the current progress of the colony, Camilla gurgled forth an ugly little laugh. Although I felt vindicated that Camilla appeared to be rejecting the excessive Fanny, I also feared that any hostility between them would reduce both sisters to unhappy solitude.

I introduced myself to Madame Frétageot who said, with typical Gallic unpleasantness, 'You must be the mother of *notre petit* Henri, who sees a plot in every kindness and can work up a complaint about every favour.' Suddenly I no longer doubted Henry's vision of the French schoolmistress – she *was* odious and merited the nickname he'd given her, 'Madame Vinaigre.'

Soon these liberated lads and lasses were prancing up and down the overheated room, which I could never forget had not long ago been a church. They seemed merry and carefree and why not? They'd replaced a jealous God with the benign if long-winded Mr Owen, whose seemingly bottomless pockets assured everyone's peace of mind. For a moment I, too, whose pockets were empty, considered living off his largess though I could never stomach the chicanery and impiety.

The spring day had been nearly warm but now the great windows let in cold breezes siphoning down out of the vast Indiana skies. Mr Owen delivered an interminable address on the newest rules of the colony and something about a financial dispute with Mr Maclure. When the speech was over the silence was celebrated by a parade outside. The New Harmony Light Infantry fired their muskets and awakened the birds nesting in the neighbouring trees. We all rushed outside to watch it drill, but when the white acrid clouds from the firearms had drifted away, we had nothing better to do than to drift back inside for more talk and a rousing song performed by the children's choir based on words written by Mr Owen:

Sick of the Old World's sophistry
Haste then across the dark blue sea,
Land of the West, we rush to thee!
Home of the brave: soil of the free.

At last we were given a performance by the Thespian Society of a verse play by Robert Dale Owen about Pocahontas. His drama was much in the same vein as Fanny Wright's own first play about Swiss patriots. It was directed by a brave little body called Mrs Chase who'd also painted the scenery. She kept scurrying about adjusting the Indian maid's feathers. When I spoke later to Mrs Chase, a convinced phrenologist, she told me that Robert Dale Owen showed pronounced organs of conscientiousness and friendship but that his Bump of Wit was virtually non-existent.

We skipped away after the first Act and hurried to the Tavern and our tidy, deep beds under pleasantly suffocating eiderdowns turned sideways in the German manner. I never saw Emily sleep so soundly despite her disquieting cough. Auguste and Henry agreed to share a bed in the room next to ours but we didn't hear a thing, not a thing. Though I thought it base to thank God for the trivial arrangements of our lives, nevertheless I couldn't help but acknowledge his benevolence in sending Auguste to protect the Trollopes.

The next morning Fanny came by in her sunniest mood. She did seem very much like a woman in love – with the whey-faced Robert Dale Owen, I presume, though I could scarcely fit that in with her schemes to banish Mrs but not Mr Flower from Nashoba. Was she in love with both men? Was she a sort of sentimental 'bigamist'? Or was she entertaining a whole harem of emotions I knew nothing about?

I realize that I am setting up shop as Fanny's biographer, dear reader, and certainly everything I am saying is true, true, true, but a mystery always seemed to hover over Frances Wright. Her public deeds and utterances are clear enough, but her private life remains obscure, partly because she was unusually discreet and seldom confided in others, at least not in me, and largely because she took no interest in such things. I don't mean to suggest she was indifferent to love and even its most sensual expression, despite her temperamental Puritanism, for she was seldom without a companion or two, but she couldn't see the gossip value in such subjects, the whole heated he-did-what and she-left-him-why repertory of questions, hints and veiled answers. She was ready, always ready, for love, but she couldn't find the interest in relating its details. Today no one remembers the sentimental facts of her life since she devoted so little effort toward broadcasting them.

When I inherited the Garnett letters I discovered that in one from Fanny to Harriet she tells her that she should be cautious about confiding anything sacrosanct to Mrs Trollope, 'who is a dear old thing but careless with the reputation of others and not overly scrupulous about veracity. Not that I hold such failings against her since they are an integral part of her exuberance.' The reader will recognize that if I dare to include such injuries I can afford to because my gravity and honesty have long since been established in the eyes of the whole world. If I have been received by Chateaubriand, Prince Metternich, Lord Shaftesbury and a daughter of George III, these entrées have proved beyond a doubt the integrity of my character. And yet it was painful for me to see in her loopy handwriting her low estimation of my regard for the truth. So that was it! I thought. That was why she withdrew from me. Like a disappointed lover who discovers decades later that his mistress threw him over due to a mis-understanding, I felt half-solaced and half-grieved.

I was given a tour of the various workshops at New Harmony but many of the old ateliers equipped by the Rappites were now empty for lack of trained artisans. Cotton-spinning had come to a standstill. The dye-house with its glowing copper vessels sat empty and the pottery wheels and kilns were occupied only by shafts of sunlight and gliding white and green butterflies. To be sure, I saw boots being hammered and hats being blocked, and butchers, bakers, coopers, tailors and sawyers all busy and pro-ductive, but there was a vague air of insubstantiality clinging to every activity, as if someone had improvised flimsy buildings and smiling artisans to impress the Empress as she rode swiftly past in her carriage.

Any idiot could have seen that this community was doomed. It had filled up with the first-comers, mostly free-thinkers and parasites. Mr Owen wanted cleanliness and found dirt; he wanted temperance and found disorder; he wanted a passion for learning and found ignorance. In any society in which hardworking labourers and idlers are paid the same wages, chaos is imminent.

Miss Wright introduced me to a teacher at the school, a devotee of the Pestalozzi method, a certain William Phiquepal from Bordeaux, where his father had held a distinguished post but had quarrelled with his rebellious son. It seems that Phiquepal had taught in Maclure's original school in Spain but that there he'd established a printing press and thereby run afoul of the newly restored and highly repressive Bourbon government. Phiquepal and Maclure fled from Spain and travelled to

Philadelphia, where the Frenchman joined Maclure's mistress, the unconventional Madame Frétageot, in running Maclure's new school. They had all removed to New Harmony recently. Henry said that the students laughed at Phiquepal, who was practically blind and given to uncontrollable rages.

I accompanied Miss Wright into the print shop where three printers (all trained by Phiquepal) were setting type for the next number of the weekly *Gazette*. I sat in a corner and read a few back issues. There were many curiosities used as column fillers – the Albification of a Negro, a Mode for Stopping Epistaxis (nosebleeds), and a Receipt for Destroying Rats (grind up fresh corks, fry them in butter, place them before the ratholes, turn off all sources of water – and *voilà!*).

There were items on comparative religion (which days are designated as the Sabbath by different religions) designed to promote atheism. A method to make a dye for linen or cotton out of horse chestnuts. And endless extracts from Fanny Wright's updated parable, *A Few Days in Athens*. She had recently written additional chapters for it attacking all religions.

The whole enterprise seemed at once universal and piecemeal, innocent and corrupt, optimistic and despairing. Robert Dale Owen came in, smiling and tripping over his own long legs, his white face looking somehow scalded, as if the original beautiful outer layer had been peeled away to reveal this squamous mass. We chatted for a while until a sudden squall blew up, black clouds rushing in from the West, the faint artillery crackle and boom of distant lightning and thunder. A big wooden shutter across the street was banging in the wind and children were rushing home through the spattering rain, laughing.

When the rain let up for a moment we decided to go on to the next point in our tour. A carpenter was going to demonstrate how to construct side-hung and centre-guided drawers. The lightning was still playing across the heavens. At the end of the deserted street was an old man with a white beard approaching us. He was carrying a slender iron rod, ten or twelve feet long, which he held straight upright, as a soldier carries a musket. His clothes were drenched through and moulded to his hollow chest and sloping shoulders. He was walking slowly down the centre of the street with all the dignity of a solemn ceremony.

'Mr Greenwood!' called Robert Dale Owen. 'What are you doing?'

'Ah! Well, my young friend,' Mr Greenwood replied with a boyish smile through his white beard, like the first crocus breaking through the snow, 'I am very old. I am not well. I shuffer much, and I thought it might be a good chance to slip off, and be laid quietly away in the corner of the orchard.'

'You hoped to be struck by lightning?' Mr Owen exclaimed as if he had been struck himself.

'You shee,' Mr Greenwood said in the slushy sibilants of someone wearing wooden false teeth, 'I don't like to kill myself. It sheems like taking matters out of God's hands. But I thought He might shend me a spare bolt when I put myself in the way. If He had only seen fit to do it, I'd have been at rest this very minute, all my pains gone, no more trouble to anyone, and no more burden to myshelf.'

So concluding, he moved away with his deliberate gliding pace, as if he were ice-skating very slowly. Thunderstruck ourselves we stood in the middle of the empty thoroughfare and watched his lightning rod sway above him like some strange antenna attuned to the fates.

These fates refused to smile on either Nashoba or New Harmony. Nashoba was an open wound bleeding money, and the communistic experiment of New Harmony had proved disastrous. In both places Fanny Wright and old Mr Owen thought they could rectify everything by publishing yet another new position paper. Faced with economic ruin, Fanny rewrote her bylaws and added new names to the board of directors. Mr Owen gave exhausting speeches about first principles, modified them, pitied himself – and finally withdrew from Indiana in a sulk. Before leaving Indiana he had expelled many colonists; now, in the spring of 1828, he rejected the entire colony.

We left on the morning of the fourth day. Henry was with us

and we were all jubilant – the girls and I and Auguste most especially, for at times he must have felt suffocated by the female principle so predominant in our midst. Men, I've noticed, are curious beasts who love the sex but cannot be with them too much. Perhaps they object to our loquaciousness; Dr Johnson said, 'I am very fond of the company of ladies. I like their beauty, I like their delicacy, I like their vivacity, and I like their *silence*.' I'm afraid, my male readers, that if you agree with the good doctor you'll never like me. I have never mastered the art of silence, I confess, nor of delicacy and beauty, but people do tell me I am vivacious.

Sixteen

We returned to Cincinnati with an exciting new scheme. I was determined that the Queen City would prove to be the nest where I could hatch golden eggs for Henry. [I can just imagine Theodosia underlining 'hatch' and filling the margins with exclamation points, but the poor girl is ill and has stopped censoring my manuscript.] [*Editor's note*: In fact Theodosia died in 1865, following a lengthy illness, just two years after her mother-in-law. They are buried under facing gravestones over a patch of green lawn in the English cemetery in Florence, as if they were just continuing their dispute about literary propriety over the breakfast table. Once, apparently, Theodosia confided to Mrs Trollope that she was afraid of being caricatured and appearing in one of the sharp-eyed lady's so many volumes a year – something she might well have feared, since she was easy to satirize and almost comically lethargic. Mrs Trollope, in her best vulgar manner, said to her, 'Of course I draw from life – but I always pulp my acquaintance before serving them up. You would never recognize a pig in a sausage.']

Our first inspiration was to have Henry offer lessons. He placed an announcement in the Cincinnati *Gazette*: 'Mr Henry Trollope, having received a completely classical education, at the royal college of Winchester [England] would be happy to give lessons in the Latin language to gentlemen at their own houses . . . terms: fifty cents for lessons of one hour.' He offered to instruct them according to a scientific method of his own devising – perhaps it was the sound of that 'method' that frightened the lazy students away, for none appeared.

We knew how deprived Cincinnati, this triste little town, was of culture and pleasure of any sort. There was absolutely nothing to do beyond hikes through the slaughterhouse countryside and interminable soirées of sexual segregation as rigid as a Turk's and of buffets as lavish and nauseating as the Great Khan's.

We visited the Western Museum at the corner of Main and Second Streets and introduced ourselves to its curator, Joseph Dorfeuille. We'd exchanged visiting cards and then one after-noon Henry and I dropped in on him. It was an April day, already suffocatingly hot outdoors, and someone had closed the venetian blinds through which lines of sunlight glittered. The floorboards creaked and groaned. The ceilings were so high that everything was strikingly cooler. I longed for a lemonade, a loose gown and a large paper fan.

We were the only visitors. The first room, totally unguarded, was filled with dismal stuffed birds and jars displaying serpents in alcohol. And all those big old bones we'd been told about – mammoth bones, elephant bones, unearthed at Big Bone Lick in Boone County. In the second room there were quartz and crystal specimens. And that shrunken head. An unpleasant smell of turpentine and dried straw hung over everything. In one corner we discovered a winding staircase and ascended it. I called out, 'Yoo-hoo!' Upstairs there were wax statues of various per-sonalities. A French cuirass recovered from the Battle of Waterloo was on display. In this military room we saw a transparency of the Battle of New Orleans, the drawing 'executed by a lady of this city,' as the legend read. 'No competition for Auguste,' I whis-pered to Henry, who nodded solemnly. He kept raising his collar, despite the heat, to cover a rather nasty blue-black bruise I'd glimpsed on his neck.

At last we discovered an immensely fat man in the corner who was dozing in the dark within a baronial chair behind the statue of Blackhawk baring his chest and teeth, a raised tomahawk in one hand. The teeth weren't well done – they looked like a set of old ivory dice. The fat man was snoring the sort of snore that becomes something close to strangulation at its acme and we felt we were watching a frail ship borne higher and higher on one vast wave after another, held in suspense at the peak of each swell. He'd open his mouth and flutter his uvula, stop all systems, turn bright red in utter silence – then crash noisily into the next grunting, gasping valley.

At the death-defying peak of one such cycle he woke up, staggering slightly forward, as if his recognition that visitors had interrupted his frightening siesta coincided with his state of bodily alarm or asphyxia.

'Wobble, google, ugh!' he mumbled then shouted, and at first I thought he was speaking Blackhawk's language.

'Forgive us, good sir,' I said, 'for giving you a fright.'

'Not at all, not at all, Madam, it is I –' and he made a half-hearted attempt to cantilever his immense rippling body out of its chair.

'Pray, good sir, remain seated. No reason for us to stand on ceremony,' I said, as if recognizing that this human behemoth could stand only for the most solemn of ceremonies. He mopped his forehead with a handkerchief.

Though I am often repelled by obesity, for some reason I found everything about Dorfeuille sympathetic.

'I am Mrs Trollope,' I said, 'and this is my son Henry.'

'Yes, yes. Dorfeuille here, Madam, at your service.'

'You must forgive us, dear sir, for being so delinquent in visiting the Western Museum. I fear we let the exigencies of settling in at Cincinnati take precedence over all cultural duties or do I mean pleasures?'

'No sin there, dear lady, since many Cincinnatians of long date have never visited the museum at all in the eight years I've been here.' When he spoke he closed his eyes and let them flutter, but

206

the minute he stopped speaking he opened them wide. As he spoke he mopped his forehead with his dirty hanky, as though his whole head needed constant oiling and draining. He indicated two empty wooden chairs sitting in the shadows. 'Please, please, accommodate yourselves.'

We perched on the edges of our chairs. We talked about one thing and another, about Mr Dorfeuille's earlier career as a naturalist, about the local citizens' indifference to culture, about their failure to subscribe for the purpose of purchasing Monsieur Hervieu's significant *Lafayette Landing at Cincinnati* and their even more lamentable absence at the Western Museum.

'Why,' said Mr Dorfeuille in his small, feminine voice with its air of put-upon gentility, 'these wax figures by Hiram Powers alone are worth the price of admission.' Here his eyelids flew open. He explained to us that Mr Powers had fashioned some thirty wax figures for him, all of an uncanny realism. There was Marat, the French patriot, covered with scabies in his hip bath, pouring out his life's blood under the assaults of Charlotte Corday and her ruthless dagger. There was an empress of Russia on her throne. There was a beautiful woman dozing on a divan while her two children played on the rug beside her. There was *The Death of George Washington*, consisting of three figures attending the prostrate Father of His Country with appropriate scenery and decorations. There was Tecumseh in his Indian garb. There were Jackson and Napoleon and someone else I forget. Oh! A 'Human Monster and Cannibal.' An additional attraction was the manufacture on the spot of nitrous oxide, which the paying public at lectures on geology would be encouraged to inhale until they were all falling about laughing.

At the mention of the 'paying public' I slapped my forehead and almost fainted from the exertion in the humid heat. 'I nearly forgot the whole matter of the price of admission,' I said, opening the drawn silk mouth of my rose-coloured purse, knowing perfectly well there was nothing inside.

'No emoluments necessary from so distinguished a family,' Mr Dorfeuille said with a wave of his surprisingly tiny hand. I concentrated on the sweating, suffering face and the flickering white hand so I wouldn't have to think about the great flowing folds of his body in its dark 'artistic' suit. In fact, there in the shadows, I half imagined that his body was a hand and arm in a loose black sleeve manipulating his head, the puppet in a strangely outsized Punch and Judy show. His big sweating face was Punch's, I suppose, and his small alto voice was Judy's.

We talked some more about the paucity of custom visiting the Western Museum. Rummaging around with a blind hand under his chair, Mr Dorfeuille located a newspaper. 'Listen to this. How can we expect people to visit a museum in a city where a leading citizen declares, "Here everything is fresh – the city is the growth of a day – you see none of those ancient and venerable nuisances called interesting antiquities – no decayed and falling houses, rendezvous for rats, bats, cats and desolation, the exuviae of past generations . . . The streets, houses, trees and people are all *new*."' Mr Dorfeuille sighed. 'How can I lure *new* people here? I have no instinct for show-off.'

Suddenly I was ignited. I thought I'd sink into dim despair in this heat if I didn't push myself forward. I remembered having told Mr Winchester back in Memphis that I had gumption; now I had to prove it. 'But I do, Mr Dorfeuille. I have a born talent for using clever, facile bits of glitter and silliness to draw attention to the heights of culture as if I'd placed a pivoting mirror and painted kernels on the peaks of Mount Parnassus just to attract Zeus as a bird – as an eagle!'

He looked startled and his eyebrows lengthened and barred his immense face like clouds crossing the full moon.

With gay irrelevance I said, 'Never forget that an eagle is a bird, too!' The heat had obviously turned my head.

Now the eyebrows tilted toward the nose like an accent grave and an accent aigu. 'What are you suggesting?'

'What I'm *suggesting*, dear Mr Dorfeuille, is that young Henry here will don a toga and veil and be seated in a stage set that will look half like the great Temple of Karnak and half like the witches' cave in *Macbeth*. Our own great French *artiste*, Monsieur

Hervieu, *peintre-décorateur*, will design the set and Henry will spout a mystifying macaroni-language made up of Latin, French, German and Italian. Oh, the poor Ohioans won't know what's happened to them!'

I have no idea how I came up with this scheme on the spur of the moment and I almost laughed when I saw Henry's eyes widen. He'd often amused us with his macaroni-gibberish which he could deliver with headlong speed and utter conviction. His voice had changed slightly but if we veiled him and padded him copiously he'd have just the right matronly look for his contralto.

Mr Dorfeuille sloshed back and forth in his chair with tidal-wave agitation and his eyebrows rose so high they disappeared into his hairline. 'But – but –' he sputtered faintly, 'won't it bring dishonour to my museum?'

'Not at all,' I said dismissively whilst smiling sweetly at him. 'Wax figures are all very well but you need something alive and mysterious. We'll put an announcement in the Cincinnati *Gazette* of great dignity. Here!' And I scribbled something on a scrap of paper:

> The proprietor of the WESTERN MUSEUM is now able to tender to the public the gratification of receiving the responses of the 'Invisible Girl.' As he has spared no expense in preparing this most interesting philosophical experiment, he relies upon his fellow citizens for a fair demonstration of a disposition to remunerate him for an attempt to present to the world a subject in which science and taste have been equally consulted.

After Mr Dorfeuille read this statement his misgivings were assuaged – I felt he was the most reassured by my phrase 'philosophical experiment', which was indeed a lucky and daring find.

Within a matter of five days the sets were built and painted, I'd sewn the costume and the announcement had run in the weekly Cincinnati *Gazette*. Since the good people of Cincinnati work so hard, we were careful to have the opening occur on a

Saturday afternoon. We thought that at best a few curiosity-seekers would appear at the stated time, but surprisingly there was a long line of young men and women down to the corner, for what we had forgotten was that everyone was bored in Cincinnati and in search of amusement. They might ignore an offer to instruct them in Latin but they would pay twenty-five cents to laugh in amazed delight at someone gibbering in a made-up dialect of European languages; as Tocqueville once said, Americans prefer to utilize learning rather than to possess it. They were particularly distrustful of anything theoretical. But when bits of learning floated to the surface like vegetables in a thick soup, they were delighted by the incongruity and would clap like children.

Monsieur Hervieu insisted that he be the one to dress Henry in his women's clothes and argued, rather persuasively, that even his underthings should be feminine, in order to give him the most thorough conviction in his assumed identity. Emily graciously lent him her petticoat and unmentionables. Henry smiled at this odd notion with serene good humour and let his friend have his way.

The success was enormous. Mr Dorfeuille was astonished and delighted as his coffers filled up. Henry was remarkably gifted behind his heavy veils – at times inert and swaying as Virgil's Cumaean sibyl, then stirred into incomprehensible prophecy, at times teasingly close to comprehensible meaning. Hervieu had placed him in one of those theatres of probation in the Egyptian mysteries; as the posters read: 'The light is admitted through transparencies painted by MR HERVIEU.' Hiram Powers had placed Henry next to Hecate's cauldron surrounded by long-nosed witches laughing fiendishly. Up above a female arm projected from a cloud; in her hand she held a small glass trumpet. Only twelve visitors were admitted at a time and each customer could propound only three questions. Everyone was sternly enjoined to observe total silence otherwise. In such a small town what puzzled the citizens the most was the exact identity of this husky-voiced female. They were certain they'd taken note of everyone, especially foreign, who'd ever visited their great metropolis. People lined up time and again just for the pleasure of hearing Henry's ridiculous pronouncements.

After eight weeks everyone with a spare twenty-five cents and a bumpkin's urge to be mystified had paid the museum a visit. Mr Dorfeuille wasn't terribly generous with us – he gave us only a third of the receipts. I was determined, however, to maintain our success. I happened to be rereading my favourite book, Dante's *Inferno*, and with sibylline inspiration of my own I proposed that we re-create the 'Infernal Regions' with the help of Mr Powers.

Mr Dorfeuille needed no convincing. He was persuaded I was a great creative mind, though I had only been imitating 'The Invisible Girl: The Oracle of Leicester Square' and Madame Tussaud's waxworks.

We were introduced to Hiram Powers, who quickly became one of our closest friends. He was then just eighteen, only a year older than Henry, though far more self-reliant, I must admit. He was tall and shambling, but he had a way of hovering over whatever came before him so long as it was inanimate. He was helpless with human beings, especially girls, who made him blush, but no matter what was placed in his hands – a broken bowl, ice-skates, an old clock – he would lean into it, scrutinize it closely, enter into its very mechanism, his long delicate fingers revolving it slowly as if he were Monsieur Louis Braille and it was written in the new system of raised letters.

Now Hiram lives near us in Florence – indeed he has been here since 1837 – and we have been delighted to observe his ascent to a position of universal esteem. He is as refined as any of our Anglo-Florentine tribe, but then he was a stammering farm boy, born in Vermont though he'd moved to Ohio in 1819. He'd done everything. He'd superintended a reading-room in a Cincinnati hotel, clerked in a general store and worked in a clock and organ factory, all before he'd turned eighteen. At the factory he'd evidenced a surprising mechanical gift and a knack for carving wood and gilding bronze. He'd studied with Herr

Eckstein, a German painter and the would-be founder of the Cincinnati Academy of Fine Arts, which he could never raise enough money to support. Cincinnatians, as we'd discovered, would not invest in art – why, they wouldn't even invest in public lighting and sewage. They'd rather stumble in foul-smelling streets, nuzzled by cold snouts, than take up a subscription for common utilities. They speak of a city of half a million in the next century that will surely become the nation's capital, but they are content to discuss such possibilities in an atmosphere redolent of swine.

In March, just a month before the Invisible Girl, Monsieur Hervieu had attempted to teach at the impoverished Academy with Herr Eckstein, but after three weeks he had stormed out in a rage over the lack of discipline. Eckstein refused to bear down on his students. He shrugged and said, 'In Europe we'd have them whipped into shape, but here you must praise their most awkward drawings, encourage their most idiotic theories and look the other way during their frequent absences.'

'I, the student of Gros – never!' Auguste sputtered. 'No! I cannot live like that!' Soon afterwards Auguste opened his own school in which strict Continental discipline reigned – and which no one attended.

He was busy enough with our frightening folly at the Western Museum. I ran an advance notice of the attraction in the *Gazette*, attributing it all to Mr Dorfeuille:

He has constructed a pandemonium in which he has congregated all the images of horror his fertile fancy could devise – dwarves that, by machinery, grow into giants before the spectator; imps of ebony with eyes of flame; monstrous reptiles devouring youth and beauty. In short, wax, paint and strings have done wonders. It is visible through a grate of massive iron bars, among which are arranged wires connected to an electrical machine. Should any daring hand touch the grate, the shocking effect is comical.

212

Hiram Powers created a huge wax statue of a cloven-footed Minos the Judge of Hell. Clad in a sable robe, Minos nodded at the spectator. At his feet spread a frozen lake on which bobbed the heads of doomed earthlings, for there was both a hell of ice and a hell of fire. There was a huge serpent who uncoiled with majestic slowness. There was even a stuffed bear reared up on its hind legs which snapped its jaws rather alarmingly. Electric sparks were flying and on some days Emily beat a tom-tom ominously off in a corner. Hervieu painted visions of Purgatory and Paradise, including Beatrice on her parade-float tours of pure white light, but those more pleasant possibilities of the afterlife were out-weighed by the vivacity in the depiction of the Land of Pain and its Lord.

In England I suppose even the most naïve lass or lad would half-pretend to be frightened by an equivalent scene, but here in the stronghold of Baptism and Methodism and their hellfire sermonizing, I thought I detected more than one local visitor trembling with genuine fright at the torments awaiting him.

We were successful. Day after day Cincinnatians lined up to gaze directly into the inferno. It's *still* an attraction at the Western Museum. We soon had enough money to rent a little house on the outskirts of town, in a village called Mohawk, a mile from the centre of the city. As summer was descending on us we escaped to a hillside next to an unpolluted stream. We had an icehouse that never failed, we were at last free from mosquitoes, we ate huge tomatoes out of our own garden and drank milk from our own cow. Both Henry and I had been very ill – Henry with a bilious complaint cured only by quantities of calomel and repeated bleedings. I had a high fever and constant delirious fantasies. In the Mohawk cottage, however, we both recovered, though Henry remained perilously thin.

We became friendly with our neighbour, Dr William Price, a free-thinker who'd visited New Harmony and Nashoba, and with his more conventional but no less charming wife and children. (Dr Price, a brewer and a prominent citizen, remained a friend to me and mine and especially to Fanny Wright till the

213

end of her days.) Hiram Powers, blushing permanently but observing everything closely, was in attendance nearly every evening. The portly Mr Dorfeuille rode out in his pony cart more than once a week; the first time he made the trip was the first I'd seen him in the daylight. His immense body shifting toward the full moon of his face, the delicate and disastrous manoeuvres to get him poured into his conveyance and installed, the poor pony's intermittent refusal to take another step uphill and the absolute necessity to brake the cart on its suicidal descents – oh, these were just a few of the dramatic details accompanying Mr Dorfeuille's visits to our cottage. We even became familiar with another neighbour, a black man, a Mr Jupiter Higgins, a blacksmith. He found a pair of second-hand shoes for Cecilia, lovely, practical shoes they were, and in countless little ways brought us comfort without ever trespassing above his station in life, though I often felt his place was by my side, helping me . . .

Of course I haven't forgotten that Frances Wright is my theme and not my own petty triumphs and tribulations. Fanny visited Cincinnati as a lecturer in an effort to find subscribers to the *New Harmony Gazette* and I insisted she stay with us at the Mohawk cottage. Our quiet, sleepy days were suddenly energized – she was up at dawn and home after midnight. As if she were campaigning in an election she boldly introduced herself to everyone of interest – and people of no interest she dismissed rudely. She immediately became friends with Dr Price, the convinced atheist, and with Josiah Warren, an anarchist and friend. I was used to moustache-twirling bomb-throwers from my old regicide-salon days and the company of the adorable General Pepe. Although my own principles were far more conservative, I certainly preferred their conversation to that of Cincinnati matrons who would be total recluses if they didn't indulge in public worship and private tea-drinking and who thought nothing of gossiping about the Holy Ghost while basting a hem.

In this town where the Western Museum was virtually the only amusement and where respectable people avoided the theatre and where reading anything but the Bible on a Sunday was considered a sin, Miss Wright's lectures were thronged. The various local newspapers were too prudish to report on the event, but Fanny *almost* filled the courthouse (although very few women were courageous enough to attend).

Mrs Price and I, armed with fans, were courageous and attended with Henry, Hiram and Auguste and we took an intense pleasure in the presence of our Fanny, whose deep voice was so full and melodious, and whose gestures, emerging out of the simple Greek folds of her muslin dress, struck Hiram as the quintessence of Attic grace. Everyone was expecting her to start belching flames, as if she truly were an inhabitant of our 'Infernal Regions,' but she confined herself during her first lecture to an exposition of unexceptionable general principles.

Between the first and second lectures we set out to visit a religious camp meeting. Its hysterical excesses I feared would stir Miss Wright into a rage.

During the trip out into the country, Fanny told me that Camilla was ailing and back in New Harmony. She'd ridden horseback cross-country and developed a carbuncle on her back due to the pressure of her corset. 'I implored her to throw off her nasty whale-boning, so absurd in any event since she weighs less than ninety pounds!' Fanny exclaimed. 'The doctor had to apply twenty-four leeches to her body and for five nights only opium could make her sleep.'

'But why would she go out on horseback in a corset,' I asked, 'especially now that she's living at New Harmony, where all the women wear harem trousers?'

For a moment I thought Fanny hadn't heard me. She stared straight ahead as we rode in our hired buggy. Finally she said, 'Camilla is pregnant.'

'Yes,' I blurted, 'but that's not – I mean, she *is* married.'

'Her husband has abandoned her.'

'That nice Quaker, Mr Whitby?'

'Yes, he's vanished. I don't mind in the least, of course, since I regard the institution of marriage as nothing but legalized

215

prostitution and sanctioned slavery, but poor Camilla feels terribly frightened.'

'But she has you?'

'Her health is not good. She's losing weight and her chest is weak, even as her little belly is getting rounder and rounder.'

'You're always there to nurse her.'

'Not always,' Fanny said, clearly irritated with my foolish repetition. 'Right now I'm on a lecture tour all through Ohio, Illinois, Kentucky. I've discovered I am an extraordinary public speaker.' She said it without emphasis as if to say, 'It's about to rain.'

'Absolutely!' I exclaimed once I'd taken in what she'd said.

She fell into a brown study then pulled out of it long enough to say, 'All her life Camilla has adored me and followed me, but something, I don't know what, has soured her towards me. When I rebelled against our aunt Miss Campbell she followed my lead unquestioningly. She applauded me when I became intimate with Lafayette, then when I broke off with him, then when I settled in Nashoba. She has paid with her very health for her loyalty. She's suffered terrible headaches, become jaundiced, endured sustained fevers, lost two stone and been greeted by all the scorn of ignorant American neighbours. And *still* she's remained unquestioningly loyal to me. But now? Something has changed. I don't know what. It's as if in losing weight she's lost an entire amative faculty. Now her mouth relaxes into a sneer, if she's forced to touch me her soul retreats into some hidden inner gland and is no longer palpable. She's gone from being the sweetest sister to a bitter stranger.' Fanny seized my hands. 'Oh, do you think I'm such an egoist that something radical in her died and I didn't even notice?'

I've always operated on the principle that people never want to hear the truth if it's harsh. Now I chuckled wisely and said, my voice pitched very low, as if the wisdom I was spouting was self-evident, 'But pregnancy invariably distorts the character. It can make some women giddy and others tragic.' I preferred winning back Fanny's friendship to telling her the unpalatable truth. There was a nasty satisfaction in seeing Fanny suffer, but that ignoble feeling was replaced within me by a sisterly concern.

Fanny turned her strong masculine face toward me and looked back and forth from one of my eyes to the other and down to my lips as if reading a document in an unfamiliar Gothic script. At last she said, as a statement and not a question, 'Do you really think so.'

Our horse plodded on through the dappled summer light. At last, as evening was falling, we pulled into the evangelical camp-site. I later heard that about twenty acres had been cleared to accommodate the 2,000 sinners who'd come to repent. The buggy driver let us descend at the edge of the encampment. He said he'd prepare us our dinner while we were out 'exploring,' but he warned that here, on the periphery of the camp, could be found the 'rough element' and we should be cautious in returning to the buggy. 'Yes, out here,' he said, 'there are the scoffers and infidels and even prostitutes. There are men selling whisky and men drinking it. There's gambling and brawling – it's like the devil tempting Jesus in the desert. Or the money-changers in the temple.' He seemed a nice tranquil unbeliever who was throwing in dimly remembered biblical tags to humour his two (presumably) pious lady clients.

As we moved toward the more respectable centre of the circle, we heard people within their individual tents praying and sob-bing or talking in quiet, everyday voices or orating in that feverish, stylized rhetorical way that Americans employ when addressing the Deity.

I knew that our neighbour Mr Jupiter Higgins would be some-where in the Negro tent and his proximity and the possibility I might see him excited me unaccountably.

We approached one tent that was glowing mysteriously in the dark against the gloomy forest (lights were moving behind the white fabric), and suddenly someone pulled back the flap and there in profile was a tall bearded preacher, dressed in black, who was exhorting about thirty people of all ages kneeling in the straw that was scattered thickly over the ground. The words rose out of him in jerky spasms as if he were merely an entranced medium conveying them but they were too powerful for him and

217

were exploding within him. The same spasms were seen in a young woman who was bobbing back and forth, almost as if she were in labour. She fell forward into the straw and the astonishingly handsome young man beside her swooped down to wrap a comforting arm around her. 'Sweet Jesus!' someone called. The Methodist minister started to fulminate against 'luxury, whisky and slavery,' which for him were 'the three devils of these latter days.' He shouted every fifth or sixth word, regardless of its meaning, and the congregation began to jerk backwards and forward with great violence and speed. As he spoke his small congregation twitched in paroxysms of acrobatic Christianity.

He suddenly began to speak of the rich man who despite all his wealth had died in torment inside his palace. Suddenly the preacher whispered, 'Hark! hear the rich man. What does he say? He says, "Father Abraham, dip the tip of your finger in water and cool my parched tongue, for I am tormented in this flame."' His listeners were shouting, 'Spare me! Oh God, forgive me!' The preacher bellowed: '"Father Abraham, cool my parched tongue, for I am tormented in this flame." Oh, my hearers, he has been making this same request for more than –' and here he punched each syllable – 'eight-teen hun-dred years! And millions of years hence he will be whispering, "Father Abraham, cool my parched tongue, for I am tormented in this flame."'

The writhing and sudden shouts had reached such a pitch that one man was hopping in place as if on hot coals.

Having wreaked such havoc the preacher now changed direction and spoke of salvation. He told the glad tidings of great joy. He knelt beside the prostrate body of the pretty girl, whom the pretty boy had failed to soothe, and he framed her tear-stained, pale, pretty face with his long, long hands, covered with wiry black hairs, and he pulled her up into his arms and gave her what he called 'good old gospel comfort.' That may be what it was but to us it looked like pure Tartufferie – and a way of stealing improper marches on her virginal, defenceless body. He even placed one of those sinister hairy hands on her pure rising breast and said, 'Be still, my daughter, you shall be washed in the blood of the Lamb.'

218

A trumpet sounded and called us all to the main worship area. As we were hurrying over there I felt a stab of hunger since in every direction fires were burning and pots were boiling, hams seething, chickens turning. We decided not to tarry at the principal service of the evening. In front of some of the tents there were mattresses and bedsteads, even chests of drawers, for sometimes these farmers in high summer (when the planting is done and the harvest has not yet commenced) feel free to take off eight or ten days to be redeemed, and they bring their furniture with them in heavy, slow-rolling carts. The woods up above the campground were alive with lovers.

We scurried into a large enclosure that held hundreds of people, all seated on long benches. When we walked in everyone was singing a good Methodist hymn, one of the milder songs. We took our place not far from the closest corner, where the exit was located. The vast square was demarcated by log cabins that had been hastily thrown up on three sides and a mountain of straw on the fourth. A preacher was addressing everyone in a powerful nasal voice. I am short-sighted but Fanny whispered to me that behind the preacher, and seated on a bench, were a dozen other ministers, all awaiting their turn.

The current preacher had chosen his text from Ezekiel, the most unpleasant and the maddest book in the Old Testament, surely apocryphal or badly in need of ingenious hermeneutics, for otherwise it makes Yahweh sound like an irritable, vengeful, dusty little desert sheik.

The preacher, who kept repeating, 'There was a noise, and behold a shaking, and the bones came together, bone to his bone,' had soon caused his congregation to shake and rattle as if skeletons were rising out of the ruins of Jerusalem.

As he spoke, more and more people drifted over to the haystack on our right. Miss Wright and I went there, too, as inconspicuously as possible, though we needn't have bothered to be discreet since each person was isolated in his or her pain. An old woman rubbed her head and cried as if she'd never wept before. Another woman, much younger, looked terribly alone as she staggered here and there and hugged her own body. We asked a lady in the congregation why these women had quarantined themselves over here. 'That theer', she said, 'is the Anxious Seat. They ain't been saved yet but they're thinking on it something powerful.'

As the preacher invoked the shaking bones of Ezekiel once again, his hearers became still more impassioned. They fell to their knees and started shouting. They were praying, their faces lifted toward the moon, their eyes closed (for in America people close their eyes to pray). Everyone was shouting now. One fifteen-year-old with a terrific Indiana twang called out, 'Satan's tearing at me but I's holdin' fast. Help! He'd be dragging me down.' As the din increased the ministers from the back bench moved slowly and expertly through the crowd. One of them knelt beside a frightened farm couple, wizened from their labours, their nerves overwrought from the continual preaching. The minister put his hands on them in a mystic embrace until they fell on their backs with their eyes closed and wove their hands slowly in front of their faces as if fending off the Furies while crying, 'Glory, Glory, Glory!' A young man next to us turned and said with a wide smile, 'Why, they're sure having a Christ, ain't they?' Someone next to him said, 'Yep, those folks are getting right. It's a real gospel mill here tonight.'

We fled the improvised chapel and were heading back to the buggy and our dinner when we heard singing welling out of a large tent – high, powerful sopranos and deep basses that made the tent pegs revolve in their holes. We peeked in and saw a congregation of Negroes, all dressed superbly and so illumined by gas lamps that they appeared to be actors on the stage. Two women had on turbans, another wore a pink gauze dress trimmed in silver and the most striking had donned a pale yellow silk dress, yellow of daffodils and gold chains against her warm, chocolate-coloured skin. The men were in snow-white pantaloons, with gay-coloured linen jackets. They were moving in a slow circle around an extremely comely youth, who was so overwrought that he shouted and jumped in place and invoked God the Father in surprisingly intimate terms. I could see my friend, Mr Jupiter

Higgins, looking somewhat older and more ponderous in this young, electric company, but that, of course, was how I liked him. He was already so much more handsome than I that it made me anxious to stand beside him. I suppose that until the moment I spied him here I had thought of the gathering as a quasi-African ceremony, certainly 'folkloric', but when I glimpsed his dear earnest face, his lowered eyes, his full, beard-wreathed lips mumbling, his forehead as shiny as bevelled anthracite, suddenly I saw the general piety, the transfiguring goodness, in this curiously animated assembly.

I pulled Fanny by the sleeve and, whispering, pointed out Jupiter to her. Suddenly I realized I cared more for him than for her. Instead of being a principal player in my life Fanny was no more than a spectator and this change in her status took me by surprise. She wasn't a very satisfactory witness, since she seemed almost indifferent to his proximity, which at first vexed me. In her place I would at least have pretended pleasure upon recognizing one of her near and dear. But in a moment I hugged myself under my cloak and took an unaccountable comfort in her lack of interest, for in some way it confirmed that Jupiter's friendship belonged to me alone.

Although Fanny wanted to stay a moment longer in order to study Negro religion in action, I insisted we depart, and it was rare for me to insist on anything around Fanny. I'm certain I was blushing.

Once we were away from the revivalist tents everything took on the silence and majesty of the night forest: the owl's hollow hoot, as if it were leaning down into a deep well and calling to itself; the moon's travels through rapid clouds like that of a pebble flying over dark waters; the smell of log fires and cooking meat; the low thumping of bullfrogs and the high peeping of tree frogs; the wonderfully languid sifting of the wind through the tree-tops and around us, tugging at our cloaks and pushing back the brims of our bonnets, as if the noise and panic of Methodism had been replaced by something older and more pagan, the polytheism of the American woods. I felt so happy I'd seen my Mr Higgins that

I tilted my head and submitted to the wind's playful massage and the moon's cold burn.

Our driver had turned a chicken over his outdoor fire and now he served it with little potatoes still in their jackets that he'd buried in the coals and big white beans of some sort that he'd cooked in water in a dented little tin pan he'd suspended over the flames from a tall metal stake he'd driven into the ground. In the dark we felt free to suck the sweet flesh off the chicken bones and to gulp the raw, grassy dandelion wine he'd bottled himself. He said he'd been raised as an adolescent by a German pietist colony (though his own parents were non-believers and had simply lodged him with the Germans); the pietists had concocted wines out of dandelions or rhubarb. I'd barely pulled a shawl over me and wiped my shiny lips before I fell asleep.

In my dreams I half-heard wonderful Negro religious songs just as the sky was beginning to lighten. I was still drowsing but I recognized that these resonant and perfectly pitched voices were singing the words, 'Oh, see God choosing the weak things of this world to confound the things that are mighty.' One soprano soared above the chorus to tell us, 'Ye were sometime darkness, but now . . .' I never found out what they were 'now' for I'd forgotten the biblical passage and our driver was talking loudly to his horse and hitching it to the buggy and even strumming the buggy wheels with a stick to awaken us and get us on our way to Cincinnati. As we pulled away from the meeting I saw many a simpering young maiden feeding cooked eggs and hot coffee to her preaching saint or howling sinner – both tribes of men seemed equally hungry and content.

The next day Frances Wright, infuriated by the camp meeting, gave a fiery lecture at the crowded courthouse denouncing religion as a 'swindle' specially designed to keep women abject through the 'sorcery' of superstition.

Fanny did not, could not recognize that the entire Ohio Valley was in the throes of a religious fever that would not burn itself out for many years to come. To be sure, George Flower had told her that in his travels along the river he'd seen normally cheerful

men and women reduced to sobbing forth their pleas for forgiveness to preachers who knew how to play on their fear and
anguish with all the skill of a master organist, pulling out the
'trumpet'-stop of the Last Judgement or even the *vox humana* of
penance and treading the bass pedals of guilt and terror. A few
years later the ever-perspicacious Tocqueville remarked that in
the United States Christianity retained 'a greater influence over
the souls of men' than anywhere else. Of course Fanny found
this influence nefarious, especially since, as she acidly pointed
out, religion and slavery were deemed perfectly compatible by
half the population.

Unaware of how out of step she was with the temper of the
times, Fanny aroused the ire of the Methodists, the Baptists and
the Prebysterians when she described the self-abasement of
revivalism: 'By the sudden combination of three orthodox sects,
a *revival*, as such scenes of distraction are wont to be styled, was
opened in houses, churches, and even on the Ohio River or in
forest clearings. The victims of this odious experiment on human
credulity and nervous weakness were invariably women. Helpless
age was made a public spectacle, innocent youth driven to raving
insanity, mothers and daughters carried lifeless from the presence of the ghostly expounders of damnation; all ranks shared
the contagion and discord would seem to have taken possession
of every mansion.' Here Fanny pulled herself up and, amidst violent booing and hissing, announced, 'Since all were dumb' it was
incumbent on her alone to defend 'the cause of insulted reason
and outraged humanity.' Poor Fanny – convinced that people
needed only to hear the truth to be cured of their folly.

And yet her own disappointments at Nashoba and New
Harmony had indeed cured her of many of her rosy views of
America. She learned at this time that a Philadelphia pastor was
calling for the founding of a Christian Party to keep all non-
believers out of politics – a movement that disproved her certainty
that in a democracy religion would naturally wither away. When
Jackson's followers waved the flag and rattled their sabres, she
denounced patriotism and jingoism. She called on her listeners

223

to love humanity rather than just their countrymen, and to esteem the universal values encoded in the Constitution rather than the document itself. She reminded the public that equality means more than the privilege to vote (which in any case was denied to women and Negroes) but also signifies 'the free and fearless exercise of the mental faculties.' In her disillusionment with America she said that she had mistaken 'the restlessness of commercial enterprise' for 'the energy of enlightened liberty.' Americans, she claimed, preferred to fill their coffers with coins rather than their urns with ballots or their minds with noble ideas.

At the end of her thrilling lecture, during which she never consulted a note nor shrank back from the insults of the crowd, a man hooted, 'Get a husband and leave us in peace!' In response Fanny called out, 'I have wedded the cause of human improvement, staked on it my reputation, my future and my life. I will devote the rest of my energy to the promotion of just knowledge, the establishment of just practice and the increase of human happiness.' Like an Anglican priest she pronounced *knowledge* as 'no-ledge.'

She swept off the stage in the midst of men chanting, 'Priestess of Beelzebub, priestess of Beelzebub, priestess of Beelzebub,' which isn't terribly easy to say.

I suppose I must ask myself what are the religious beliefs I espouse. As is usually the case the truth, I'm convinced, lies somewhere in the middle. Christ was born of Mary, but she wasn't necessarily a virgin. He was undoubtedly a very great philosopher – the greatest! – but not necessarily the literal incarnation of God. Humanity has never forgotten him, and in that sense alone we can speak of his 'resurrection.' But I certainly would not want to offend anyone, not even a Mahometan, and I think after all the most important thing is that we all be moral and loving, each after his own fashion. There! I suspect I've worked out my theology, though I assure the reader I'm never obstinate and could be persuaded otherwise by the first well-spoken comer. You see, wisdom lies in moderation.

Fanny left us for controversies in nearby cities and Mr Owen departed for Scotland. I had at last received a letter from Trollope who seemed overwhelmed by bad luck and reversals of fortune. He feared being thrown into debtors' prison, and our income was now heavily encumbered. He admitted he was incapable of work and that Anthony and Tom had become charity cases at Winchester. His letter lacked all warmth beyond the high fever of anxiety. Not a single word of affection for me was in it.

At last he announced that he and Tom would be travelling to New-York sometime in September and thence to Cincinnati. With the return of the cooler weather Henry and I both experienced a complete restoration of health, though Henry remained irritable. He got it into his head that Auguste had become too close to Hiram, though I knew with certainty that Hiram scarcely saw other men and reserved all his bashful affection for women and girls and for the inanimate puzzle of broken objects he longed to repair. Maybe he saw women and mechanical failures as somehow related, both in need of his expert touch.

I was reassured that Trollope was making the effort to come and see us but I was still angry that he had written me so seldom and so tepidly. Later I learned that all of Harrow had been scandalized by my secret departure for America. The treacherous Harriet Garnett, for instance, had written her mother, 'The grates of the most rigid convent are not so insurmountable a barrier betwixt the world & the nun they enclose, as public scorn makes against a woman who has joined such a community as Nashoba.' I was stung by the passage when years and years later I read through the Garnett family correspondence.

When I admitted to her in a letter that I'd decided not to stay at Nashoba but to try my luck in Cincinnati, at the time Harriet wrote to her mother, still more illogically, that she was shocked by my 'inconstancy' to 'poor Miss Wright.' She'd already decided that Trollope was 'poor Trollope' because I'd abandoned him and Harrow and ruined my reputation. Surrounded by such tut-tutting, no wonder Trollope felt authorized to ignore my pleas for a few words from him. Though he refused to work and subjected us all to his calomel-induced foul moods, he was the one our neighbours and friends pitied.

225

Fortunately I knew nothing of Harrow's universal condemnation of my actions. Such a knowledge would have made my exile in America seem all the more forlorn and irreversible.

I feel wonderfully free of my daughter-in-law's spying (always well-intentioned) since she is at last hard at work on a book of her own, *Social Aspects of the Italian Revolution in a Series of Letters from Florence* (not the most singing title). The poor girl was dreadfully ill and (but she mustn't see this passage) is not long for this world. We've always teased her for her indolence, which is perhaps nothing more than a symptom of her constitutional weakness. I love her dearly and am grateful to her for her attentiveness, though (dare I admit it?) I am enjoying this new amnesty of neglect. It's true that my mind is more and more clouded and that I forget from one page of mss to the next what I am relating; Theodosia has been my memory for years, standing behind my chair during receptions and whispering to me the names of my oldest friends as they approach. It's not that I don't recognize them. It's not that I don't remember every detail of their personal sagas down to the tiniest joy or affliction, but in company I panic – yes, that must be it – I panic and can think of their names only when the information is no longer of any use. In the same way Theodosia, like a good capable archivist who has read through every letter drafted or received and carefully filed it, remembers my life for me.

She knows the chronology of my travels and publications far better than I. She has even *read* all my books, which I've never done, and she knows when my characters Mr and Mrs Barnaby first arrived in America and exactly where they sneaked to shore after lying about their aristocratic titles (or some such flummery, it's all slipped my mind yet again). But I welcome the slight retreat she's taken away from me. My memories are free now to wander where they will, even if they're considerably less orderly and precise than they would be under Theodosia's supervision. Ah, for an old woman enjoys but three things – sitting in a warm garden, sifting through her unedited memories,

226

and babbling with her infant granddaughter (in my case my little Bice!).

But although I certainly relish these memories and delight in exploring them, I will seal the next twenty or thirty pages with a warning, *Secret: Do Not Read* and *Destroy After My Death*.

[*Editor's note*: Here Mrs Trollope is being disingenuous, for no professional writer ever commits anything to paper that he doesn't want published. When Virgil asked his friends to destroy *The Aeneid* after his death because it was imperfect he was only striking a pose. Some vengeful widows have burned their husbands' letters to other women, but the world's loss must be counted as greater than the wife's angry satisfaction. To be sure, what Mrs Trollope is about to relate will raise some eyebrows very high, but she thrived on scandal or at least excitement. In the interest of the truth the editors have decided to preserve this text exactly as they found it.]

Seventeen

It was during the autumn of 1828, while waiting for Trollope to arrive, that I began to pay impromptu visits to Jupiter Higgins. Although I'd been taught that Negroes were savage by nature and inferior intellectually and spiritually, I soon learned that his sable skin and exaggerated features masked a quick mind and a noble soul. At first I told myself that I wished to discover from him something about the condition of the Negro in America. I'd already begun to take notes for an eventual book, though I had no idea what form a book about America should assume. All I knew was that it would not be abstract and Masculine but gossipy and Feminine, full of the little facts that all readers enjoy though few will admit it.

As a consequence I wanted to know what Negroes ate, how they worshipped, how they arranged their homes, even how they courted one another and made love. Ever since I'd seen that slave couple at Nashoba, I was convinced that blacks were tenderer than whites. And how did they regard us? As deities or fools? As monsters of caprice or as sage parents?

In the long golden Cincinnati autumn we'd moved our chairs and couch out onto the grass beside our house as if it were a natural salon. So few people passed by and our few neighbours were all so delightful that we felt free to occupy even the woods and Emily and Cecilia and I would stitch or tat in the long, shadowed cool of the evening. We even moved a big pier glass outdoors and propped it against a majestic old maple. The girls would dance in front of it and I'd join in and become so exhausted tossing myself about that at last I'd collapse in a heap and like Cleopatra calling out to her maid Charmian I'd gasp, 'Cut my laces!' That became our byword for tomfoolery. An embarrassed but amused Henry (the man in him was embarrassed, the boy amused) would complain with a smile, 'Mammy is cutting her laces again,' for that's what everyone called me, 'Mammy.'

One day I could see Mr Higgins standing in his doorway, dressed in his great leather apron with the fringe at the bottom, a still-glowing horseshoe between pincers in his hand, in the background the little black boy who sometimes worked the bellows for him and ran errands, and Jupiter said, 'My, you ladies shure enough knows how to delight in life. But why do you keep talking about lace? That puzzles me since you ain't wearin' no lace I's can sees.'

I found my Shakespeare and read him the passage which he enjoyed with a Negro's natural pleasure in fanciful language, but it was a long path from Cleopatra's exclamation to our silliness in the Ohio woods and Mr Higgins at last rubbed his chin and said, 'I do declare I think you English a tarnation more given to triflin' than the good citizens of Cincinnati,' which was true and pleased us infinitely, since we admitted our love of play bordered on lunacy.

Although Jupiter enjoyed teasing us and remarking on our quirks, he never overstepped himself. He was just very dear and twinkly. Some days, if he was busy, I'd see him arrive and depart from the forge, nothing more, but I took comfort from the constant clanging inside and his powerful exertions. Sometimes he'd stand out in front of the yard in his backless slippers, wearing his special farrier's apron split at the bottom so that he could straddle and bend a horse's hoof back between his knees and claw off a broken shoe and file down the foot before hammering on a new shoe. I would sometimes place something for him to eat on the stone just outside his door, a portion of whatever I'd prepared for us – a leg of chicken or a slice of Cincinnati's famous ham, sometimes a brook trout I'd sizzled in butter. At first my offerings (not always burnt, I hope) embarrassed the blacksmith, but eventually he learned to accept them gracefully. Sometimes he'd leave a bouquet of wild flowers on my open window-sill and sometimes a loaf of bread from town or a pannier of strawberries. One day I caught him repairing the broken hinge of the green wood shutters over the windows letting into our tiny salon. When I protested he simply raised a finger to his lips and got on with his work. I noticed that if white people he didn't know visited us he eclipsed himself wordlessly.

As the days turned colder and rainier in October we hurried our furniture back indoors. Now I had nothing to do but worry about Henry's future and wait for Trollope's arrival. I pottered about the house and made thick soups of pulse and streaky bacon. One day I was carrying a bowl of it to the forge and I thought it idiotic to let it turn cold on the stone, so I ventured into the narrow hot room without knocking. Mr Higgins seemed greatly discomfited since he was working without a shirt on and he hastened to throw an old cape over his shoulders, but not before I saw how powerful his upper body was – biceps round and black as cannon-balls, a furry chest thick with muscle but burned free of all fat, forearms as tendoned as a horse's withers. He could have posed for an anatomy demonstration at a college of surgeons or artists and I wondered why Monsieur Hervieu had never been tempted to draw him: 'Vulcan at his Forge' would be an excellent subject, especially a New World *black* Vulcan.

I, too, was embarrassed but I said, 'I didn't want the soup to get cold,' and he said, 'I thank you,' and cleared a place for me. I sat and stared into the flames, which he banked by shaking wet twigs at the coals, producing a hissing sound and white smoke. I smelled the odour of honest labour and of burning wood and something exquisitely and indefinably Negro, a smell like heated leather and liquid coal, a bit offensive until one stopped resisting it and accepted it as a comforting pleasure. He had a slab of cornbread (he cut it with a knife he'd made) and shared it with me, which I ate greedily even though I don't really like it.

'Oh Mr Higgins, it's so warm and dry and cosy in your forge, whereas at our cottage everything is dreary and damp.'

In the windowless darkness of the building (which was something like a barn but small like a shed, with sliding doors high enough, none the less, to let in a horse), his smile lit up the room. I looked at his lips and thought I could never kiss them, they were obscenely full and shone like overripe fruit through the scratchy, woolly wreathing of his beard. I remembered, however, how my feelings toward him and his appearance had progressed. When I'd first met him I'd thought he was as ugly as a chimpanzee but now in his monstrous features – his everted lips and wide nostrils and low brow – I saw the very 'lineaments of desire.' I suppose for me he was like a wheezing, frowning pug that one comes to love by dint of holding it so often on one's lap.

'Mr Higgins?'

'Yes, Mrs Trollope?'

'I wanted to ask you about being saved. As you know I saw you that night at the camp meeting, but I scarcely understood what was happening.'

'We was trying to get right with the Lord.'

'Through dancing?'

'Oh the Negur has his ways that are different from the white man's. We do dance and prance and shout hallelujah 'cause we are longing for the Promised Land. The slave see hisself as an Israelite in bondage in the Land of Pharaoh, and heaven he see as a return to a rebuilt Jerusalem.'

'Then you are not afraid of death, Mr Higgins?'

'Death is a homecoming, Mrs Trollope.'

By then he was working his bellows again, which blew a fine stream of air down through a tube that he called a 'tuyère,' onto the exact spot where the iron melted. He operated the overhead bellows by pulling a chain and releasing it. When the metal was

231

glowing he moved it to the 'bick' or round nose of the anvil, which was resting on a tree-trunk, and shaped the length into a curved horseshoe. He immersed it, hissing, into a barrel of water; when the metal cooled he knocked off the black scale that had formed. Sparks flew and the heat was overpowering, as was the noise – a foreglimpse of hell, I thought. Or of heaven.

As he swung his great arm, he sang very slowly in his big bass voice:

> In that morning, true believers,
>> In that morning,
> We will sit aside of Jesus,
>> In that morning,
> If you should go 'fore I go,
>> In that morning,
> You will sit aside of Jesus,
>> In that morning.

I could see he wanted to work and I slipped away with the empty bowl.

I became obsessed with him. Early in the morning, sometimes before dawn, I'd see him arriving, or if I was still in bed I'd awaken and look at him through the half-closed shutters so he couldn't see me. I'd watch him empty the spent slag from his cold forge into the pit he'd dug behind his shanty and unload coal from his one-horse cart. Before long the smoke would begin to curl gaily from his chimney and soon I'd hear the wheeze of his bellows and the clangour of his hammer. Sometimes his voice would well up in a dirge of lamentation or in a joyful hymn in which I'd hear the words, 'Crown of glory, palms of victory,' and I'd see him as he had been in the tent that night, his eyes closed, his Herculean body stepping forward with confidence, his whole being bright with the certainty of salvation.

Customers would come by with all sorts of jobs – they'd want him to trim cows' and goats' feet, mend children's toys and hoops, even put a new ferrule on the tip of a walking-stick. He'd shoe horses, first grasping their hooves between his knees, then placing the whole hoof on a steady three-legged tabouret and filing off the rough edges with a rasp. He'd fashion iron hoops to go around wooden cartwheels. He'd repair fancy cast-iron work – fences, fireplace screens, gates – though he said that such things were very fragile and easily broken.

One day he told me that he'd been a slave in Kentucky and that he'd escaped. 'My Massuh sent me to Lexington to sell some hosses for him but when night fell and I still was far from the Big House I was scared of hiding, Colonel Tom could hardly forbear a whipping –' And here he smiled most inappropriately and even laughed, which I found exceedingly strange, a weird private joke only he understood. He said, 'The curfew was nine in summer for all niggers and I *knew* it was way later.'

'Didn't he know how long it would take you to get home?'

'That didn't matter. He beat me any chance he got.'

'And so you ran away because you feared the harsh punishment of your master?'

''Zackly,' he said.

His talk was sometimes hard for me to follow. To be fair he had trouble deciphering my speech as well.

'I tied up ol' Joss' – the horse, no doubt – 'and I ran all night due north as best I could tell by the stars, and I slept all day in the woods. I could hear wolves at night, but now it was too late to turn back. The next night I saw a vegetable patch and I pulled up carrots and ate them dirt and all and a dog commenced biting me but I kicked him past the kingdom come and then I lived on what roots I could grabble.'

'Evidently you escaped safe and sound.'

He merely bent his head at my fatuity and murmured, 'Like you says, Ma'am . . .'

It was only on another day when he told me the rest of the tale, how he'd seen on the open road two Methodist ministers travelling all alone in the countryside and he'd thrown himself on their mercy, stepping out of the bushes and begging them to take him North with them. He'd heard his Colonel Tom curse the Methodists as abolitionists and like a good servant he had laughed and nodded his way through these imprecations, all the while secreting away this information as possibly relevant to his own future. He recognized these two ministers as itinerant preachers who'd come by the Big House and asked most politely to be taken in for the night but Colonel Tom, drunk and impious as always, had fired a shot just above their heads before falling into a stupor at which the Missus and her older gal, Miss Alice, had sent Jupiter running after their buggy to invite them back. They were hidden from Tom in the overseer's house (the overseer himself was off in Lexington selling corn) and plied with good things to eat but no drink since the Methodists don't indulge. Now Jupiter, half-crazed from hunger and fear, babbled all this out to them there on the open road, reminding them of their recent visit. The two ministers, once they'd comprehended his story and accepted his plea as valid, agreed to hide him (and first to feed him) and eventually to spirit him North to Ohio and freedom. Apparently they hid Jupiter under a lap-robe in the back of their buggy but when the road was clear they'd all three break into a rousing chorus:

> Farewell vain world I'm going home,
> My Jesus smiles and bid me come.

'You heard of the emancipationists, Mammy?' For Mr Higgins, following my children's lead, had also taken to calling me 'Mammy.' I nodded, eager for him to go on. 'Well, them preacher mens had a system all rigged up. At night we met a rowboat down in the reeds of the Ohio River and we all rowed, as fast as we could, against the powerful current. We was nigh destroyed by a riverboat all lit and churnin' and musical like a Big House ball, but we jes' slipped through its wake and come up the further shore and said our prayers, for we done crossed that lonesome valley *and* the River Jordan.'

'Hallelujah,' I said, a bit hypocritically, since it was a word I'd never *said* once in my life though I'd sung it in Mr Handel's

234

'Hallelujah Chorus'. But I felt a genuine relief and a sense of his triumph. He'd been fed and then hidden by day in a cemetery under a false tombstone that swung to one side though the whole experience had whitened many of the hairs on his head, as he solemnly pointed out. Luckily, once he arrived in Cincinnati he had a valuable skill – he'd been Colonel Tom's blacksmith – and soon enough with the aid of Mount Auburn Methodists he'd set up his own forge and found lodging in Little Africa at a black widow's house. Within a day or two he had his first important job, repairing the bell of the Presbyterian church, which had cracked one Sunday on a day of extreme cold. Now it rang out with a drone of beautiful sound, which made Jupiter very proud.

Once, on another day, when I brought him a thick beef and onion soup, I complimented him on his classical name and he produced that strange rictus of a smile and inappropriate laugh and said, 'But these fancy names are just a belly-slapper for the Massuh, same as you call a house cat Ophelia or a black one Othello. Ol' Colonel Tom named his slaves Daphne and Mercury, Venus and Pallas, Nero and Pompea, but we had our secret African names like Quaco and Cudjo, Quamana and Wolk.'

I asked him what his secret name was and he looked at me strangely. The silence dilated between us but at last he must have made a decision to trust me, for he said it was Cudjo, which meant Monday in African, the day he'd been born.

'Then why do you keep your name of Jupiter,' I asked, 'if you find it insulting?'

''Cause I hope my family is gonna get free and join me and I want folks to know where I'm at when they ax.'

He told me that Colonel Tom had sent a white man to his forge here in Ohio asking him to return. All would be forgiven, he'd never be whipped again and he could set his own hours and conditions of work. 'Colonel Tom was just thinkin' I'm gonna miss him and his family 'cause he thinks I *love* his family but I don't.' Here he paused and said something surprising: 'He never taught me to read.'

'And is there nothing you miss at the Big House?'

'Mammy, I missin' my missus, Dine, and our little wood house where we'd sleep together with our children on the floor next the fire, where we'd be pigged lovingly together.' And here he laughed, but not the frozen rictus of a laugh when he spoke of his master, but a good free laugh of pleasure in recollection.

'And why are you called Higgins?' I asked.

''Cause that was Colonel Tom's name. Here up North a black man needs a family name so I took his'n.' The straightforward way Jupiter said that made me shiver.

One day he asked me if I knew how to cook collard greens with bits of hamhock in it (*jarret de porc*) and I asked him for his receipt and after that I made it often for him and for the boy who worked the bellows, his 'helps' as he called him. Henry and Cecilia actively disliked the taste, which they thought was greasy and bitter. I suppose we all like what we ate as children. Mr Higgins spit out the cup of tea I served him once but he couldn't get his fill of corn bread and greens.

After his explanation of his names – Jupiter as a condescending joke and Higgins as the equivalent to his master's brand on his flanks – I found myself embarrassed every time I addressed him and I ended up calling him Cudjo, though I knew he thought I was presumptuous.

One day he asked me whom I was waiting for while I stood at the top of our hill and I said, 'My husband and my oldest son Tom. They're coming from England. They wrote that their ship would arrive – well, ten days ago if all went according to schedule.'

Mr Higgins laughed his high, free whinny of a laugh and slapped his side for he found it 'wondrous strange' that people could communicate from one world to another by letter and walk on the water like Our Lord. Then he said, a bit sadly, 'Mammy, we alike for we both be attending our beloved, but your Mister is gonna come for sure but my Dine is never, never gonna come,' and here he wept and I touched his sleeve with compassion.

Tom and Trollope came walking up the hill one evening and I embraced them and I was about to present them to my Cudjo but he just doffed his cap and hurried away with his horrible little laugh mumbling, 'Yessuh, yessuh,' and I knew he was jealous of Trollope. At least I hoped so.

Henry and the girls and even Hervieu were delighted to the point of hysteria and danced around Tom and Trollope as if they represented everything desirable in life and memorable about England. For the last week I'd felt unfairly that I alone was anxious about their long-delayed arrival, but now I saw that the others had also been disquieted in their own oblique way, so noisy and sincere was their welcome. Now we were all reunited except for Anthony.

The Pater took to his – or rather my – bed, within seconds of his arrival, though he looked healthier than I had seen him in years. It was as if he'd remembered he was a perennial invalid the moment he'd seen me. Tom appeared genuinely happy to hold his old mother in his arms and laughingly recounted the tribulations of their voyage out. Because he was both stoic and mean, Trollope had bought them steerage tickets on the *Corinthian*. Tom had taken one look at – and one whiff of – the crowded bunks and announced he was going to sleep on deck. The other passengers scoffed at him but he kept to his resolve all the thirty-eight nights of the journey, wrapping himself in his greatcoat, or 'dreadnought' as it was called back then, sleeping through wind and rain and the punishing cold of the high seas in September. By day he'd look after his ailing father, whose headaches were so brutal he scarcely noticed the squalor all around him, though Trollope did begin to feel better after a week at sea. In a sense each man proved himself – Trollope that he was so ill no mere discomfort could affect him, Tom that he was so above the herd that he would suffer any inconvenience to preserve his solitude.

If anyone had been listening he would have concluded that the legend of English reserve was utterly misleading since we did nothing but talk night and day, all rushing forward with our stories and fighting for attention, even little Emily. I realized that Emily had simply dried up in the New World, unable to understand American girls or to emulate their fierce democratic self-esteem, spurned by Henry, ignored by Auguste, neglected by me, preoccupied as I had been for so long with our very survival. Even Cecilia avoided her, since she disliked someone who so resembled her here in the alien corn. Now with her beloved if difficult father present once again and her brother Tom in constant attendance (a brother so much older that he was like a kindly uncle who was always teasing her though he quite obviously delighted in discovering her anew), she sprang back to life. She even resumed her flutey English 'accent' and her droll foot-stomping fits of pique, which made us all laugh because they so obviously disguised a shockingly compliant heart.

But if I was happy to see my children merry and reassured, I was dismayed to have to acknowledge that nothing remained between Trollope and me. He never embraced me nor seated me on his knee nor explained his long epistolary silences nor whispered sweetly into my ear. On the contrary. He revealed in his way of cocking one shaggy eyebrow whenever I said something frivolous, or of pressing his thin lips together whenever I cut my laces that he thought of me as a fallen woman in danger of compromising her whole family's reputation. Whenever Auguste would come into the room without knocking or show me a sketch and lean over me to observe my first reaction, Mr Trollope would produce an exasperated sound that fortunately Monsieur Hervieu failed to notice.

Snow began to fall and fall in great pure drifts and I had ever fewer occasions to wander outside where I kept hoping I'd run into Cudjo. I began to plan elaborate Christmas charades and plays and concerts with my children and the neighbours, especially with the Prices and Hiram Powers and Mr Dorfeuille, and our cottage was redolent of pine swags and a fine fruitcake I was ageing in whisky-soaked rags, of apple pies and hams and the gigantic turkey, which Mr Trollope refused even to taste though its white meat is reputed to be suitable for invalids and delicate organisms. I kept imagining an impossible moment when I could invite Cudjo in to share in our merriness. I wrote a play which contained a prize couplet:

238

> For Tories I care not a fig.
> My only terror is a Whig.

Emily and Cecilia were singing scales in one corner and in another Tom was bellowing out Falstaff's lines, since the Prices would soon be presenting *The Merry Wives of Windsor* in which I'd play Mistress Quickly. And yet all my merriness was forced, affected for the children's benefit. At night I'd lie awake beside the sleeping Mr Trollope and tears of self-pity would sting my eyes when I'd think that this person was empty, wrung dry, and that I would never again receive a kiss from his dry, fleshless lips. Nor, for that matter, from lips embarrassingly ripe.

One day as we were walking over to dinner at Dr Price's I knelt to adjust my shoe in the snow and fell behind and when I looked up I saw Trollope from behind, his narrow, nearly paralysed back, his crablike gait, one shoulder pitched higher than the other, his scrawny neck, his old man's shuffle. Suddenly I realized that his bad health was not a pose, or if so he'd held it so long it had deformed him.

Hiram introduced us to his patron, Nicholas Longworth, the richest man in town, who had those long white sideburns the French call *favoris*, which framed a great strawberry nose, huge and misbegotten. He'd moved to Cincinnati in 1803 when it was still a log village of just eight hundred citizens (a village frequently attacked by Indians), and by clever trading he had accumulated property that was soon worth three million dollars – a large part of downtown. In 1828, when we met him, he'd retired from his law practice and was devoting himself full-time to horticulture. He'd developed the only successful grape in America, the Catawba, which was the basis for an amusing little white wine, more fruity than flinty, but which of course the Americans insisted must rank higher than the subtlest Moselle or Sauvignon.

At first I thought Mr Longworth might back one of my projects or another but I soon enough learned from his own lips that he never gave money outright to the enterprising but rather leased them land at a low rent or gave them a favourable rate at one of his mills or tanneries or wineries (nothing of any use to me). Later he would prove to be fatally difficult with me in money matters.

All the coming and going to the Prices' house or ours made, in my imagination at least, the forge seem even more isolated. I knew Cudjo's secret name but I couldn't say it out loud, any more than I could disgrace myself before Trollope or Tom by paying a friendly call on a black man. Of course it was obvious, but I'd never meditated on the truth before, that a real friendship between a Negro man and a white woman could occur only in the most stifling privacy, one that was equivalent to an admission of something shameful. There were no social forms or forums to house our feelings. One day I left half a roast partridge beside Cudjo's door but later I noticed he hadn't touched it and that a stray dog was devouring it. I wondered if he simply didn't like game (which Mr Longworth had provided) or whether he was sending me a message; I didn't test him a second time. One Sunday in town I saw Mr Higgins in a handsome costume in tandem with the pretty woman I'd first spied at the camp meeting, the one who'd worn so much gold. She was in her daffodil-yellow dress. They were obviously on their way from church and looked so solemn I had to laugh, but my derision stuck in my throat as tears are said to come out dry in hell.

Tom liked everyone and everything. He took the girls skating on nearby ponds and flirted with the Prices' two pretty daughters. Since he'd learned nothing at all about America at Winchester, he had a whole Faery Land to discover. He evidenced an intense interest in Mr Longworth's viniculture as well as his attempts to create hermaphrodite strawberries, which in my troubled mind kept rhyming with his nose. Tom wasn't as snobbish as I. The way American men lounged on chairs or draped themselves over couches and protruded their dirty boots into one's path did not disturb him and he thought their constant spitting was 'funny.' Perhaps because he never imagined for a moment that he might actually try to live amongst these comical boors he had no need of setting himself apart or essaying to reform them.

Everything I found reprehensible he deemed colourful. He made me see things through his eyes and everything became doubly interesting.

Over the years I have learned from him. We moved to Florence together in 1843 (when I was already sixty-three years old) where we've remained ever since. Tom showed me how to esteem or at least tolerate Florentine ways and instructed me by example how to keep an open mind despite my advanced age. To be sure the Tuscans were never as raw or prickly as the Ohioans – and if anything the average Florentine domestic erred in the direction of oiliness and obsequiousness. And in Florence we've always enjoyed the *crème* of English and American expatriate society: Sir Henry Taylor, the friend of Southey and Carlyle, Lord and Lady Holland, Hiram Powers and an American lady, Mrs Brooks, who seems to know everything, for when an American is cultured no one can rival her in erudition and refinement. Mrs Brooks goes to the Duomo nearly once a week.

One day at the end of 1828 I had an inspiration – a *fatal* inspiration, I might add. I decided that the best way to build on our success with the Invisible Girl and the Infernal Regions was to construct a Bazaar, a coffee-house where wits could gather and a theatre where amateur plays could be staged and a shopping arcade where unusual trifles could be purchased. We immediately agreed that I would stay on in Cincinnati another two years to make sure the Bazaar was well launched and that during the following decade Auguste and Henry would manage it. By then I imagined they'd be so rich they could retire and return to England in glory.

I convened my whole clan after Boxing Day and made my proposal as gravely as I could because a visionary must first convince her entourage that her chimera is already half-real (something I learned from Fanny). 'We will provide this town with all its civilized needs. We'll put some sin back in Cincinnati. Upstairs we'll serve tea and ice-cream to the ladies and juleps to the men. We'll think up something exciting for the children. We'll have a large lovely globe at the top of the stairs. There will be exhibitions and entertainments, a ballroom with a minstrels' gallery. We'll combine sociability with commerce. We'll even sell local crafts, for Cincinnati ladies are *tireless* with their fancy sewing and quilting and baking.'

Trollope was rubbing his forehead with one hand and shielding his eyes with the other. Henry was seated on the floor with his shoulders leaning back against Auguste's knees and both of them seemed politely enthusiastic but unconcerned, as if I were sketching out a purely abstract question rather than their concrete future. The girls were genuinely thrilled; at least Emily was already clapping her hands and bouncing in her chair.

Because the general silence was so shaming, Auguste made an effort and asked me about the architecture of the place.

'It must be eclectic and you and I, Auguste, will design it,' I said.

Here Trollope's shaggy right eyebrow shot up above his screening hand.

I decided that there should be medieval battlements, Greek columns framing arabesque windows, the whole topped by a Turkish dome. The back of the Bazaar would be mainly Egyptian. The building would summarize all the epochs of man and bring that missing note of the Romantic to this pedestrian place. I'd picked up the Egyptian note from William Bullock, a rich Englishman who lived in Kentucky just across the river and who'd built the Egyptian Hall in Piccadilly based on Denon's drawings of the Egyptian ruins.

We bought the property for fifteen hundred dollars. It wasn't exactly in the main, bustling section of town, but it did have the honour of gracing the site where Cincinnati's original fortress against the Indians had stood. Mr Trollope signed the deed, since as a married woman I couldn't own property.

He seldom spoke to me (though he was often huddled away with Tom). If Auguste entered the room, Trollope went silent in mid-sentence. I thought he'd selected the wrong man to be jealous of. Trollope didn't even approve of Auguste's friendship with

Henry. To be sure Auguste could overexcite himself and flap about or drench himself in too much eau de Russie, and, agreed, he did touch Henry too often by an Englishman's lights, but he was an artist, after all, and a Gallic one at that, and what is an artist without temperament? Tom thought him an intolerable bounder but recognized that he'd saved my life. He did, however, bitterly take exception to Auguste's pea-green waistcoat. Tom was planning to read Greats at Oxford that spring. I thought I detected a moment of panicked envy in Henry's eyes. In his impetuous way he'd dropped his studies and only now were we securing a future for him but in bleak little Cincinnati, not in London, that vast rumbling metropolis, the foggy centre of the world.

Trollope acted as if our whole North American trip were a lark of mine in dubious taste; he refused to admit that his withdrawal from his legal practice had ruined his family and that I alone had had the pluck to save us. But he did come up with an 'inspiration' of his own (ill-fated as well). He thought we should sell small English items at the Bazaar – leather goods, cutlery, China, napery. I was so absurdly grateful for his making any suggestion at all that I foolishly agreed, though neither he nor I knew a thing about buying or selling. Trollope argued that our success would lead other merchants to rent stalls to sell their own goods and we'd profit from the rentals – and the swelling crowds. Dr Price objected that the Bazaar would be too far outside the usual shopping district. In fact, its neighbours would be a distillery and Goodloe & Brown, a steam-engine factory.

I wrote to Harriet,

Mr Trollope has entered into an equal division with Henry of all profits proceeding from this institution till he shall be of age, after which he is to have the whole, as long as he chooses to remain here to superintend it. When he leaves it, Mr Trollope hopes to sell it to advantage. The rapid and almost daily increase of this extraordinary city certainly warrants the expectation.

Before this I hadn't written Harriet for many long months since I'd had nothing positive to say till now.

As soon as Trollope arrived in England he sent me 2,000 dollars. I engaged builders and bought materials, but I instantly came up against the dishonesty of tradesmen. As I later discovered, bricks cost me thrice the normal price. An Englishman promised to install the first system of gas lighting in Cincinnati but he vanished with my initial payment.

I kept expecting an additional 4,000 dollars from England with which to purchase goods, but wily old Trollope (forgive my bitter tone) sent trumpery goods instead – pocket-knives and pepper boxes and bits of French finery already available in greater variety in a store just a street away. I wrote Julia that 'the sight of those dreadful and utterly unsaleable goods, and the consciousness of the considerable sum still to be paid to the workmen' sent me to bed for eleven weeks with jaundice and fevers and chills: malaria.

I was reading the whole of Fenimore Cooper and sank into a hot, sticky sleep only to have a Redskin with the face of my rascally English gas supplier take a tomahawk to my scalp. I'd wake up with my teeth rattling. I drank beef broth and ate grilled bread and allowed Emily to fan me for the entire sweaty summer, which was even more stifling than the preceding one.

I was lost and all my plans had come to naught. The New World had taken its revenge on me. I'd scorned it and it had punished me in kind. I was yellow but I felt red from humiliation. Nothing had gone according to my light-hearted plan. I, the gay Miss Milton, had always believed no distinction should be made between work and play, but Cincinnati did not agree. I had the soul of an artist and was always goading myself on to ever greater frankness, more extravagant and penetrating self-disclosure, but in Cincinnati the merchants played to win with their cards close to their chests. They gave nothing away. Though I loved the sociability of whist and here in Florence I'm ever ready to go on till two in the morning, at my ridiculous age – though I've played whist all my life I've almost never won and then strictly by accident. I am too eager to gossip, to groan or exclaim – to *dramatize* every moment in the game, for I delight in expression and nothing lives for me unless it's narrated or acted out (which once I decided to write became a professional skill after all).

Jaundiced and skinny, I looked at my face in the mirror as seldom as possible and saw in it nothing but an abnegation of any man's future interest. I was irreversibly old, definitively ugly and whereas just a year ago one in a hundred strangers might have glanced up from his journal or his desk to acknowledge my presence or passage, now I was invisible. If to be is to be perceived, as Dr Berkeley tells us, then I'd become nothingness.

I was too weak to cross the room and every alternative I contemplated in my future fatigued me into extinction. I had nothing but debts in England and in America, I couldn't pay for our passage home on a ship nor did I have any prospects there. Now Henry had no future either. We no longer even had the illusory but comforting prospect of racing off to America and succeeding there. We'd not been cautious or disciplined enough to win in Cincinnati, nor hard enough nor cunning enough.

Fanny wrote me a newsy letter, unusually chatty for her. In 1829 she and Robert Dale Owen had moved to New-York, where they'd relaunched their journal, now called the *Free Enquirer*. She'd taken up the cause of organized labour and the enlightenment of the working classes and she had helped to found the first political organization representing syndicalists in America, the New-York Working Men's Party. She and Owen were campaigning for the ten-hour day and were backing workers in strikes against their bosses. She wrote:

But a note of dissension has already crept into our organization. A radical named Thomas Skidmore has called for a revolution that would lead to the equal division of property. I'm most opposed to this issue, not as a goal but as a strategy. America is not yet ready for communism. Robert Dale and I are repeatedly saddened by the ignorance of the working class. We want to educate workers. Equalize fortunes at this hour and in one year knavery will have beggared honesty. Credulous simplicity will have yielded all to the crafty hypocrite.

The letter was a choice cutting from the burned-out bush of Fanny's style: all those dead abstractions ('credulous simplicity', 'knavery') and the strangely oblique functions ('beggared honesty' or 'equalize fortunes') – and I detest all neologisms that end in -*ize*.

Despite my stylistic caveats I couldn't help but apply Fanny's words to myself. I was the credulous simpleton and I was about to lose everything to crafty hypocrites.

Fanny included a newspaper clipping hostile to her in which the members of the New-York Working Men's Party were called 'Wright Reasoners' and she herself was denounced as 'a crazy atheistical woman lost to society, to earth and to heaven, godless and hopeless, clothed and fed by stealing and blasphemy.'

Stealing? I'd never known Fanny to steal. The rest sounded about right.

Fanny's idea that workers should be educated was sound and generous, but typically she carried it too far. She fervently believed that the children of the rich and the poor could become equals only if they lived far from the 'contaminating' influence of their parents in state-supported boarding-schools.

Fanny knew little of human nature if she seriously imagined parents would agree to give up their children to an impersonal, imperious institution. Nor would the rich want their sons and daughters to rub shoulders with poor children, nor could poor parents permit their children to learn to despise them. The New-York Typographical Society criticized Fanny's scheme for being recklessly visionary and destructive to working-class social ties. Fanny wanted to hand her principles down to workers without consulting them, but naturally they were shocked by her arrogance, her atheism and her contempt for the family.

There! Now that I've written about Fanny I feel that I've earned the right as a biographer to return parenthetically to my own life, since it is so clearly interwoven with many of the themes in Wright's story – our double portrait could even be called Fanaticism vs. Sweet Moderation.

Except my love for Cudjo [Destroy these pages! My sons must not see any of this and my public reputation would be permanently besmirched] wasn't moderate at all. [My books would be banned and Tom would have none of the benefit of my two decades' worth of rising at four in the morning.] Cudjo was visible again now that the autumn had come back. My husband had returned to England, my illness was in retreat and the house had calmed down. It was as if I'd lost a whole year or that I'd been put under a glass bell for a year, but one that withered rather than preserved me.

One cold day the girls had been invited by the Prices and their daughters to go on a buggy ride in the country to look at the glorious changing leaves. Henry and Auguste were supervising the last details at the Bazaar, which was about to have its grand opening. I was alone in the house, much better now that the cooler weather had returned. I'd assured everyone I'd be fine but suddenly I wasn't. I was seized by a new fit of trembling. The door had blown open and the stray dog of the neighbourhood had entered the cottage at first fearfully but soon boldly as he tap-tapped on his long hard nails over the wood floors and went into the pantry to see what it had to offer.

And all the while I was powerless to do anything but lie on the floor and wrap a rag rug around me for warmth. It wasn't even very clean and I was conscious of the grit in my hair and on my lips. I longed for a cool draught of water but I didn't have the energy to seek it out. I lay in my rag rug, rolled up like jelly in a pastry but a green jelly, a bitter mint jelly.

I must have fallen asleep for when I awakened the sun had shifted its pattern on the floor and I felt something cool against me. I assumed it was the stray's cold nose, but no, when I opened my eyes I saw Cudjo's cool hand and though a feeble protest arose in me against his seeing me so weak and dirty and ugly, he just said in his rich bass voice, 'My poor girl.' He unrolled

247

me and took me up in his strong arms and laid me on my bed and I regretted the wrinkled sheets and the wilted flowers on my chiffonier and the faded flowers in my cheeks – I who'd always been strawberries and cream long past my prime. I loved the touch of his thick muscles under my hands but I was so feeble he felt like a different kind of animal altogether.

I was that funny little picayune doll I'd bought Emily in New Orleans, the one she'd lost with the yellow hair and the big button eyes sewn on and the stiff straw stuffing that smelled of mould, not at all like the pretty porcelain English doll with the weighted lids above blue crystals that glided shut. I looked up at Cudjo's face, so close and so dear though monstrous, surely, for part of me held out against accepting him entirely. Yet hadn't he called me, 'My poor girl'?

He pulled the covers over me and plumped my pillows and then he was off somewhere boiling water and then he was making me sit up and sip tea which warmed me through and through; the tea even caused me to perspire. And then a moment later he was back with some cornbread he'd gone to fetch from the forge and though officially I hated it and had ridiculed it in many a mocking letter home, nevertheless here I was devouring it grate-fully, even the charred edges. 'They left you all alone, little girl.'

'I'm not a little girl,' I protested, using all my energy to smile an instant.

'You are for me. You're *my* little girl.'

I closed my eyes in a sunburst of pleasure and floated a wiz-ened yellow hand against his sleeve and my very weakness per-mitted me to say nothing more than 'Yes,' and in that way I affirmed in a great simplifying monosyllable that I belonged to him. My 'yes' made him laugh, not in his delighted whinny but in a big roar of joyful spontaneity, which was like a necessary physical process – like eating or sleeping.

He never dared come into the cottage again but he had no need to since soon I was strong enough to visit him in the forge – I should say once a day but it was more often. I told him I owed him my life but I was exaggerating, as we both knew. I suppose I wanted to acknowledge that he'd given me a new reason to live. I was still a sickly thing, a hank of limp hair on a stick like an old hobbyhorse, but I put a bright ribbon in my hair as one might pin a satin rosette to a nag in honour of the king's birthday: the occasion, not the creature, was being honoured.

When I was at last restored to health and began to show some of my old plumpness, his big sable hand actually squeezed one of my buttocks through my skirts and he said, 'That's what I like to see, some flesh on them bones – let these bones live, as Ezekiel says.' I laughed like an alehouse coquette, but no matter, at least I was laughing. Never in a hundred years (and that was my age, or so it seemed) would I have tolerated such impertinence in England, but now I felt my husband was far away and had betrayed me stupidly and he'd become my aged, complaining father, whereas I had turned into big black Cudjo's little yellow girl and he could do with me what he wanted.

[These pages, so full of fluttering life, must die with my death or else all that I've struggled to become will pass into obscurity and the patrimony I've left my sons will die with me and they will be laughed at in Florence and London, people will speak of the Old Trollop, I'm sure they will.]

One day I asked him what slavery had been like.

He said, 'Oh, there were good masters but they didn't *stay* good.'

'What do you mean?'

We were eating a bit of the ham and spinach in cream I'd prepared with some of Mr Longworth's Catawba grapes thrown in so that I could call the whole dish *Jambon véronique*. I was sitting in Cudjo's only chair and he was hunkering in his curious crouching way with his back pushed against the wall. The fire had died down but was still toasty and I felt it irradiating my whole being.

'Colonel Tom married a good religious woman from Maryland. Her family didn't have no slaves and she was *so* polite next to me for the first year. She wanted to teach me to read 'cause I was already fixin' to be a preacher man and I had to read my

Bible, but Colonel Tom caught her at it and he shouted 'Woman, don you know thas illegal to teach a nigger to read?' and he struck me like he was going to whip the letters outta my haid.'

After that the Colonel's wife became more and more querulous with Cudjo and even ordered the overseer to flog him more than once.

'Was she hoping to atone for teaching you to read?' I asked.

'If you put the whip in someone's hand, they're gonna *use* it.'

He told me horribly specific wounding things about slavery that saddened me and sickened me. He cited prices – Colonel Tom had sold a slave trained as a carpenter for 2,500 dollars and Cudjo's own blacksmith helper for 1,114 dollars. 'A field nigger goes for seven hundred dollars to nine hundred dollars,' he said. Almost proudly he added, 'I'd fetch 3,000 dollars.'

'But you speak of them, of yourself, as if you're domestic animals!' I said.

'Yessum, Mammy, there are dealers who pay for slaves in horse flesh – it's an exchange.'

'Mammy,' he said a bit later, 'if I'm worth 3,000 dollars no wonder the old Colonel doesn't like it if I lurked out.'

'If you *what*?' I asked, uncomprehending.

'Lurked out. Run away.'

On another day he told me the reason he'd run away was that once he'd missed his curfew he knew he was in danger. Anyone could legally kill a runaway and receive ninety-eight and three-quarter cents if the slave was found within ten miles of his home and three and one-eighth cents for each additional mile.

'Weren't you afraid someone would catch you and enslave you? You're worth more alive than dead. Three thousand dollars is worth more than ninety-eight cents.' I wondered if I'd fetch as much as a dollar.

'Mammy,' he said, smiling, 'that would be slave-stealing and a white man thief like that gets minimum five years in prison and maximum fifteen years.'

'And what if someone captured you here and took you back to the Colonel?' I asked.

'That could happen but it sure enough is illegal now. Slavery ain't legal in Ohio. And even if it was, no one could legally *sell* me to Colonel Tom 'cause interstate slave trading ain't legal now noways.'

I was impressed by how much he knew about the law, even if he was illiterate. Doubtless the Negroes downtown talked about every last detail, though I understood knowledge would do little to help a slave if his master decided to recapture him. Cudjo was frightened that the Colonel wanted him back at any price and he lived in daily fear of being kidnapped. I wished I had the 3,000 dollars to buy him outright.

I confessed to Cudjo how worried I was about the opening of the Bazaar. 'I know all my dreams will evaporate with the first whiff of ridicule.' My vocabulary and accent and turns of phrase all made him laugh with delight, but he was intelligent and could hear the depths of my despair. Nor did he utter futile reassurances.

I decided to teach him to read every evening as he drank his beer and I my tea. His 'helps' brought him a tin pail of beer, which he heated up. After all, I'd taught my children to read in an amusing way and I was droll and brisk.

He made rapid progress, especially when we worked from the Bible, for he'd already memorized whole passages of it with that peculiar aptitude reserved to the illiterate and with great joy he made out the familiar words from the unfamiliar signs. He'd struggle over the first few words and then the rest would flow out spontaneously and he'd touch the book, the thin pages and leather binding, as if it were the mind and body of a wonderful friend.

One day, after he read a whole psalm in his low, warm voice, I was so thrilled I pecked him on the cheek and he took me in his arms and looked me right in the eye and then as if he were puzzled but determined to understand me he inched still closer and looked even deeper into my eyes and then his eyes closed

251

and his mouth opened and his big pink tongue started systematically washing my teeth and my tongue and the roof of my
mouth, a big slippery *sangsue* tasting of hops.

He stood up and closed the door of the forge and locked us
in and he slowly undressed me by the glow of the banked embers
and seated me on his leather apron and though each revelation
of a new part of my body made me search his face with new
terror I failed to see any manifestation of disgust.

Of course there was something comical about the reading
lesson and the book cast aside, about this elderly white Francesca
and her burly black Paolo. I knew my Dante too well not to anticipate the whirling wind of eternal punishment that awaited us.
And even those obsessed lovers hadn't embraced each other over
the Bible.

But these fears of future damnation and the even greater fear
of repelling my lover now were nothing beside the panting
pleasure of – well, of pleasure. The reawakened body's bliss. The
sweet, vulnerable validation of a man's tender but ungallant attentions. The fascination of this foreign brand of male beauty. Cudjo's
irrepressible sensuality, the whole hip-smacking, aureole-licking,
ear-bathing thoroughness he brought to the job. I thanked the
goddesses and gods (since I dared not thank God) for granting
me this capsizing joy at least once in my long life. I asked him
what the black woman in the yellow dress and gold jewellery was
to him and he said she was like a sister. I wondered if I was like
a mother.

Why am I writing these dangerous words now, two decades
after the event? Why do I keep fearing and hoping the letters
on the page will catch on fire and consume themselves before
it's too late? I suppose that after years of covering page after
page, quarto after folio with the black bite of my tiny, pecking
letters, after the indirection and often feebly figured invention
of my half-hearted imaginings – that after all that, some silent,
waiting sibyl within me is speaking out. I want to recall and re-
create for myself those painful black hands lifting my pelvis, that
fruit-pink mouth and tongue obscenely battening off my very

life's force, that sweet, exhausted tangle of our limbs and the heart-slowing return to what felt like an old, a very old friendship. 'My dear,' I said, 'my very dear one,' and he said, propped up on one elbow and stroking me like a river god laving a Nereid with a cold, barely flowing stream, 'My girl, my little girl,' and these words of possession rang out strangely in a country where people really and truly, legally, could own one another and where Cudjo had been property.

I couldn't share my happy news with anyone, not even that flaming radical Frances Wright. She needed me to be conservative that she might be the revolutionary. She would have been shaken to her foundations if I'd voiced such a thing as my love for Cudjo, for even if she might have embraced a slave she would have buried the act of human congress under obliterating abstractions and high-minded rhetoric. No, I was alone with my America.

I knew that what we had just done was very dangerous. I could be whipped and Cudjo hanged. No one must know even about our highly suspect friendship. Luckily, few people came to our house or forge, but Cudjo did have the odd customer, and the Prices did pass by from time to time. We knew we had to be more secretive.

The Bazaar opened on 16 October 1829. One critic said that its *mélange* of exotic styles in a city of brick boxes and neo-classical trim made it look like a belly dancer in a procession of Greek maidens. I'd thought it would be a magnet for fashionable society but it attracted nothing but ridicule. The workmanship had been poorly done and a medieval battlement was half slipping down over a Venetian flame-shaped window like a droopy eyelid. Inside there was sawdust everywhere and though I'd provided cuspidors the men insisted on spitting against the freshly painted walls. On the opening night the whole place smelled of rotting eggs – the leaking gas. I immediately decided to replace the gas lamps with oil and spermacetti.

Except for our very particular friends – the Prices, Hiram Powers, Joseph Dorfeuille, and the preacher and writer Timothy Flint, the most civilized man in America – everyone scoffed at the architecture, the bad smell and the shoddy goods for sale on the lower level.

In the theatre upstairs we put on variety evenings of popular songs, sung by the English actor Joseph Cowell, and great moments in Shakespeare recited by Alexander Drake and his wife, who'd been ousted from their own Cincinnati theatre after its dismal failure. All we were asking for admission was twenty-five cents, but that sounded dear to these boorish men for the return in entertainment and in any event local preachers were denouncing our sinful stage and rival merchants were laughing at the shoddiness of our goods. Very few people came, no women, and during the theatricals men in the audience, who smelled of cooked onions and home-made whisky, would spit, talk loudly, and hang their rear ends out over the edge of the balcony while they addressed other men in their party. Poor Mr Cowell refused to return to the stage after his first song was ruined by a fit of laughter provoked by someone's sneeze. He ran off into the night.

We'd finished the building on credit and now that the workers (and the bankers) could see the Bazaar was a failure they were all clamouring for their money. Henry, having auctioned off the trumpery goods the Pater had sent over, for a fraction of their original cost, handed the money over to the workers but they were howling for more.

We lost everything and were penniless. Everything was seized by the creditors. Mr Gano, our landlord in Mohawk, whom we'd thought of as a friend, had the justice of the peace and the sheriff's assistant remove us bodily from the cottage and seal the doors shut. All of our furniture – the beds, the dressers, the pier glass, the lanterns, even that rag rug in which Cudjo had dis-covered me – was carted away. I'd been able to rescue one good Turkey carpet from the parlour which I gave to Major and Mrs Lionel, who operated a nearby boarding-house. In exchange for the carpet they let Emily, Cecilia and me sleep in one small bed for a few nights. Henry and Auguste lay on the floor in the kitchen.

I tried to let the Bazaar but no one wanted it. My son Tom

had been planning to come back for a leisurely trip through America but now I wrote him a frantic letter begging him to send instead a one-way ticket for Henry home to England. Henry was very ill with malaria (and exhaustion, no doubt). And consumption. The doctor wanted to bleed him again but I refused to permit it – I knew the cure would kill him. Another more gifted doctor told us that only the climate of his native land could restore Henry's health. Hervieu's painting of Lafayette landing at Cincinnati had won him such praise in the local journals that he received a few portrait commissions and that's what kept us alive. From time to time Cudjo also gave us a 'mess of greens' to eat cooked with streaky bacon.

Every few days I visited him secretly at the end of his work and we sat beside the still warm forge. If near his smithy I encountered someone I kept on walking and only later doubled back. Sometimes we just held hands like a respectable old couple. We never had much time together and I scarcely knew whether I preferred confiding in him (for he was my only friend) or embracing him (for our intimacy was an appetite I couldn't stop feeding).

We would begin by talking and holding hands. 'Today, dear Cudjo,' I'd say, 'the bailiff has sealed the Bazaar shut. It no longer belongs to the Trollopes. Every last farthing we had went into it and much, much more and now we have nothing and we owe everyone.'

He just smiled and began nibbling my palms and wrists as if that would make up for my loss and somehow it did. He said, 'But you're a plucky little thing, Mammy, and your way of talking and thinking is worth more than money in the bank.'

I sat on his knee and felt his huge hands undoing my stays with great delicacy like a horse knitting – a ridiculously strained image but expressive of his awkward dexterity. What sustained me during these terrible days was the knowledge that soon – in a day or two – I'd have Cudjo to myself again, moments that were islands of tranquillity in the storm of debt and disgrace.

At this time Lafayette, who all along had thought my children and I were in New-York, at last was informed of our residence in Cincinnati. He wrote me of his fatherly concern for our welfare and included a letter of introduction to one of the wealthiest citizens of the Queen City, none other than Mr Amelung. When I delivered the letter and my own note at the house of this great gentleman I was ushered into his study with all due ceremony. Imagine his discomfort when he realized I must be the pariah of Trollope's Folly, and picture his wife's horror when she took in my old, torn dress and faded, greasy bonnet – my last clothes and not only shoddy but not really respectable enough to earn an admission into decent society. The gentleman must have been puzzled by Lafayette's devotion to such an adventuress (one who travelled everywhere, moreover, with a much younger bearded French artist, the breadwinner for her and her children). He offered to return my call but I told him I had no place where I could receive a visitor.

I'd lost all pride. I admitted the truth – all the truths (but one!) – to everyone and in the simplest way, without ameliorating smiles or disarming words. I stood there in a sumptuous library beside a lightly crackling fire in my rags, my hair grey, nearly white, and disarranged by the removal of my bonnet. I didn't make it easy for the gentleman of Cincinnati nor for his lady by concealing or shrugging off the disasters that had befallen me. I took tea from a Sèvres cup that, if sold, would have bought my whole brood another week's worth of food and shelter.

The Amelungs were as agreeable as possible. Oddly they'd decided that I was leaving the city on the morrow, though I'd clearly admitted I didn't have enough money once the ice broke at the end of February to pay our passage down the Ohio and Mississippi, much less to buy the tickets from New Orleans back to England. No, they'd worked out, husband and wife, this useful fiction of my imminent departure, which absolved them of all need to help me and rescued them from the duty to present me to the other notables of the city. 'Oh, if only we'd known you were in our midst all this time,' the lady cried. 'How we would have loved to invite you to our provincial little collations. No, you were too wicked not to call on us sooner,' though the date on Lafayette's letter was quite recent and we all knew that without it I'd never have had a passport into their midst.

Husband and wife accompanied me to the door while their King Charles spaniel yapped and they assured me of their sorrow and vexation at the brevity of my stay in their city – and there I was! Alone on their elegant *perron*, the black lacquer door sealed shut behind me, never to open again, and the snow swirling around me.

The one favour I'd been able to wrest from them, despite their wiliness, was a portrait commission for Hervieu. He was going to paint the distinguished couple together and she was already asking herself which of her frocks should be immortalized.

The money from that commission was what we lived on for the next few weeks, though Hervieu had to listen to many criticisms, more than usual, and make adjustments accordingly. And Hervieu was submitted to many questions about me, my family and my background. For the most part Hervieu pretended his English wasn't up to it.

Eighteen

Suddenly everything changed. In December 1829 I received a letter from Fanny Wright asking me if I'd like to accompany her to Haiti. She'd finally accepted the failure of her slave-freeing scheme at Nashoba. She now knew the slaves would never earn enough to feed themselves, much less to buy their own freedom. Her emancipation scheme had foundered. And yet she'd publicly promised to liberate her slaves sooner rather than later – but where would they live? Not that she herself believed Negroes were unsuited for living in the United States. On the contrary. They were some of the earliest settlers in America, she often pointed out, and had built the nation with their arms and backs. They deserved to rule America, she declared.

But she'd also seen how badly black freed men were treated – in New-York, where she happened to be living, or in any city or town in the States she'd visited.

What to do? She'd heard about the scheme to 'return' blacks to the new country of Liberia and its capital city of Monrovia, but the Negroes she'd met and who'd even published essays in the *Free Enquirer* violently opposed repatriation. They were supposed to go to Liberia as Christian missionaries, but many of them were illiterate and some even considered Christianity to be the religion of white oppressors. Fanny herself, of course, detested what she labelled the 'priesthood of superstition.' She called for a more stringent morality and an end to the entire religious conspiracy, which she always maintained was especially designed to subjugate women and Negroes.

But they had to be removed from America. Everywhere in the States freed bondsmen were being re-enslaved. A new law stated that no slave could be freed unless his owner *immediately* removed him from the state where he'd lived. If the owner who wanted to liberate him did not provide adequate funds for passage and six months' support in Western Africa, the local state clerk was to hire out the ex-slave till the resettlement money was raised. Of course many masters, especially in Virginia and Maryland, dispatched their most rebellious slaves to Liberia in order to get rid of them. Years later I discovered that after a difficult first decade in Liberia American ex-slaves began to dominate the local population. American blacks became colonists, exactly like the Belgians in the Congo. The whole dreadful system was simply re-created.

Cudjo told me that he and his fellow slaves on Colonel Tom's plantation had dreaded most being sent to Liberia, which they thought was a death sentence. They couldn't speak the African languages, the level of civilization there was reputedly very low, the climate treacherous, they wouldn't be able to resist the local diseases, and their role as Christian missionaries invited ridicule and harm.

In her own inner debates about what to do with her slaves, Fanny kept remembering Monsieur Granville, the envoy from Haiti whom she'd met in Philadelphia. Fanny wrote to him and he handed her letter over to General Inginiac, the second highest official on the island after President-for-Life Boyer. Fanny had also begged Lafayette to write on her behalf, and his letter obviously was more effective than the one he'd written for me to Cincinnati. Fanny received a letter from the presidential palace: she was offered everything she'd asked for and more. Her slaves

259

would be given land and tools on President Boyer's own estate. They would not be forced to practise Catholicism, though they would have to learn French and obey the laws of the land. Two years previously President Boyer had abandoned his experiment of resettling American Negroes in Haiti at the government's expense since so many of the new settlers had become disgruntled and returned to North America even if the trip home meant enslavement anew. But Boyer said he would make an exception in Fanny's case. He knew from Granville that she was considered a friend to the African. She would be the first white woman to be received officially by the new republic where some twenty or thirty years earlier the white French settlers had been slaughtered by their rebellious slaves.

I was a friend to *an* African and I gladly accepted Fanny's invitation to accompany her, especially since she said she'd reward me with a ticket home to England from New Orleans (a ticket I would of course turn over to my sickly Henry). Fanny said that she'd be accompanied to Haiti by William Phiquepal, the professor from New Harmony, since he had travelled extensively in the West Indies and understood the region. I remembered how Fanny had laughed at Phiquepal in New Harmony and I wondered what had changed her mind about him. Henry had told me Phiquepal was choleric and hard-headed and not very honest or intelligent. And I knew that Mr Maclure, after having invited Phiquepal first to Spain, then to Philadelphia and New Harmony, had now turned against him. Maclure had written to me that Phiquepal was ignorant, vain and capricious. His 'irritable bad temper' had driven away half his students and turned those who remained into whimsical madmen like himself. Robert Dale Owen was just as negative though he rated Phiquepal's natural gifts higher. Owen called him suspicious and headstrong but 'a wrongheaded genius whose extravagance and wilfulness and inordinate self-conceit have destroyed his usefulness.'

I read Fanny's letter to Cudjo and he said, 'Mammy, we could go together. I could pretend to be one of Miz Wright's slaves when we travel through the South. I'd like to settle in Haiti, though I don' like no voodoo!' And here he rolled his eyes and made his hands tremble in front of his face – how I laughed!

'But, dear Cudjo,' I asked, more seriously, 'why would you give up your quiet life here and your friends and your forge? Believe me, once upon a time I too imagined a change could only be for the better, but I was wrong. I've been punished for my presumption.'

He kissed my eyelids and said, 'Is this punishment, our being here like this?'

'If this be the food of love then feed on!' I murmured, which made him laugh. Whenever I quoted Shakespeare, no matter how approximately, or one of our poets (Southey, Pope, Byron) Cudjo always attributed the cleverness to me and applauded my wit. Shamelessly I accepted it.

But I was waiting for a response to my question and eventually he said, 'If I were a freed man I'd stay here, but those slave owners want their property back. I know they gon' to pass some *nefarious* law.' (He pronounced the word as if it were linked to an evil pharaoh's will, and indeed in his biblical imagination there was no history, or little of it, only a simultaneity of parables, of current American events and Old Testament stories.)

'What kind of ne-pharaoh's law?' I asked, for my father had taught me to mispronounce a word exactly as a friend or guest had mangled it lest he be embarrassed.

'A law giving slave hunters the right to reclaim stolen property, even in the North. Sure as spring follow winter, that's acomin'.' And of course he was right – in another decade the Fugitive Slave Act, which was indeed nefarious, was passed, only to become another blight on the nation's honour.

'You see, Mammy,' he went on, shifting me from one knee to the other, 'I escaped but it be like I stole myself. I am stolen property. Thas why I want to go to Haiti. Mammy, they speak English there?'

'No,' I said, 'French. Or their own kind of French. You'll be a foreigner there.'

'I am like a foreigner here in Ohio.'

We went back to our reading lesson, working from Deuteronomy, but after a while he said, 'What do you think, Mammy?'

'About Haiti?'

'Yes, Ma'am.'

'Well, Sir, privately I'm delighted because there we can walk down the street hand in hand.'

He laughed and kissed me on the lips. Sitting there on his knee, his huge hands around my waist, I felt like his possession. I can't emphasize enough how beautifully we felt we belonged to each other.

I wrote to Fanny and asked her if a freed black man who had been kind to my family could come on our trip to Haiti as well. I explained Mr Jupiter Higgins's reasons for wanting to leave America.

When two weeks later I had a new letter from Fanny she told me, almost in passing, that of course Mr Higgins could come along. But then she broke off and gave me some terrible news:

Alas, poor Camilla! Her little boy has died and she is blind and senseless with grief. The child, who had large blue eyes, a broad forehead and round and dimpled cheeks, looked like Napoleon. He was but seven months when he died of cholera infantum, associated with teething. Camilla had to be forcibly separated from the little corpse, for she clung to it and kissed it and even sang to it funny little sea chanties I had no idea she knew.

Camilla, I must tell you, no longer likes me. She may even hate me. When I went on my great lecture tour of the West, riding on swift horses overland, wrapped in a buffalo robe, I left her behind in Nashoba expecting her baby. Other people were scandalized that I could thus abandon her but I felt then (and do now) that I was struggling for the very soul of America and that I could not betray this sacred cause out of a strictly personal concern for my sister. I was fighting the formation of the so-called Christian Party in politics; I had to argue that by that detestable party's standards Washington, Jefferson, Adams and Franklin would have been turned away from public life, since all four dismissed the particular claims of Christianity.

But Camilla did register my desertion, though she loyally wrote Julia and Harriet Garnett that she had a slave girl there at Nashoba to tend to her needs during childbirth. Until then I think she'd felt she had to protest her love for me and her devotion even to the most strenuous of my causes, since following me had cost her so dearly. After I 'abandoned' her all the weight of the reproaches accumulated over thirty years fell in on her.

Now she says that she has no reason to live. She is in New-York and her estranged husband at Nashoba, where he is going to register the transference of the slaves to New Orleans, a delicate task, for they could be seized in Louisiana by some half-drunk official claiming they are stolen property. Camilla is sinking into worse and worse health and she is convinced she has no more reason to live. She said to me this morning, 'I've already lived a long life in thirty years, been orphaned in Dundee, fêted in London, educated in Glasgow, received in Paris, liberated in America. I've preached against matrimony and I've married and been disappointed in my choice of husband. I've watched my sister enter history and I've tired of time. I've known the bliss of motherhood and the tragedy of maternal loss, all in less than a year. I am weary of existence. My soul's best treasure is departed and there is naught on earth that can yield me satisfaction.'

I know I have failed her and when I return from Haiti I will immediately escort her to France, where I trust she will recover her health and her bright spirits.

Mournfully,
Frances Wright

Although Fanny had only mentioned in passing the difficulties of transporting her slaves through the South, I took her comment as a subtle warning of the risks Cudjo would be running, and of the possible danger he might inflict on Fanny's whole enterprise.

'Darling,' I said to him, 'what if you're discovered *en route*? How will you get from here to Memphis without being arrested? Presumably you can pose as one of Fanny's slaves on the trip down to New Orleans and thence to Haiti, but even there an official might demand to see the bill of sale for each slave.'

'But staying here is dangerous, too.'

A few days later I heard the rumour that a runaway slave had been captured in Illinois and returned to his master in Tennessee and that story convinced me of the urgency of removing Cudjo from the United States.

When he spoke to me of the joys of living in an all-black nation where he would have a chance to 'study on freedom', as he put it, I tried to convince him that black Haitians were not black Americans and that the differences of culture might be more significant than the fraternity of colour. But he pointed out that President Boyer expressed racial solidarity with American Negroes. I argued that he and his friends could perfectly well imagine a hostile Liberia. Why were they so certain that Haiti would be benign, especially since so many black American settlers had already come back?

We went around and around in circles as we debated versions of a future no one could foresee. The minute attention we brought to the debate, however, proved our mutual affection, my fierce protectiveness of him and his longing for freedom.

I wrote to Marcus Winchester and Richeson Whitby, who were in charge of getting the slaves to New Orleans, and I asked them both for advice about what to do with Mr Jupiter Higgins. I soon had their replies, which I handed over to Cudjo as a reading lesson. He couldn't make out anything – I'd forgotten that though he could read the printed word he had yet to learn to decipher cursive handwriting.

Richeson Whitby counselled us to abandon the scheme altogether since it would be tempting the devil to return an escaped slave to the slave states. 'If you trick out false papers and give your friend a new identity as a free black man under a different name, there is no reason to think that even if people down South accept his new identity they would respect his freedom. A strong healthy black man, especially one with a skill, could be enslaved on the slightest pretext even if it was illegal.'

Marcus Winchester, writing without having consulted Whitby, said that he might be able to convince a riverboat captain to engage Jupiter in Cincinnati under another name as if he were one of Winchester's own slaves who'd been hired out for wages. Hiring out slaves happened all the time, but there was always the risk that someone who'd seen Colonel Tom's leaflets offering a reward for Jupiter's return would be able to identify him. Or that someone who'd known Jupiter in the old days (Colonel Tom was a very sociable man) would recognize him and turn him in.

Once Jupiter joined the Nashoba slaves he'd have to be out-fitted with new papers and a new bill of sale and passed off as one of Frances Wright's slaves. Winchester added, 'Needless to say if this fraud were exposed it could jeopardize the whole trans-action as well as the freedom of the complicitous.' By this ele-gant periphrasis he meant Whitby and himself.

After I'd read all this to Cudjo he put his hands on his knees, pushed himself up to a standing position and said, 'There's my answer. It's too dangerous for your friends and that's all there is to say. If I can find my own way to Haiti I'll go, or I might ship out to Canada where I'll be safe.'

My little fantasy of walking hand in hand with Cudjo through the streets of Port au Prince had evaporated – as well it might. What had I been dreaming of? He, too, seemed to have regis-tered that we were approaching the end of our friendship. When I entered the forge his complex feelings were condensed in a big, outstretched hand that brushed me aside and the other hand that pulled me to him. In the past for me the act of making love had always been a muted, twilit moment of spiritual union but even in those crepuscular embraces I had had to recognize that the body played a part, even a rather athletic part. Now that I was old and stiff and sagging if still driven by a quite youthful ardour, I kept fearing my body would let me down, that there would be positions or acts required of me that I would, tragically and comically, be incapable of performing. Our staging the previous Christmas of *The Merry Wives of Windsor* had reminded me that for the great authors an old person who dares to make love is always a figure of fun.

And yet Cudjo treated me kindly and now that twenty years have flown by since I last saw him I can easily admit that he was the one man in the whole world who made me accept myself as a woman (the language of lovers demands uniqueness, eternity and a universal scale, but in my case I swear, I swear it was true). He explored me, almost as if he were holding aloft a torch, and I stood beside him, as amazed as he by what we were finding. I would whimper or groan and once I wept copiously, I suppose for joy, and every emotion was completely new to me. I'd never uttered these sounds before, I couldn't explain these convulsions nor these spasms of delight but they restored me to myself, just as one might, if prodded by the right interlocutor, suddenly recover a lost childhood language, the first one, the one in which all of one's primitive joys and terrors had been inscribed.

Nineteen

When the ice cracked at the end of February the Cincinnatians were elate, thinking of the rich goods the transport ships might bring them and of the profitable goods they might export again, but Henry and I seized the occasion for our own departure downstream. We slipped away almost unseen and certainly unnoticed, just two valises between us. I left my daughters with Mrs Price, who was delighted to take them in and to use my Cecilia and Emily to inspire her own daughters with a bit of respect and femininity, for Mrs Price's girls had become shockingly brash. I had such respect for Cecilia's good sense and Emily's innocence (for she seemed much younger than her age, which was thirteen) that I had no fear of entrusting them to the motherly Mrs Price. At last my girls would have a room of their own in their comfortable old Mohawk neighbourhood. I promised them all that I would be back for them in two or three months after my exciting adventure.

Henry and Hervieu had a long fraternal embrace on the levee which made the tobacco-spitting Ohio merchants shake their heads in disgust, since they were unused to Continental exuberance in men. I couldn't help but wonder how they would have reacted if they'd witnessed my last clench with Cudjo, a moment that was more awkward, less fluent than the boys' embrace because less optimistic. We were two old people who might never know love again; even this time it had had to surprise us in its completely unexpected and forbidden form.

We descended at Memphis to link up with Whitby and Miss Wright's slaves. When I looked at their thin, sickly faces, jaundiced eyes, cracked bare feet and slat-thin legs I was pleased, after all, that Cudjo hadn't come with us. Quite aside from all the dangers his presence would have posed to our enterprise and to his own security, I think my heart would have broken if I'd seen his distinguished countenance and his exemplary physique amidst such *misère* and *maladie*. And surely the inspectors would have noticed the suspicious difference – Cudjo's robustness, his intelligent glance, the beauty of his skin and the pride in his carriage. Once again everything had turned out for the best.

In New Orleans we were greeted by Fanny and her much older friend whom we were no longer to call William Phiquepal but rather Guillaume Sylvain Casimir Phiquepal d'Arusmont, his correct aristocratic name, which the ever-unpredictable Fanny preferred.

She embraced me with almost a parody of femininity, as if she could adopt the giddy affection and the whispering remonstrations of a middle-class woman only by putting them between inverted commas. She hugged me and almost touched my cheek with hers as she produced the cooing contralto burbles one addresses to a baby, but I caught her winking at Whitby, almost as if to say, 'See, I remember how to be part of the absurd menagerie of women, if I earnestly put my mind to it.'

I found Monsieur d'Arusmont an old man at fifty. He had the breath of someone who ate badly, digested not at all and refused to have his rotten teeth pulled. His hair was lank and thin and if he brushed it to one side it remained there out of insipidity. In the same way if he frowned, the creases, once imprinted, remained indelible on his brow. His stooped shoulders were covered with dandruff, his walk betrayed a worrying shuffle and lack of co-ordination, and his body froze in whatever position he'd last put it. In fact everything – his hair, his frown, his posture – seemed a fossil of itself. But let there be the slightest chance to express an opinion and this whole broken mechanism suddenly functioned with lethal accuracy. He had an opinion on every subject and he held to it tenaciously and attacked all doubters with hissing scorn.

I suppose in many ways he was like Trollope, but whereas the poor Pater had once been a brilliant man now sorely degraded by illness, one felt that d'Arusmont was a *pauvre type* – vengeful, petty, wilful – who'd been elevated by circumstance. Trollope loved his family, though he thought me imprudent, Henry disobedient and the girls of no interest whatsoever. I suppose I mean to say he was a good father to Tom and Anthony . . . Perhaps I'm forced to acknowledge that Fanny seemed to be deliberately courting a man similar to the one I'd ended up with through bad luck. I know I shouldn't blacken the Pater's name, but my intimacy with Cudjo had shown me what a man could be.

I couldn't help but look at black men on the streets of New Orleans if only to acknowledge their beauty, their supple waists, blinding smiles, rhythmic walk, as if every act of crossing the street were an entrance made before hundreds of spectators. No one resembled Cudjo but I found his beard here, his nose there, his different laughs at the end of an alleyway (the whinny) or floating down from a balcony (the unending guffaw). Maybe what my friendship with Mr Higgins had done was to sensitize me to the allure of black men, an awakening that necessarily led to a perception of their myriad differences.

Henry was shipped off to England after many tearful embraces. I feared I'd never see him again in this life – at least that was a reasonable fear, given his bad health, though my love for him was so strong it had nothing to do with reason. If he lived I knew he'd have to strike out on yet another new path, but I was convinced that his experience in America, and his disillusionment, would give him a new . . . shall we call it 'realism'? – though in fact that's a word for nothing but cynicism and cunning.

Fanny engaged a fine little brig of 163 tons called the *John Quincy Adams*. She was transporting thirteen adult slaves, eighteen of their children, herself, Whitby, Monsieur d'Arusmont and me. The voyage out would take twenty to thirty days and the voyage back, if favoured by the winds, between ten and twenty.

I call her people 'slaves' but they'd been freed while still in Tennessee, which meant that at any moment before the *Adams* sailed an unscrupulous official could always have claimed they were runaways and imprisoned them. They, too, knew that, and scarcely could decide which to fear more, a Louisiana jail or a Haitian farm. Fanny, who'd never treated them better or worse than servants, had said nothing to reassure them. I knew from Cudjo how he and his Cincinnati cronies would be disturbed by the prospect of settling in an unknown land.

To help finance the journey Fanny had been talked into transporting lard and pork as cash products to Haiti. On the return trip she'd bring back Haitian coffee. Although Fanny needed money – she'd lost about 17,000 dollars at Nashoba, a third of her fortune and a sum comparable to the totality of the vanished Trollope fortune, lost on the Bazaar – perhaps she erred in combining philanthropy with trade now. It certainly laid her open to criticism later.

When the *John Quincy Adams* pulled out of American territorial waters I looked to see if Miss Wright's former slaves would raise even the faintest huzzah, but they stared aimlessly around them, no two in the same direction. Nor were there any clusters of children around their parents – Miss Wright's pedagogical fear of 'parental contamination' had dissolved even those bonds. I wondered what the Haitians would make of these malarial, broken-spirited colonists, none of whom was responsive to the universal human family ties.

The nights were hot and still and the keel cut slowly through stagnating kelp and seaweed. Fanny and I had our hammocks moved to the deck but the smell of the vegetation in the water kept us awake. After a smooth trip we made the harbour of Port au Prince. The two sides of the harbour swallowed our ship like the submerged jaws of an alligator. Between the two coasts was an uninhabited island – in fact, everything looked uninhabited, even the coasts. No smoke rising from cooking fires, no cleared fields to push back the dense, tropical vegetation, no villages looking down on the steamy bay, no fishing boats to ripple the glassy surface of the water, no cries of birds or somersaults of dolphins: nothing.

When at last we approached Port au Prince the city seemed deserted. The houses were all just one storey tall, the pitched roofs held up on slender wood columns, some of them not quite perpendicular. Grass grew down from the hills and into the city. The land had been ravaged by recent floods and ruts of red mud oozed on every side. Along the shore mangrove trees extended their grotesque roots into the water. In the streets there were no wagons or diligences, just a few almost naked barefoot children and a soldier. Men in rags materialized out of the shadows under the eaves of the customs house and resentfully tied to half-rotting stumps the hawsers thrown down to them on the dock. I looked at our ex-slaves and saw crystals of fear forming in their eyes.

The sun falls fast in the tropics and always at six in the evening, dividing the hot, sullen day from the hot, dangerous night. By the time we were ashore the sun was in precipitous decline and a slow drum, the rhythm of a sleeper's pulse, had begun its ominous beat somewhere out of sight. Two huge buildings arose over the uneven lines of little houses – the Cathedral on one hill and the Presidential Palace on another. The palace was a rambling white structure, the windows glowing with light. We could see a delegation on horseback descending from the palace in a cloud of dust accompanying a small uniformed man in a carriage.

Up close we saw he was a mulatto with pale blue blinking eyes and a white-gloved hand that kept shaping his already brilliantined moustaches into ever-stiffer antennae.

He descended from his carriage with the greatest alacrity. 'Miss Wright?' he asked in a high, nasal voice, very aristocratic. When she smiled loftily and held out her hand he bent to graze it. 'Mrs Trollope,' she said, indicating me.

271

He made another reverence though he raised an eyebrow for a fraction of an instant at the state of my attire or perhaps out of confusion as to who I might be. He said, 'I am the Secretary General, Inginiac.'

Miss Wright presented Phiquepal with his full mellifluous name and Inginiac gave him a very deep bow and even raised his tricorne. She then named Mr Whitby as her brother-in-law – oh, and the captain of the ship was also introduced. Then Miss Wright, indicating her freed bondsmen with a sweep of her hand, said, 'And these are your new Haitians.'

General Inginiac merely pursed his lips and tapped on them with his small gloved index finger.

'I bear a second letter from Lafayette,' Miss Wright said in her lovely if Scottish-accented French, which meant that the usually swallowed *r*s were rolled with Burgundian relish and the *u*s were impeccably rendered. 'It is addressed to your great President as a salutation from lovers of liberty everywhere, addressed to the leader of the first black Republic in the New World, a man we must all –'

'Black?' Inginiac echoed, clearly peeved. 'Well, at least not white. You may be astonished that all individuals of African blood, no matter how diluted and no matter where they were born, will be granted residency in Haiti and eventually citizenship. But whites are not permitted to own land here nor to marry our citizens nor to become citizens themselves. We may admire certain white nations, especially the French –' and here he bowed deeply again to Phiquepal – 'but we regard all whites as our natural enemies. All except you, *chère* Madame, and your friends and the great General Lafayette.'

And here he bowed again and slapped at a mosquito on his white-jacketed forearm, which set the fringe of his heavy gold epaulettes swinging and left a bright point of blood on his sleeve.

Night had fallen.

'But let us not linger here, where the air can be mephitic. Your blacks will be taken somewhere nearby and fed and watered and given bedding and you shall be able to inspect them soon to make certain everything is to your satisfaction. Now I must address a few words to them. Will you translate, Miss Wright?'

She nodded and soon I heard her speaking in English to her astonished freed men on behalf of Inginiac:

'We are born with the same interests because the same blood – the blood of Great Africa which should render our union indivisible – runs equally in our veins. Renounce for ever – for yourselves and for your posterity – those lands where you were bent under the most intolerable abasement known to man. Ah! far from blushing because we owe our existence to Africa, let us glory in it!'

The poor freed men looked stunned, even more so when Inginiac went on and called on all whites to renounce pride of skin. After this torrent of words (and the incomprehensible reference to 'blushing') the black Americans were speechless. Miss Wright thanked the Secretary General in their stead.

'Now,' Inginiac said briskly, changing the subject, 'Mrs Trollope, Monsieur d'Arusmont, Mr Whitby and you, dear lady, will return to the Palace with me, where you will be given accommodations of your own and made most comfortable. President Boyer is hoping you will dine with him at nine.'

We were handed up into the carriage, an open barouche, and we set off at a dusty clip, surrounded by mounted soldiers carrying torches. In the lurid glare, I noticed that these uniformed horsemen were barefoot but had spurs strapped to their naked ankles. One of them had a tailor's list wrapped around his waist as a belt and an old straw hat crushed down over his head.

Once we arrived at the Palace, laid out as a solid two-storeyed house to resemble the Petit Palais at Versailles, we were ushered to our rooms, brilliantly lit with gas lamps of the latest model if otherwise sparsely furnished. My room had a bed under a mosquito net, a chair and a dressing table. I rushed to the window to look down on the city but it still seemed uninhabited. No cooking, no lights, no movement.

To the north were the plains of Cul de Sac defined by a chain of low mountains that swooped all the way to the sea, the Channel of Ste Marie, as a pretty lady-in-waiting explained to me in school-room French. On the other side of the harbour these mountains were matched by others, called 'La Coupe'. She extended her chubby hand in one direction and then the other, saying, 'It's almost a league from one gate of the city to the other,' and she rounded her eyes with wonder, though I couldn't help noticing that the city walls were in bad repair and had collapsed in several places. 'There is Fort Pétion,' she said, pointing to a low, decrepit building. 'That is the sacred tomb for the bowels of our first President – Anne-Alexandre Pétion.'

'Bowels?' I asked.

She nodded gaily. I wondered about burying the bowels of a man named Anne. She then designated the different districts of the city and named them in her charming, sing-song way: 'La Croix, Le Marre, Bazilles, Hôpital, Léogâne . . .' She pointed out Fort Islet at the entrance to the harbour. Every district was covered with dark, interchangeable hovels. I noticed, now that we were looking at it from a different angle, that a large part of the Cathedral was a charred ruin. My companion explained that the fires of 1820 and 1822 had damaged much of the Cathedral and all the important buildings in the city. '*Très triste,*' she said, and turned her lips down in her pudgy, delightful face, an incongruous expression that instantly melted away and gave way to her more natural exuberance.

She seemed a bit shocked that I had no lovely gown and diamonds to change in to, but she sent for a fabulous flowered shawl of her own which she decorated with a bouquet. She did wonders for my coiffure and set me generally to rights. I explained to her I was very poor and was in her paradisal country thanks only to the generosity of Miss Wright. Mention of Miss Wright elicited a brilliant smile: '*Mademoiselle Vite est une dame extraordinaire – une grande amie à tous les gens de couleur!*' I kept wishing I could steal this fragrant, sunny child and give her as a present to Cudjo, who would know how to appreciate her.

It turned out everyone did. She was called Hersilie and was President Boyer's favourite, his adopted daughter and the daughter of his predecessor, President Pétion, whose bowels she had so casually mentioned. She told me that President Boyer, in his mid-fifties, was '*un vrai amour*,' who never forgot to send her little affectionate letters whenever he was away pacifying another part of the island. He wrote letters as well to his only child, his daughter Azéma. 'In fact he's surrounded by women. His wife, Joutte Lachenais, who also happens to be my mother and formerly the consort of President Pétion. There's also a lovely girl called Fine, Azéma and me. My sister Célie died five years ago and was given a sumptuous funeral. And now there's *you*, dear Madame Trop Lotte.'

The President was waiting for us at the entrance to the magnificent reception rooms, surrounded by all the Port-au-Princiens and -Princiennes. He kissed each woman's hand with a dreamy look – he was evidently a famous charmer, a practised *vieux beau*. He had permanently lifted eyebrows, curly hair, a long nose, sensual but not thick lips and a gold hoop in one ear exactly like Lafayette's. He was slender, with high cheekbones and an aloof poetic air that was an affectation he often forgot to maintain – and then he was all soft smiles like his beloved Hersilie. Despite his martial airs he wasn't a military man but rather an autocrat who wanted to be loved. Later, when we became friends, Hersilie would show me her stepfather's letters in which he often professed to be astonished by how warmly cheered he was by his people in Santo Domingo or on the peninsula of Samaná or elsewhere. He was a mouth-breather, which made him appear less intelligent than I later discovered him to be.

I was escorted into dinner by the English consul but I couldn't take my eyes off President Boyer, who seemed such a comedian. He was always in motion, he drank nothing but water and he was extremely slender and looked wonderful in his military uniform, which my dinner partner, the consul Charles MacKenzie, told me was merely a colonel's kit and thus considered the height of modesty for the head of state to wear. He pulled out her chair for Fanny, who was magnificent in a white ball gown.

I was astonished that she had had the wit to bring with her such finery – or that she still even owned a gown. She must have known that she would be expected to appear *en grande tenue*.

President Boyer was a master of the flowery phrase, though I learned he was from humble beginnings – the son of a tailor and his mother a slave from the Congo. No sooner were we seated than Boyer began to make toasts to Miss Wright. One, I remember, ended with the surprising formula, *'Je me félicite déjà d'avoir une occasion aussi solenelle de manifester hautement les sentiments dont je suis pénétré'* ('I congratulate myself on already having such a solemn occasion to proclaim the feelings with which I am imbued'). Miss Wright, who would have scoffed at such tributes from a mere white man, touched the place above and between her breasts and smiled with the womanly grace of a Pauline Bonaparte.

Since no one seemed to speak English, Mr MacKenzie launched into a long anecdote about his frustrations of the day with his lazy servants.

The dinner was for forty guests seated at two tables. The large windows on opposite sides of the formal room with its cool marble floors and cream-and-gilt ceiling were wide open, though almost invisibly screened with fine gauze stretched tight against the mosquitoes. A cool breeze circulated around us and bore the scent of old-fashioned roses and banksia. I noticed Monsieur d'Arusmont seated at the lower table, wedged between two jolly, portly Negresses. He looked intensely uncomfortable and his whiteness suddenly struck me as something like a skin disease.

Mr MacKenzie had a wicked tongue and delighted in ridiculing the Haitians. He'd already been on the island for five years and longed to be reassigned. He was accompanied on his mission to advance and protect British commerce by two vice-consuls, John Fisher and Francis Bishop, who waved gamely but a bit sheepishly to us from the lower table when they sensed we were discussing them.

'Where are all the people in this city?' I asked.

He smiled. 'You'll see them and hear them – and *smell* them! if the wind blows in the wrong direction – bright and early tomorrow morning. Almost all Haitians go to bed at eventide. They're an indolent people, incapable of work or anything more strenuous than cheering their champion rooster on in a cock-fight.'

'Who is the gentleman who met our ship?' I asked, not wanting to use Inginiac's name or look his way.

'He is the second-in-command and is known as the Talleyrand of Haiti, so cruel and scheming is he. Whereas our host is a sentimental man who never forgoes a chance to quote the verse of André Chénier or some words of our local Haitian poets –' (and here Mr MacKenzie rolled his eyes to express his contempt).

'But to turn to the bright side, our host's adopted daughter –'

'Oh! Isn't she adorable!' MacKenzie exclaimed, his one outburst of enthusiasm and so uncritical it made him blush at sounding so youthful.

'Adorable. She kept mentioning our host's wife –'

He laughed. 'I know, I know. The marital or rather amorous complications in the lives of the men around us would need a professional genealogist or gossip to sort out. Let us simply say no one here is married and no two children have the same two parents. But it's the same on every social level. A woman isn't married in Haiti but rather *placée*.' He folded his hands neatly over his considerable belly and I began to hate him.

'Why do they all have such swinish morals?' I asked, playing along.

'Well,' the Consul drawled, 'they *are* savages, after all, and then the French were no better. They were all bedding down with their black mistresses, begging your pardon. Where do you think all these mulattos surrounding us came from? They make 110 distinctions of colour here. There are *nègres*, the usual word for blacks, there are *griffons*, who are three-quarters black, *marabouts*, *mulâtres*, the *sacatra*, the *métis*, *quaterons*, who are one-quarter black, and *octavons*, one-eighth. The mulattos are especially arrogant, since they were already free *before* the Haitian Revolution.

277

Often they owned slaves. They are the *anciens libres*, the 'formerly free'. Of course there *are* those who set great store by being black. The late King, for instance –'

'You mean Emperor?'

Mr MacKenzie laughed. 'Well might you be confused, but Christophe was a king – King Henry I is what he called himself. He ruled the North, which was predominantly black, and our host or his predecessor Monsieur Pétion ruled the West, which as you can see is the mulatto paradise.'

'What happened to the King?'

Mr MacKenzie smiled mildly. 'If you're very lucky the President will show you after dinner the suicide pistol the King used to shoot himself once he realized his own army had turned against him. He was a monster but brave and decisive. By the way, the President might also show you the rusty anchor of the *Santa Maria* that Christopher Columbus dropped here when he discovered America. It's twice as tall as a man and the Haitians are talking about bartering it for ready money.' Here Mr MacKenzie winked.

'What makes these people so diabolic?' I asked. I could see that Boyer was raising another glass of champagne to toast Miss Wright. Her cheeks were rosy from the drink perhaps but for a moment in this light she looked young and healthy once more.

'I must insist, dear lady, the French were no better. One *grand seigneur* had the road leading up to his plantation lined with stakes on which were skewered the rotting heads of all those slaves who'd dared to disobey him.'

I pushed my plate of fish away and the barefoot major-domo, dressed in an impeccable white uniform, rushed up to remove it, carrying it away while holding it out at arms' length and turning his mouth down as if the fish had offended us all.

'Sorry, sorry,' the Consul said, chuckling. 'And the *grandes mesdames* were no better. One French lady was so furious when she discovered the pastry was overdone that she had the black chef hurled into the white-hot oven and roasted alive. All the guests had a good laugh.'

'Ah, the French,' I said.

'Not to say they're not damn wily,' the Consul continued, insensitive to irony. 'Why just five years ago a French officer, the Baron de Mackao, sailed into the harbour here with his fleet and demanded huge reparations from Haiti for the property it had confiscated from French citizens during the Revolution – the price was set at some sixty million English pounds! Our host sank into a half-stupor of fear and confusion. They were all certain the French were going to re-enslave them.'

'Oh, the poor people!' I said in spite of myself, picturing the manacles on Cudjo's wrists.

The Consul looked at me with fire in his eyes and ran a hand through his bright red hair. 'How touching, your concern,' he said with contempt for me. 'In any event you need not waste your sympathy on the Haitians since it all turned out moderately well. The President and the Senate voted to pay the ruinous indemnity in five yearly instalments of 150 million francs, which led to a new issue of nearly worthless currency.'

I suppose I didn't gurgle here with the right condescending laugh, for the Consul added, 'Ah, dear lady, you'll find they're all like big children. The President imagines he's terribly dashing and every Sunday he reviews the troops. He lives for parades or for patriot plays put on by the local *circus*, of all things, plays with titles like *The Siege of Port-au-Prince*, though the script doesn't mention that Boyer was ready to burn down his own city rather than defend it. King Henry actually did burn Cape Haitian when the French weighed anchor in the port; he was imitating another of his favourite moments in history, the Russians' burning of Moscow when Napoleon invaded. The King inhabited an operetta world. He made almost all his officers into nobles with amusing titles like the Count de Limonade and the Duke de Marmalade. My poor Mr Fisher, the vice-consul, was trying diligently to flatter the President by telling him he could be "greater than Hannibal", *plus grand qu'Annibal*. The President was deeply offended and drew himself up to his full five feet three inches and said, "*Comment, Consul, moi cannibal!*"'

279

I put my hand in front of my mouth and mimed a rocking laugh. When I'd let a sufficient pause for mirth tick by I said, 'What is that drum that's always beating?'

'It could be anything, for the city is often given over to wild municipal dances that last four and five days at a time and that occur at least once a month when the President isn't in one of his suicidal moods. Haitians, you should know, dear lady, are partial to suicide and if they're the least vexed they'll do themselves in – which they imagine is a quick way to return to Africa.' Here he raised his eyebrows before continuing. 'But in fact it's a voodoo drum. The descendants of fugitive slaves, called Maroons, live in the jungle and there they practise their horrid rites at night.'

'Have you ever attended one?' I asked sceptically.

'To be sure,' he said, tasting his yam *dauphinoise*. 'One day I was talking to a very sophisticated Haitian who was educated in France and he was rolling his eyes and pretending that voodoo was nothing but an invention of European journalists and whenever I brought up a bit of counter-evidence he'd drown me out with his tsking – when, all of sudden, out of his pocket fell his *ouanga* bag, an evil charm. We both stared at it, this foul sack in our path, black with dried blood and glued shut with the feathers of a slaughtered chicken, and we both gasped and then he said, very quietly, "All right. Be ready at midnight and we'll attend a mass."'

'A midnight mass!' I kept wishing Fanny could hear all this, but of course she would have expressed her indignation right away and ruined everything.

'Wait, wait,' he said. 'Although the government officially persecutes Voodoo priests and priestesses, everyone here is a believer, including our host, who has been bathed publicly in the blood of goats and has made gifts to the Voodoo clergy. Reputedly he has buried a charm in the garden here to make sure none of his successors rules more than a year. There are even those who say he has eaten what is politely called in African "the goat without horns" or human flesh.'

'They actually *are* cannibals?' I asked, incredulous.

He said, 'They cook human flesh with Congo beans, which are small and bitter, and I saw them bury a severed child's hand in a pail of yams and meat from a black goat sacred to Satan – the child's palm eaten raw is their favourite delicacy. When a mother was reproached for eating her own daughters she said coolly, "And who has a better right – aren't I the one who made them?"'

I knew he was trying to make me too sick to eat my yams but I finished them with total self-control and asked, 'But the midnight mass?'

'Well, we went far into the jungle, guided by the constant drums, and at last came to a clearing where the many adepts, men and women, were wearing red bandanas around their waists. There was a sort of shack or temple, called a *haumfort*, papered over inside with engravings from an illustrated London newspaper as well as pictures of the Virgin Mary and other saints. On a banner were written the words, "Société des Fleurs za Dahomian," for they all imagine they originally came from Dahomey. Each religious fraternity or *compagnie* has a king, a name and a flag. The night I went the *compagnie* were all facing the altar, a box that reputedly housed a sacred snake. Everyone present was sworn to secrecy. The Queen stood on the serpent's box, went into a trance and answered the questions posed by the congregation.

'A novice was initiated into the religion. The Voodoo King, who's called the Papaloi, drew a black circle on the earth and traced it with shiny stones, some crescent-shaped, that my guide said came from Africa. Then the Papaloi gave him herbs and horsehair and pieces of horn to hold. The adepts chanted an African song. The novice began to tremble and dance. When they dance, the women isolate and gyrate their pelvises while holding the rest of their bodies stationary.'

'That must be diverting to watch,' I said.

'Yes, Mrs Trollope, it's a filthy business. They believe the dying must be fed at all costs and they force food on their dying friends with their last breath. One must not leave this world with an empty stomach. When the person dies he is laid out in his house and the wake lasts *nine* nights as the family and friends laugh and drink and make merry and the body nearly rots away. Then there's the magic death cult, but we'll leave that for another evening.'

I smiled weakly. There was one question I'd been longing to ask all evening and now, as I sensed I was about to be separated from this supremely opinionated and cynical man, I simply had to articulate it: 'Tell me, Consul, what will become of Miss Wright's slaves?' I looked over and saw that she and the President were huddled closely together, discussing politics, no doubt. He must have been thrilled that she wasn't a grim little abolitionist, just as she was deeply honoured to be the first white woman to be received as a guest of the new nation.

'They'll hate it here, of course, since they will be mistreated as blacks and as English-speakers and foreigners and non-Catholics, not to mention non-Voodooists. Our host has two fates reserved for them. Either he'll send them to the peninsula of Samaná, a disease-ridden place, low and swampy, where they'll no doubt succumb to fevers and ague. Previously, some of the American ex-slaves were sent to the border to protect it before Boyer took Santo Domingo away from the Spanish. Or the President will conscript the adult American men into the army. The soldiers must clothe and shoe themselves, though most are barefoot, and they must feed themselves as well. If they become ill they must also cure themselves, for Haitian doctors are all charlatans.'

'But why did Boyer and Inginiac and Granville encourage American ex-slaves to come here?'

I half-feared Mr MacKenzie's answer. I felt that all my life I let myself believe in something earnestly only to be seated next to some fluent cynic who in a single remark could disabuse me of my illusions. I was still capable of being rudely undeceived.

'The country is badly underpopulated – there are just one million people here and the island is four hundred miles long. And then Boyer hoped it would make a good impression, inviting all these black Americans to Haiti – he's obsessed with impressing white foreigners. And Inginiac thought that Granville would find the best and most skilled blacks, but when he discovered Granville had just swept up the worst refuse from Philadelphia and New-York he wrote an angry letter to your abolitionist journal, *The Genius of Universal Emancipation*, and here in Haiti he had poor Granville demoted and made a *lycée* principal. The other evening we had to sit through the graduating students' recitals in Latin, if you please, from Cicero and Sallust! Of course they were just parrots and had no idea what they were saying.'

The President, who had scarcely touched his food since he'd been so busy talking to Miss Wright, now led her off to the ball-room and I was forced to abandon my delicious stewed guavas on a fragile meringue. As Mr MacKenzie offered me his arm I said, sighing, 'It all sounds frightening and sordid and hopeless.'

'Oh, but you must see it as opera buffa, Mrs Trollope. I do.'

'That would be hard to do,' I said, 'since like Miss Wright I am concerned about the future of the African Nation. Don't forget that Miss Wright is the first woman in America who ever acted publicly to oppose slavery.'

Here he tucked in his chin, or rather chins, and with his finger quite literally wiped away his smile. 'His Majesty's government asked me to write a report on my observations of Haiti and whether I thought that slaves in the British colonies should be freed. In short, I was solicited to say whether in my best judge-ment the black race, or the African Nation as you so poetically put it, was capable of ruling itself. I was obliged to state cate-gorically *no*. It's a particularly dramatic question now because the whites in Jamaica fear an invasion by a Haitian liberating army – all nonsense, I'm certain. Though to be sure, some escaped Jamaican slaves founded Liberia in 1822.'

I let the implications of his remarks spread their ripples through my mind. 'Does that mean your report will condemn tens of thousands of Africans to continued slavery throughout the English colonies?'

'I wouldn't put it like that,' he said peevishly.

'You odious little man,' I said, withdrawing my arm and walking away to join Hersilie in the ballroom.

'You are shaking all over,' Hersilie said, patting me sweetly.

'I've just had a most unpleasant conversation,' I said.

At this moment President Boyer came waltzing up beside us with a coolly abstracted-looking Miss Wright in his arms. Phiquepal, who'd been watching ferociously, now hurried up and danced Fanny away. Boyer said, 'You're quite pale, Mrs Trollope. Not our treacherous tropical nights, I trust.'

Hersilie produced a little moue and said, 'Mr MacKenzie has upset her.'

The President's eyes lit up and made a quick, merry trip around my poor old face. 'Bravo!' he said in a low, prolonged sigh. 'I'm sure he's been filling your ears with frightening things about our dear Haiti.'

'He is a wretched man,' I said, looking away, cross-eyed with fury, which only made Boyer laugh uproariously – Cudjo's warm, spontaneous outburst, not his high whinny but his low laugh as thrumming as the boom of the Presbyterian bell he'd repaired.

That night in bed I wept. Without quite noticing it, I'd been holding out with my fantasy about settling some day in Haiti with Cudjo. Now I recognized there was no place for him, nor for me – certainly not for us as a couple – in this country or anywhere else.

Twenty

The President took a liking to me, possibly because I'd defied the hateful English Consul or perhaps because Hersilie, his darling, had vouched for me. He and his whole family but not his courtiers decided to accompany us into the high hills or *mornes* to his country estate for a few days. His genuine pleasure in life and his intense self-satisfaction made him a most agreeable companion and I kept thinking it a pity that every small-minded white plantation owner in the South couldn't spend a day with him as his guest.

His highly developed capacity for enjoyment found its expression in the flowery phrases he was always producing. He actually said to me that 'my visit had given him the most sensitive pleasure and that he had always considered the English nation as one of the most worthy of his esteem.'

I knew that Fanny had a horror of all the outer display of the *couple*. In fact, as her biographer I've found it maddening that I could never be certain whether she was having an affair with Lafayette or not or with George Flower or not or with Robert Dale Owen or not. All the evidence and rumour pointed to the reality of these intimacies, but in front of me, at least, Fanny never betrayed through lingering looks or tender smiles or solicitous words any sentiment other than idealistic fervour or businesslike partnership.

The reader can thus imagine my astonishment when Fanny let the unappetizing Phiquepal sit beside her in the President's carriage and hold her hand and whisper his foul breath into her face. At first I thought she was shrewdly producing all the manifestations of an amorous commitment to Monsieur d'Arusmont in order to discourage Boyer's attentions. But then I realized Fanny was genuinely colour-blind though she was highly sensitive to distinctions of power and rank and worldly importance. She liked the President and welcomed the verbal bouquets he tossed her way and registered his every move, just as she was totally unalive to the feelings and actions of her ex-slaves. She didn't see them, not because they were black but because they were humble. Fanny, who'd been a radical since her first childhood rebellions, had always been subject to the magnetism of powerful men – Bentham, Lafayette, Jefferson, the Owens, Flower (whose appeal was more sexual and personal than political and public). Fanny might argue for the rights of women in as vigorous a manner as poor Mary Shelley's mother, Mary Wollstonecraft, but Fanny, without even being conscious of it, was fully awakened only when a great man walked into the room. The man could be as much a *poseur* as Lafayette or as decrepit as Jefferson or as misogynistic as Bentham, but Fanny would still build him a shrine in her heart. In retrospect I thought one reason she'd been so disagreeable to Lafayette at Monticello was that in the presence of two powerful ancients she was tempted to give up the serial monotheism of her devotion for an uncomfortable dualism, which her every instinct made her reject. She preferred to wound Lafayette than to worship two gods, to overthrow Cronus rather than disappoint Zeus.

If my analysis explained why she was gratified by Boyer's courtesies, it didn't account for her middle-class wifeyness around d'Arusmont. Every day produced new concessions to his growing power over her. During our second evening at the country estate

286

of Monimance, d'Arusmont decided that Fanny, whom I'd never seen inebriated, was drinking too much wine; he waved away the servitor who approached her dessert glass with an exquisite bottle of Château d'Yquem. Fanny merely smiled, a most unaccustomed expression on her face, the look of a little girl who's been caught doing something naughty. The next night Fanny was explaining Nashoba's successes and failures to the President. At one point she made a very broad gesture and d'Arusmont, who was glued to her side, caught her hand on the upsweep and returned it to her lap. Fanny's first reaction was indignation but then she mastered her smouldering and smiled meekly at Phiquepal.

We went out riding on horseback and in carriages every day and often we moved on to a different presidential estate – I vaguely recall the names of Métivier and Pois la général, Vaudreuil, Pois la ravine, Drouillard and Robin, Brache and Deschapelles. One was as small as an English cottage, sheltered by a dirty kapok tree whose pods kept exploding white filaments onto the low eaves. Another was a rambling white wood mansion that had a whole wing falling into ruin, bare floors and sisal rugs beside the bed but heavy eighteenth-century silverware and eggshell-thin dishes.

Wherever we went I kept seeing the same hand-painted French wallpaper showing up in the principal room. I couldn't figure out this ubiquity until I looked closer and discovered that the paper was held in place just by straight pins and that it was dismounted and spirited from house to house in the middle of the night.

The President loved light banter, dancing, music, a game of whist and even a shrieking, childish game of Blind Man's Buff. The lovely Hersilie Pétion was the centre of every activity, though she found the evenings long and often fell asleep in one of her perishable gowns, leaning against her august stepfather's shoulders. Once he was so afraid of awakening her that he pulled out a pearl-handled knife and cut off his uniform sleeve so that he could steal away. I was so touched by his gallantry and consideration that I mouthed a silent 'Oh!' and clutched my hands together in the air in front of me with excitement, but when I turned to Phiquepal he merely breathed a snicker through his nose and returned to his book. Everyone was engaged in frivolities that could have been painted by Watteau, except the dainty girls in swings and the satin-suited swains plucking lutes were all Moors, whereas we the attendants were white. Monsieur d'Arusmont brought a touch of winter into so much spring. He was reading one of Condillac's ponderous volumes of moral philosophy that, if I'm not mistaken, relies on mathematics to prove virtue!

Boyer sometimes shared with us his political concerns, especially when he saw that Miss Wright was informed and interested. He said that France was attempting to recolonize Haiti by crippling it economically. At this very moment his envoy was in Le Havre treating with French officials, negotiating to lower the yearly indemnity that Haiti must pay. 'The French bankers have set the rates so high that our entire yearly national income goes toward paying just the interest and the debt is never reduced by a centime. My envoy has pointed out that the treaty stipulates that the debt is to be paid in the Haitian currency, the gourde, but Charles X doesn't like that one bit, especially since the gourde has lost seventy-five per cent of its value in the last five years.' He smiled his gentle smile and remembered suddenly that as a great leader he should turn a beautiful phrase or strike a romantic pose. In one of his houses he had even hung a portrait of himself in a Roman toga, and here at Deschapelles in the stairwell there was a painting of a laird in a kilt with a sporran in front and a tartan slung over one shoulder as he stood against a background of mountain and stormy sky – except the laird was black, was Boyer himself!

Whenever we plied him with serious questions he'd answer them seriously. One afternoon we went walking through an overgrown garden of pines dropping their slender needles on the ground, and we stopped by a fountain and basin in which the water was so pure it looked invisible, so that the fish in the pond appeared to be floating in the air. The President broke his silence and said, 'You mention the French threat. I should tell you that we're building a new city up on the Coupe above Port-au-Prince, a salubrious new city that French warships will not be able to threaten from the harbour. We also need an administrative city where we can store our national archives in an impregnable fort. It will be named Pétionville after the George Washington of our Republic, Hersilie's revered father.' And here he smiled at the sweet child who was wearing white lace gloves and carrying a matching parasol, pacing the old, gloomy garden paths. When we looked up from the invisible water and turned to glimpse the villa in the sun's last rays, the balconies and verandas were rioting with bougainvillaea like Turkey carpets hurled out the window to be beat clean.

One evening after a superb dinner (we were just eight, *en petit comité*, as the President said) I pronounced the dreaded word 'voodoo'.

He sighed and said, 'Did Mr MacKenzie tell you his famous story of the child's hand in the cocoa-bean stew? That's one of his favourites, which he always trots out to new members of the foreign community. Mrs Trollope, I rule a small country of extremely poor people who are only now emerging from two centuries of brutal oppression. Magic was the only thing that gave a nation of slaves a sense of power – over their masters, over life and death and love and sickness, sometimes over each other. It sustained their dream of a continent of their own and the nearly mythical freedom of the distant past. The French slave owners wouldn't allow the slaves to speak in their own languages – in fact the Africans were deliberately assigned to groups so that the only common language would be a debased pidgin French the masters taught them. Not real French but a ghastly *patois* devoid of grammar and anything but a rudimentary vocabulary. The miracle is that the children of these pidgin-talkers evolved a complex, fluent creole of their own devising, a wonderful poetic tongue that I must teach you one of these days.' The President smiled at Hersilie who poured us out thimblesful of pungent coffee from the gold stem, shaped like a swan's beak, of a white Napoleonic pot. She then handed around the gold-bordered demitasse cups and a plate of the most pungent chocolates I ever tasted, chocolates with the density of black diamonds. The pause for this elegant, spoon-swirling ritual set Boyer off on a different tack: 'Of course the Christians are no better than the Voodoo clergy. We just had to endure a disgraceful battle between an Irish priest and a Roman cleric each claiming to be the official appointed head of the Haitian Church. The denunciations on each side were so vile and acrimonious and childish that I had to exile both men. The Italian, I fear, departed on a ship that sank in the Atlantic and the Irish priest is now stumbling drunkenly through the United States. And the Pope is so angry that we rejected his nuncio that he refuses to send us a new one. The priests here, especially the Jesuits, have been excessively adaptable and have even incorporated many of the African deities into the church calendar as new "saints" or perhaps just "blesseds." Judas, I fear, has been given a strange role of redemption that might surprise the Vatican.' He smiled the delicate smile of the connoisseur of human absurdity and lifted his permanently lifted eyebrows still higher. With almost no transition a deep sadness washed over his face. 'So many conflicts: Catholics and Voodooists, French and Haitians, whites and blacks and among my own Africans so much contempt by the mulattos for the blacks – and of each lighter degree for every darker gradation.' Hersilie rose and stood behind him and ran her cool little hands over his troubled brow, her fingers so attentive to his chagrin and so eager to soothe away his heartache that I suspected her of some sort of gentle filial voodoo of her own.

Here I am in Florence so many years later and I'm sitting here scribbling in the coolness of our wonderful loggia, which looks out on a garden shaded by thickly blooming wisteria vines and I'm hoping my son Tom will come by and give his mother his arm and walk her about the garden for her little daily trot. I'm at peace but I can't help but think of all the deaths that separate me from my tale. President Boyer – exiled by his own people and divested of his properties, dying in Paris in the arms of one

290

of his decrepit black generals. His darling Hersilie mysteriously dead in Jamaica during the first years of their exile – she was just twenty-five. And all the others, my darlings . . . And I, all the while, whether ill or well, rising every morning at four to grind out my five pages, writing to pay for life and pay for death, so many deaths, sometimes so tired that I could not think of the most common words and I longed for a quick, witty conversation with a clever woman that would deposit bright new currency into my depleted verbal account.

Next week, when he comes back from a trip, I'm to have a seance with the great Scottish spiritualist, Mr Home (pronounced 'Hume,' like the philosopher), who's all the rage in Florence and by whom Mrs Browning absolutely swears (though Mr Browning scoffs at him and has written a most unpleasant poem about him called 'Sludge the Medium', composed in the master's worst style, at once obscure and long-winded, and extremely offensive to poor Mr Sludge, I mean Home).

I'm afraid that now my mind is clouding over more and more rapidly and I judge this manuscript to be an unshapely muddle. There is too much spite in it, the best passages must be censored and Fanny herself remains irritatingly elusive. I really didn't keep up with Fanny in her later years, but it would be a pity to let this book, which represents a whole month's work, come to naught. Perhaps I'll dictate it all to Miss Knowlton, that efficient little Englishwoman who's looking for work and is so poor she attends absolutely any reception so that she can get a dinner off the hors d'oeuvres. I could read out the whole manuscript to her, adding and suppressing where necessary as I go along, cutting judiciously, eliminating all the impieties and irritating bits of French and Italian and making myself sound calmer and wiser.

During our Haitian *villeggiatura* I saw Fanny, who'd always been a tireless talker so long as the topic was political or philosophical, turn more and more silent. Whenever she'd launch into a discourse in her old, authoritative manner Phiquepal would stare at her. Once he even raised a finger to his lips and Fanny came

291

strangely undone and quickly stuttered into inanition. He himself liked to go to bed early, whereas Fanny was normally dull by day but took fire at night. Due to his influence, as poisonous as his breath and as relentless as his voice when he chose to 'clarify' a moral subject, Fanny was soon shuffling off to their room at ten, before the *digestif*.

I say *their* room since she made no secret of their cohabitation. I wanted to draw her aside and ask her how at this late date (she was thirty-five), after her sister's tragic loss of her baby and her unhappy marriage, after a long, vigorous life of preaching against the evils of matrimony, how she, the Free Enquirer, could submit to – well, to a Mr Trollope. If her lover had been the moody, mercurial, intelligent President Boyer I could have understood the concessions she was making to a man, but what woman would choose to serve and obey a petty tyrant like Phiquepal if she knew what she was getting?

I couldn't help but worry about how Miss Wright's ex-slaves were faring in Haiti. Perhaps I was especially sensitive to their lot since so recently Cudjo had considered joining them. The English Consul's terrible predictions haunted me. I doubted that Fanny herself would inquire after them. She must have been relieved to have brought the whole sorry affair to an honourable conclusion. Once when I started to mention the subject, Phiquepal rushed in with, 'There, there, Mrs Trollope, you don't want to be labelled a meddler, do you?' He, of course, was the one in charge of selling the pickled pork that the *John Quincy Adams* had transported to Haiti, and he was the one rounding up the highest quality of coffee bean for the return voyage – he didn't want even to contemplate taking up valuable cargo space with disgruntled, returning American Negroes. Nor did he want to refund President Boyer's generously offered reimbursement of some of the cost to Fanny of bringing the ex-slaves to Haiti. My question was out of season.

But my love for Cudjo had transformed me. Fanny might see her slaves as mere ciphers in her idealistic calculus, but to me they weren't a group but individuals, each a hopeful, fearful aspirant toward happiness or at least toward the cessation of pain and danger, individuals subject to toothache, bellyache, earache, heartache, poor disoriented creatures seeking to re-establish due North in their feelings and longings. They'd never been consulted about their future or asked if they wanted to settle in Haiti. For that matter they'd never been told what Haiti *was*. Perhaps they still didn't know exactly where they'd ended up. Had they already been sent to the malarial swamps of Samaná? Or had the men been conscripted into an army that was unprovisioned and un-billeted, unruly and unshod?

That night we'd just taken up residence at Brache, a stone house with small windows and thick walls like a Provençal *mas* on top of a *morne* where the constant warm wind had trained the castor bean trees to lean all in one direction and to chatter to themselves (their long flat pods were clacking like castanets and Boyer told me they were called 'old woman's tongue' in Creole). Despite the possible reproach in his botanical comment, I asked just as we were being served our goat *gigot*, 'Tell me, General, what has happened to Miss Wright's slaves?'

Phiquepal looked apoplectic and was clutching at his scrawny neck to loosen his cravat and to push down his stiff raised collar. The copious grey tufts of hair in his ears bristled with electricity. Fanny merely raised her eyes. The President said without hesi-tation, 'Well might you ask, Mrs Trollope. I'm delighted to say that they're living within a few leagues of here and you can see them for yourselves tomorrow. We'll go over there on horseback or in a cart and pay them a call. I've asked Inginiac to see after their every want, to make certain their quarters satisfy them and that they're fed foods they're used to, to the degree our climate and terrain permit. I've also asked Inginiac to provide them for the first month of their residence here with a translator. But you can ask them everything tomorrow . . .'

We did go and the ex-slaves did seem genuinely happy with their new occupations as farmers and their habitations, which were clean little cottages scattered in the hills like the summer mountain shelters of Swiss herdsmen. I kept wondering if they were being coerced to smile and if they'd just been moved here overnight, but then I regretted my suspicions and felt reassured by how they looked already a bit plumper and healthier.

On the way back to the windswept fastness of Brache, Fanny had to dismount. She vomited in the bushes and emerged from them looking green. We persuaded her to take a place in the cart. She was nauseated and in such pain she had tears in her eyes. When we descended at the manor house, Hersilie and I hurried Fanny up to her room, undressed her, washed her brow and stretched her out on her high metal bed.

Looking at her through the etherealizing veil of the mosquito net I said, 'Fanny, is it a return of your fevers?'

'Oh, no, Madame Trop Lotte,' Hersilie said with a wonderful grin. She was obviously Fanny's confidante. 'Mademoiselle Fanny is pregnant!'

I looked at Fanny, thunderstruck. She opened her eyes quickly then squeezed them shut and slowly nodded.

In one of her rare moments of woman-to-woman confiding-ness, Fanny told me she had decided to marry Monsieur d'Arusmont. She was like one of my characters (I've forgotten in which novel) who says that for a woman marriage means only one thing – the loss of money – but she'd now decided that an ille-gitimate child's woes outweighed the dangers run by her mother.

Once I had envied Fanny her freedom and wealth but now she was about to have a child and to marry a difficult pauper. I had attempted to emulate her independence, but she had ended up taking up my burdens. The same bourgeois streak in Fanny that had made her treat her slaves as servants and court the approval of Lafayette and Jefferson was now convincing her to marry. Motherhood turns us all conventional, but I was surprised to see how readily Fanny acquiesced to this inevitability.

Her morning sickness made her wretchedly ill. I suppose she suffered more because she was older. Despite their refinement, President Boyer's circle honestly didn't lift an eyebrow over Miss Wright's condition. None of them seemed to have had their unions consecrated and yet all had a strong sense of family.

Being pregnant made Fanny even more subservient to Phiquepal. He had to leave for New Orleans a few days in advance on the *John Quincy Adams* to deliver the famous cargo of coffee, the commercial pendant to the humanitarian goal of liberating her slaves, a money-making scheme that ultimately was used by Fanny's enemies to besmirch her reputation further. They claimed she'd traded on her prestige as an abolitionist to convince Boyer to waive all Haitian duties on her pork and beans, although the profits she made did not even begin to defray her expenses (despite Boyer's help) and she ended up by losing another four hundred dollars on the venture.

Once Phiquepal was gone Fanny moped around on Inginiac's estate just above Port-au-Prince; she was incapable of enjoying the endless parties of that endless summer. She wrote Phiquepal that she was 'oppressed with lassitude and passed the day reading on the sofa, feeling my solitude and often speculating respecting the progress of the *John Quincy Adams*.' Uncharacteristically, she showed me the letter.

It would have been natural for me to leave with Phiquepal and make my way to Cincinnati to gather up my girls and Hervieu, but I hoped I could be of use to Fanny – and besides I despised Phiquepal and shrank from the idea of spending two weeks alone in his company. Fanny kept sinking into reverie, however, and I had a sustained conversation with her only once in Inginiac's gardens along the shores where her eyes kept drifting to the sailboats skimming past, spinnakers full of the wind coming up behind them, bound to Jamaica with their cargoes of cotton, tobacco, mahogany and coffee.

'Will you live in France or the United States?' I asked Fanny, half-resentful that after so many years together I still knew so little about her plans and was still intimidated by her.

'My first duty is to get Camilla back to Europe – exactly as you've done with Henry.'

'Of all my children he's the one who's burdened my mind the most,' I said. 'In fact I've neglected the two other boys frightfully in order to make something out of Henry. Tom and Anthony inherited their father's bulky frame and strong muscles and I think they're built for survival. But Henry is delicate, resentful, sensitive.'

'Thank heavens he has Monsieur Hervieu as his lover,' Fanny said, squinting into the sunlight. She'd reclined on a *chaise-longue* that Inginiac had had brought into the garden for her.

I laughed at her odd word and said, 'Yes, they are the dearest of friends and Hervieu seems to be in love with our whole family.' To change the subject I said, 'How do you think Camilla will respond to your . . . expecting so soon after the loss of her own baby?'

Fanny pressed her fingers to her temples and her eyes filled with tears. 'Oh, Mrs Trollope, I have no idea. She's said farewell to life. Certainly to love, though she once agreed with me that sexual passion is the strongest and noblest of human sentiments and the source of the best joys of our existence.'

I smiled, thinking of Cudjo, until I realized every respectable woman would be shocked by Fanny's brazen promulgation of an appetite as perverse as female sensuality. Only the houris of Egypt were expected to own up to such filth, or so Mr Trollope had once told me when I asked him soon after our marriage if the wife was supposed to find any pleasure in intimacy.

'Will Camilla see my child as a lien on the future, a promise that our poor doomed line will continue after all, or will she hate my baby and think that once again I have won where she has lost?'

That must have been the most honest, unmediated moment that ever transpired between us.

Fanny set sail on the *Enterprise* and arrived in Philadelphia on 23 April, 1830. She became violently ill due to the sudden transition from tropical heat to a freezing gale that swept up the East Coast.

She made her way to New-York after a six-month absence from the city, and saw that Camilla was slipping away day by day. On 1 May Fanny announced in the *Free Enquirer* that personal business was obliging her to return in June to Europe with her sister.

During her last days in America she kept up a gruelling speaking schedule. Luckily, she was only three months pregnant and was able through dress to conceal her condition. In her final speech in Philadelphia (where she was protected by a bodyguard of Quaker ladies in the full costume of their sect, lace bonnets and all) and in New-York where she addressed three thousand people, her audiences were at least half composed of women, an unprecedented phenomenon in America. She spoke out against the arbitrary division of people into social classes and declared that only the interests of the working class 'more nearly approached to the great natural interests of man.' It was hard to imagine that this woman had once known how to flirt with Lafayette and win over Jefferson, for now she had put aside all feminine charms and even her body had become less supple, more stolid, and her voice had become so deep that if one heard her speak without seeing her, one was startled to learn that she was a woman.

Fanny and Camilla sailed on 1 July, 1830 for England on the *Hannibal*. Robert Dale Owen, who was probably in love with Camilla by now, wept openly on the dock. A New-York newspaper published a 'song' of several verses that ended:

> And if you want to raise the wind
> Or breed a moral storm
> You must have one bold lady-man
> To prate about reform.

Fanny was so proud – perhaps even proud of her masculinity, her 'lady-man' ambiguity – that she wanted no one to know she was pregnant. She had insisted that Phiquepal sail to France weeks earlier; she didn't want to be seen with him. Not yet. She and Camilla moved to Paris and though they found lodgings in the heart of the city on the rue Montaigne they lived in the deepest obscurity. No one saw them. In January 1831 Fanny gave birth to a daughter, Sylva, and on 8 February Camilla died of consumption. She was just thirty. She had been the witness to Fanny's life, a sweet girl on whom Fanny had tested all her theories. These ideas may have made Fanny unhappy but they had killed Camilla. Now Fanny felt she had no one she could count on except the Garnetts, but Harriet, as her letters to me and Lafayette (which he once showed me) proved, was treacherous. She had been grateful to Fanny for introducing her to Lafayette, though she prized him more as a social lion than admired him as a radical.

I would have given my love to Fanny despite the disappointment and resentment she'd awakened in me, but she didn't trust me – probably Harriet's doing again. Fanny didn't keep letters from her women friends, only from her 'historic' men, but I'm certain Harriet convinced Fanny I was a gossip. She also disliked me not so much for my politics as for the use that had been made of me; my book on America was seized on by the Orleanists as proof that democracy was impracticable.

In July 1831, Fanny married Phiquepal in Paris at the town hall after having obtained the necessary consent of his mother, whom he hadn't seen or written to in years. Fanny took Phiquepal's aristocratic name of d'Arusmont as her own.

A French father who had entrusted the upbringing of his son to Phiquepal and who had embraced Phiquepal's theories of a Rousseauist and Pestalozzian education now discovered, after the boy returned from several years in Philadelphia and New Harmony, that he could barely read or write, had no skills befitting a gentleman, had acquired not even a smattering of Latin and Greek and had been impressed into hard work as an unpaid typesetter for the *Free Press* in New-York. The boy knew nothing, could not even write a decent French and spouted heretical and Jacobin ideas as if they were accepted wisdom. Outraged, the father took Phiquepal to court in Bordeaux for damages but lost his case; the judge reproached the father for entrusting his offspring to 'an obvious lunatic.'

Fanny had assumed her testimony on behalf of Phiquepal would be decisive but the judge silenced her after a minute. He didn't seem to know who she was.

Curiously, back in America, everyone forgot her as well. In 1829 she had been the most controversial and notorious woman in the country but two years later no one ever mentioned her. Considering she was the first woman in America to oppose slavery, the first woman ever to address a mixed audience, a notorious atheist, the first leader of the first labour party, the most radical journalist in the land, the oblivion that swallowed her whole is a stunning (I could say *deliberate*) act of effacement. She was too challenging, too uncomfortable to be remembered. In any event Americans denigrate ideas by attaching them to colourful personalities, whom they decide should be replaced by new, even more bizarre eccentrics. Personality is all in America. An odd hemline or a becoming stutter will always upstage a worrying thought.

Fanny withdrew into the seclusion and mourning appropriate to a Sicilian widow. She wore black. When Harriet called unexpectedly on her she found little Sylva wandering about a dirty flat stark naked (one of Fanny's new pedagogical notions). D'Arusmont was seated at one desk and Fanny at another, both of them scribbling away; Harriet had the impression they lived in monastic silence and scurried out only to buy food. There was the smell of food cooking, no sign of a servant. Harriet wasn't even asked to sit down or offered a cup of tea. She told me that Fanny responded only to her every third letter. It was as if Phiquepal's repressiveness and hatred of humanity had won out and that he'd weaned her away from all her friends and activities. Even Lafayette was unable to see her, though he did receive from her a long pedantic letter criticizing his support of Louis Philippe, the new king. Fanny wrote that the kiss Lafayette had conferred on the Orleans pretender on the balcony of the town hall while the mob looked on had made him the monarch, whereas what France clearly needed was to become a republic once more. Lafayette died in 1834 without ever seeing her again.

When the hateful old Madame Frétageot, back in France and enjoying the fortune bestowed on her by her lover Maclure, called unannounced one afternoon, Fanny couldn't have been colder. After all, Frétageot had made no secret of her dislike of Phiquepal.

Fanny said explicitly that she no longer received visitors. When Frétageot said with a certain jauntiness, 'Then you must call on me,' Fanny said nothing and refused to take the card that the Frenchwoman extended to her.

Fanny – always so brilliant and, in her 'off-stage' moments, so tender and affectionate – now seemed like a woman who'd taken a vow not to smile, not to talk, not even to register a human presence that wasn't Sylva's or Phiquepal's.

A year after Sylva was born Fanny had a baby who died at birth and Fanny managed to corrupt an official at the town hall into assigning the dead baby's 'birth-date' to Sylva, assuring her the illusion of legitimacy. For the rest of her days Sylva will no doubt believe she was born on 14 April, 1832.

Fanny read all the papers in Paris, especially the radical ones, and she would conceive intense sympathies for oppressed people in remote countries while brushing aside a Paris beggar's hand.

She and Phiquepal were often ill. He liked to dine at two in the afternoon, since he thought that hour better suited to a good night's sleep, but if he wasn't well he didn't eat and when she, too, was ill they ate nothing, nor did Sylva.

Phiquepal, who felt an alien in France after all his years in America and who sometimes groped for words in French, had no friends in Paris and no professional activities. He devoted himself entirely to Sylva's education, which, given his methods, produced variable results. Sylva was a pretty girl, small for her age, inevitably bilingual, who wore her hair in rather greasy sausage curls and had a bulging brow that a phrenologist, I doubt not, would have interpreted as a Bulge of Wilfulness.

While Fanny was residing in the heart of Paris though far from the world, I was leading a decidedly more active existence. After Haiti I went back to Cincinnati and collected Hervieu and the girls. Though I rushed to the forge I found it cold and empty but the next day the little black boy who'd worked the bellows for Cudjo came to my boarding-house and told me Mr Higgins had moved to Canada. He handed me an envelope on which 'Trolup' was written in big letters. Inside, it said in the letters I'd taught him to write, 'Godbie my little gall.' I said it to myself and recognized he meant *girl*, for he often called me his girl or child, which was so winningly ridiculous.

*   *   *

Once, a few years later, in Florence I saw an announcement that a Signora Sacqui would be performing in a theatre some of the most difficult known tricks on the high wire. I thought she must be a descendant of the already somewhat *mature* Sacqui I'd seen in my youth – but no! it was the same old lady. She did all her feats with stupendous agility and strength and for the climax to the spectacle walked across a rope stretched close to the painted ceiling of gods and nymphs. When she'd reached the middle of the rope she stopped and boldly waved two flags she held in her hands and the horrified, thrilled audience began to shout and stamp in fear and admiration. Only at that point did she coolly descend a dangling rope, dressed in the spangled costume of her prime which now showed her sagging buttocks, jiggling under-arms and dismally ruched thighs. I thought surely she should have covered these deformities out of consideration for the sensibilities of the young. She, no doubt, reasoned that she'd earned the right to display her body exactly as it was. Her effrontery impressed me – I could see the point of it.

I can still picture that old lady with her buttocks dripping down out of her costume, her arms strong if wobbling, eyes blazing in a heavily rouged face though her moustache was revealed in the cross-lights. I can see her there, rotating her flags above us, her wizened body silhouetted against an allegory of the Seven Graces dancing far more demurely in an eternal circle around a bearded god.

In Haiti I had already decided to write something, possibly a biography of Frances Wright or a satirical look at American manners, especially when Basil Hall had had such success the year before with his *Travels in North America*. I was busy taking notes as I travelled to New-York, Washington, Stonington, Niagara Falls

– the places I thought my future readers might want to learn about. We were still living entirely on Auguste's meagre earnings, and our clothes were in such disrepair that respectable men weren't quite certain they should lift their hats to me nor women that they should say, 'How d'ye do?' to my daughters and me.

At last, after our beggarly hejira across the United States we sailed to England. I had to threaten Mr Trollope to force him to yield to us the eighty pounds we needed for our passage; I warned him that if he didn't make this sacrifice for his daughters' sake I'd have to apply to his family for the funds. He succumbed to the pressure and we arrived at last in Woolwich at the end of the summer of 1831 after an absence from England of nearly four years.

If anything the situation at Harrow was even more desperate than I'd imagined. Trollope still blamed Henry and me for the débâcle of the Bazaar in Cincinnati, but I soon enough learned that his misadventures in farming had gone on to lose us another thousand pounds. As Anthony said after his father's death,

> The touch of his hand seemed to create failure. He embarked in one hopeless enterprise after another, spending on each all the money he could at the time command. But the worst curse to him of all was a temper so irritable that even those he loved the best could not endure it. We were all estranged from him, and yet I believed he would have given his heart's blood for any of us. His life as I know it was one long tragedy.

To my horror upon my return to England I discovered that Mr Trollope, while in Cincinnati, had signed a large loan from the botanical Mr Nicholas Longworth and that by the terms of this document it was not enough that we'd lost the cursed Bazaar but we must continue paying back the loan year after year and at a very high rate. I couldn't help but associate our dilemma with France's exploitation of Haiti, and I only wished we'd contracted to pay Mr Longworth in gourdes!

I had little time to bewail our lot. I put the finishing touches

302

on my satirical book about America and soon enough I'd sold it to a publisher. It had been rushed into print – and like Byron I awakened to discover I'd become famous. I ridiculed Cincinnati, pigs and all, unmasked Fanny Wright's utopian colony, expressed my revulsion at American rudeness and impertinence and the horrors of constant spitting. I had a laugh at American speech (which soon everyone in England was imitating), American servants, American vanity and humourlessness. I exposed the indecency of rabid American revivalist meetings. And above all I showed the iniquity in that dangerous American slogan, 'All men are created equal.'Although I still counted Fanny as a friend, I was shocked by the way I treated her in print. Apparently I was more bitter than I thought.

Despite my grand success and the hundreds of pounds I earned we still had to flee the country in total secrecy. As Lord Northwick's bailiff, Mr Quilton, was banging at the door, ready to seize all our belongings, Cecilia and Emily were passing my pretty-pretties through a gap in the hedge to our faithful neighbours the Grants. The rest of our things were sold off under the hammer, and we crept away from England on the Calais packet. I installed us all – my sickly Henry, my sometimes violent and always complaining Trollope, my meek daughters (Emily never more than twenty-four inches from my elbow), the ever-fiery and ever-loyal Hervieu – in the Château d'Hondt in Bruges.

I haven't the courage to write out the end of this story. Suffice it to say I suffered much and Henry more. He developed a 'late' interest in geology, the only subject he'd excelled in at New Harmony, and he was proud to be made a member of the Geological Society in 1832 (he was proposed for membership by Basil Hall). As I researched *Belgium and the Belgians* Henry travelled with me, recording his geological observations while Auguste drew every site we visited, though I sometimes felt he spent more time studying the feeble Henry than the castle or fortified town or crumbling bridge we were meant to be scrutinizing.

Henry died two days before Christmas in 1834 in Bruges. Throughout his last months he was an extremely demanding patient. For some reason he took up carpentry and was banging things late into the night. (I wonder where he found the strength.) Often he would collapse in a fit of bloody coughing. He wanted me by his side at every moment, reading to him, leaning in to hear his disordered thoughts as he whispered them, promising him he was about to get better. I thought up several schemes to send him to the tropics that never materialized. Although Bruges could be lovely in summer with its swan-heavy canals gliding under humpbacked stone bridges and its medieval covered stone market and fruited trees poking up above time-blackened walls, in the winter it was heavily sedated on fog and rain and silence, a torpor broken only on Saturdays when peasants stunned by beer swung past below our windows gurgling songs, for even drunks observed the universal law against noise and seldom out-sang the lapping waves. My only consolation was a regular visit to the house of a friend, the mayor of the town, who had in his collection a Memling of a boy in an apple-green waistcoat with a raw white face and above it a splendour of gold filaments of hair radiating out into the surrounding darkness like energy boiling up out of the sun.

Henry would seldom leave me in peace though I finally cre-ated a sanity-saving moment in the afternoon when I descended to take my tea. If Henry wasn't sleeping then, Auguste would creep up to keep him company though the poor 'Her-view' truly was hopeless. Seeing Henry's transparent white face with the blue-green artery ticking in his temple and the hands so tiny and hot reduced the Frenchman to unmanly floods of tears. My most painful job was convincing poor delicate Emily not to visit her dying brother, since I knew she was too weak to resist his infec-tion. I would rise earlier and earlier each morning to scribble out new pages of my three-volume *Tremordyn Cliff* (or was it *The Abbess?*). But no sooner had I stumbled half-asleep through one or two pages than I'd hear Henry's cough, his endless spell of coughing, the loudest sound in Bruges.

When he died I went to my room and sat on my bed and started to get up to write, to help, to read to him – but then I

304

knew there was nothing I could do and I sat back down heavily and let time claw at me like a marrow-sucking, eye-extracting vacuum, not a warm bath of grief, nothing surrounding and delimiting, nothing that might mean anything except a dull negation, a leeching out of all meaning.

Perhaps in anyone as capable as I am there is always a nearly equal temptation to give up completely and pull the covers over one's head. Certainly the deep passivity of sitting on my little Belgian bed and watching the slanting rain pock the window-pane then slide, pock and slide, did not come to me with even a shade of unfamiliarity. Might it be that in honour of Henry's death I was imitating the principal condition of death, that it has no future, no need, not even any consciousness? (Of course my impiety here is unpardonable, but I can assure the reader that my own feeling of extinction in no way affected my belief in Henry's everlasting life.)

Henry was buried in the Protestant corner of the Bruges cemetery. On the day of his interment Monsieur Hervieu appeared to be deeply affronted, as though Fate had personally slapped him in the face. He wore an expression of indignation. His nostrils flared and his lips turned down, but then, when the coffin was lowered under its single bouquet, a great lion's roar of grief broke out of this frozen muzzle of vexation and I understood that that look had been just an accidental by-product of holding back so much suffering. As I watched his effort to fling himself into the grave and the energy exerted by the gravediggers and even the Lutheran chaplain to hold him back, I said to myself that after all we English might learn the French language and even live in France, but we could never permit ourselves these histrionic displays. They would always remain foreign to us.

My husband no longer wanted to share my bedroom nor even to speak to me civilly. His coldness earned me my children's sympathy. They would have been surprised to learn that I appreciated his indifference and welcomed my solitude. Alone, I could still imagine in some way I was faithful to Cudjo. Sleeping with my husband would have struck me as adulterous.

I knew I must feed my girls, one of them ailing, and nurse my husband, who was seriously ill. I could not return to England until after his death since until then every farthing I earned could be seized by his creditors – Lord Northwick and Mr Longworth. No, I was in harness. I had had my unexpected last affair, and now like Signora Sacqui I had to walk the high wire and earn my keep.

Trollope, to be fair, believed that as a gentleman he had to work as hard as I did. He decided to write – all alone and with no assistance – a massive *Encyclopaedia Ecclesiastica* that would give, in hundreds of entries arranged not chronologically but alphabetically, the comprehensive history of the Church – Primitive, Catholic, Orthodox, Nestorian and Protestant, every rite, every saint, every sacrament, every martyrdom, every sacred synod, every bull and encyclical, every heresy, every crusade, every schism and every inquisition. The project struck me as grotesque but it kept him busy, though he would live to finish only the first volume.

We all travelled to Paris where I hoped to take the temperature of this city that changed faster than any other, where every generalization was constantly given the lie. I needed to understand the new Paris of Louis Philippe, the bourgeois monarch Lafayette had kissed into life. I knew that Fanny was in Paris on the rue Montaigne and twice I paced the street slowly, looking and half-hoping to run into her, but I didn't see her and she didn't respond to the note I sent her.

For her I was a Tory since I'd scoffed at America in my book and it had been held up as proof that democracy couldn't work and the vote should not be extended in England to the lower orders. It was discussed in Parliament and at the Tuileries Palace. I suppose I enjoyed the attention by the right wing or the left but I hadn't intended to write a political tract. I could only describe, as a woman must, the follies and foibles of an age and a place. All I had were my powers of observation, a touch of irony, no analysis – and that was all.

Fanny, of course, was our thinker and in this grim period of her life, when her wings were clipped by Phiquepal and their

306

shared but slightly unhealthy focus on Sylva, Fanny decided to construct a *system* out of all her random thoughts and intuitions, to create a philosophy out of her sympathies. When Madame Frétageot, cobbling together an excuse for Fanny's rudeness, had said, 'Then I suppose you write much?' Fanny had replied, 'I do not. I am totally occupied with my family,' but that was a lie.

Fanny had endured an almost fatal attack of fever at Nashoba, which some say had gone to her brain, and then she had become further enfeebled during her editorial and speaking career due to too constant a mental effort. She'd been shocked by her sister's death and plunged into a guilty grief. Childbirth and a year later a dead baby had drained her body. Paris was in the throes of a great cholera epidemic, which was so serious that it had already killed half the population of Provence. Out of all this unhappiness, guilt, melancholy and bad health, poor Fanny was attempting to fashion a book.

Miraculously, in 1835 Fanny sprang back to life and returned to the United States without Phiquepal. She was armed now with a doctrine she'd hammered out – an end to the class system, the abolition of slavery, an equalizing of wealth – reforms that would require no violence or even inconvenience. It was a programme that required nothing but a universal desire for moral reform. Her new manner was oracular, her imagery shadowy, her ideas out of step with the times. Her programme, she declared, would satisfy the wants and calm the anxieties of every individual, 'assailing no class, disputing with no prejudices, forcing no habits, sacrificing no interests . . .' Well, you see what I mean. It was spineless reformism she proposed, she who had become famous for fiery revolution. Her new ideas were so abstract that no one would rally under such a pale flag.

Oddly enough the public was now interested in her old inflammatory ideas. Her once virulent abolitionism was a stand many people in the North were now ready to embrace, but Fanny had transformed it (in line with her new intellectual pleasantness) into a policy that avoided all controversy. People came to Fanny hoping she'd drape herself in the revolutionary flag and lead them into a holy war. Instead, she now told them that slavery was a 'minor issue' that would not be solved soon. The real problem, she said, was wage slavery.

Fanny didn't want the government or the courts to intervene to free blacks or improve working conditions. No, she wanted planters and factory owners to reform out of their own goodness and reasonableness. Her new policies were coherent with her old respect for authority – her own social class, finally.

As soon as I finished one book I would start another. I was furiously writing my anti-slavery novel, *The Life and Adventures of Jonathan Jefferson Whitlaw: or Scenes on the Mississippi* (illustrations by A. Hervieu), 3 vols, later reissued under a better title, *Lynch Law*. I remembered all the horrors Cudjo had told me and I patterned my appallingly cruel plantation master Whitlaw after Cudjo's Colonel Tom. As a sort of happy ending for Cudjo – just in case he'd gone on reading in Canada and was keeping up with my books – I had the slaves rebel and kill their master. My book was the first abolitionist novel, published well before *Uncle Tom's Cabin* though unfortunately it was not nearly as lucrative.

Fanny's audiences melted away. At last she had found a way not to offend anyone – or to interest anyone. She and Phiquepal were no longer living together. They were travelling their separate ways – Fanny to lecture to smaller and smaller audiences, Phiquepal to manage Fanny's investments, many of them in Cincinnati. He was going blind and had to be accompanied everywhere by his little girl, whose position in the world obsessed him. He and Fanny had each abandoned their youthful radicalism, he to reclaim his aristocratic name and to enjoy Fanny's wealth, which he was carefully husbanding, Fanny to refashion her wild public personality into that of a mild reformer and an universal intellectual.

In Paris I had consulted the leading medical specialists. About Emily all they would say was that she was 'a delicate case,' nothing more, a girl in need of rest, warmth and plentiful, nourishing food. Since the London doctors had prescribed the same cure for Henry a few years earlier, the vague recommendations of the French physicians filled me with dread. As to Mr Trollope, they were far more explicit. They said he would be dead within the year. Dr Mojon in Paris guessed that Trollope was a man in his early eighties; in fact he was just sixty-two.

The Pater died on 23 October, 1835. His attending physician in Bruges, an ageing army doctor who'd served under Napoleon, had never suggested to me that the end was so near and Trollope's sudden 'disappearance,' as the French say, shocked me profoundly. He'd just seen through the press the A–F volume of his *Encyclopaedia Ecclesiastica* (which ended with the entry 'Funeral Rites') and I had just handed in the first volume of my *Paris and the Parisians*. I buried Trollope next to Henry, a headstone for the father and an Ionic column for the son. In the Protestant corner the monuments are becomingly modest, compared to the big stone *houses* erected by the Catholics.

Trollope had worked hard all his life but every seed he had sown had died and every field he'd ploughed had been barren. He'd married a minister's daughter, sweet and pliant, but she had developed into a clever woman, a famous writer and an indefatigable fighter. He'd signed away our fortune and covered us with debts without even once telling us what he was doing. He insisted on playing the old-fashioned patriarch though he had no judgement and suicidal instincts. He'd been a violent man and had often beat the boys and struck me. We all struggled to dream up excuses for his foul temper, but though there were medical explanations there were no moral justifications. Under as much pressure as he was, I never behaved in the same contemptible fashion. He was vile because our society let him be – there! I almost sound like one of Fanny's funny old feminists!

The first practical result of the Pater's death was that now we could return to England. I was no longer responsible for his debts – nor was he, sad man. My only regret is that now no one visits Henry's and Trollope's graves. It's not that I think that even a single shred of their spirits swirls around the headstone and the column, but some voodoo-primitive part of me feels we should still be there offering flowers and prayers. I don't like it that strangers might see these neglected graves bearing such recent dates and a name I have made famous.

We moved into a London flat in Northumberland Street across from the Marylebone Workhouse, a dreary place but then as Tom says all London flats are grim. Just as I'd been afraid to expose Emily to Henry, now I didn't want Cecilia in the presence of Emily – luckily our old Harrow friend Lady Milman took her in.

Emily died on 12 February, 1836; she had just turned eighteen. Unlike Henry she didn't demand every second of my attention. She knew I had to write to pay the bills. Now that Trollope was dead, life – even our sad little underpopulated tragic life – seemed so much easier. We'd always tiptoed around his headaches, cringed before his rages, feared what new economic disaster he was brewing – but now Blue Beard had departed from the castle, the Minotaur had fled the Labyrinth and all the doors had flown open – but it wasn't a happy day.

When Emily died I regained a bit of my faith because she looked so lovely, angelic, really, and I believed that if she'd drawn her last breath and would never again be conscious it would be too unfair. Like the Duke de Broglie I preferred to think she hadn't died but just gone to America. She deserved immortality. I consoled myself by claiming that at least I'd led her on a merry chase and crowded all of America into her short life. We were pioneers together and together we'd sailed the Atlantic, mounted the Mississippi, gone hungry, fled the bailiff, built our Cincinnati Folly and buried Henry and the Pater. We'd done everything together.

I was publishing book after book, alternating my travel accounts with my novels. Even if my talents were limited I was always bubbling over with good ideas – why, look how often I've been imitated! Harriet Beecher Stowe imitated my anti-slavery novel, and Dickens, who sometimes dismisses me, keeps following my lead. His American novel, *Martin Chuzzlewit*, copied my Nashoba scenes very closely and his tobacco-spitting braggarts in his *American Notes* had already been described in my first book. Even his diatribes against the exploitation of child labour, especially his magnificent *Oliver Twist*, had its model in my rushed novel, *Michael Armstrong, the Factory Boy*. Like me he's written about grasping parvenus and grieving mothers, virtuous gutter-snipes and tyrannical fathers. Of course he has much more flair, but I was always there first, which must count for something. Fanny's influence on me was decisive – she made me, the hard-hearted old Tory, into someone progressive and Whiggish.

Now I've contracted with that nice Miss Knowlton to come by tomorrow morning. Apparently she's been trained to take down dictation rapidly and write out a fair copy in a neat hand. This book can possibly be set to rights if I reshape it as I go along, a process that will let me hear repetitions and contradictions. I shall also watch Miss Knowlton while I speak the text out and pay attention to the passages that make her cringe (I hope she's a conspicuous cringer), which I can easily drop.

My mind, however, keeps clouding over. To write a page or two that sticks to the subject, I need a strong dose of India tea, a preceding night of perfect repose and an ambient tempera-ture neither too warm nor too chilly. If it's warm I doze off and if chilly my arthritic claws close up and I can't hold my writing instrument. Ah, when I think how I used to write in the early morning and still have time to pluck fresh roses from our garden and dot the house with bouquets, all before anyone was stirring. But now, at age seventy-six, I find that if I have to search for a word I've soon ambled down some winding path of reverie and let my page slip off my lap. Thank heavens Tom married a rich girl! I now write only to keep my name before the public and I have a strong hunch that soon Anthony (after a disastrous beginning with several novels about Ireland of all unappealing places) will be sustaining the family reputation. He's just brought out a little jewel, *The Warden*, destined for some success, I'd hazard. At last he's found a voice of his own, which if anything owes something to my conversational style but nothing to my rather uninspired writing style.

311

While I was making my way to Florence with my faithful champion, my boy Tom, an ever-more disconsolate Hervieu was heading off into the Swiss mountains. He'd found a pretty girl to marry, one who curiously resembled Henry. Soon he was no longer responding to my letters.

At the same time poor Fanny was settling in Cincinnati, all alone. She'd divorced the odious Phiquepal after a long dispute over her fortune, which had been augmented at the death of an obscure but wealthy Scottish relative. Phiquepal wanted to guarantee that Fanny did not dissipate her new funds and took legal steps to make certain he had complete control over the family finances. Of course a wife has no legal rights even when it's a matter of her own money. The wicked and unpleasantly precocious little Sylva, who unfortunately had become her father's child, took his side in all of these unsavoury negotiations. Her mother, in any event, seemed indifferent to her. Fanny was too busy writing and publishing her weekly journal, *The Manual of American Principles*, and campaigning for Martin Van Buren. Like her he was an enemy of the Bank of the United States and hostile to all national financial institutions. No sooner did her candidate become President in 1837 than the entire American market of speculation burst like a bubble. Tens of thousands of Americans faced starvation. Fanny's only solution to the problem was to argue in her columns for the dissolution of the national bank. Fanny detested big government.

I find all these positions she assumed puzzling and grotesque given the collapse of her personal life. My life at the time seemed to be going well – in 1838 Cecilia announced her engagement to one of Anthony's fellow clerks in the Post Office, a charming and devoted John Tilley. A year later Cecilia gave birth to a child, a little girl she named Frances Trollope! In the end she became the mother of five adorable children, but her own health continued to deteriorate. She died on 10 April 1849. Tom just showed me, at my request, a letter I wrote him at the time. I was seventy-one then and I find in the letter this line: 'Though I feel that I am almost too old for a *rally*, I will do the best I can to get over it.'

*

Fanny brought out a dull book called *England the Civilizer* a decade ago which fell from my hands, though I do remember she praised the French Revolution as the most glorious moment in history and the English 'bloodless revolution' of 1688 she labelled a cold-hearted financial transaction.

She was familiar with such transactions from personal experience. Her husband had granted her a very small yearly allowance. When she died, just three years ago on 13 December 1852, she was alone in Cincinnati. She had finally won a divorce and regained control over a portion of her wealth as *feme sole*, to use the legal expression that she repeated and murmured night and day as if it were a talisman, both a blessing and a malediction. She was indeed a woman on her own, spiritually as much as legally. She had a string of young women working for her, since she'd never learned to do the simplest chores and could no more sweep a room or stitch a hem than she could avoid an abstraction in conversation. But those girls found her frightening and regarded her as virtually a member of an alien species.

Her daughter came to visit her and spent five hours with her. Sylva writes me:

At first I was so moved by the simple sight of her – her eyes huge and filled with torment. Maybe madness. She embraced me – I had to stoop down since she could not rise from her chair. She told me that the year before she'd fallen on the ice and broken her thigh bone. For weeks her broken leg had been kept fully extended with weights posed on it so that it would not heal incorrectly. As if that suffering weren't enough she had ordered a dentist to pull all her teeth and make her a set of dentures, which she paid for with old gold. I sympathized with her agony that was mental as well, as could be seen by looking at her head, which had become as male and mad as the old Beethoven's – marionette lines carved deep and falling from her nostrils to the corners of her lips as if tracing out the deep furrows of her tears. She said she loved me and wanted us to be friends again, but

313

soon she was raving against my father and cursing the laws that harm a married woman and even a *feme sole*. I suggested that God had made these laws for our edification, which triggered a new burst of abuse against religion and the state and her ex-husband. She was voluble as never before and I wondered if she were delirious from some pain-lessening opiate. I sat there stony-hearted and resolved never to see her again. As Papa says talking to her is a waste of time.

Fanny had moved into an unfinished house and while the two carpenters worked to put a roof over her head she slowed their progress by hectoring them the whole time about the lot of the working man. She had, according to one of the carpenters, Joel Brown, an opinion on everything. At my prompting he wrote me a detailed letter and said she had taught him, for instance, that the wife not the husband should determine how many children they should have – and the children should bear her family name, not his. He said she ate almost nothing – a potato or an egg. I'm no better, but then I'm twenty years older than she was. Mr Brown writes:

Madame d'Arusmont had few friends, spent most of her time reading and writing, and walked everywhere looking neither to the right nor the left. As she walked she'd practice her speeches out loud until she got them right. In a public speech she never consulted a note and never searched for a word. Everything interested her, that is, every subject, though she scarcely seemed to notice the people around her. When she died she was reading *Uncle Tom's Cabin* and Prescott's *History of Mexico*.

She had requested those books because she wanted reading matter that would make her forget her pain; only Fanny would have found such titles to be palliatives.

Like many idealists, when writing her will she had forgotten her

314

various causes and in some feudal reflex of family loyalty had left all her wealth to the traitorous little Sylva. (By the way, Sylva arrived in Cincinnati the day after her mother died.) When the American Congress had a hearing about the feasibility of giving women the vote, Sylva spoke out against it loud and clear before all those bearded men. She said, 'I lived with a feminist mother and I know the vice and madness that lie behind women's rights and the destruction to the family.'

Tonight I'll see Mr Home and I'll ask him – or rather Fanny's summoned spirit – a few pertinent questions. I mentioned to Mrs Baker, his friend, that I'm working on a biography of Fanny and need to know a few things about her rapport with her sister and her daughter and her various lovers.

I suppose I'm secretly pleased, in the manner of most old people, that I've outlived my friends, even much younger ones such as Fanny. As a writer I will have the last word, even the last laugh. There have been many moments in the composition of this biography when I've imagined Fanny objecting, but with the serene finality of the scribe I have overcome her protestations and finished my phrase. I was half in love with Fanny – at least I was invariably thrilled in her presence, as if she conferred favour on me through proximity – but I also resented her superiority and relished her downfall. For years I dreamed about her. In most of the dreams we were young together and bathing naked in hot, bubbling springs that exhaled clouds of steam into the cooler night air. I never went to such a place in this world, though the reality of the spa is most present. Perhaps it is a foreglimpse of the future.

Twenty-one

A complete rout! I've never been so humiliated! I've just arrived home and though I'm exhausted I want to get this all down as notes for my chapter on spiritualism in my new novel, *Paris and London; or Fashionable Life*. I'm sitting here in my hat and cloak and writing at my little desk and trembling all over.

We were all literary at the seance – the American novelist Hawthorne, the unstoppable Browning and his earnest, spiritual Ba and their little Pen, the elderly American poet William Cullen Bryant, whom I never spoke to though Mr Hawthorne told me he's a cheerful old man but not affectionate. 'He cannot get closely home to his sorrow,' Hawthorne said, 'and in consequence of that deficiency the world lacks substance to him.' Mr Bryant certainly looked substantial enough – his waistcoat buttons were about to burst! Of course there was Mr Home and his hostess, Georgina Baker, a familiar member of the English colony. Her old villa is said to be haunted.

I was happy to see Browning. His nonsense is of an excellent vintage, the true bubble and babble and effervescence of a powerful mind.

Mr Home I had observed in action several times before and I

316

have always had a highly favourable impression of him. He is tall and slim, his eyes are of a most penetrating blue and his features are irregular but distinguished. He could not be more than twenty-five years old but he has the manners of an English butler or, one might say, of an Ukrainian prince. In fact he speaks with a highly unstable accent which includes a Scottish burr, a Yankee twang and something indefinably Continental.

Browning says that Home's mother was Elizabeth McNeill, whose family is supposed to be gifted with second sight, and his father the natural son of Alexander, tenth Earl of Home (in Scotland). When little Home was only nine he was adopted by an aunt and removed to Greensville, Connecticut. 'There he became a weird little boy,' Mr Browning is telling me. 'He had telepathic conversations with the dead and produced or induced strange rappings all over his aunt's old wooden house. Remember spiritualism was invented by the Fox sisters not far away in New-York about the same time – their raps were all supposed to be due to double-jointed big toes! Maybe Mr Home is similarly gifted. Never forget that the New Englanders are all puritans –'

'You needn't remind *me*, Mr Browning!' I said, rewarding him with a pitying smile.

He blushed. 'Sorry! Hmnn . . . careless, naturally, Mrs Trollope, I'm frightfully, hmnn, the Domestic Mannerist herself – *what*!?'

'There, there, steady on,' I said, teasing him since so much apologetic sputtering was endearing but quite unnecessary. Anyway, I know no one reads my books now.

'The puritanical aunt couldn't tolerate the knocking and rapping and had the local clergymen – *all* the local clergymen of *all* the denominations – called in for prayers and hymns and exorcisms, but nothing availed and the poor weird lad was summarily moved out. And the bizarre noises went with him. To the degree the aunt had been intolerant of raps, the boy's new friends delighted in them and soon he drew about him a distinguished circle including our friend Bryant the poet and a Supreme Court judge and a Harvard professor or two.' Browning could always talk a wonderful quantity in a little time.

317

I thought it ironic that Mr Browning, whose conversation is always so clear and to the point, unlike the latent meanings and obscurities of his verse – ironic that he, of all fathers, should bang on about a weird little boy when his own Pen was helping all the guests to cake and strawberries as if he were the daughter of the family. There he was with his long curly hair, a girl's frock and short hose, gliding solemnly around with Mrs Baker's best china in his tiny blue hands. Then, when everyone was served, he retreated to a couch, the nine-year-old, climbed up on it and composed himself, even closed his eyes. 'He's enjoying his own meditations,' Ba whispered to me in her gently impulsive manner, delighted instead of alarmed, as another mother might have been. 'Pen' (or as the Italians call him, 'Pennini'), since he's so small and there's a colossal statue by the same name in Florence – Pen prides himself on being Florentine. Like his mother he is sweetly disposed towards the human race though only remotely akin to it.

Ba and I fell into an ecstasy of praise for Mr Home (we felt the 'Mr' was a deceptive stab at modesty by a seer who should obviously be addressed as 'O Great One!' at the very least). Spending a sociable evening with Mr Home (who always maintains a certain distance) is like spending a casual weekend shooting at Balmoral – religion disguised as everyday life.

'But he's a humbug with his priestly airs,' Mr Browning was saying, wiping the double cream from his lips.

'My darling,' Ba said with that certain artificiality of a famous wife addressing a famous husband in public before other journal-keeping, letter-writing authors, 'when a thing *is*, the time is past for considering the probability of its being. Anyway, so many people can attest to its truth – you may as well deny that men saw a comet last summer. You're like the man who shuts his eyes at midday and says it's dark.'

Of course what she and I shared was that we'd each had conversations with our dead. Ba was in touch with her beloved brother whom she'd not been able to see for years after she broke with her father. I'd talked to my daughter. One day, when I was seeing Sophia Eckly, another local spiritualist and a 'sister' to Ba, I wrote questions down for my little Emily ('Are you happy?' and 'Is Cudjo

318

dead or alive?'), sealed them in an envelope and threw it in the fire. Two slates that were bound together with string and laid on the heavily draped dining-room table commenced to jump about furiously and I could hear the scraping of chalk.

At last Miss Eckly handed me the boards, which I unbound and there, painted on the inside, was a fresh rose, and I remembered how Emily used to tease me always for gathering roses every morning and putting a bud vase on each breakfast tray. The first answer was, 'Dear Mother, I've never been so happy, except I miss you. Come join me soon.' The second: 'Yes, he's still alive and most content and a happy old hound.' Hound? Obviously Emily – or whoever wrote the words – thought Cudjo must be a dog's name. But surely Emily would have – no! Of course not! She knew him as Jupiter. I resolved that the next time I'd ask after the fate of Jupiter Higgins.

Now Browning was saying that Dickens had very recently declined Theodosia's invitation to a seance with Mr Home. 'You ladies will be vexed by this,' Browning said with a big caddish smile, 'but Theodosia showed me the letter wherein he wrote: "I have not the least belief in the awful unseen world being available for evening parties at so much a night."'

Ba turned to me and said, 'Why are men such sceptics? In *Blackwood's* I read an essay by a Mr Aytoun in which he said he rejects the railway, obscure new poetry, free trade and spiritualism. I, at least, am all for the free circulation of the spirits and have been guilty of poetic innovation.'

Robert was back at it. 'It all started in New-York, spiritualism, where as you've told us, Mrs Trollope –' and here he was making up for having forgotten my books on America – 'life is gloomy, the men all drink whisky and spit, and everyone is longing for novelties, though not necessarily *obscure* new poetry, as my lamentable American sales attest.'

Strange, I thought, that Browning's name should be synonymous with delicacy and indirection yet he's not above guffawing about his 'sales'!

Browning concluded, 'I can't help but agree with the man in *The Times* who reported one of Home's seances in Jermyn Street.

The reporter said that the spirits might very well exist but that they never revealed anything of the least importance and were just frivolous bores.'

As if to express supernatural wrath at so much scorn, the double doors banged open and there was Mr Home, his face dramatically pale and his hands folded in front of him but with his fingers held oddly as in a symbol from the Mysteries. Mr Hawthorne helped me rise from my chair. He said, 'I've been talking to Hiram Powers. I know what he means – I've been American Consul to Liverpool the last few years – but talking to Mr Powers makes me think exile is a very unsatisfactory life. We are always deferring the reality of life until a future moment and, by and by, we have deferred it till there are no future moments.'

This little speech made me testy and I said, 'At least Hiram makes the most of all his moments no matter where he is.'

At my age the least movement, even walking from one room to another, can leave me breathless and with a throbbing head and a pained lower back, but my son Tom took my arm and trotted me to the dining-room with its single very dim gas lamp on the sideboard.

Everyone except Mr Home was seated. He smiled a bit helplessly and shrugged: 'You all recognize that often the spirits aren't co-operative. Or maybe it's my own powers that are failing. I go through rather long periods of . . . *incompetence*, that's the only word.'

He stood with his hands on the back of a wooden chair. 'When I'm graced with a bit of luck,' he said almost sadly, 'a way of pushing back the veil just an inch, then my critics spring to all sorts of conclusions. Some sceptics suppose that I magnetize or biologize my audience, and that they only imagine they see what they see. Others say I administer a thimbleful of chloroform to each of the sitters. Then there are those who believe I've tapped the odd force and fluid action, or a nervous principle, and they speak of collision, illusion and delusion.'

Here he smiled and sat down. 'It's all beyond me. There are a few people who have a certain knack, perhaps a sensitivity, neither more nor less, something like a daguerreotype plate.

Maybe I'm one of them. But not tonight . . .' and he sighed.

He asked us all to close our eyes and place our hands on the table, palms down, but none of us was to touch anyone else. I suddenly remembered that Hiram Powers, who's become a Swedenborgian, thinks Home is a knave but *organized* in such a way as to be a particularly good medium. 'It all has to do with his wiring,' Hiram said. He thinks that Mr Home helps us to 'dream awake,' and as in a dream the dead during a seance always appear alive. But I think I'm getting confused. I long for my bed. I'll just finish this.

After a lengthy, unbearably long wait, we began to hear a distant rapping not under or on the table but somewhere in its own ethereal space – decidedly *not* from Mr Home's big toe. Mr Browning whispered to me, 'Heavenly mice . . .' I was vexed and whispered back, 'I'm hoping to hear from Miss Wright.'

'Oh, is Home a spiritual postal clerk?' But then Browning must have thought I'd take that amiss, given that my son Tony works for the terrestrial Post Office. He subsided into silence.

An eerie accordion, suspended in the air above us, played a sad little tune. If I squinted I thought I could just see it, the bellows opening and squeezing shut, the keys depressed and released without the intervening agency of visible fingers.

Suddenly there was a terrible crash and the furniture started dancing about. Our table was rumbling and all the crystals in the chandelier above us began to shiver and one fell on the table and broke.

The table was now bucking like an enraged bull stuck full of banderillas.

Then silence. A cold wind blew over us and a wordless chorus of children's voices was singing and I wondered if Cecilia and Emily were part of the heavenly choir and I strained to pick out their voices.

A low, incomprehensible growling, like the sound of a real voice speaking too slow to be understood, was hissing and cursing, an explosion of genuine hatred.

Mr Home stood and said, 'We're in for a bad one. I'm going

to have to bind you all together for your own safety. There's a Miss Wright who's visiting us.'

He and Mrs Baker quickly wrapped a rope around the five of us and tied it tight, then regained their own chairs and slipped in under the rope as well.

Heavy white flowers were plopping on the floor beside me, the table was tipping and a wall-sconce of old Venetian glass just beside me started shaking like a tambourine.

'Mrs Trollope,' said Mr Home in a ghastly woman's voice rolling Scottish *r*s. It was Fanny Wright's low, masculine voice. I looked over at him and saw his eyes closed, his face waxen as in a coffin.

'Yes,' I squeaked in a high voice I scarcely recognized. 'Is that you, Fanny?'

'You filthy bitch!' hissed Mr Home or Fanny (for surely she'd possessed him). The others were palpably alarmed at the horrible word because they were pulling on the rope, as they leaned away to escape her truly diabolic vehemence.

'You traitor!'

I gulped. My poor old knees were knocking together. 'How – how could I have betrayed you, Fanny? I'm writing your biography and it's full of praise.'

'Lies! All lies!' the deep voice boomed and Mr Home's normally inscrutable face was now twisted into an appalling sneer. He suddenly spat on the table and then his head was violently thrust back so far he was looking up at the ceiling and shouting, 'You stinking little profiteer, thriving off the corpses of your superiors . . .'

'Mother, let's go,' said Tom somewhere in the dark.

But Fanny was talking: 'I never slept with all those men – that was your filthy mind. I never quarrelled with Camilla – she was a saint and I worshipped her like one. You have dirtied everything you've touched. And my ideas! My great intellectual contributions have been cheapened and sullied and belittled in your pages. My little Sylva never betrayed her mother –' and here she began to sob hysterically and lights wheeled and dipped like foxfire through gauze and Mr Home shook from side to side and we all felt it since we were tied together by the one rope. A pure violin was mounting

322

higher and higher in another room somewhere upstairs in Mrs Baker's haunted old villa and after Mr Home slumped heavily forward, Mrs Baker called, 'Lights! *Luce*! Lights!'

The *camerista* rushed in with candles, but they all blew out in an otherworldly back-draught and the maid had to fumble with the glass globe of the gas lamp which shook in her hands. At last it was lit and Mrs Baker and the maid helped the extenuated Mr Home shuffle off. Mrs Baker kept whispering confidentially, 'He's very tired. Very vulnerable. Don't say anything. I've called for your carriages.' The butler untied our rope.

In the light everyone looked at me with curiosity or even reproach, as if I really were a grave robber. I felt my last bit of energy draining away from my body and mind. I wondered if I'd have the strength to make it to the carriage. The irrepressible Mr Browning said, 'I think you're in the celestial dog house, Mrs Trollope.'

I wanted to rap him with my fan but I didn't have the gumption and I was leaning heavily on Tom. Is that the right word – *gumption*?

Now it's the next morning and my granddaughter has come in with the maid and my hot coffee milk. Darling Bice . . . I'm still in bed, which is most unusual, and though I feel my fingers twitching I can't remember what I'm supposed to be writing. Maybe nothing more than just this journal entry. I don't think I have a novel or travel book on the hob at the moment. Or do I? I can't remember, which makes me anxious. Until I saw Bice I wasn't even sure where I was exactly and at first I imagined I was back at Harrow. Then I started daydreaming about that time I was wrapped in the rug, ill and shivering, and Cudjo saved me. I have the worst feeling that something dreadful happened last night but for the life of me I can't think what it was. It's exactly like a really unpleasant morning after excessive drinking.

The major-domo has come in to announce a Miss Knowlton.

'Who?' I ask. 'I don't know a Miss Knowlton, do I? Send her away.' And then instead of using the more usual word, *arrivederci*, I say, 'Tell her *addio*.'

Acknowledgements

I wish to thank Princeton University for a sabbatical semester during which I was able to work on this manuscript.

Jenny Uglow, my editor at Chatto & Windus, has brought to this novel all her flair and knowledge of the period and passion for effective writing. In America I am grateful to my new editor and old friend, Dan Halpern at Ecco, for encouraging me at every point in the writing of this book. My partner, Michael Carroll, has heard every word of it many times and has often turned on the light during yet another dark night of the soul. Friends such as Russell Banks, Marie-Claude de Brunhoff, Patrick Rose, Peter Carey and especially Marina Warner and Hermione Lee have given me advice and shared with me their knowledge of history and literature. A Trollope scholar (and wonderful friend), Geordie Greig, helped and encouraged me at several junctures. My friends and hosts in Princeton, George Pitcher and Ed Cone, have become my ideal readers. Kate Bucknell read an earlier draft and gave me copious notes. I have received encouragement from such enthusiastic and constant readers as Zachary Lazar, David Leavitt, Mark Mitchell, Felice Picano, Andrew Holleran, Jeremy Reed and Stephen Barber.

I wish to thank the British Library, where I worked for four months, the Firestone Library at Princeton and the Bobst Library at New-York University.

My agent, Amanda Urban, has never failed to share with me her enthusiasm for this project. And I thank Deborah Rogers, my English agent, for her kind counsel and good meals and abundant love. Patrick Merla, a dear friend of long date, helped me prepare this manuscript.

I have relied heavily on the standard biographies of Frances Wright and Frances Trollope: *Fanny Wright: Rebel in America* by Celia Morris, *Frances Wright* by William Randall Waterman, *Frances Wright: Free Enquirer* by A.J.G. Perkins and Theresa Wolfson, *The Life, Manners and Travels of Fanny Trollope* by Johanna Johnston, *Fanny Trollope: The Life and Adventures of a Clever Woman* by Pamela Neville-Sington, and Mrs Trollope's daughter-in-law's biography, *Frances Trollope: Her Life and Literary Work from George III to Victoria*, by Frances Eleanor Trollope. I drew a few details from her son's book, *What I Remember*, by Thomas Adolphus Trollope.

I have read dozens of accounts by British travellers of their experiences in the United States, half a dozen slave narratives, scores of biographies and autobiographies, three books about blacksmiths and their art, several about Cincinnati, copies of the *New Harmony Gazette* and of obscure scholarly articles about Marcus Winchester. I read ten books on the Haiti of the period, several on nineteenth-century New Orleans and several on spiritualism. Of course this book is a novel and as such relies on invention. Mrs Trollope never went to New Harmony or Haiti (though Frances Wright did) and no one before me has suggested that Mrs Trollope had a Cudjo in her life or that Henry Trollope was sexually ambiguous. I should make it clear that I have quoted directly only from two paragraphs in Mrs Trollope's *Domestic Manners of the Americans*, her first book, the one that made her famous. My usual method has been to take an occasion only briefly presented by Mrs Trollope and to re-imagine it entirely (the visit to New Orleans, for instance, or the revivalist camp meeting). I have played fast and free with the chronology in several places. Auguste Hervieu, for instance, actually entered the lives of the Trollopes somewhat later than in my account.

In an essay written about the historical novel in 1830, Niccolo Tommaseo suggests that the genre is best served when it is about real but obscure people. Some of my characters were famous then and now – the Brownings, Lafayette, Jefferson, James Fenimore Cooper – but they play only cameo roles. My leading characters, true to Tommaseo's recommendations, lived great lives but have been largely and unfairly forgotten.